acclaimed mystery series . . .

Praise for
A Connecticut Yankee in Criminal Court

"An enjoyable tour of 1890's New Orleans . . . Twain can take a bow for his performance. Heck takes a colorful city (New Orleans) and a colorful character (Mark Twain), adds a murder, a duel, some voodoo and period detail and conjures up an entertaining sequel to Death on the Mississippi."
—*Publishers Weekly*

"A period charmer . . . Against the background of this famous city with its colorful mix of characters, cultures, food, music, and religion, the famous author and his loyal sidekick worm their way into the heart of a scandalous murder."
—*Alfred Hitchcock Mystery Magazine*

"Packed with casual racists, unregenerate Civil War veterans, superstitious rationalists, and poseurs of every stripe—exactly the sort of colorful cast that brings its satiric hero's famous passion for unmasking pretension into brilliant relief."
—*Kirkus Reviews*

"Crescent City mystery simmers."
—*Booklist*

"The second of Heck's Mark Twain detective novels is a charming winner. Twain is as fabulous a personality in fiction as he was a real-life writer . . . A unique, intriguing reading experience."
—*Ed's Internet Book Review*

"Exciting."
—*Book Alert*

Berkley Prime Crime Books by Peter J. Heck

DEATH ON THE MISSISSIPPI
A CONNECTICUT YANKEE IN CRIMINAL COURT
THE PRINCE AND THE PROSECUTOR

The Prince

and the

Prosecutor

A Mark Twain Mystery

Peter J. Heck

BERKLEY PRIME CRIME, NEW YORK

THE PRINCE AND THE PROSECUTOR

A Berkley Prime Crime Book / published by arrangement with the author

PRINTING HISTORY
Berkley Prime Crime hardcover / December 1997
Berkley Prime Crime mass-market edition / November 1998

The Penguin Putnam Inc. World Wide Web site address is
http://www.penguinputnam.com

ISBN: 0-425-16567-1

Berkley Prime Crime Books are published
by The Berkley Publishing Group,
a member of Penguin Putnam Inc.,
375 Hudson Street, New York, NY 10014
The name BERKLEY PRIME CRIME and the BERKLEY PRIME
CRIME design are trademarks belonging to Berkley Publishing
Corporation.

PRINTED IN THE UNITED STATES OF AMERICA

10 9 8 7 6 5 4 3 2 1

For Dan, and the boys in the band.

Historical Note and Acknowledgments

As with my previous Mark Twain mysteries, this novel walks a line between history and fiction, using historical figures as fictional characters, and introducing them into situations that they never faced in real life. While Mark Twain met Rudyard Kipling on more than one occasion, they never crossed the Atlantic together on the same ship. Nor did they ever collaborate to catch a murderer—Carrie Kipling would certainly have mentioned such an event in her highly detailed diaries, had it occurred.

I have done my best to portray Mark Twain and his era as faithfully as possible, and to make him and the Kiplings (the only other historical figures here) act and speak as they probably would have in the circumstances they face here. The historical Twain's financial difficulties in the early 1890s, stemming from a series of bad investments and worse luck, sent him to the brink of bankruptcy. He sent his wife and daughters to Europe, to take advantage of a cheaper cost of living, while he made several trips across the Atlantic, going on lecture tours and tending to his finances in the U.S. By the end of the nineties he had paid his debts. I show him at the beginning of this period, although I have rearranged his itinerary for my own purposes.

I have taken certain other liberties with fact. These include my resuscitation of Mittel Reuss, a German prin-

cipality that ceased to exist in 1616, as well as my whole-
sale remodeling of the *City of Baltimore*, the historical
version of which was a much older and smaller ship than
the one portrayed here. I hope the reader will take these
inventions in the same spirit as my creation of the various
imaginary characters who play supporting roles to Mr.
Clemens and the Kiplings.

My fictional Mark Twain tells a number of jokes and
stories that the historical Twain wrote or told on many
occasions. As a practiced public speaker, he had on hand
a stock repertory of witticisms and anecdotes, which he
expanded and modified for different audiences, so it is
no surprise that he would do so during the voyage portrayed in these pages. I stand ready to accept the reader's
verdict that my own inventions (there are a few here!)
fall short of Mr. Clemens's enviable standards, but I hope
they are at least in the proper spirit.

As always, too many people to mention individually
have had some hand in helping me bring this novel to
completion. I owe special thanks to my editors, Laura
Anne Gilman and Natalee Rosenstein; to my agent, Mar-
tha Millard; and to my wife, Jane Jewell, my first and
most demanding reader. Thanks also to Charles Chaffee,
for information on early ocean liners. The book would
have been far less than it is without their contributions;
of course, any flaws that remain are my own responsibility.

The Prince

and the
Prosecutor

"William, someone is calling you on the telephone." I looked up in surprise at my mother, who had interrupted my leisurely breakfast with this remarkable announcement. Until then, I had been dawdling over my coffee and reading a newspaper.

"Really," I said. "I wonder who it could be." The telephone had been installed in my parents' home in New London only a few months before, shortly after my graduation from Yale in 189—. Having left home very soon thereafter, I had never before gotten a telephone call at home.

With a feeling somewhere between excitement and anxiety, I arose from the dining room table and walked out to the front hallway, where the instrument had been mounted on the wall near the foot of the stairs. I picked up the earpiece, and spoke into the conical black tube. "Hello, are you there? This is Cabot; who's calling, please?"

"Wentworth, is that you?" came a familiar drawling voice, recognizable even over the telephone as that of my employer, Mr. Samuel Clemens, a writer and lecturer of some repute. "I've hung around this blasted telephone office half the morning trying to get hold of you—you'd think they'd give faster service, for what they charge for long distance. Good thing there's only one Cabot with a phone in New London, or the operators would never have found you. I was about ready to give up and send a telegram, except I hate cramming my whole damn message into ten words, and I'd still have had to wait for the answer. How'd you like to go to Europe?''

"Europe!" I exclaimed. "When do we leave?"

In the capacity of traveling secretary, I had recently accompanied Mr. Clemens (who was better known to the public under the pen name Mark Twain) on an extensive lecture tour of the Mississippi Valley, New Orleans, and the South. The tour itself had been a great success, with overflow crowds in every town where we stopped. Upon our return to New York, Mr. Clemens had proclaimed himself satisfied with my performance of my duties, paying me a bonus of a hundred dollars above my salary for the tour.

But it had been over a month since our return. I had sat idle for all of September and into October. True, I had spent a few hours each day working on my notes of the tour, with the notion of turning them into something publishable. My father, who had expected me to follow in his footsteps and take up a career as a lawyer, kept dropping hints about "coming back to the real world" and "taking up respectable work." It did not in the least impress him that I had found employment with a famous writer, or that I was meeting important people in the world of literature. So the invitation to accompany Mr. Clemens to Europe came as something of a godsend.

"I've talked Henry Rogers into sponsoring a European tour starting in November," said Mr. Clemens. "I reckon I can wrap up my affairs here in a week or so, and jump on the first boat leaving after that. If you can come on down to New York by Monday, I'll have plenty of work for you. And maybe this time we can manage to take a trip without anybody getting murdered."

"I certainly hope so," I said. One of the unexpected duties of my position as Mr. Clemens's traveling secretary had been my participation in the resolution of two murder cases—one that began in New York and came to its conclusion aboard a Mississippi riverboat, and another involving two deaths among the New Orleans aristocracy.

"I'm in the Union Square Hotel again," said my employer. "I'll tell them to reserve you a room starting Monday night. Pack your trunk—we'll probably be gone right up till spring. And if you know any French or German or Italian, brush up on it now. I reckon we'll see most of the continent before we're done."

"I'll start packing right away," I said, excited that my dreams of foreign travel were at last about to come true.
"Look for me midmorning on Monday."

I broke the connection, and turned to see my mother standing behind me, a sad expression on her face. Her arms were folded across her bosom, and she had on an old, dark blue dress that in the dim light of the hallway seemed to emphasize her melancholy. "So, you're leaving again," she said quietly. "Your father will be very disappointed, William." She and my father were almost the only people I knew who called me by my first name. It made me feel like a small child, despite my being a good ten inches taller than Mother.

"How else am I to see Europe?" I asked. "If it weren't for Mr. Clemens, I'd never have been out of New England."

"Your father and I have never been to Europe, and it has not hurt us in the least. Besides, if it weren't for Mr. Clemens, you'd never have been in jail," she said accusingly. My parents had been deeply shocked to learn of my having spent several hours in a New Orleans jail cell following a duel with pistols. (I had done my best to keep the knowledge from them, but some well-meaning person had seen the New Orleans newspaper accounts and passed on the story.) She cocked her head to one side and looked up at me. "I don't think that man is a good influence on you. Mr. Digby tells me that his books are unwholesome and that he openly mocks respectable people of our sort."

"I am sorry to hear that," I said. Mr. Digby was the minister at our church, and my mother put great stock in his opinion on all subjects. I personally found his manner rather pompous, but had generally refrained from criticizing him in my mother's presence. "I can only tell you that Mr. Clemens's circle of acquaintance includes some of the most eminent people in the country. If Mr. Digby had spent as much time in his company as I have, I hope he would be of a different opinion." As I said this, the image of my employer came to me, puffing great clouds of cigar smoke, knocking back full bumpers of Scotch whisky, and swearing like a stevedore. Perhaps it was just as well that Mr. Digby had not made his acquaintance. . . .

"I see I am wasting my time talking to you," said my mother. "Your father will have something to say about this when he comes home." She raised her chin, then turned and walked away.

"I am sure he will," I said, as calmly as I could manage. I was angry at her opposition to my plans, but I had no desire to hurt her. "But if I don't take this opportunity now, it may never come again."

She turned and looked at me, and I could see a hint of moisture around her eyes. "And what opportunities are you passing up in favor of this notion of seeing Europe? Why not settle down and make a fair start at establishing yourself in some worthwhile profession? You know how your father is eating his heart out at your refusal to follow him into the practice of law. But I think he would be satisfied by your commitment to any steady and respectable occupation."

"Perhaps he would," I said. "But I have made my commitment to Europe, and to Mr. Clemens."

When all was said and done, my parents had no choice but to acquiesce in my continued employment as Mr. Clemens's secretary. After all, I was a grown man and in full possession of my senses. In fact, my father's attempt to get me to listen to reason—or, more precisely, to my mother's pleas—seemed almost perfunctory. It made me wonder whether he might not have his own unfulfilled wish to see some of the world, even if it didn't qualify as a steady and respectable occupation.

In any case, the following Monday found me once again in New York City, in the lobby of the Union Square Hotel, where I had first learned what it meant to be part of a police investigation. Mr. Clemens had reserved a room for me adjacent to his own, and within an hour of my arrival I was immersed in the now-familiar business of helping him with his correspondence, and taking care of last-minute arrangements for our journey to Europe. It felt good to be busy again, and to be a part of the great world beyond Connecticut.

My employer lounged in a comfortable easy chair, his feet propped up and a pipe between his teeth. The hotel had sent up an urn of hot coffee and some sweet buns for our late-morning refreshment. I sipped at my coffee in between scribbling down Mr. Clemens's instructions. Fortunately, his slow speech made it easy to keep up with him; my education had included many things, but instruction in shorthand was not among them.

"I've been in touch with my English publishers," said Mr. Clemens. "They're anxious for my new book, and if I get a little work done on the boat, it'll be just about ready for the press. I'm planning on meeting Livy in London, so she can go over the manuscript—she's the only editor I really trust—and then I'll hand it in and start to see some money from it."

"I'm surprised you wouldn't publish it first in this country," I said. "Don't your fellow Americans deserve first look at your writings? I'm sure they'd support your work as well as the British would." I was a little taken aback by his intention; it seemed out of character for a staunch admirer of all things American.

"I'm sure they would, but there's the damned copyright problem," he growled. "It's been the plague of my existence, Wentworth. The English won't recognize copyright for any book first published elsewhere, so I have to let the stiff-necked swindlers put it out before the American edition, even if it's only by twenty-four hours. Otherwise, I'd never see a penny from England.''

"That's dreadful! I can imagine the difficulties it must create,'' I said. "Still, with today's fast ships, and the transatlantic telegraph, it ought be considerably easier to coordinate the two editions, shouldn't it? Why can't you simply send your corrected manuscript directly to New York, once the English have finished with it?''

Mr. Clemens knocked the ash out of his pipe and shook his head. "You don't know the half of it, Wentworth. The fast ships cause more trouble than they prevent. With a couple of my books, the Canadians got hold of the English edition and ran off pirated copies for sale in the U.S before my American publishers had the type set. They cost me thousands in royalties, and thousands more trying to stop their goddamned thievery. Howells and George Putnam and I went to Congress a few years ago, and we convinced them to plug up some of the loopholes. But there's still no guarantee I'll get the benefit of my labors unless I pay attention to every jot and tittle of the law. Writing's hard enough work, without having to be a damned lawyer, as well.''

"I can believe you,'' I told him, recalling my own efforts at turning my notes into something resembling passible prose. I thought I had a solid grounding in the use of my native tongue, but while my sentences were correctly formed, to my eye they lacked a certain vigor. I had expected my employment with Mr. Clemens to bring about some improvement in my writing, but my carefully revised pages looked even less presentable to me now than they had when I was still a student.

"We'll be traveling on the *City of Baltimore*,'' said Mr. Clemens, standing up and walking over to pour himself another cup of coffee—his third since the urn had been delivered. "I figure an American writer ought to patronize an American ship when he can. Besides, she's a little older and less fashionable than the others leaving at around the same time. So she'll save us a few dollars.''

"Yes, I suppose that's important. It would have been nice to travel on one of the big new ships, though.''

"Oh, the *City of Baltimore* is big enough," said Mr. Clemens. "You should have seen the old *Quaker City*, the ship I took on my first visit to Europe in '67. I thought she was pretty well fitted out, but she was already thirteen years old, and barely a dinghy next to these modern ocean liners. Only nineteen hundred tons, with paddle wheels, and sails! They'd laugh her out of the water, these days."

"I shan't complain," I said. "I'm getting to see Europe at last. If I had to stoke the boilers on the crossing, it wouldn't be too high a price to pay."

Mr. Clemens looked at me with a twinkle in his eye. "Maybe I'll take you up on that, Wentworth," he said. "I do have to watch my expenses these days, and two passages to England for the price of one may be too much of a bargain to pass up!"

After lunch (at which I was treated to a string of amusing stories about European travel), Mr. Clemens sent me to the American Steamship Line's terminal at Pier 43, on the Hudson River near Christopher Street. The bellboy in the hotel lobby told me that the Fourteenth Street tramway, which stopped not far from the hotel, would take me directly there, and (after a somewhat crowded ride that my mother would undoubtedly have considered undignified if not outright dangerous) so it did.

I had gone past the Hudson River piers on my previous visits to New York, but this was my first chance to see them up close. I was pleased to learn that our pier was near those of the Cunard Line, where I had the opportunity to observe the red and black funnels of the *Campania*, which had recently established a record for the Atlantic crossing, just under five and a half days. And the *City of New York*, which had held the record only a few years ago, was tied up at the American Line's docks. So there were two of the fastest ships ever built, sitting within a hundred yards of one another. Though Mr. Clemens and I would be sailing on an older, slower boat, for a moment my imagination conjured up the vision of these two "ocean greyhounds" racing side by side across the waves. Perhaps another time I should have the pleasure of crossing the ocean aboard one of them.

The office I was searching for was in a sort of warehouse on the shore end of the pier, and there were several people ahead of me at the ticket window. I had all afternoon to transact my business, so I took my place in line, content to enjoy the unfamiliar sights and scenes of a steamship terminal. At first all went quite pleasantly, if slowly. I overheard conversations in several languages and accents, and saw a variety of gentlemen and ladies in their best traveling clothes preparing to board the *New York*, which was scheduled to sail that very afternoon. Through a door opening onto the docks, I saw the smartly uniformed employees of the steamship line readying the great ship for departure.

But before long I became aware of a disturbance up ahead at the window. Actually, it would have been difficult to ignore, since the large, loud fellow who was the evident cause of the problem was less than ten feet away from me. "This is an outrage," he bellowed. "I have given you the full fare for a first-class passage over a month ago, and now you tell me there is no room for me on the *New York*."

The clerk attempted to explain the situation. "I'm sorry, sir, but your check was returned by the bank. We tried to get in touch with you, but you weren't at the address you gave us. The best we can do now is find you a second-class cabin on *City of New York*. Or I can give you a first-class cabin on *City of Baltimore*, this time next week." I felt sorry for the clerk, a fresh-faced young fellow who was clearly trying to be as diplomatic as possible under the circumstances. I wondered whether, if I were in his position, I would be so polite to someone who had given me a bad check.

But the man would hear none of the clerk's explanation. He brandished his cane, and for a moment I was afraid he was about to swing it at the clerk, although he would have had a hard time doing any damage on account of the barred window between them. His little white goatee fairly quivered as he shouted, "The bank has made a mistake, and you have made a bigger one, you impudent whelp! If I am not on the *New York* when she sails, I will see to it that you lose your position. Why should I absorb another week's hotel bills? I demand to see your superior this instant." The fellow's face was red, and his gestures were wild. The man behind him in the line had stepped back, as if he feared being struck by the fellow, even if accidentally. Others around the office had stopped what they were doing, staring at the growing altercation.

The poor clerk stepped back from the window and said in a tired voice, "Very well, sir. Please wait here while I call my supervisor." He turned his back, and disappeared, while the angry customer planted his cane on the floor with a loud thump, and stood there in a posture that radiated hostility, even from behind. I saw several of the onlookers make faces and roll their eyes at one another, and one young woman struggled to suppress a giggle.

After an uncomfortable interval—it could hardly have been much more than two minutes, but the tension made it seem like fifteen—a balding fellow with a walrus mustache appeared on the other side of the window. Behind him I could see the worried-looking clerk. "I am Mr. Saunders, the manager," he said, "Now, what seems to be the problem, mister?"

Perhaps the brief wait had calmed the irate passenger. He managed to outline his complaint in a normal speaking voice, and his gestures were considerably restrained, although he still waved his hands more than the occasion demanded. Listening to him, I thought I detected something of an accent—German, perhaps.

"I am Prinz Heinrich Karl von Ruckgarten," he said. "One month ago, I deposited my check for four hundred American dollars with your company, to secure a first-class passage on the *New York*. Now I am told that you have not held a cabin for me, and I am reduced to traveling second-class or else to waiting a week for the next ship. Why, if I wanted to wait another entire week, I would have asked for that date to begin with. I have a mind to walk over to Cunard and see if the English understand better how to treat a gentleman."

"Is that so?" said Mr. Saunders from behind the window, leaning on his elbow while the passenger spoke. "Well, you may have given us a piece of paper with the bank's name on it, but the bank says you never gave 'em the four hundred dollars to back it. I don't know what the English call that, but in New York we call it *writing a bum check*. Sometimes it's an honest mistake, and I'm willing to give you the benefit of the doubt on that. We tried to find you and straighten it out, but you must have given us a bad address, as well. You can't hardly expect us to hold a first-class cabin for you, not when there's other passengers waving cash money and begging for a ride to Southampton." Some of those waiting on line snickered at this, although they quieted down as the angry passenger looked around in annoyance.

Turning back to the window, he raised his voice again, although some of the wind seemed to have gone out of his sails. "A gentleman's word should be sufficient to hold the cabin. I do not write the bum checks, as you call them; your bank must have made a mistake. I have been traveling, and so your message must have missed me. But see, I will give you the four hundred dollars for my cabin right now." He pulled a wallet from his breast pocket and displayed a thick wad of greenbacks.

Seeing the money, the manager took a more conciliatory tone. "Well, I can see you've got the wherewithal, and I wish I could tell you I had the cabin. But it's God's own truth, every first-class cabin on the *New York* is taken. I'll put you into a second-class cabin this minute for one-fifty."

"Impossible!" said the prince. "What would it look like for a gentleman to travel with the common herd? I must have a first-class cabin. If you cannot provide it, I will have to see what the *Campania* has open. Or perhaps the White Star Line can accommodate me."

"I can't dictate whose ship you travel on," said the manager, shrugging. "But here's a suggestion. Give me a fifty percent cash deposit now, and I'll guarantee you a first-class cabin on *City of Baltimore* next week. If you get a berth on another ship before *City of Baltimore* sails, I'll refund every cent."

The passenger seemed mollified, but had one last protest. "I cannot live a week in a New York hotel for free. You will be costing me a good bit of money."

"No, look at it this way," said Mr. Saunders. "You were ready to pay four hundred for *City of New York*, and I can give you the same class of room on *City of Baltimore* for three-fifty. Now, I don't know about you, but I could live pretty comfortably on fifty bucks a week in New York City. Unless there's some reason you have to be in England by this Saturday, you'll be just as well off waiting for *City of Baltimore*, maybe even better off. Think about it, mister. There's no way you can lose."

After a pause, the passenger nodded. "Very well. If you will put your promise in writing, I shall give you a one-hundred-seventy-five-dollar deposit for the best first-class cabin on *City of Baltimore*. By what time do you require the full amount, should I decide to sail with you?"

"Twenty-four hours before sailing will do fine," said the manager, smiling. "And I think you'll be glad you decided to stay with the American Steamship Line."

After seeing the passenger's arrogance and unruly temper, I thought that both the American Line and I might be happier if he were to find a berth with Cunard, after all. But I was just as glad to see him finish his business so I could get on with my own errand at the steamship office. In a few minutes, I had handed over the necessary fee to upgrade Mr. Clemens's reservation to a small suite, with a private bedroom for me, and I was on my way back to the Union Square Hotel.

2

The next few days, my time was divided between looking after my employer's affairs and enjoying my stay in New York City, one of the social and cultural capitals of the world. My travels with Mr. Clemens—especially our stay in New Orleans—had spoiled my palate for the plain and wholesome cooking I had grown up with in Connecticut, and I enjoyed this opportunity to expand my culinary experience. Mr. Clemens made certain I had the chance to sample the offerings at some of the better restaurants and private clubs around Manhattan. He had a knack for persuading publishers and editors to buy him (and his secretary!) lunch or dinner, dangling in front of them the offer to write something for their houses. And so we ate handsomely without much depleting Mr. Clemens's pocketbook.

"So, Wentworth, do you see how the literary game is played?" he said. We were strolling back to Union Square after dinner and billiards at The Players Club, of which Mr. Clemens told me he had been one of the founders. The fare had been excellent: a dozen raw Little Neck clams, turtle soup with a splash of sherry, a fresh watercress salad, and then a brace of pheasants with wild rice and all the trimmings. A couple of bottles of champagne washed it all down, with good coffee and a snifter of fine brandy to complement Mr. Clemens's after-dinner cigar. Mr. Putnam, the head of a large publishing house, had been our host, and Mr. Clemens had repaid him with a colorful account of our trip down the Mississippi, and the shocking events in which we played some small part.

"I believe I do," I said. "The first principle seems to be to persuade the publisher that you have something worth his time and effort. I can understand why he would think so, in your case. But how does a novice such as I get taken up by the likes of Mr. Putnam?"

"There are about as many ways as there are writers," said Mr. Clemens. "You could send in a manuscript on some kind of bright-colored paper, or written in extra-fancy script. You could send it in by special messenger, and maybe hire a brass band to play when he delivers it. You could include a bottle of wine, or a box of cigars, or anything else of the sort, as a bribe. You could get a few well-known people to commend your writing and promise to buy hundreds of copies as gifts. Those are the common methods."

I was startled to hear this. "Good Lord, I had no idea. I would never have thought to try anything of the sort."

We stopped for a moment on the curb at the intersection of Seventeenth Street and Fourth Avenue, as a string of carriages hurried by. Mr. Clemens was silent for a moment, waiting for the traffic to clear. Then he turned to me. "I'm sorry you have so little imagination, Wentworth. Thousands of writers have used those methods, and no doubt others I haven't heard of, to draw attention to their manuscripts." There was a break in the traffic, and we stepped out into the street. Halfway across, he turned to me and said, matter-of-factly, "Of course, most of 'em don't work worth a damn."

I turned to him in exasperation and said, "Then why on earth did you tell me such a tale? For a moment, you had me convinced that an author has to use all these tricks to catch a publisher's eye." I had barely been back in Mr. Clemens's employ a day before falling for one of his leg-pullings. At least I had learned to recognize them, instead of continuing to believe in his nonsense for as much as a week, as I had with some of his hoaxes during our riverboat journey.

"Don't dawdle in the middle of traffic, Wentworth. These New York carriage drivers are like to run you down," said Mr. Clemens, grinning as he stepped ahead of me toward the far side of the street. Laughing, I scurried to catch up with him.

The next morning after breakfast, Mr. Clemens and I were on our way to the elevators when a short, dark-skinned man strode up to us and said in a deep voice, "Good morning, Mr. Clemens. I trust you remember meeting me?" He was a sturdily built fellow, with a cleft chin and a huge mustache. His piercing blue eyes, surmounted by bushy eyebrows, peered at us through thick glasses.

Mr. Clemens looked at the fellow, and his eyes opened wide. "Kipling!" he exclaimed, reaching out to shake the fellow's hand. "What brings you to New York? Come on up to my room and have a cigar!"

"I'm afraid I haven't a minute to spare just now," said the newcomer, whose accent tagged him as an Englishman. "I'm on my way to an appointment. But perhaps we can have dinner, if you're staying here. I'll be in New York for the rest of the week. My wife and I are going to England next Monday, but I hope we can find time to get together before then."

"Why, we're going to England, too," said Mr. Clemens. Then he remembered me and introduced us. "Rudyard Kipling, this is my secretary, Wentworth Cabot. He went to Yale, but it doesn't seem to have spoiled him."

"Mr. Kipling, a pleasure to meet you," I said. "I've read one of your books on India." We shook hands.

"What boat are you sailing on?" asked my employer.

"We're on the *City of Baltimore*, next Monday."

"What luck, so are Carrie and I!" said Kipling. "We should have a capital crossing, then. Nonetheless, let's get together in the city before we leave. Are you free this evening?"

As it happened, Mr. Clemens had no engagement for the evening, and so he and Mr. Kipling agreed to meet for dinner. The Englishman then took his leave, and we crossed the lobby and waited for the elevator. "Kipling will be good to travel with," said Mr. Clemens. "First-class storyteller, and a hell of a fine poet, too. He lives in Vermont now, but he must have spent ten years in India, learning the country and watching the people. He came to visit me at my summer place in Elmira, New York, a few years ago. Between the two of us, we cover the entire field of human knowledge."

"Really?" I said, impressed that my employer would have such a high opinion of a man not so much older than I.

"Yes," drawled Mr. Clemens. The elevator door opened, and we both got in and told the boy our floor number. Then Mr. Clemens fixed me with his gaze. "Kipling has mastered all there is to know," he said. "And I know everything else." The elevator door closed, and I found myself speechless again.

Dinner that evening was at Solari, a pleasant restaurant on University Place between Ninth and Tenth streets, a few short blocks from our hotel. I was pleasantly surprised to be included in the dinner party, having often been left to my own devices when Mr. Clemens was asked out to dinner during our riverboat tour a few short months earlier. I was not about to complain; the New York restaurants were considerably more expensive than those in the West, and I hadn't the option of eating cheaply on the boat, as I had often done on the tour.

We were joined by Mr. Kipling's wife, Caroline, a Vermont woman of good family (and, as quickly became evident, the repository of a great stock of New England common sense). Solari's cuisine had been highly recommended, and Mr. Clemens seemed determined to put the restaurant's reputation to the test. I myself thought the wine was overpriced, not to mention a bit thin, but everything else was as good as I could have asked for. I especially enjoyed my first taste of terrapin stew, the flavor of which belied its reptilian origin. For dessert I had a sinfully rich chocolate cake with chocolate icing, and by the time Mr. Clemens and Mr. Kipling lit their after-dinner cigars, I was beginning to wonder whether I would be able to walk back to the hotel unaided. If I or any of my companions ate or drank another iota, we might well have to find a cab for the four-block journey.

However, Mr. Clemens showed no sign of being ready to bring the evening to a conclusion. He ordered brandy and coffee, and he and Mr. Kipling began "swapping yarns," as my employer called it. As always when Mr. Clemens dined in public, he had been recognized by many of the restaurant's patrons, and he was enjoying the spotlight. A number of them had come to the table to extend their good wishes, or to express their appreciation for something he had written, and Mr. Clemens returned their attentions by playing to the crowd: telling his best stories, with a wealth of colorful detail, and in a rich variety of accents and voices.

Mr. Kipling held up his own end of the conversation in fine style, as well—I was almost ready to believe Mr. Clemens's declaration that he knew everything there was to know. His brief residence in Vermont (barely five years) had given him a surprising familiarity with New England life. He told stories about the fishing boats and their sailors that made me wonder how I had spent almost my entire life within five miles of the Atlantic without learning even half of what this Englishman seemed to know as well as the palm of his hand.

But it was his tales of India (he pronounced it *In-ja*) that brought out his true wealth of knowledge. After hearing him tell of teeming cities and primeval wilderness, beggars and maharajahs, Hindus and Moslems, deadly cobras and royal white elephants, and all the variety of life in that populous British colony, I promised myself that some day I would visit that mysterious land. If only half of what Mr. Kipling said of it were true, then it outstripped my wildest imagination. Even Mr. Clemens seemed impressed. After the Englishman told a fantastic tale of a boy raised in the jungle by wolves, my employer remarked, "I can see I'm going to have to make it my business to go see India, if only to find out whether Kipling's a better storyteller than I am, or just a better liar."

"It would be presumptuous of me to claim superiority to Mark Twain in either respect," replied Mr. Kipling, smiling broadly. Mr. Clemens and Mrs. Kipling laughed, as did the eavesdroppers at several nearby tables, and the storytelling continued.

Finally Mr. Clemens recounted the tale of our trip down the Mississippi, and our stay in New Orleans, with special emphasis on how he and I had brought two murderers to justice. "Now that's what I call an incredible story," said Mr. Kipling. He leaned his elbows on the table and peered at Mr. Clemens with an envious expression. "It's rare enough that anyone not a policeman has anything to do with solving a murder case, let alone two of them in the space of a few weeks. It's unprecedented, I tell you. Will you be giving up writing and become the American Sherlock Holmes, Mr. Clemens?"

"If I thought there was any money in it, I might," said my employer, leaning back in his chair. "But I haven't gotten a nickel for my detecting, and I reckon I won't anytime soon. As far as the glory, I can do without it. There's only so much excitement a man my age can take. Maybe a young rascal like Cabot can enjoy fistfights and getting thrown in jail, but I'd just as soon save my energy for something a little less strenuous. Smoking cigars, for example."

Finally, we were ready to return to our hotel. And while the restaurant owner had undoubtedly been pleased to see us ordering up his best brandy, and keeping other diners buying food and drink while they stayed to listen to Mr. Clemens, it was clear he was ready to close his doors for the evening. But when we came to the front of the restaurant, we discovered several of the other patrons huddled in the entryway, peering anxiously into the street. The reason was not far to seek: Rain was falling in sheets, and a flash of lightning threw the empty streets into stark relief. "We'll never find a cab in this weather," said Mr. Clemens. "Anyone with a lick of sense is going to be indoors. We'll have to wait it out."

"Yes," said Mr. Kipling. "And we'll have to wait our turn after these people already here. If I know the signs, this storm won't let up any time soon."

Even as he finished speaking, a stylish double brougham—clearly someone's private conveyance—stopped in front of the restaurant, pulled by a nicely matched span of bays. The driver, dressed in oilskins against the weather, leapt down from the seat, holding a large umbrella for his passengers, a prosperous-looking middle-aged couple who were standing in the doorway just in front of us. "It's too bad that one's not for hire," said Mr. Clemens. "There'd be room for all four of us, and we'd be at the hotel in five minutes."

"Five minutes?" The gentleman had begun to step forward toward his coach, but now he turned to look at us. "Why, I think I can solve your problem. Louise, would you be willing to wait ten minutes while Roger takes Mr. Clemens and his party to their hotel?"

"I could hardly object, seeing as how he's been so kind as to provide our evening's entertainment," said the lady, smiling at my employer. She wore a fox coat and matching cap; the head of one of the animals peered over her shoulder, glassy-eyed.

"Well, that's settled, then," said the gentleman. "Roger, take Mr. Clemens and his friends wherever they're going, and then come straight back for me and Mrs. Babson."

"I hardly expected this, but I'm mighty pleased," said Mr. Clemens, extending his right hand. "You have my hearty thanks, Mr. . . . ?"

"Julius Babson, of Philadelphia," said the gentleman, shaking Mr. Clemens's hand. He was a tall, distinguished-looking man, and his silk top hat made him appear even taller. "The pleasure is all mine, believe me."

"Well, if I can return the favor in any way, be sure to let me know," said my employer. "Much obliged, Mr. Babson." With the driver holding an umbrella for us, we thanked our benefactor and hurried into the coach. We managed to get back to our hotel without getting more than a little damp. Not for the first time, I reflected on the benefits of having a well-loved celebrity for my employer, and decided that I had made the right choice of career, after all.

3

The next few days passed rapidly. Mr. Clemens was finishing a magazine article about our journey down the Mississippi, and I was kept busy running errands connected with our upcoming sea voyage. I had never had a passport, and I spent more time than I would have thought possible at a government office, filling out forms and waiting. Luckily, Mr. Clemens had a few acquaintances he could call on to expedite matters, and I eventually had my papers well before our sailing date. Meanwhile, I was responsible for getting our baggage to the ship before sailing, for arranging mail forwarding, and for finding accommodations at the other end of our voyage. My experience as Mr. Clemens's secretary on our Mississippi tour stood me well, but there were whole new dimensions called up by international travel. I was greatly relieved when we finally found ourselves on the dock at Pier 43, ready to board the *City of Baltimore* en route to Southampton, England.

You could easily have persuaded me that the entire population of New York City had taken a holiday to come down to the docks that morning. The crowd was so thick that one could barely breathe, and little mountains of luggage spaced about the pier made free movement for more than a few steps in any direction an impossibility. Every few minutes another cart or cab would pull up and discharge more passengers and luggage, with their retinues of porters and servants, all of whom crowded forward in the deluded expectation that they would be allowed to board the boat the instant they arrived. And without exception, when they learned they would be required to wait their turn, they began to complain bitterly—whether anyone would listen or not.

Mr. Clemens, an experienced traveler, turned a weary eye upon the scene. "It never fails, Wentworth," he said. "They've had two or three days to get this ship ready to leave, and they still aren't ready to let anybody on board. And when they finally do start letting us on, half the damn-fool passengers will charge the gangplank as if they were staking out mining claims, instead of going to cabins they've already reserved. We'll be lucky if nobody gets drowned. Any man with a lick of sense would find a quiet place to sit, so he won't get knocked down and stepped on. And that's what I'm going to do."

I followed him to a corner of the dock, somewhat out of the press, where he sat down on a wooden box and began loading his corncob pipe. From here we had a fine view of the ship, and I realized just how large she was. While *City of Baltimore* was not the American Line's largest or fastest ship (*City of New York* and *City of Paris* shared those distinctions), she measured close to five hundred feet long. And, as I knew from the steamship line's advertisements, she could comfortably house over a thousand souls, counting passengers and crew, for the week-long Atlantic crossing.

But I was more surprised to find that a machine—for that is all a giant ocean liner really is—could appear so graceful. Having grown up by a seaport, I had been around ships and boats all my life, from the humblest of fishing dories to the blue-blooded racing yachts that used to come down from Newport in the summer, not to forget the ferryboats and freighters plying New London Harbor. I had seen a different style of nautical design out on the Mississippi, where the riverboat builders had outdone one another in the search for baroque splendor. But nothing had quite prepared me for the sleek elegance of *City of Baltimore*. For size, power and pure geometrical beauty, she outdid anything I had ever seen. (I later learned that she was considered a mere drudge in comparison to her sister ship, *City of Rome*.)

In contrast, the crowd gathering to board her seemed to be made up of tiny, unruly beings, scrambling about between their piles of luggage, pushing and shoving and bawling in an amazingly heterogenous mixture of languages. On the face of it, one could hardly credit that the great ship had been designed and built by such creatures, and existed only for their convenience in crossing the ocean. And yet, for the most part this was the cream of our American society, captains of industry and leading professional men (with their families and servants) on their way to visit the Old World, whether for enjoyment or for trade and profit. Relatively few passengers were likely to travel in steerage on an eastward crossing—the Land of Opportunity lay on this side of the Atlantic.

As often when looking at a large crowd, I began to wonder whether anyone I knew might be among the group. I would not have been surprised to find some of my schoolfellows along the dock. In fact, the crowd included a fair number of young men and women of about my age, and I began to reflect with some pleasure on the prospect of having agreeable companionship for the voyage. While Mr. Clemens's company was by no means onerous, one shares a certain bond with others of one's own age and class. It struck me that my mother would be much mollified to learn that, despite my having betrayed her hopes of a respectable career, I would at least be traveling with exactly the sort of person she most approved of.

Then my eye lit on a familiar face—and not one I was pleased to see. Not fifteen feet away, wearing a dramatic cape and scowling through a monocle, stood Prinz Heinrich Karl von Ruckgarten, who had made such a nuisance of himself during my previous visit to the docks. Evidently he had decided to travel on *City of Baltimore* after all. Most likely, he would be on the same first-class deck as Mr. Clemens and I. Well, with any luck, he would leave us alone, and we could make the crossing without any unpleasant encounters with this particular fellow traveler.

But as the prince swept his gaze over the crowd, he turned to look in our direction, and to my dismay, his eye fell on Mr. Clemens and his face lit up in a smile. As he stepped in our direction, I bent over and whispered to my employer, "Be careful with this fellow—I'm afraid he's going to be difficult." But Mr. Clemens merely nodded and held his ground, puffing on the corncob pipe.

"Meinherr Mark Twain!" said the prince, stopping in front of us and making a little half-bow. "I am Prinz Heinrich Karl von Ruckgarten, at your service. Am I correct in assuming we are to have the honor of your presence on the crossing to England?"

"I'm not sure how much honor there'll be to it," said Mr. Clemens, raising his bushy white eyebrows. "According to the New York papers, I'm a failure in business, and according to the Boston press, I'm a corrupter of American youth. I haven't read the reports from New Orleans, but after my last visit I wouldn't be surprised if they listed me as an enemy of polite society. I'll be on board the *Baltimore*, if that's what you're asking."

The prince threw back his head and gave a hearty laugh, much to my surprise—I wouldn't have expected him to have the least sense of humor. "Oho, Herr Twain!" he said, still chuckling. "You are every bit as amusing as I could have asked. I am very much pleased to know you will be one of the company. I had feared the voyage would be ever so tedious, but now I know otherwise." His countenance was measurably less obnoxious with a smile upon it. Perhaps the fellow's display of temper at the ticket office had been an aberration. If he were this jovial most of the time, he might not be such bad company after all.

"Well, I hope I don't disappoint you," said my employer. "I don't plan to exert myself any. I'll have to spend a lot of time in my cabin, finishing up a book.

Other than that, I'll do as little as I can get away with. I've just come off a long lecture tour, and I plan to take it easy.'' Even so, I could see from Mr. Clemens's smile that the man's flattery had hit its target.

''An excellent plan,'' said the German, nodding. ''With your permission, I will see that a bottle of the best champagne on board is sent to your cabin, so you can begin your voyage in a proper state of relaxation. Please call me Karl—all the men in my family are named Heinrich, so the second name I use with friends, so to avoid confusion. Oho, I do look forward to our ocean voyage, Mark Twain.'' He gave another of his little bows, spun on his heel, and strode off purposefully in the direction of the ship.

Mr. Clemens looked after him with a surprised expression for a moment, then said, ''Well, that fellow may be a bit stiff, but he introduces himself graciously enough, and doesn't intrude or linger. I doubt he's going to be as difficult as you say, Wentworth. Nothing like a taste of champagne to start off an ocean voyage, especially when somebody else pays for it!''

''I suppose you're right,'' I replied. But privately, I wondered what Prinz Karl might want in return for his generosity.

At last *City of Baltimore* blew her whistle, signaling that it was time for boarding. As my employer had predicted, there was a great rush among the throng lining the dock, with everyone shouting and trying to push forward at once. I was ready to grab my bag and make my way forward, until Mr. Clemens said, ''Feel free to join in the riot, if you want. You can get a black eye or a broken nose as easily here as on the football field, so maybe you'll enjoy it. I used to get up and scuffle with the best of 'em, but I'm too old for that kind of entertainment.''

Somewhat reluctantly, I sat back down. While I could understand his disinclination to shove his way through a large crowd, I had no reason to believe it would be any thinner if we waited to board. At least I'd had the fore-sight to send our heavy trunks ahead, to be loaded by the crew, so we each had only a small carpetbag to carry. Even so, I didn't fancy the notion of struggling aboard in the middle of a last-minute rush.

But it only took twenty minutes for the crowding to subside, and then Mr. Clemens knocked out his pipe and said, "Well, I reckon we can get on the boat, now." I had to admit that he had gauged the situation exactly.

We took our carpetbags and walked toward the gang-plank, actually a long stairway leading from the pier to a large door well up the side of the ship. But even before we got there, I could see there was some sort of trouble in the boarding area. At the foot of the gangplank I could hear raised voices. I knew the signs of an argument when I saw them, and as I might well have expected, Prinz Heinrich Karl von Ruckgarten was right in the middle of it. I was surprised to see another familiar face: Mr. Julius Babson, the man who had so graciously lent us his coach a few days ago in the rainstorm.

Prinz Karl was standing chest to chest with a young man about my own age, who was dressed in the sort of casual elegance that bespoke considerable affluence. Even as we drew close, Prinz Karl shook his fist and shouted, "I will not give way to persons of no merit or importance. Have the courtesy to stand aside and let a gentleman board, and you will have your turn."

The young man did not back down. "We were here first, I'll have you know," he said. "First come, first served, is the rule in this country. If you won't stand back, I'll push you back."

"Robert, please," said Mrs. Babson, who stood next to her husband, a nervous look on her face. Mr. Babson stood stiffly, looking down his nose in the general direc-tion of the prince. From their attitudes, it was easy to guess that young Robert must be their son, and his next words confirmed it.

"Don't worry, Mother," he said. "This pompous tub of lard may be used to cowing the peasants back home, but if he hasn't learned not to tread on an American's toes, it's time somebody taught him the lesson.'' Young Babson turned back to the prince. ''Stand aside, mister. This is the last chance I'm giving you.''

I was convinced the two men were about to exchange blows, and wondering whether I ought to intervene to keep the peace—although experience had taught me that the man who steps between two others determined to fight often takes a harder blow than either. I had no reason to take either man's side. I took one step forward, holding out my hand to keep Mr. Clemens from straying too close to the altercation. For myself, I intended to stay clear, but I was ready to do whatever became necessary.

I was saved from any such necessity by an authoritative voice from the deck above. ''Ahoy! We'll have none of that. Both you men, step off the gangplank and let the other passengers board.'' The speaker was a tall, bearded man, in a blue uniform covered with gold braid: one of the ship's officers, I decided. When neither Prinz Karl nor young Babson gave a sign of moving, the officer frowned and said, ''Mr. Gallagher, will you please clear the gangplank!''

A wiry fellow with a weather-beaten face and a short-trimmed black beard stepped out of the ship and onto the gangplank. He was not much more than five foot six, and cocky as a bantam rooster in his uniform, though it was far plainer than the officer's. Behind him were two burly seamen, neither of whom I would have been pleased to see across the line from me on a football field. They stepped down the gangplank in a purposeful manner, with that curious sway in their step that is the hallmark of a sailor. ''You heard the captain,'' said Gallagher, conveying a clear sense of menace without particularly raising his voice. ''Step aside, now.''

Prinz Karl looked as if he might be ready to contest this order, but a look at the crewmen changed his mind. He stepped backward off the gangplank, still holding himself arrogantly erect. Young Babson stood his ground a moment longer, looking at the three men calmly advancing toward him. "Come on, lad, we don't want any trouble," said Gallagher, with a half-smile that suggested that while he mightn't want trouble, he was fully prepared to deal with it.

Then Mrs. Babson said, "Robert! Come here this instant!" Her husband had been supervising two servants collecting their luggage; now he strode back to the gangplank and spoke in the tone of one used to being obeyed: "Robert, this is absurd. Come down and help your mother board the ship." Looking somewhat peeved, the young fellow backed down, going to his mother's side. His expression bespoke resentment, but the confrontation was over. Mr. Gallagher looked around, spotted Mr. Clemens, and smiled. "Here, I know that face," he said. "You're Mark Twain, aren't you? No reason for *you* to wait here. Come aboard, and I'll sort the rest of this out."

And so we strolled up the gangplank onto the *City of Baltimore*, leaving Gallagher and his crewmen to resolve the question of precedence between Prinz Karl and the Babsons. I was just as glad to leave it in his hands; I'd had more than my share of fights and confrontations during my brief employment with Mr. Clemens, and had no interest in any more. For now, all I cared for was to find our cabin and pursue the exact same course of action as Mr. Clemens had planned for the voyage: sit on the deck, relax, and do as little as possible.

4

A businesslike man wearing an officer's uniform and carrying a clipboard met us at the top of the gang-plank. He introduced himself as Mr. Leslie, the ship's purser. After a quick but thorough inspection of our tickets and passports he detailed a steward to lead Mr. Clemens and me to our cabin.

The steward, who was introduced to us as Harrison, set off at a brisk pace through such a maze of stairs and passageways that I quickly lost track of all the twists and turns. Meanwhile, he kept up a steady stream of commentary, indicating various points of interest as we passed them. "Here's the purser's office, and right down that passageway you'll find the first-class barbershop, and the ship's doctor is just opposite. Now we'll go up to the cabin deck. Watch your step, please, gentlemen. Just aft of us is the ship's library, which I'm sure you'll find of interest, Mr. Clemens—we have over six hundred volumes on all subjects, and the Grand Saloon is aft of that. That's the main smoking room, there—there's another smoker up by the prow, and another on the deck below."

I did my best to keep track of all the facilities he mentioned, but by the time he finally brought us to the door of our cabin I was certain only that the ship was even larger on the inside than she had appeared from the dock. It was obvious that we would find every amenity on board that one would expect in a first-class hotel ashore. Perhaps the only thing missing was a billiard room, but

it did not take much thought to realize that lining up a
carom shot on a rolling sea might be more akin to torture
than to diversion.

Our cabin was actually a small suite of rooms, with an
opening from the main room directly onto the deck. The
sitting-room, paneled in blond oak, had two large arm-
chairs and a small table, and a comfortable-looking set-
tee. Two doors opened off it, leading to a pair of
bedrooms with brass bedsteads. Two portholes offered
ample sunlight, and there was an electric bulb in each
room. We also had our own sink (cold water only), and
Harrison showed us to a bathroom on the inside corridor
only a few doors away. Mr. Clemens took the slightly
larger bedroom; but even my smaller one was more comfortably appointed than the stateroom I had inhabited for
several weeks on the *Horace Greeley*, our Mississippi
riverboat. I had thought the three-hundred-fifty-dollar
price for the crossing excessive, but now that I saw the
accommodations, I began to revise my estimate.

The trunks containing the clothing we would wear on
the voyage had been delivered to the main room, and Mr.
Clemens and I directed Harrison in sorting the contents
and placing them in our bedrooms. (The bulk of our luggage was stored somewhere below, until we reached
Southampton.) The steward was finishing this job when
there was a knock on the door. "Who could that be?" I
wondered out loud.

I opened the door to discover Mr. Kipling, dressed in
a serviceable brown tweed jacket and a well-broken-in
felt hat. "Hullo," he said. "I see you two are getting
settled in nicely. Carrie and I are just around the corner
in number seventeen. Shall we go see if we can all get
seated at the same table for meals?"

"That would be fine with me, but it may not be as
easy as you'd think," said Mr. Clemens. "The captain
will probably insist on having me at his table. I'm not
sure he'll want to take on all four of us as the price of
it."

"We shan't attempt to read the captain's mind," said

Mr. Kipling, smiling broadly. "Let's go make our own arrangements, and we can adjust our plans to the captain's wishes when he makes them known."

"Fair enough," said Mr. Clemens. We left the steward to finish stowing our belongings, and walked out on deck. We had a good view of the harbor from this point, well above the sheds that lined the dock. It was a clear day, and I could see well up the Hudson beyond the currently vacant dock of the White Star Line, and across to the steep Palisades on the New Jersey side. There were numerous boats of one kind or another in the river, sail and steam alike: the Hoboken ferry, barges coming downriver from Albany and Poughkeepsie, pleasure craft and fishing boats. Yet all of them seemed inconsequential next to the great liner we were about to sail on. It was exhilarating to contemplate the voyage that lay before us.

I followed Mr. Clemens and Mr. Kipling aft toward the purser's office to make our seating arrangements for meals. Being experienced travelers, they seemed to have a good idea where we were going; I was still a bit disoriented by the layout of the ship. But I followed them into a broad passageway, down a couple of flights of stairs, and into a sort of lobby, where there was already a small crowd waiting, presumably on the same errand that brought us there.

A murmur went through the group as some of the waiting passengers recognized my employer. Of course, his long white hair and mustache, and his white suit (which he wore despite the fact that summer was long gone) made him a distinctive figure, and his recent lecture tour had been written up in a number of newspapers. So he was perhaps more of a public figure than most writers who spent their time alone in a room "turning blank paper into prose," as he described his trade.

"Hello, Mr. Clemens," came a familiar voice. We turned to see Julius Babson (a prosecuting attorney in Philadelphia, as I learned later on), who had evidently gotten on board in spite of his son's confrontation with Prinz Karl at the gangplank. "I'm delighted to see we'll have the pleasure of your company on the way to Europe.''

"Well, I'm delighted to be going," said Mr. Clemens. "It'll be the first I've seen my wife and family in several months, and I can't tell you how much I'm looking forward to it. I want to thank you again for the loan of your coach the other night; it was a mighty civilized thing to do for a stranger. But I'm glad to see we're on the same boat, because it'll give me the chance to buy you a drink.''

"My goodness, that's hardly necessary," said Mr. Babson, but his beaming face clearly betrayed his pleasure at the invitation.

"Oh, I insist," said Mr. Clemens. "I reckon being on the same boat for most of a week makes us neighbors. It wouldn't be neighborly to let somebody give you a ride and not return the favor some way or another.''

"Well, then, I'll take you up on your offer once we're under weigh," Mr. Babson replied.

As he said this, the young man I'd seen arguing with Prinz Karl on the gangplank came through the door and walked over to Mr. Babson. With him was a very pretty young woman whom I hadn't seen before, but who certainly caught my eye. "Excuse me, Father," he said. "I found our deck chairs after all. They'd been stowed with Mr. Mercer's things, so we can get them any time we want to.''

"Good, I'm glad that's straightened out," said Mr. Babson senior. Then he turned to my employer. "Mr. Clemens, permit me to introduce my son, Robert. Robert, this is Mr. Samuel Clemens, whom you've heard of under his pen name, Mark Twain.''

"Hello, Mr. Clemens," said young Babson. "Pleased to meet you; Father's talked a lot about your books.'' Then he turned to the young woman with him. "May I introduce Miss Theresa Mercer. Tess has consented to become my bride, after we return from Europe.''

"Hello, Mr. Clemens," the young woman said. She blushed prettily as she gave a little curtsy, but she did not lower her eyes. She was a very fair-skinned blonde, with twinkling blue eyes, and I found myself envious of Robert Babson.

"Well, my congratulations, young man—and it's a pleasure to meet you, Miss Mercer. It's good to know there'll be something aboard for these old eyes to look at besides the ocean waves." My employer smiled broadly, and Theresa Mercer blushed again. I thought I saw young Babson stiffen as my employer paid this harmless little compliment; then she took her fiancé's hand and he relaxed, and the moment passed.

As Mr. Clemens had predicted, the chief steward had already placed him at the captain's table for the duration of our crossing. The other seats would be filled (by invitation) with a selection of the more important or influential passengers, changing from one evening to the next. So by the time we reached Southampton, a fair number of guests would have had the honor of dining with the captain—and with the famous author Mark Twain.

Meanwhile, Mr. and Mrs. Kipling and I reserved seats together at one of the other tables for dinners. Mr. Clemens shrugged. "Now you see the price of fame, Kipling. I'll be sitting next to a bunch of businessmen most of the way over, providing the only amusement at the table. I'll tell the captain you're aboard, though. That'll probably get you and your wife invited up for at least one meal, and I'll have somebody I can actually talk to. With any luck, you'll be invited for a couple more meals—assuming you *want* to help me entertain the stuffed shirts." My employer concluded his speech with a broad wink at Mr. Kipling and myself, from which I deduced that he meant his remark facetiously. After three months in Mr. Clemens's company, I was becoming accustomed to his sort of humor, which often consisted of belittling observations about the respectable classes of society—of which he was, willy-nilly, a member.

Mr. Kipling laughed. "Your American businessmen can't be very different to some of the *pukka sahibs* in

India. The ones I've met have been decent enough chaps. You never know when a friend with money might come in useful, do you?''

''You're right about that,'' said Mr. Clemens. ''I'd be in sad shape if Henry Rogers hadn't been willing to help bail me out. He's paying my passage over, and Wentworth's, too—giving me the chance to work my way back into solvency. I used to think the Carnegies and Rockefellers were parasites on the human race. Now I think maybe millionaires have some purpose in the world, after all.''

''Aye, making it possible for writers to live by their wits,'' agreed Mr. Kipling. ''Shall we go see how the smoking room is set up?''

''Best suggestion I've heard today,'' said Mr. Clemens. ''No, make that second best—assuming that German makes good on his offer of a bottle of champagne. We'll have a smoke, and then we'll look back in my cabin and see if he's remembered his promise.''

''And if he hasn't, we can send for our own,'' said Kipling. ''Be a shame to cast off without a proper celebration. I'm looking forward to meeting this Prinz Karl; sounds like a capital fellow—although a bit of an odd one.'' He laughed again, and we went in search of the first-class smoking lounge, while Mrs. Kipling made her way to the Grand Saloon.

I have never been one of the brotherhood of smokers— my one childhood experiment with a pipe and tobacco that one of my playmates ''borrowed'' from his father ended in such a way as to discourage me from further efforts along the same lines. And when I went out for football and other sports, I quickly learned that I had an edge in endurance over the fellows who smoked. But Mr. Clemens was an inveterate smoker, and his brain seemed to operate at full speed only when properly fumed with pipe or cigar smoke. So I had gotten used to doing much of our work, during his travels, in smoking cars and in hotel rooms with a thick aura of tobacco in the air. Knowing that the smoking lounge would be, in effect,

our second home during the voyage, I saw no reason not
to scout it out along with my employer and Mr. Kipling.

We found the area we were looking for not far from
the dining room. The room was laid out much like a
gentleman's club on land, with card tables, plush sofas,
several electric lights, and a supply of current newspapers
and magazines. Half a dozen other passengers had already arrived in this sanctuary, and were putting it to
good use—there were a pair of bewhiskered older men
pegging away a hand of cribbage, two more quietly poring over the New York papers, and all adding their quota
of smoke to the air. A few, evidently recognizing Mr.
Clemens, looked up and nodded as we entered.

"Well, this is pleasantly laid out," said Mr. Kipling,
settling down on one of the sofas and pulling a cigar case
out of his pocket. "Let's hope it doesn't get too crowded
to have a quiet talk."

"Oh, there are two other smoking lounges if we want
to go hunt for them," said Mr. Clemens, looking around
at the appointments. "You young fellows are spoiled
when it comes to ocean travel. Hell, I remember the old
days, when we had to go out to the 'fiddle' for a smoke.
That was just a shed covering the main hatch, with no
place to sit, a stinking oil lamp, and cracks in the walls
big enough to throw a tomcat through. I'd as soon smoke
in a chicken coop—no, I'd *rather* smoke in a chicken
coop. A well-made chicken coop is cleaner and keeps the
weather out more efficiently, though I'll grant you the
company is a bit dull. But this room is as comfortable as
you'll find in most hotels—hell, I've been in German
hotels that didn't have a smoking room at all."

Mr. Kipling leaned over to me and asked, in a stage
whisper, "Is he going to give us his lecture on the old
days, when the passengers had to row all the way across
and catch their own fish to eat?" We all laughed, and I
decided that Mr. Kipling was a fellow very much to my
liking.

Mr. Clemens scowled at Kipling. "Now, don't mock
your elders, young man. You're likely to make poor

Wentworth think I'm not entirely veracious. He's been with me since early summer, and I don't think he's caught me in a lie yet. Don't go spoiling my reputation.''

''I don't know,'' I said. ''There was some sort of tale you tried to tell me about alligator nets . . .''

''There, Kipling, see what you've done?'' Mr. Clemens knit his brows fiercely. ''You've roused up Wentworth's suspicions, and I reckon I'll never be able to impose on him again. You have no idea what a loss that is. Now I'll just have to shut up entirely—or worse yet, confine myself strictly to the truth. See if I let *you* have any of my champagne!''

''Hoist by my own petard,'' said Kipling, a wide smile on his features. ''Could I possibly change your mind by offering you one of these excellent Havana cigars? I bought a box specially in New York, thinking they'd be just the thing to help pass the voyage.''

Mr. Clemens took the proffered cigar and sniffed it, then smiled. ''That's what I like about you, Kipling— you have a good sense of the priorities. Let's see if these things want to burn properly.'' He snipped the end of the cigar with his pocket knife, and struck a sulfur-match to light it. Soon the two writers were happily smoking, and I sat back to look around the room.

The cribbage players were still locked in combat, calling out the scores and watching each other's hands like hawks for stray points they could steal: ''Fifteen, two. Fifteen, four. Run of three, seven. And nobby, for eight.'' They gave the impression of being old rivals, who had met over the card table more than once. Another fellow of about the same vintage had joined them, and was looking over the shoulder of the nearer player with manifest interest.

A lean man with a fringe of gray hair around a balding pate and an expensively cut dark blue suit had sat down next to the gentleman who had been reading the newspaper, and they were now engaged in a sober discussion of the stock market. ''My broker says to stay away from the railroad stocks for the next six months,'' said the newcomer, and the other shook his head gravely. "Can't imagine what the fellow's thinking about. There's nothing sounder than railroads, nothing at all. I just took on ten thousand B and O, myself. If I were you, I'd do the same." My own familiarity with stocks and finance was extremely limited, but I had the instant impression that I was hearing two of the prime movers of American commerce in conference, and wondered how much money might be gained or lost when one of these gentlemen decided to change his portfolio.

I became aware of a bit of noise at the entrance, and looked up to see a uniformed steward attempting to prevent several younger-looking men from entering. At second glance, I was startled to recognize two of them as former Yale classmates of mine. What a surprise! I stood up and said, "Excuse me a moment," to Mr. Clemens and Mr. Kipling, and walked over to see what they were doing here.

"I'm sorry, this is the first-class lounge," the steward was saying. "Steerage passengers strictly forbidden. You'll have to go back to your own deck."

"Oh, bosh, old man, we're not going to break anything," said one of the fellows. "We just want to come in and have a smoke like everyone else."

"Hello, Bertie," I said. "What, are you going to Europe?"

"Good Lord, it's Wentworth Cabot!" said Bertie Parsons—he'd had a room just down the hall from me our last year at Yale. "Hullo, old boy, what on earth are you doing aboard? Tell this chap we're regular fellows, will you? You remember good old Johnny DeWitt, don't you? And this is his brother Tom—he's finished his first year up at New Haven."

I turned to the steward, who seemed overwhelmed by the sudden influx of sons of Eli. "I know these fellows," I said. "Is my word enough to let them in?"

"It's hardly regular," said the steward, flustered. He was a little worried-looking fellow with a red face and blond hair parted in the middle. A premature bald spot

The Prince and the Prosecutor 37

had started to show toward the back of his skull. He kept
glancing around as if he hoped to find someone of higher
authority to back him up.

"Oh, they can be my guests, if you need authoriza-
tion," I said. "They're none of them ruffians, if that's
what you're concerned about."

"I'm sorry, sir, but I can't just let you bring in a pack
of people who don't belong," said the steward, although
he was clearly beginning to waver.

"Here, what's the problem?" It was Mr. Clemens,
who'd come up behind me. "Do you know these fellows,
Wentworth?"

"Why, yes," I said, and quickly introduced them to
my employer. I was secretly pleased to see that Bertie
and the DeWitts seemed properly impressed to learn that
I was traveling with none other than Mr. Clemens, whom
they probably knew as Mark Twain.

"Well, I'm pleased to say that I'm a Yale man myself," said Mr. Clemens. "If a man that can get into Yale
College ain't good enough to sit in the smoking lounge,
then you might as well throw all five of us overboard
and get it done with. Are you going to let these boys in—
as my guests?"

At this, the steward had to confess that he was out of
his league, and he beat a hasty retreat as Mr. Clemens
and I escorted the three Yale men over to sit with us.

Bertie and Johnny and I had spent more than one late
night with a bottle of wine and an endless stream of talk
on every subject under the sun. Those were still some of
my fondest memories of college. I had been looking forward to my Atlantic voyage, but now I was even more
convinced it was going to be great fun.

5 ~

M r. Clemens and Mr. Kipling entertained my Yale
classmates with stories and small talk for the better part of an hour. My friends had saved up their
earnings from summer work and were now on their way
to see the sights of Europe on the cheap by crossing the
Atlantic as steerage passengers, after the prime season
for eastbound travel. They had brought along bicycles to
reduce their expenses on the European side, and were
treating the entire expedition as a jolly adventure. Indeed,
it sounded like grand fun—although, having had a sample of first-class accommodations with Mr. Clemens, I
suspected that my taste for steerage travel was already
spoiled. Certainly, there was something to be said for
going to Europe first-class and being paid for it, especially if traveling on a shoestring were the only alterna-
tive. (Although, to be honest, Mr. Clemens was on a
tighter budget than it must have seemed to our fellow
passengers, and he would be earning his keep on the
other end by giving a series of lectures and readings.)

As I had seen many times before, for Mr. Clemens
merely to sit and hold a conversation in a public area was
tantamount to issuing an invitation for all who recognized
him to come introduce themselves, however slight the
pretext. One of my normal responsibilities as his traveling secretary was to pry him away from such intruding
members of the public when their demands grew excessive. But for the time being, he was clearly enjoying the

crowd's attention, and utterly charmed not only my friends but most of the others who ventured within ear-shot.

Among those who introduced themselves were several Philadelphians, who as it turned out were traveling in a group to explore the museums and architectural monuments of England, France, and Italy. Julius Babson and his family we had already met; now we made the acquaintance of Mr. Vincent Mercer, a prominent banker, and the father of young Robert Babson's fiancée, Theresa. He had a somewhat pinched countenance, and the reserved manner of a man whose station in life depends upon his ability to convince others to trust him with their money. Nevertheless, he claimed familiarity with Mr. Clemens's writings, and seemed genuinely pleased to make my employer's acquaintance.

With him was Wilfred Smythe, a young man of about my own age, and the son of a Methodist minister in Philadelphia. (His parents were on board the ship, but his father was another who abjured the use of tobacco, and therefore had not come to the smoking lounge.) Young Smythe had something of the seriousness I had seen in other ministers' sons, but I caught a twinkle in his eye as he listened to Mr. Clemens's stories, and decided that his upbringing had not left him without an independent spirit. Vincent Mercer had promoted him to a position of responsibility in his bank, and clearly looked on him as a young man of promise. Observing Smythe's quiet demeanor and obvious intelligence, I decided that Mr. Mercer's confidence in him would likely prove to be well-placed.

Mr. Mercer also introduced us to Signor Giorgio Rubbia, an Italian artist who was to be the Philadelphians' guide to the artistic treasures of Europe. Although he stood no more than five foot six, Signor Rubbia must have weighed something over two hundred fifty pounds, and his fleshy jowls were accentuated by bushy white side whiskers. His attire was as distinctive as his figure: a wide-brimmed black felt hat, a flamboyant purple-lined cape, and a long, colorful scarf worn instead of a necktie. He seemed incapable of uttering a sentence without an extravagant gesture to accompany it. I could tell by Mr. Clemens's expression that he was not impressed by Signor Rubbia. Amused, perhaps, but not at all impressed. For myself, I found the man an interestingly exotic specimen, and determined to see what I could learn from his observations on art (although his thick Italian accent might make that something of a challenge).

Signor Rubbia appeared to have only a vague notion of who Mr. Clemens was. But he soon discerned that my employer was the focus of all eyes in the lounge, and that even Vincent Mercer was paying more attention to the American writer than to him. Rubbia's eyes narrowed as Mr. Mercer asked Mr. Clemens his advice on the sights to see in London; clearly, he considered this request an intrusion on his own prerogatives as guide to the Mercer party.

"What to see depends on what you like," said Mr. Clemens. "There's plenty to see in London. Don't miss Westminster Abbey, the Houses of Parliament, or the British Museum—and make sure to get a look at the Tower of London. It'll remind you how the kings and nobles have kept the people under their thumb for so long. I've always wondered how some Americans pretend to admire those rascals—a king's not much better than a slaveholder, in my opinion."

Mr. Kipling chuckled. "Now, watch yourself, Clemens. I'll make allowance for your opinions of kings. You're an American and a humorist besides, but don't forget you have a loyal subject of the Queen sitting here next to you."

"What is there to see in the way of art?" asked Mr. Mercer, ignoring Mr. Kipling's sally.

"I'd suggest the National Portrait Gallery," said Mr. Clemens. "Don't bother with the other National Gallery—if you want my opinion, the portraits are the only paintings in London worth a second look. Even if most of them are of dead people, at least they're *real* people.

There's no other art in England worth walking across the street for.''

Signor Rubbia instantly seized this opening. "No art in England? What sort of foolishness is this? Have you not seen 'The Hay Wain' of Constable? Or the 'Fighting Temeraire' of Turner? Did you not see the Elgin Marbles?''

Mr. Clemens looked up at the Italian, raising his eyebrows. His pipe had burnt out, and he carefully tapped the ashes into the ashtray before he replied. "Sure, I've seen all of 'em. I'd rather sit by the Thames and watch the boats passing, if you want to know the truth. Nature's the oldest master of them all, and the only one that's never let me down.''

"Aha! A man after my own heart!'' exclaimed a hearty voice from the back of the room. I looked up to see Prinz Heinrich Karl von Ruckgarten, who had just come through the door. "Herr Mark Twain, I hope you have received the magnum of champagne I had sent to your cabin! I consider it a doubly deserved gift after hearing your astute criticism. No man who follows the teachings of Nature can go far wrong.'' He gave a little bow; out of the corner of my eye I saw Mr. Clemens smile.

For his part, Signor Rubbia was far from pleased with the new arrival. "That theory no doubt does very well in Germania,'' he said loudly. "Without imagination or *brio*, the artists there can only draw what they see—one Giotto is worth the whole bunch of them.''

"I've heard of Jotto,'' said Mr. Clemens. "Is he dead?'' The audience burst into laughter, although I was not quite certain what the joke was, and Signor Rubbia turned red.

Before the laughter had subsided, Mr. Clemens stood. "Well, Prinz Karl, Kipling and I were just about to go down to my cabin to see if your bottle was there. Why don't you come along and find out if you got your money's worth? Sounds as if there's plenty for all of us.''

"I would be most delighted to join Herr Mark Twain,'' said the prince, and the four of us swept out the door together, leaving a smiling crowd behind—with the exception of Signor Rubbia, who looked as if he had a sudden case of indigestion.

The champagne had indeed been delivered, and was already well chilled. I pulled the cork and filled four glasses. Mr. Clemens waited for the bubbles to subside a bit, then turned to the prince and said, "To your health, and many thanks for the fine going-away present!"

"My pleasure entirely, Herr Twain," said the prince, beaming. We clinked our glasses and drank. The champagne was sweeter than most I had tasted, but very full-bodied and delightfully cool. All except Prinz Karl took seats in the comfortable chairs and sofa provided. Mr. Kipling propped his feet up and said, "If you don't mind my asking, what brings a German prince to America? Most of the time, the poor Yankees have to go to your side of the pond to rub elbows with royalty."

"Ah, that is a long story," said Prinz Karl. He had remained standing, and his erect posture gave a lively sense of his aristocratic upbringing. "I will give you the brief version. America is now what Europe will be—almost for certain in the lifetimes of you two young gentlemen. Now is the last act of the play for kings and princes, I believe, and the start of the time for parliaments and ministers. In my great-grandfather's time, things were different—a whole division our little principality raised, for him to go to Austerlitz and fight against Napoleon. Alas, the French artillery did not let him bring many of his men home again. My father still believed for many years that our principality could exist by itself, but Prinz von Bismarck became more and more insistent. The Prussians can be very persuasive, you know."

"I believe so," said Mr. Kipling. "The man with a big enough army can usually get his way." There was general nodding of heads in agreement with this.

"Though another fellow with a bigger army can often make him stop and think before he does something stupid," said Mr. Clemens. "So I take it that Ruckgarten has been swallowed up by the German empire.''

"So it has," said the prince, spreading his left hand in front of him, as if balancing something on the palm. "To console him in his old age, my father still has his title and his little palace and his hereditary honors, but I do not think they will much benefit me. In fact, I am sure they will not—since I have been so improvident to have been born my father's second son. To be perfectly frank with you, I do not in the least regret it. My brother Heinrich Maximillian is quite competent, and very serious. And as I say, I think the time for kings and princes is not long. So I travel about the globe, and enjoy what there is to enjoy in life, and let my brother govern as best he can without consulting me."

"A melancholy thought, in a way," said Mr. Kipling. He sipped at his champagne, a meditative expression on his face. "I hope that England will never find itself in such condition, but I'm not such a fool to think it will avoid those straits without strenuous efforts to stem the tide of history."

"Well, if there's any kind of tide in history, it rolls in and out just like the ocean," said Mr. Clemens. "You can't bet on progress, only on change. I'll tell you one thing about democracy, Prinz Karl. A senator can rob you just as blind as a duke—there ain't hardly any difference between them, except when you get tired of one senator you can usually bring in another one to rob you some new way."

Prinz Karl and Mr. Kipling laughed heartily, and Kipling raised his glass. "Well, Clemens, I see you haven't taken up diplomacy in your old age. I look forward to watching you properly scandalize the British lecture audiences. It should be a sight to remember."

Mr. Clemens waved his hand disparagingly. "Scandalizing the British is child's play—Wentworth could do it, if he put his mind to it. Now, a real challenge would be scandalizing a Frenchman—or possibly an Italian."

"You didn't seem to have much difficulty with that artist, Signor Rubbia," I remarked.

"Oh, that was no challenge at all," said Mr. Clemens, grinning broadly. "You can always rile up an Italian by making fun of art—or opera, if you're in the mood for a real argument. I knew Signor Rubbia for a sham the instant I saw that scarf of his. It was hard to resist exposing him right on the spot. But I guess we should be glad he's aboard—if we run out of other entertainment on the crossing, we can get hours of amusement pulling his leg."

I was at a loss to understand Mr. Clemens's reaction to Signor Rubbia. For all I knew, the artist *was* a sham. But I was not so confident of my own knowledge of art (though I knew what I liked) to judge another's expertise. Still, a few minutes' conversation in the lounge seemed to me too short a time to dismiss Rubbia's opinions entirely, or to decide to make him the target of jokes and taunts. But I was not being paid to contradict my employer, or to chide him for behavior that appeared unseemly to me. Certainly, neither Mr. Kipling nor Prinz Karl took exception to his remarks, except in a spirit of fun. So I held my tongue, and resolved to listen and learn—from Signor Rubbia as well as Mr. Clemens, and even from Prinz Karl, who seemed a pleasant enough fellow when he managed to keep his temper under control.

After the first glass of champagne, Mr. Clemens suggested that we invite Mrs. Kipling to join us. "Of course," said Mr. Kipling. "I'll go fetch Carrie directly."

"No need of that," I said. "Tell me where to find her and I'll bring her back. I'll trust you gentlemen to save at least one glass for me."

"And one for the lady, as well," said Prinz Karl, smiling. "To invite her to share an empty bottle with us, it would be most inhospitable!"

"We can order up another bottle, if it comes to that," said Mr. Clemens. "But I reckon there'll be some left by the time Wentworth gets back, if he don't get lost—or spend all afternoon stopping to gawk at the boat."

"No danger of that," I said. "I've got most of a week to see the ship. Where should I expect to find Mrs. Kipling?"

"She was going to the Grand Saloon," said Mr. Kipling. "If she's not there, she'll probably be back in our cabin—number seventeen. Around the corner—do you know where it is?"

"I think I can find it," I said. "If not, I'll come back and ask directions." I drank up the half-inch remaining in my glass, and went to look for Mrs. Kipling.

There was a good bit of activity on the decks, with passengers gathering at the rail to enjoy their last view of New York City, and crewmen wrestling with a few last pieces of latecomers' baggage. The anticipation of our departure was a tonic in the air, and most of the passengers I passed were talking animatedly, or pointing out the sights to their companions. The excitement was contagious, and I found myself smiling and nodding to my fellow passengers as if we were all old friends, instead of people who had never laid eyes on one another before this very moment.

Actually, I realized, that wasn't quite true. Ahead of me I saw young Robert Babson, leaning over the rail and pointing out the sights of the docks below and of the city beyond to his pretty fiancée, Miss Theresa Mercer. I smiled and touched the brim of my hat as I passed them, but they had eyes only for each other, and so I went on my way.

A short distance after, I encountered another familiar face: Wilfred Smythe, the young assistant to Miss Mercer's father. He was ambling slowly along the deck toward me, a pensive expression on his face. I was surprised—he had seemed an eminently cheerful fellow when his employer had introduced him to Mr. Clemens and me, a short while ago in the smoking room. Then I saw his gaze light on something behind me, and a frown came across his face; for a moment, I considered whether it would best to walk on by, pretending not to notice him. Then he saw me coming toward him, and he managed a little smile, and a quiet "Hello," as we passed. I replied in kind, and went on my way, wondering at what could have caused his evident annoyance.

It was some time later when it occurred to me that he must have been looking at Robert Babson and Theresa Mercer, whom I had just passed as he came into my view. And it was later still that I understood what had caused him to frown so.

I returned with Mrs. Kipling to the cabin, where in the company of Mr. Clemens, Mr. Kipling, and Prinz Karl, we finished the magnum of champagne, laughing a good deal. I think the anticipation of our departure had as much to do with our high spirits as anything we drank. Certainly, between my employer and Prinz Karl, the quips flew fast and furious. I think Mrs. Kipling had never been so outrageously flattered in her life. Had her husband not been present, and making as many jokes as Mr. Clemens and the Prince, I think she would have been scandalized.

When the bottle was at last emptied, we strolled out on deck to observe the final preparations for casting off. Already I could feel from somewhere deep below the throbbing rhythm of the great steam engines—a feeling with which I had become familiar (though on a smaller scale) during my trip down the Mississippi with Mr. Clemens. A glance upward showed smoke gathering above the three tall smokestacks of our vessel. Alas, it also revealed a bank of dark clouds swarming over the New Jersey Palisades to our west; we would be lucky to get out of the harbor without a rainstorm.

But we were not about to let something as trivial as an impending storm spoil our jolly moods. Somewhere in the direction of the ship's bow, a band was playing, and we let the music draw us toward it. On the foredeck we found many of the first-class passengers gathered to watch half a dozen smartly uniformed fellows, in blue jackets, peaked caps, and white trousers, playing a sprightly march on an assortment of wind instruments. A tall fellow with hawkish features and an iron-gray ''Imperial'' beard directed them with a slender white baton. While his erect posture and gold-braided uniform radiated authority, he was clearly enjoying the music as much as any of the listeners. It would have been difficult, in the foulest of moods, to resist tapping a foot and breaking into a smile.

Though mid-October was well past the prime season for ocean travel, the ship appeared to have attracted a goodly complement of passengers. I had already met many of those whom I saw watching the scene with the same evident enjoyment as I. The Babson family stood in a group along the starboard rail, the father nodding his head in time to the rhythm, and his wife and daughter—a pretty young woman in a black traveling dress that set off her blond hair to good effect—arm in arm beside him. Robert Babson and his fiancée, Theresa Mercer, stood slightly apart from them. Young Babson leaned back with one foot propped against a lower rung of the railing behind him, and a straw hat cocked at a rakish angle on his head; Miss Mercer whispered something to him and he nodded, smiling. Not far away stood Vincent Mercer, the banker, next to a severe-looking woman wearing a fur wrap, evidently his wife.

One young man waved to the Babsons and said, ''Here, stand right where you are, against the rail and I'll take your picture.'' He was carrying a little black box in his hands, which on closer inspection I recognized as one of the Kodak portable cameras that had become such a fad the last few years. One of my uncles had bought one of the first models the year I went away to Yale, and had spent almost the entire summer lining people up and telling them to smile, then locking himself in a dark closet to mix up strange-smelling chemicals so as to develop his films. Despite everyone's skepticism, the little camera actually made quite acceptable photographs. The Babsons dutifully posed, with artificial-looking smiles, and the young man pressed the button. He thanked them, then wandered off in search of other photographic subjects. I wondered how he was going to keep his chemicals from spilling on board the rolling ship.

Signor Rubbia looked at the amateur photographer with a condescending expression. The artist would have made a fine subject for a picture, himself—his cape catching the breeze and his scarf fluttering dramatically behind him. Indeed, it seemed to me that he was striking a pose rather than standing naturally: His feet were spread apart, and his chin was lifted as if to add an inch or two to his height. Under one arm he carried a stout walking stick, with an ivory handle carved in the shape of an eagle's head.

Against the opposite rail stood Wilfred Smythe, flanked by an elderly couple who were unmistakably his parents: a tall, thin, scholarly looking gentleman in a clerical collar, wearing thick spectacles and a plain black hat, and a stout, gray-haired woman whose modestly cut dark dress was in stark contrast to her bright eyes and ready smile. Young Smythe seemed to have recovered from his bout of melancholy; he tapped his foot along with the band, and applauded enthusiastically when the tune came to an end.

The bandleader turned and bowed to the audience, then faced his men again and struck up a new tune, this one in waltz time: the sentimental "After the Ball." Prinz Karl turned to Mr. Kipling and asked his permission to dance with his wife. "Why, certainly, if Carrie would like to," said Mr. Kipling, and to my surprise the two of them began waltzing gracefully across the deck. Several other couples followed their example, and soon the deck resembled nothing so much as an open-air ballroom. The sense of fun was contagious, and I began to think that the whole voyage would be one continuous party.

But as I looked around, I realized that not everyone found the scene as charming as I did. Mrs. Mercer, the banker's wife, curled her lip, as if she found the spon-

taneous outbreak of dancing somehow distasteful. Some
of the other ladies seemed to share her feeling; I saw one
or two of them give a sniff of displeasure. Nor was Signor Rubbia impressed; as soon as Prinz Karl had begun
dancing with Mrs. Kipling, he rolled his eyes ostenta-
tiously, turned his back, and strode away from the scene.
I wondered briefly whether it was the dancing or the dancer he found so little to his liking. Then the band swung
into another tune, "The Sidewalks of New York," and I
turned my attention back to the music.

Prinz Karl proved to be an excellent dancer. I could
see that Mrs. Mercer's reaction to the dancing was by no
means the prevailing sentiment among the ladies. When
the band had concluded its medley, the prince led Mrs.
Kipling back to her husband, bowing as he handed her
over. Then the musicians struck up "Daisy Bell," and
the next thing I knew, the prince was waltzing with another lady—evidently a perfect stranger!—while Mr.
Kipling led his wife out on the floor and showed himself
a very smooth and stylish dancer in his own right. I found
myself a bit envious of Prinz Karl's easy grace and con-
tinental manners, and wished for an introduction to some
of the young ladies on board so I might find a dancing
partner of my own. Perhaps the opportunity would present itself soon.

At last, the impromptu party was interrupted by a double blast of the ship's whistle—loud enough to drown
out the band for a moment. This was evidently a signal
that we were about to cast off, for it was followed by a
cry of "All ashore that's going ashore" by an officer
with a megaphone. This unambiguous (if not entirely
grammatical) order led to a hasty exodus of those who
had come aboard to bid their friends "bon voyage." For
the next few minutes, departing visitors crowded the
gangplank, and the passengers moved to the rail to wave
farewell to those ashore as the great ship prepared to set
out on its voyage. The bandleader, recognizing that the
time for dancing on deck had passed, had his fellows
strike up a lively march again.

Mr. Clemens and I moved to a position with a clear view of the dockside, and watched the crew busy itself with the details of casting off the sturdy hawsers that tied us to the dock. The engines throbbed more purposefully and, guided by a little red and green tugboat that seemed barely adequate to the task, *City of Baltimore* backed away from the dock. A cheer went up from the passengers, and the crowd ashore began to wave and blow kisses even more frantically. Then, as we cleared the dock, the tugboat moved up to point our bow downstream, and the band echoed our mood of excitement with the strains of "Ta-Ra-Ra Boom-De-Ay!" I felt a quickening in my blood; at last, I was on my way to Europe!

We were not far down the Hudson when the clouds that had loomed so threateningly over New Jersey began to sprinkle us with rain. The bandleader dismissed his men, and—as much as I wanted to enjoy the last sight of my native country I expected to have for many weeks—I followed Mr. Clemens into our cabin for a little rest before dinner. We had both been up since early in the day, and after partaking of Prinz Karl's gift of champagne, it was hardly surprising that we felt somewhat fatigued.

Inside, Mr. Clemens seated himself in an easy chair, took off his shoes, and propped his feet on the table in front of him. "Well, I'm looking forward to this," he said. "A chance to sit back and smoke a few cigars and tell lies, and do nothing in particular until we're in England. And it looks as if the company won't be entirely boring, either."

"I should think not," I said, settling into a chair opposite him. "Prinz Karl is a lively fellow, for one."

"Yes, I wonder what his game is. I won't object to a fellow buying me a bottle of champagne, mind you. But he's got something up his sleeve, and I'd like to know what it is before it costs me more than just a little time and breath."

"What on earth do you mean? Are you suggesting he isn't really a prince?"

"Maybe he is, and maybe he isn't. Even if he does have a drop or two of royal blood, he might still be a fraud. Why, I'd bet you two bucks of my own money he's a fraud, though I grant you he's an entertaining one."

"How long have you suspected this?" I asked.

"I smelled a rat almost as soon as he started talking about where he comes from. I find it mighty interesting that I *lived* in Germany for several months, and never heard tell of Ruckgarten until just this afternoon."

I was astonished. "Why, that's incredible . . . isn't it?" I tried to remember whether I had ever heard of such a place, but my geographical knowledge was too spotty to provide the information.

"Maybe," he said, cupping his chin in his hand. "I suppose it could be some backwoods place of no interest to anybody from the outside world—like Arkansas, say. But the name's a bit strange, too. Do you know any German?"

"I'm afraid not," I said. Languages had never been my strong suit, although I had struggled manfully through the requisite courses in Latin.

Mr. Clemens shook his head. "To think a fellow could graduate from Yale, and know so little of any real use . . . Well, I can't pretend to speak German very fluently, myself, so I shouldn't give myself airs about it. It can be a real jawbreaker if you're used to a sensibly organized language like English. But unless I'm mistaken, *Ruckgarten* means something like 'back garden.' Not a likely name for what the prince says used to be an independent principality. I'll have to ask Kipling about it—if he hasn't heard of it, there's no such animal."

"But what could Prinz Karl expect to accomplish by such a blatant imposture—assuming that's what it is? Surely, he can't believe he won't be exposed!" I rose to my feet, and went to look out our porthole; the rain was still falling, and the sky was darker than ever. Vaguely I could make out the shoreline, and a few buildings in the distance, so we were evidently still within the confines of New York harbor.

I looked back at Mr. Clemens, who spread his hands and shrugged. "I don't know what he's up to. That Italian artist, now—he's as transparent as plate glass. He's bamboozling the Philadelphians by setting up as an expert in something they don't know enough about to spot him as a fraud, and getting a free tour of Europe out of it. But Prinz Karl's got some other game going— and until I figure it out, I'm not about to play high-stakes poker with him."

"He bought us a magnum of champagne," I said, trying to reconcile the prince's generosity with Mr. Clemens's doubt of his genuineness—a doubt I had no way to refute. My employer had shown himself to be an astute judge of character during the time I had known him. Even so, I liked to think I was a bit more seasoned than the naive young fellow who had come down from Yale to offer himself to Mr. Clemens as a traveling secretary a few short months ago. I could look back with some amusement on my willingness to accept my fellow passengers at face value during our riverboat journey. A certain young lady had pulled the wool over my eyes quite effectively . . . then again, I recalled that she had managed to fool Mr. Clemens as well.

"I haven't forgotten the champagne," said my employer. "Hell, I'll buy the prince a drink or two in return, as long as he doesn't do anything worse than lie about where he's from. But I'll keep a grip on my wallet while I do it, and I advise you to follow suit."

I had no ready rejoinder to this. Instead, my memory called up the image of my first encounter with Prinz Karl, when he had created a scene at the ticket office. Had he really tried to pay for his passage with a check drawn against insufficient funds in his bank account? Even if he had, he had quickly produced cash to make good the deficiency. Was it simply a misunderstanding, or were his finances more irregular than one would assume from his self-proclaimed status as the younger brother of the heir to a principality—even one that had fallen on hard times? And what, if anything, did he expect to gain from the imposture, if such it was? I searched my brain for answers, but found none.

After a while, Mr. Clemens and I roused ourselves to dress for dinner. The rain continued, and so we made our way to the dining room through an inside passageway. The motion of the ship was more perceptible now. We must have come out of the harbor into the open sea, where one would feel the influence of the ocean waves as well as the stormy weather. While I was by no means uncomfortable, it crossed my mind that many activities I took for granted on dry land would become more difficult on a moving ship—drinking a cup of coffee, for example, or eating soup. I wondered if the ship's cooks took the weather into account when planning a day's menu, or if they went ahead, unheeding, with a predetermined bill of fare.

The end of the passageway opened into a larger hall-way, where we found a good-sized crowd waiting for the dining room doors to open. There was a buzz of conversation as people introduced themselves to other passengers or simply carried on the usual small talk among strangers brought together for a social occasion. Mr. Clemens's entry caused a little stir. As people became aware of the famous writer in their midst, heads turned, and there was a noticeable change in the tempo of the conversation. If experience were any guide, the novelty of his presence would soon dissipate, and he would be able to go about his business without constantly being stared at.

Over to one side, I spotted a small group of people my own age. My first instinct was to look for my Yale friends, until I recalled that steerage passengers wouldn't be allowed in the first-class dining room. (Even so, I wouldn't have put it past Bertie Parsons to put on his best suit and try to bluff his way in; he had been a great party-crasher in our college days.) But Robert Babson was there, talking loudly, to a group that included his fiancée, Theresa Mercer, and the blond young lady I'd seen with the Babsons earlier that day, and who I guessed was Robert's sister. Before, seeing her in her street clothes, I had thought her quite pretty; now, in a more formal dark green velvet dress, she was stunning. I decided it might be worth my while to further cultivate her father's acquaintance, and perhaps get an introduction.

Near them, Mr. Clemens spotted the Kiplings. Since I would be sitting at the same dinner table with them, I went with my employer as he ambled over to greet the couple—not at all sorry for the chance to see Miss Babson at closer range. "Hullo, Clemens," said Kipling. "I see you're ready to entertain the captain and his millionaire guests."

"Oh, I doubt we have too many millionaires aboard," said Mr. Clemens. "Most of them will have been seduced onto one of the newer and faster ships—nothing with less than four smokestacks will suit the fancy crowd. Mind you, I wouldn't have turned down a ticket on a fast four-stacker, myself. But with Henry Rogers footing the bill, I reckon I'm obliged to economize where I can."

"Yes, economy's one of the cardinal virtues," said Kipling. "Not such a great one as to persuade a fellow to take passage in steerage, of course."

"Well, you're too young to remember the old-time steamships," said Mr. Clemens. "These days, I reckon even steerage is better than anything the richest man alive could buy, back then. The cabins were about as dismal and uncomfortable as the greatest minds of the day could contrive to make them: no electrical lights, no place to sit and talk except the dining room, no decorations or paintings or music. The decks were awash even in calm weather—why, on one trip I took, the captain told me he'd pumped the whole Atlantic Ocean out of his hold sixteen times during the crossing. Or maybe it was only fifteen times. It's a pity I can't recall the exact figure; a man shouldn't quote such an important statistic without being certain it's completely accurate.''

Mr. Kipling laughed, as did several of the bystanders, who as usual seemed to consider any of Mr. Clemens's remarks (even in private conversation) to have been made for their own entertainment. Just as the laughter was subsiding, another voice cut through the noise of the crowd: ''There's that pompous ass again. He's as tiresome as Rubbia—let's hope he isn't sitting near us at dinner.'' It was Robert Babson's voice. When I turned to look, I saw him staring with ill-disguised hostility at Prinz Karl von Ruckgarten, who had just come into the hallway, dressed in a semi-military uniform and carrying his gold-headed cane.

One or two of the group around Babson giggled in response to his rude comment, although I was pleased to notice that his sister did not seem amused. Instead, she laid a hand on his elbow and said something to him, too quietly for me to overhear. It was easy to guess what she had told him, though: He glared around the room to see who might have noticed what he said. His eyes locked with mine for a moment, and I looked away, feeling uncomfortable at having drawn his attention. From what I had seen of him, we had little in common; but neither did I have any reason to start off on the wrong foot with someone who had given me no particular offense or injury. Especially someone with such an attractive sister . . .

My thoughts were interrupted by a burst of light, which I realized came from the suddenly opened doors leading to the dining room. The light was emitted by numerous electrical bulbs reflecting off dazzling crystal chandeliers. The tables were covered with pure white linen, with fine gold-trimmed china at each place, flanked by sparkling cut-glass goblets and an impressive array of silverware. For a moment, the crowd seemed stunned by the sheer brilliance of the vista that had opened before them; then, as if of a single mind, we surged forward into the light, each of us searching for our proper place in the huge dining room.

≈7

Dinner that first evening at sea turned out to be memorable; not so much for the food (excellent as it was) as for what happened at the end of the meal.

Seated at the same table with the Kiplings and me were Dr. Lloyd Gillman, a retired surgeon, and his wife, Elizabeth; Lt. Col. Sir Henry Fitzwilliam, a retired British army officer who had served in Africa and India, and his wife, Helen; and Angus Rennie, an engineer whose broad accent betrayed his Scottish origins. (Having no previous experience with British titles, and whether they take precedence over military rank, or the other way around, I was not certain whether to address Fitzwilliam by his title, his military rank, or both, until Mr. Kipling came to my rescue by calling him "Colonel.")

The colonel had finished straightening his silverware (as if to arrange it in a more precise military alignment) and was busy perusing the wine list, when Mr. Kipling introduced himself and Mrs. Kipling to the others at the table. "Kipling, Kipling," the colonel said, looking intently at him. "Any relation to that writer fellow, the one out of India?" (He pronounced it *In-ja*, just as Mr. Kipling did.)

Mr. Kipling smiled modestly, and admitted that he was indeed related to the writer—"very closely related, in fact." At this, Mrs. Kipling laughed, and everyone at the table joined in, getting the joke. We were on easy terms from then on.

"You know, I've read your stuff about India," said the colonel, beaming. "I was stationed there a good fifteen years, and I daresay I know it better than most. I might pick a bone with you here or there, but I must admit you've got India spot on. I say, when you were in Lahore, did you happen to meet Dr. Hogworthy? Extraordinary chap—why, he used to go out into the Punjab without even a native translator. He's back in London, now—you really ought to look him up."

The two of them were soon embarked on a lively discussion of India, which I found fascinating. Here were two men who had been practically on the opposite side of the world, speaking with easy familiarity of exotic places and customs. Their conversation almost made me neglect my dinner of poached salmon in a delicate wine sauce, until Mrs. Kipling gave me an anxious look and inquired whether I was feeling well. After that, I remembered to eat.

Our table was near the aft wall, and I was seated with my back to it. So while I was on the periphery, I had a good view of the entire room whenever I chanced to look beyond my own dinner companions. There was a constant coming and going of waiters and their assistants, and the diners were keeping the wine steward busy, as well. At the captain's table, which was a double-sized table (seating sixteen) at the center of the room, champagne was being poured. Even from my seat in the hinterlands I could occasionally hear the captain and his guests laugh at one of Mr. Clemens's stories. "Why, Noah would never pass muster as a captain these days," said my employer, and spun a fanciful scene of the Hebrew patriarch applying for his license with a punctilious German inspector.

Closer to us were the Philadelphians, split among several tables along generational lines. Robert Babson and his sister, Theresa Mercer, and several others I'd seen with them just before dinner were seated together, at the table right next to ours. Somewhat to my surprise, Wilfred Smythe was not with this party, but seated with his parents at another table with the older Babsons and Mercers, and Signor Rubbia, the Italian artist. The two tables were a study in contrasts: the young Philadelphians loud and boisterous, while their parents were models of propriety. Robert Babson, in particular, seemed in high spirits, laughing immoderately and sending the waiter on one errand after another—usually for more wine. His conversation consisted mostly of rude comments on his elders, and I thought I saw some of the older Philadelphians shoot disapproving glances in his direction, but if so, he paid them no attention.

By coincidence, Prinz Karl was also seated nearby, at a table directly between the young Philadelphians and the captain's table. Seated with him were ladies and gentlemen of around his own age. As I might have expected, the prince had established himself as unofficial head of his table—much as Mr. Clemens had (despite his nominal status as one of many guests) at the captain's table, or (in a very different way) Robert Babson at his. I could see the eyes of Prinz Karl's dinner companions focused on him, smiles on their faces, and every so often, I heard laughter as he made some witty observation or delivered a florid compliment to one of the ladies. I wondered again whether Mr. Clemens was right in his assessment of the prince's *bona fides*, and resolved to ask Mr. Kipling's opinion on the subject.

The main courses had been cleared to make way for dessert, and dessert to make way for cheese and fruit, coffee and brandy. To be frank, I had stuffed myself, and was thinking that it might be a good idea to retire to my cabin early tonight—although not without following Mr. Clemens to the smoking room for a bit of after-dinner conversation. (If nothing else, that might give me my chance to sound out Mr. Kipling about the prince.) Mr. Kipling and Colonel Fitzwilliam were discussing the use of Indian natives as agents of the British crown—a fascinating topic on which Mr. Kipling said he was planning a book. Of course, I had no knowledge whatsoever of the subject, and therefore nothing useful to contribute. So out of the corner of my eye I happened to see Robert Babson just as he flicked a wine cork in the direction of Prinz Karl's table. I have no idea whether anything except sheer mischief was behind this prank; nonetheless, Babson's aim was true. The cork flew in a graceful arc over Prinz Karl's shoulder and landed squarely in his coffee cup—just as he had raised it to take a sip.

The splash startled the prince, who managed to spill a good bit of the hot coffee on his jacket and trousers. He leapt up with an angry shout, looking around to determine whence the missile had come, and his eye quickly lit on young Babson's table—where several of the young Philadelphians were trying to suppress giggles. "Who is responsible for this outrage?" roared the prince, advancing on the Philadelphians with menace in his eye. Not surprisingly, everyone in the room turned to see what the trouble was.

Robert Babson stared at Prinz Karl with an expression of utter incomprehension. "I have no idea what you're talking about, mister," he said. He pointed to the prince's trousers. "Did you spill your coffee?"

"You very well know what I mean," said the prince, his face red and his hands raised belligerently. "My uniform is ruined, and someone will pay for it."

"Oh, I'm sure someone will," said Babson, still seated calmly, raising his voice only a little. "They don't clean them for free, you know." At this witticism, two of his table companions nudged each other, grinning.

By now, the chief dining room steward had arrived on the scene, his expression anxious. "Is there some sort of difficulty, sir?" he said to Prinz Karl.

"Without question, there is," said the prince. "This arrogant young monkey, or one of his fellows, has thrown something and coffee has splashed on my uniform. I must have satisfaction from him." He turned briefly to look around the floor under his table, evidently for the cork that had caused the spill.

"I did nothing of the sort," said Babson. "This fellow was over at his table, and I was sitting right here, minding my own business. He must have spilled the coffee on himself, I don't see why he comes looking to me for satisfaction. Perhaps he's had a few too many drinks."

Robert Babson's arrogance astonished me. Evidently no one else but his table companions and I had seen him flick the cork, although Prinz Karl was clearly convinced he knew the culprit. I wondered why Babson—or one of his friends—did not simply own up to the prank and plead that it was an accident—perhaps that they had been aiming at each other and missed. High spirits and bad aim might not be the most dignified of excuses, but as I had seen after a few embarrassing incidents in my own college days, a quick confession and apology often sufficed to put things in proportion.

I wondered whether it would be wise of me to tell what I knew—perhaps without admitting that I had seen who had flipped the cork, just that it came from that direction. Certainly the prince deserved better than to be made the butt of a malicious prank by an arrogant young devil. On the other hand, I did not see any advantage in taking sides or making enemies. But if none of Babson's party were willing to confess, I might be forced to testify. Meanwhile, Babson's father had risen to his feet and come forward as if to intervene. For her part, his sister sat with her head lowered, as if deeply embarrassed.

I was saved from having to make a decision by the arrival of Captain Mortimer. "Here now, we'll not have any more of this," he said in an authoritative voice. He turned to Prinz Karl. "If you'll give your uniform to the cabin steward, it'll be cleaned and returned to you by tomorrow noon, at our expense. We won't let our passengers' enjoyment of the cruise be spoiled by something so easy to set right." His expression made it clear that he would tolerate no further discussion of the matter.

"Herr Captain, you have my humble appreciation," said the prince, making a little bow. "I am not accus-

tomed to having childish pranks played upon me, and I
hope you will excuse my irritation.''

''I will excuse it,'' said the captain, ''and I hope it will
be the last I hear of the matter.'' He looked sternly at
young Babson, then back at the prince, who bowed again
and excused himself—presumably to go change his
clothing. Apparently satisfied, the captain returned to his
seat, as did the elder Babson. But I thought Robert Babson had gotten off far too easily as the perpetrator of the
prank. I was even more convinced of it when I saw him
arise from the table shortly afterwards, smirking with evident self-satisfaction. Then and there, I resolved to have
as little to do with him as the close quarters aboard ship
would permit.

After dinner, I was still somewhat tired, and went to
tell Mr. Clemens of my plan to retire early. But he reminded me that he wanted me handy at the formal Bon
Voyage reception, which I had forgotten. This took place
in the Grand Saloon, a large, brightly lit room directly
forward of the dining room. The Grand Saloon could
double as a lecture hall, a concert chamber, or merely as
a large sitting room for the day. There was a grand piano
in one corner, and at least four fireplaces in the room, as
well as ample electric light. A huge skylight was set into
the center of the ceiling, so as to provide as much natural
illumination as possible during the daytime. And, of
course, there were comfortable chairs and sofas all about,
conveniently arranged so that passengers might converse
in groups, read quietly, or engage in other solitary activities.

As always in a new group, a large portion of the crowd
was anxious to meet Mr. Clemens. While he had met a
few at the dinner table, and more in the smoking room
before dinner, here he was practically besieged—especially by the ladies, who of course were not among the
devotees of tobacco. He chatted with them amiably,
strewing his speech with little jokes and compliments in
the manner of a born entertainer. Presently I recognized

a person in the crowd whom I had noticed earlier on deck: Wilfred Smythe's father, the Methodist minister, who waited patiently until my employer was somewhat free of the initial press of admirers.

"I am especially pleased to meet you, Mr. Clemens," said the minister, stepping forward and smiling broadly. "I am the Reverend Dr. Charles Smythe, pastor of Trinity Church."

"A pleasure, Dr. Smythe," said my employer, shaking hands. I thought I detected a wary look in his eye. "That would be Doctor of Divinity, I assume."

Dr. Smythe beamed. "Yes, I must confess I take a measure of pride—not an unbecoming measure, I hope— in having earned that distinction. But you know, Mr. Clemens, I take more pride in a distinction that I share with you."

Mr. Clemens raised his eyebrows. "Really? Let me guess what that could be. Were you a riverboat pilot?"

"No, sir," said the minister smugly.

Mr. Clemens peered intently at him, as if to learn the answer from his physiognomy. "Then maybe you were a gold miner, or a newspaper editor."

"The latter is a close guess," said Dr. Smythe. "I will not keep you any longer in the dark. I am an author in my own right."

"You are? What a surprise!" said Mr. Clemens. "I meet so few fellow authors. Here, Kipling, here's another author among us! Dr. Smythe, this is my friend Rudyard Kipling. He's an author, too."

Mr. Kipling looked at Mr. Clemens and said dryly, "How extraordinary. We shall have a regular literary salon aboard if this continues." He turned back to the gentleman with whom he'd been speaking, a big, red-faced man with a bulbous nose and a wide gap between his front teeth.

"Tell me, Dr. Smythe, do you publish under your own name, or do you follow my example and use a pen name?" asked my employer. Now his eyes were twinkling, and I sensed that he was up to some mischief.

"I must confess that I use my own name," said Dr. Smythe. "I know that some may look on it as undue self-aggrandizement, but I see it as promoting the cause of the Church itself. My humble hope is to bring a few additional sheep to the fold, and if allowing my name to appear on the title page of my book can accomplish that, then I rest content."

"And what is your book, if I may ask?" said Mr. Clemens. "I will have to make an effort to find it in the bookstores when we reach England."

"Oh, I fear my little book has not spread as far as England," Dr. Smythe replied. "Perhaps on this journey I will have the opportunity to rectify that in part."

"Well, if the stores don't have it in England, I'll try to get it sent over from America," said Mr. Clemens. "It'd be a shame to miss it, seeing as how we're traveling together."

"Why, there's no need for that," said Dr. Smythe, reaching into his coat pocket. "I just happen to have brought a number of copies with me, and I will be delighted to present one to such an eminent author as Mark Twain." He handed Mr. Clemens a small volume on the cover of which I could see the title: *A Christian's Duty*, by Charles H. Smythe, D.D. "Would you like it inscribed?" said the minister.

"Yes, that would be a kindness," said Mr. Clemens, holding out the book. "Could you sign it 'To my good friend Sam'? It may be useful, some day, for me to lay claim to the connection. Policemen and customs inspectors often place undue importance on such things."

"You do me too much honor," said Dr. Smythe, but he took the book back, went over to a nearby table where there was a pen and an inkwell, and signed the title page, blotting it carefully before returning it to my employer.

Mr. Clemens opened the book and looked at it, then turned a page and looked again. "This is remarkable," he said, turning another page. He flipped through several pages, then skipped to a page toward the end, while Dr. Smythe looked on. Presently he glanced up from the book with a troubled expression and said, "I hope you won't mind my saying this, Dr. Smythe, but this is very familiar. In fact, I believe I have a book at home that has every word of yours in it."

"No," said the minister. "That can't be—this is my own composition. I will grant you that the theme is a traditional one, and of course I quote freely from the Gospels. But I have certainly not plagiarized."

"Nevertheless, I believe the book in my library has every word of yours in it. I wonder if they have a copy on board ship."

"I should certainly like to see it, if they do," said Dr. Smythe, a look of indignation on his face. "I cannot pretend to be among the giants of literature, but I would never stoop to borrowing another's words and publishing them as my own."

"I'll tell you what," said Mr. Clemens. "The ship's library is right down the corridor. Wait here just a few minutes, and I'll go see if they have it. This is really quite remarkable."

We waited perhaps five minutes before Mr. Clemens returned to the room, a large volume under his arm. "I found it, Dr. Smythe," he said cheerfully. He held the book up in both hands, and every head in the room turned to look at the title. After a moment of shocked silence, Dr. Smythe doubled up in laughter, and the rest of the room followed suit.

Finally, Dr. Smythe recovered his composure enough to speak. "You're absolutely right, Mr. Clemens," he said, chuckling. "But what you neglected to mention was that you have taken every single word of *your* books from it, too!" He was correct, of course: The book was *Webster's Unabridged Dictionary*.

Later, in the smoking room, Robert Babson was prominently seated at the card table with several of his fellows, grinning broadly. One would have thought he had accomplished something noteworthy, instead of embarrassing a gentleman twice his age by playing a childish prank. He was a loud and arrogant card player, although evidently not a successful one. Every time I glanced in his direction, his opponents were taking another trick. I was glad to see Babson get his comeuppance, although it did neither me nor Prinz Karl any tangible good.

Having been effectively "on stage" for the last three hours, Mr. Clemens was content to sit at a little corner table, smoking cigars with Mr. Kipling, without making any effort to entertain the room at large. For myself, I was still thinking of an early bedtime, although my employer had prevailed upon me to stay and have a glass of whisky and soda water before retiring. After we had settled in, Mr. Clemens glanced around as if to make sure nobody was listening too closely to us, then leaned forward and tapped the ash off his cigar. "Well, Kipling, I reckon you know as much about geography as anybody," he said in a low voice.

"That depends on where you're talking about," said Kipling. "I know the Orient, but South America's another story. And I'd think you know more about the United States than I do."

"How about Germany?"

"I've never gone there, to tell the truth," said Kipling. After a moment, he raised his thick, dark eyebrows. "I thought you *had* been there. What do you expect me to know about it that you don't?"

Mr. Clemens took another glance around the room, then lowered his voice again and said, "Ever hear of Ruckgarten before today?"

Kipling's eyebrows went even higher. "Aha, I see what you're getting at. No, I don't think I have heard of it. You know, I wondered about that when he introduced himself, but it slipped my mind afterward. I say, Clemens, this is an annoyance."

"I suppose we might do some research in the ship's library, if we want to be dead certain. There should be a map or two there. Or maybe some history books," said my employer. "But I have a pretty good idea what we'll find, if we look."

"I believe so," said Kipling. He picked up his glass and took a sip, then scowled. "I shall have to warn Carrie about him. I wonder what possessed me to let her dance with the bounder!"

Mr. Clemens took a puff on his cigar. "Well, even if we had proof that our German friend isn't quite what he pretends to be, that doesn't go very far to tell us what he *is*. My guess would be he's some sort of swindler."

"If not an outright thief," said Kipling, nodding. "What d'you say we inform the ship's officers, and let them investigate the matter? Then we can forget about him and enjoy our voyage."

"Why would a thief buy us a magnum of champagne?" I asked. "What's more, he's traveling first class. He can't expect to make much of a profit if he keeps spending like that."

"Oh, he's not going to make any profit at all off me," said Mr. Clemens. "Nor Kipling, either, I suspect. But some folks aboard are traveling with a good bit of money. Some of the ladies are wearing some mighty impressive jewelry tonight, if I'm any judge. A diamond necklace or two is all a thief would need to turn a nice profit. And our prince wouldn't be the first to give himself a phony title, hoping to ingratiate himself with gullible victims."

"But if the two of you have unmasked him so easily, how does he expect to fool anyone?" I pointed out. "Others on board will surely detect the imposture; he can't believe he won't be exposed."

"A thief doesn't need to deceive everyone," said Mr. Kipling. "One would be enough, and I would be surprised if there weren't someone aboard rich enough and gullible enough to serve the fellow's purpose. But my instincts tell me he's not just a common thief—he's got something else in mind."

"Well, I reckon your instincts are worth something," said Mr. Clemens. "But whatever he's got up his sleeve, so far he hasn't done anything except impersonate German royalty. That may be suspicious, but there's no law agin it in America, far as I know. Hell, out in San

Francisco there used to be a fellow name of Norton, who
called himself the Emperor of California and Mexico and
God knows what else, and nobody saw any harm in it.
As for Herr von Ruckgarten, I wouldn't be a bit surprised
if it turned out—Oh, oh—mum, boys, he just came in
the door. We'll talk about this later.''

I looked toward the door, in time to see Prinz Karl
walk a few steps into the room and look around. Almost
at once, his eye lit on Robert Babson sitting at the card
table, and a scowl came over his face. I watched with
interest, wondering whether he was about to renew the
confrontation here; others must have noticed his entry, as
well, for there was an expectant hush in the buzz of conversation. Then the prince turned abruptly on his heel and
stalked out of the room. Seeing the expressions of his
companions at the card table, young Babson turned and
looked behind him, just as the door closed. Seeing nobody there, he shrugged and resumed playing his hand,
and the tension waned as rapidly as it had risen.

But while I expected the conversation to return to the
prince's apparent duplicity, and what he expected to gain
by it, the arrival of Colonel Fitzwilliam prevented us
from pursuing that topic. He sat right down and resumed
the conversation he and Mr. Kipling had begun over dinner. Naturally, Kipling introduced him to Mr. Clemens,
and they began to discuss travel, especially to India and
Africa, two areas of the world about which Mr. Clemens
was curious—as was I, in normal circumstances. But my
long, active day (not to mention a sufficiency of food and
drink) began to catch up with me. Shortly after the colonel's arrival, I found myself struggling to hold back one
yawn, then another. There was no point fighting the inevitable. I bade the three men good night, leaving my
whisky unfinished, and made my exit.

I had meant to go directly to my cabin, but since this
was my first night on a ship at sea, I decided to look out
on deck to see if the rain had stopped. If the weather had
cleared, I could walk back to my cabin by the outside
route, and perhaps get a look at the stars. The ship did

seem to be moving a bit more gently than before, although it was possible I was simply getting used to its motion.

I opened one of the doors that led outside, and sure enough, the rain seemed to be over for the moment, although the deck was still a bit slippery, and there was a hint of chill in the air. I walked over to the rail and looked out into the night. To my disappointment, the clouds were still covering most of the sky, although there was a hint of light ahead of us, where the clouds appeared to be thinner: the moon, I thought. I turned to go to my cabin, and realized that I was not alone on deck. Leaning on the rail, looking pensively out to sea, was Wilfred Smythe, the minister's son.

"Good evening," I said, feeling I should at least acknowledge his presence. I wondered if he had been in the Grand Saloon to see Mr. Clemens play the dictionary joke on his father—and to see his father turn the tables on my employer.

He looked up as if startled out of a reverie. "Hello, Mr. Cabot," he said, recognizing me. "Are you enjoying the night air?"

"I'd enjoy it more if the sky were clearer," I said. "But I guess we'll get our share of that before we get to England. Actually, I'm just getting a breath of fresh air before turning in. It was a bit stuffy in the smoking room."

"I suppose so," he said, turning to look out at the waves again. "I've never been a smoker or a gambler, so I doubt I'll spend much time there. In any case, neither the atmosphere nor the company really agrees with me."

"Well, I'm neither a smoker nor much of a card player, myself," I told him. "Still, one can find an enjoyable conversation now and then."

He was silent for a long time after I said this, and I began to grow uncomfortable. Perhaps, I reflected, I should leave him to his thoughts; he was clearly in no mood for talk. I myself had no great desire to linger. I was just about to take my leave when he broke the silence again. "I'm sorry, I'm afraid I'm being rude. I don't mean to be. But here I am aboard a ship with the one person I'd most enjoy being with, and I can't be with her because someone else—someone I loathe—has won her affection. I fear I'm not going to be very good company tonight, Mr. Cabot. I suppose I shouldn't bore you with something that's not your concern in any case."

"No offense taken, Mr. Smythe," I said. There was another awkward silence, and an abashed look came over Smythe's face, presumably at having blurted out his secret to someone he had barely met. It was not hard to guess that he must be referring to Theresa Mercer, who was now engaged to marry Robert Babson. I saw no reason to prolong his embarrassment, and so I yawned and said, "I doubt I'd be very good company, myself. I'm dog-tired, and just came out for a quick look at the ocean before going to bed. So if you'll excuse me, I'll wish you a good night and be on my way."

"Thank you, Mr. Cabot," he said. "Good night, and perhaps we'll have a more pleasant talk another time." We shook hands, and I made my way to the cabin, where I fell asleep almost as soon as my head touched the pillow.

≈8

The next morning, Mr. Clemens and I both slept late and went to breakfast together. Breakfast seating was catch-as-catch-can, as opposed to the more formal seating for dinner, so we sat at the same table. As usual, he ordered up a beefsteak and fried eggs, with plenty of black coffee. I had the eggs and coffee, but decided to substitute bacon and toast for the beef. We had both polished off our main courses and were sipping our second cups of coffee, when a man and woman came over to our table.

"Excuse me," said the man, holding his hat in his hands. "Aren't you Samuel Clemens, the writer?"

"Guilty as charged," said my employer, setting down his coffee cup. "What can I do for you?"

"I don't expect you'll remember us," said the man, "But I'm Michael Richards, and this is my sister, Susan—Mrs. Daniel Martin, she is now. You were friends with our parents in San Francisco, nearly thirty years ago."

"I'll be tarred and feathered," said Mr. Clemens, looking at the pair with suddenly heightened interest. "Would that be John and Emily Richards who lived on Mason Street?"

"The very same," said Susan Martin. "You used to come to our home for dinner. We were very young, but we still remember those visits."

Mr. Clemens stood up and shook Mr. Richards's hand.

"What a surprise! Of course I remember you. You couldn't have been much more than eight years old back then, full of mischief unless my memory's playing tricks on me. Your parents are well, I hope?"

"Mother's very well, still living in San Francisco," said Mr. Richards. "Dad passed away some years ago, I'm afraid."

"I'm sorry to hear that," said Mr. Clemens, then turned and introduced me. "I haven't been back to San Francisco in a coon's age, but I remember your mother well. She used to cook the best meals I ever had in those days."

"We remember you, too," said Susan Martin, a twinkle in her eye. "We used to hate it when our parents said you were coming to dinner."

"What?" said Mr. Clemens, raising his eyebrows. I had never seen him so surprised. "I can't believe it."

"Oh, yes," said Michael Richards, with a shy smile. "We had to eat out in the kitchen and listen to you grownups in the dining room, talking and talking—it seemed like forever. I suppose you must have been very amusing, because I still recall my parents laughing. But we children must have missed the jokes, because all I can remember is wishing you'd leave, so Mother could tell us our bedtime story. I guess nobody ever thought to ask you to tell us a bedtime story."

"Well, that was before I had children of my own," said Mr. Clemens, recovering his composure. "There's no telling what kind of story I'd have told you—probably something scandalous. Nowadays I have a large stock of appropriate stories, tested on my own three little girls. But it's probably too late to do you any good." He took Mrs. Martin's hand and held it in both of his, smiling. "I implore you to forgive me for being such a boring guest."

"You were forgiven long ago," said Mrs. Martin, with a laugh. "I just wish we had been old enough to come into the dining room, so we could recall all the stories you did tell back then. Mother has told us some of them, but I'm sure there were others just as good.''

"Well, I certainly remember Emily very fondly. You'll give her my best regards when you see her again, won't you?''

"We certainly will," said the woman. "And it's a pleasure to see we're traveling on the same ship. But we'll leave you to finish your breakfast now—I'm sure we'll get a chance to speak again.''

After she and her brother left the dining room, Mr. Clemens took a sip of his coffee, then looked at me with a melancholy expression. "I can't believe I used to know those two as small children, and now they're on the brink of middle age. I wasn't much older than you at the time, Wentworth!'' He shook his head and fell silent. I myself could only think that on first glance, I had thought of Mr. Richards and Mrs. Martin as being of an age with my own parents. Perhaps it would be best not to mention this to Mr. Clemens.

Meanwhile, I became aware of Signor Giorgio Rubbia speaking loudly at a nearby table, where he sat with Mr. Babson and Mr. Mercer and their wives, all of whom were members of the art tour he was leading. "The artist's business is not to copy what he sees,'' Rubbia said, and I perked my ears up, hoping to hear the expert's opinion on a subject I found fascinating. "Any simpleton with a little black camera can do that as well as Michelangelo. But his photograph can never express what that face makes him *feel*. For that you need the soul of a true artist.''

"What does it matter what the silly artist feels?'' said Robert Babson, who had just wandered into the dining room. He looked as if he had been up very late, but he still managed a sneer at Rubbia as he plopped himself into a vacant seat next to his father, the lawyer, and said, "Somebody else will feel differently about it, and another man will have *his* own feelings, different from the first two. There's no end to it, and no telling whether one picture's better than another.'' Then he turned to a nearby waiter and barked, "What does a fellow have to do to get a cup of coffee?"

"Directly, sir," said the harried-looking waiter, who was loaded down with a tray of food for another table.

"Well, don't be too slow about it," said Robert Babson, clearly irritated. I wondered if he had a hangover.

Meanwhile, Signor Rubbia had turned to Mr. Mercer, who seemed a more receptive audience for his comments on art. "The soul of a true artist will always reveal itself. The mere representation of a subject, this is only the surface. Any idiot can learn to draw correctly—give me time enough, and I could teach a monkey to draw." Rubbia shot a significant glance toward Robert Babson as he said this, but the young man paid him no attention, so he continued. "With a true artist, the representation of the subject is only the medium for his perception of the essence of things." He made an expansive gesture with his hands, as if to suggest the vastness of an artist's perceptions.

"Very true," said Mrs. Mercer, and her husband, the banker, nodded. "Art is so much deeper than copying what you see."

But Robert Babson was not convinced. "All anyone wants from a painter is a picture to hang over the fireplace," he said. "Who wants to pay hundreds of dollars for some awful muddle where you have to look at the label to tell whether the fellow's drawing a house or a sailboat? Or the kind of tripe you get from these self-appointed geniuses who make a woman's skin green and speckled to express their precious feelings. What are they feeling, anyway—a toothache?" He grinned, and looked around the table as if to invite approval for his jape.

Babson's father and one or two others at their table laughed, although neither of the Mercers seemed to find the quip amusing. In any case, Signor Rubbia was not ready to give up the contest. He slapped his hand on the table and said, "One who has drunk nothing but small beer may think that all wine is the same, but let him taste a few bottles of a good vintage and he will mend his opinion. When you have seen the great treasures of Europe, you will begin to understand better what art is about. Then perhaps your opinion will count for something.''

"And until then, you get to lord it over us, and tell us what provincial boobies we are,'' said Robert Babson. "Well, I don't care what some painter feels. You might as well worry about what a plumber or carpenter feels.''

Signor Rubbia stood, visibly checking his temper. "I believe I am finished with breakfast. Gentlemen and ladies, I will see you later.'' He bowed to those still at the table and left. Young Babson watched him go, smirking.

"Well, a ray of morning sunshine,'' said Mr. Clemens quietly, with a sour expression that belied his words. "Young Babson wouldn't be my idea of steady company—he needs to work on his manners, for one thing—but he's not afraid to call a spade a spade. Or in this case, call a phony a phony.''

"I wouldn't want to share a stateroom with him, either,'' I said, shifting the angle of the conversation away from a subject on which Mr. Clemens and I were evidently doomed to disagree. It surprised me that a man who made his living from one branch of the arts could so easily sneer at another. I wondered if it could be professional jealousy. Then again, he seemed to have no difficulty making friends with his fellow writers—Mr. Kipling, or Mr. G. W. Cable, whom we had met in New Orleans. "Did you see that skirmish between him and Prinz Karl last night?'' I asked.

"I saw what happened after the prince stood up; that was pretty hard to miss. What did you see, Wentworth?''

"Babson pitched a wine cork at the other table and it landed in the prince's coffee—exactly as the prince said. So Babson was lying when he denied it.''

"I figured as much,'' said Mr. Clemens. He cocked a wary eye toward the table where Robert Babson and his parents were seated. "He was shooting off his mouth all night long in the smoker. The later it got, the louder he got, though he never got funny enough to make it worth listening to. But why don't we go catch a breath of fresh air out on deck? It'll probably be a lot more pleasant than in here, and maybe the company will be better, too.'' He slid back his chair and rose to his feet.

I gulped down the last of my coffee and stood to join him, and we headed for the exit. Behind us, I could hear Robert Babson grumble, ''What's taking that fellow so long to bring my coffee?'' The more I saw of him, the less I liked him. I was glad that Mr. Clemens and I had basically finished our breakfast before Babson had arrived.

Out on deck, the rain had entirely gone away, and the sky was bright blue with wispy clouds directly above us—the kind the old sailors around the New London dock called ''mares' tails.'' *High wind's coming,* I thought to myself, remembering some of the yachtsman's lore I'd picked up in my youth. The ship seemed to be making excellent headway; despite her age, she was rated at just over eighteen knots on the eastward passage, a respectable speed even by today's standards. And while the motion of the waves was readily perceptible, I found it exhilarating rather than disturbing.

A good number of other passengers had already come out on deck. Some were sitting in deck chairs reading or conversing; others were leaning on the rail and looking out on the waves. Mr. Clemens and I had rented deck chairs in New York, but the wet weather the day before had kept us from having them brought out. If the fine weather held, I would ask our cabin steward to bring the chairs out today. It would be pleasant to lounge on deck in the warm sun—despite the lateness of the season, it was quite temperate today. But the North Atlantic had a reputation for nasty weather, and we would be lucky to have such fine days all the way across.

Toward the bow we found Mr. and Mrs. Kipling, he in his old tweed coat and soft felt hat, she in a sensible wool dress and knit shawl. They were passing a pair of binoculars back and forth, looking at a speck on the southern horizon that I decided must be another ship. "Good morning, Kipling," said my employer. "What are you looking at—pirates?"

"Ho ho, that would be a rare sight, wouldn't it?" said Mr. Kipling, laughing. "What if I told you it was the Royal Navy, coming to reclaim the colonies at last?"

"Hell, they already tried that once," said Mr. Clemens. "Burned Washington to the ground and chased away Congress. Now, that could have been a real service—Congress is the only indigenous American criminal class. But the invasion didn't do us a bit of good, in the end. After the war was over, the damned congressmen came back and built the whole mess up again, worse than ever. I suppose it couldn't hurt to burn it down again, especially if you could be sure the congressmen didn't get away this time. In fact, I'd contribute to the cause."

Mrs. Kipling smiled and wagged her finger at my employer. "Why, Mr. Clemens, you ought to hold up our American side more firmly. I'm afraid you've left it to me to contradict Ruddy, and that would hardly promote domestic tranquillity."

"Oh, I'm perfectly willing to contradict him, as long as it don't mean I have to stand up for Congress," said Mr. Clemens. "I'll leave them to handle that job themselves. Half of them are lawyers, anyhow, so they're used to defending thieves."

Just as he said that, Mr. Kipling's jaw clenched, and I heard him mutter, "Speak of the devil." I turned to follow his gaze and saw Prinz Karl von Ruckgarten stroll into sight at the far end of the deck, wearing a beaver top hat and a knee-length cape fastened at the throat. His gold-handled cane rested across his right shoulder.

Prinz Karl's face lit up as he spotted our little group and waved to us. "Good morning, my friends," he called out in a hearty voice, and he quickened his step to join us.

It was obvious that Mr. Kipling was in no way pleased at the prince's arrival, but Mr. Clemens raised his hand and returned the wave. Out of the side of his mouth, he said to Kipling, "Make some excuse if you want to get away; I'll keep him occupied."

"You're a better man than I am," said Mr. Kipling, looking relieved. Then, in a louder voice, he said, "Poor Carrie hasn't been feeling quite herself this morning. I think I'll take her back to the cabin and let her rest."

"Sorry to hear it," said Mr. Clemens, nodding as if in sympathy. "I hope we'll see you both at lunch."

"I'm sure a bit of rest will be just the thing," said Mr. Kipling, taking his wife's arm. "Good day, sir," he said, nodding to the prince, who had just come up.

"Good day to you," said the prince, doffing his hat and bowing to the departing couple. Kipling touched the brim of his hat, and his wife gave a perfunctory nod, and they walked off in the direction of their cabin.

Prinz Karl looked after them, a concerned expression on his face. "I am sorry to hear the lady is unwell," he said. "It is nothing very serious, I hope."

"Probably not," said Mr. Clemens, leaning back against the rail. "I don't think she's used to travel."

"Ah, say no more," Prinz Karl responded. "I remember my own first venture on a ship, back in my student days. I and a group of my university friends were silly enough to book an English Channel crossing in midwinter, and the waves were higher than the Alps, I thought. We were on a little tub out of Calais, and to take her out in that weather the captain must have been mad. My friends and I were too young to know better, of course. Besides, we had drunk enough wine to float the ship. Before we reached Dover, I thought the ship would capsize at least six times. I was so sick, almost I wished it *would* capsize and put me out of my misery. If I live to see a hundred, I hope I do not see a storm like that again. But after that crossing, I have never again suffered with the *mal de mer*."

"If it takes a storm like that to do it, I hope you never will again," said Mr. Clemens. Then, after a pause, he added, "At least, not on this trip," and the prince laughed and nodded.

"But I know what you mean about the old-time steamers," my employer continued. "At best, they were a real education in discomfort. I remember some mighty rough days on the ship I took on my first trip to Germany, back in '78 . . ." He shook his head. "But seeing Germany was well worth the trouble, you know? I don't have to tell you about it, I know. I don't think I got down to your part of the country, though. Just where is Ruckgarten? Maybe this time I'll get a chance to visit your country."

"Oh, it is a very small principality. Many modern maps do not even show it. And I fear there is not much for visitors to see," said the prince. "We make excellent beer, and very good cheese and sausage, but we have no fine buildings or dramatic landscapes. Still, if you were to visit, you would certainly be welcome. Of that I would make certain."

"Well, I'll have to see what my plans turn out to be," said Mr. Clemens, staring out at the horizon. "Depending on how much I have to work, I may have less time for travel and sightseeing than I'd like. But where precisely is it?" He turned and looked the prince directly in the eye.

The prince appeared uncomfortable at being quizzed in this fashion, but he said, without meeting my employer's gaze, "It is near the border of Bohemia."

Mr. Clemens grinned mischievously. "Oh, yes, on the sea coast, I suppose?"

For a moment, Prinz Karl looked at my employer with incomprehension on his face, while I struggled to picture the map in my mind. Geography had never been my strong suit, but I had been under the impression that Bohemia was some distance from the coast. Then the prince laughed and said, "Oho, *The Winter's Tale!* You make a literary joke! We are acquainted with Shakespeare in Germany, you know. Thanks to Professor von Schlegel, he is almost one of our own poets."

"You're welcome to him," said Mr. Clemens. "But speaking of literature, I'm afraid I've been putting off my own writing too long this morning. If you'll excuse me and my secretary, we'll go put our noses to the grind-stone for a while.''

"By all means," said the prince, and Mr. Clemens and I took our leave of him. I wondered what my employer had up his sleeve, since I knew very well that any work he had did not require my assistance.

A s soon as were out of sight of Prinz Karl, Mr.
Clemens said to me, "Wentworth, I want you to
go to the ship's library and find a map of Germany. Look down near Bohemia—do you know where
that is?"

I tried again to remember my European geography.
"Somewhere inland, isn't it? Near Austria, I think."

"Part of Austria, actually. Find Prague and look on
the German side of the border, to the north and west.
That'll be close enough, I think. You're looking for
Ruckgarten, or anything that sounds like it. The place is
probably small, but if it's a real place, it still ought to
show up on a good map. If they'll let you borrow the
map, bring it to Kipling's cabin—I'm going there directly. If not, tell us what you find. I can double-check
it later."

"I'll do my best," I said. "Why are we suddenly so
concerned with where it is?"

Mr. Clemens glanced both ways down the deck, making certain no one was close enough to overhear him,
then continued in a quiet voice. "I'm not going to spoil
our trip, or the Kiplings', just because we don't know
whether von Ruckgarten is a real prince or an impostor.
If we have to keep dodging him, and pretending to be
seasick, it's going to become the only thing on our minds
until we're off the ship. So we need to find out whether
Prinz Karl is what he claims to be, or some other kind

of critter entirely. Besides, if people see me associating with the prince, they're going to take him at face value and say, 'He's Mark Twain's friend, so he must be all right.' Then, if the rascal uses my supposed friendship as collateral to weasel his way into their confidence and rob them, I'm practically an accomplice. I don't need that on my conscience—I already feel guilty enough about the friends I persuaded in good faith to throw away their money investing in a damned typesetting machine that didn't work. Let's erase the doubt, so we can enjoy ourselves.''

I nodded, understanding the reason for his urgency. ''I'll find out what I can,'' I promised.

''Good. Cabin seventeen, when you know something.'' He sauntered off down the deck, while I turned in at a doorway and went to find the ship's library, which I remembered was on the same deck, near the Grand Saloon.

The corridor led me past a row of cabins, then a smaller smoking lounge and a ladies' sitting room, before I reached the ship's library. I opened the door and entered quietly, knowing from experience that librarians frowned on unnecessary noise. As with libraries on land, the first thing one noticed was a profusion of bookshelves, with several tables and comfortable chairs for reading. There was a good-sized globe on a stand in one corner, and next to it on the wall a large map showing the Atlantic Ocean, the nations bordering it, and the various sea routes between major ports. In the center of the room was a tidy desk for the librarian.

I was impressed; the library would have been the pride of many moderate-sized towns in the United States, although of course it could not compare to what I was used to at Yale. There was only one other person there—a young woman in a blue dress, staring at one of the top shelves, evidently at a book out of her reach. *The librarian,* I thought at first; then, hearing the door close behind me, she turned to see who had entered, and I recognized Robert Babson's sister.

"Good morning," I said quietly. "I thought for a moment you were the librarian."

She laughed, then put a hand to her mouth and looked around, as if afraid the librarian would suddenly appear to chastise her. "No, I'm afraid she has stepped out of the room for a moment. Although my father sometimes calls me 'the little librarian' to tease me," she said. "I *do* enjoy reading." Then she looked at me more closely. "You're Mr. Mark Twain's secretary, aren't you? My father said he met you in New York."

"Is your father Julius Babson?" I asked, and she nodded, still smiling brightly. "Yes, we met briefly. I'm Wentworth Cabot. And to whom do I have the pleasure . . . ?"

"Rebecca Babson," she said, then turned and looked back up at the shelf. "Oh, I'm lucky that you came in just now, Mr. Cabot. Could you possibly get me down *A Portrait of a Lady*? It's on the top shelf, and I can't quite reach it. I'd be ever so grateful."

"I'll be glad to," I said, pleased that my height had turned out to be useful. I plucked the book off the shelf and handed it to her, noting that it was one of several on the shelf by Henry James, a current writer whom I had heard praised as a model of style. I should have to read some of his work some time.

"Oh, thank you so much," she said. "Now, at least, I can begin reading it. When the librarian comes back, I can take it out with me."

"Very much my pleasure, Miss Babson," I said. "I hope you enjoy it."

"I expect I shall," she said, smiling brightly at me again. "Thank you again, Mr. Cabot." She blushed slightly, then turned and walked to one of the seats, near a porthole admitting the morning sun. The rays striking her blond hair from behind lit it up like a halo, and I must admit that I stared at her for a moment longer than might have been polite, before I remembered my mission for Mr. Clemens.

I found the reference section without any difficulty,

next to the map and globe I had spotted upon entering the room. There was a set of the *Encyclopaedia Britannica,* and a good selection of dictionaries of various languages (no surprise, considering that the library was designed for the use of travelers). On a bottom shelf filled with oversized books were two or three atlases of the world. Choosing the largest, I took it to a nearby table and spread it out.

While I cannot claim a special familiarity with geography, I have always enjoyed maps and globes. As a child, I used to go into my father's study and spin the globe there, watching the colors blur and then, as it slowed, poke a finger at it and see where it stopped, imagining the strange people who must live there. The colors and shapes of the maps, as well as the foreign names, had a sort of incantatory magic for me. So it was a brief exercise in nostalgia, and a distinct pleasure, for me to flip through the pages of the atlas. At the same time, I was aware of Miss Babson's presence near the window. Rebecca Babson—what a lovely name, I thought.

I found the Austrian empire quickly enough, and in the northern part I located Prague, the main city of Bohemia. To the west was Bavaria, and to the north the former kingdom of Saxony, both now in the German empire, and to the east Moravia. I scanned the area, still as amused by the outlandish place names as I had been as a child. Oelsnitz—Sebnitz—Meerane—Zschopau—I hadn't the least idea how to pronounce them. But I traced the border between Germany and Bohemia all the way from Javernig to Aigen, and unless German pronunciation and spelling were completely divorced from one another, there was not a name on the map I could twist into anything resembling ''Ruckgarten.''

The librarian still had not appeared, and I felt uneasy about taking the atlas away without her permission. I was about to return it to its shelf and go report to Mr. Clemens when the door opened, and a little gray-haired woman in a plain dark dress entered. ''May I help either of you?''

she asked. "I am Mrs. Tremont, the librarian," she added. Her voice was high-pitched but melodic enough not to be grating, and I thought I detected a hint of Boston in her accent.

"Yes," said Rebecca Babson, rising from her seat. "I would like to borrow this novel, please." She brought it to the desk, and Mrs. Tremont noted down her name and cabin number.

"The book must be returned here, in good condition, by noon of the day we dock in Southampton," said Mrs. Tremont.

"Oh, I expect I'll be done with it before then," said Miss Babson. "I read very quickly."

Mrs. Tremont smiled approvingly at her, then turned to me. "And can I help you with anything, young man?"

"Yes, ma'am. I think I've found what I need, but I wonder if it's possible to check out the atlas for a short time? I would like to show someone one of the maps."

"Reference books can't be taken from the library," said Mrs. Tremont, a stern expression on her face. "The person will have to come here to look at the atlas."

I had expected as much. "It doesn't matter," I said. "If Mr. Clemens wants to double-check what I've found, I'm sure he can find time to come here himself. What are your hours?"

"We are open from ten until five every day except Sunday, and weekday evenings from seven till nine," said the librarian. Then she stopped and looked directly up at me. "Is that Mr. Samuel Clemens, the writer Mark Twain? He visited us last night, asking to borrow a dictionary."

"Yes, ma'am. I am his secretary."

"How nice," said Mrs. Tremont, smiling. It made her look much less imposing. "If Mr. Clemens had come in person, I would be happy to let him borrow the atlas, but I fear I cannot take your word that you are here on his business—I hope you understand. Perhaps he could come to the library with you to verify your association? Then

I would be happy to let you take him whatever books he needs.''

The librarian paused, and I nodded my understanding; it seemed a reasonable condition. Besides, I had found— or rather, *not* found—what I had come looking for. Then she continued: "Perhaps you could do me a favor and ask Mr. Clemens a question. He seemed to be in a hurry last night, and so I did not have the chance to ask him myself. I am in charge of our evening cultural program, and I wonder if he would like to present a little talk to his fellow passengers. I can guarantee him a good audience.''

"Well, I can't answer for Mr. Clemens, of course. But I'll pass along your invitation," I said. "I'm sure he'll be flattered." Actually, I was not at all certain what sort of welcome the invitation would get, but I would let Mr. Clemens make his own decision, and deliver his own response.

"Thank you, young man," said Mrs. Tremont. She was smiling very sweetly now, and I realized that her blue eyes were sparkling. She must have been quite pretty as a young woman. "Normally, when I learn of a passenger who I think would be an interesting speaker, I seek him out myself. But this will get the message to him all the sooner. And please do urge him to pay us another visit.''

I turned to go, and saw that Miss Babson had waited for me. I was somewhat pleased by this, since I had been hoping that our chance meeting would give me an opportunity to talk to her at greater length. I rather liked the young Philadelphian woman, in spite of her boorish brother.

"I do hope Mr. Clemens will give a lecture," she said. "Are you doing research for one of his books?''

"He asked me to do some geographical research," I said, opening the door to let her precede me out of the library. "I really don't know whether it'll end up in a book or not." This was perfectly true, in fact—Mr. Clemens was still busy with revisions of his book on our

Mississippi River journey, and had not started a new one. But from what he had told me, the most unexpected things had a way of insinuating themselves into his writing. Perhaps the apparently nonexistent principality of Ruckgarten would somehow set his imagination to work.

"It's very curious to have a writer on board," said Miss Babson. We had stepped into the corridor outside the library, and she stopped and turned to look up at me, smiling pleasantly. "When I see Mr. Clemens sitting at dinner, or watching people on deck, I wonder what he's seeing, and what he thinks of it, and whether he's planning to put it in a book. I think it would give me a queer feeling if I were to read a book by someone I'd met and find a character in it who spoke and acted like me."

"You shouldn't worry about that," I said. We turned and began walking down the corridor toward the cabins. "He's written a book about the journey we took down the Mississippi River, and he had almost nothing to say about me, although I was with him nearly the whole time. In any case, I don't think he'd write anything unflattering about a young lady."

"How interesting," she said. "I shall have to find his book about that journey. It will be interesting to compare what he says about you to my own impressions." She held her novel against her bosom, a mischievous look in her eyes.

"And what are your impressions, Miss Babson?"

"Oh, I can hardly say, just having met you," she said. We reached the doorway to one of the ladies' salons, and she paused. "I think I shall have to get to know you better, so I can form a proper opinion." She turned to the door, then looked back at me over her shoulder. "Good day, Mr. Cabot." Her smile was brilliant.

"Good day, Miss Babson," I said. I watched the door close behind her, then turned down the corridor toward Mr. Kipling's cabin. On the way I passed the elder Mr. Smythe, the minister, who gave me a very puzzled look. It took me a moment to realize the reason; I was grinning as broadly a schoolboy who'd found a silver dollar on the street.

I knocked on the door of cabin 17, and Mr. Kipling let me in. The cabin was decorated in exactly the same style as ours, but the layout was slightly different, with only one porthole instead of two. As I'd expected, my employer was there, lounging in an armchair. Mrs. Kipling sat on the small couch opposite him, reading some loose papers—one of her husband's manuscripts, perhaps.

"What's the verdict, Wentworth?" asked Mr. Clemens.

"There's no Ruckgarten on the map, as far as I could see," I replied. "The librarian wouldn't let me bring the atlas here, but you can check for yourself, any time you want."

"No reason to doubt you," said Mr. Clemens. "It was what I expected. So, what do we do about this fellow who wants us to think he's a prince?"

There was an awkward silence as everyone in the cabin contemplated my news about the prince—I still thought of him by that title, although it was becoming more and more apparent that he might not have any right to it. "I suppose it's possible I made a mistake," I said. "Perhaps Ruckgarten is on a section of the map I overlooked."

The others turned to look at me, and I realized they were expecting me to continue. "But I was very careful," I said, not wanting to seem to defend the impostor. "I looked all along the border between Bohemia and Germany, and in the index, as well. Perhaps the atlas is too old."

"Or maybe too new," said Mr. Clemens. "Ruckgarten might have been a real place in Napoleon's time—the name could have changed since then, and not show up on modern maps. Or maybe it's the family name, and the place itself goes by some other name these days. There are dozens of principalities and duchies and so forth all over Germany—or were, until Bismarck and the Prussians made them toe the line. It's all one country on paper, now, but a lot of them still try to keep the memory of the old days alive, even if they're no bigger than a Missouri farm, and twice as poor.''

"That's a very charitable assumption, Clemens," said Kipling, raising his bushy eyebrows. "It's possible young Cabot overlooked something small on the map, but it seems far more likely that Prinz von Ruckgarten is no more royal than the boy who carried our bags aboard. I say we tell the captain, or someone else in authority. Then they can act as they think proper, and we can wash our hands of it.''

"I'm not sure we have to go that far," said Mr. Clemens. "Ruckgarten may be just a social climber, puffing himself up to insinuate himself in a better circle of society. It's too bad if he's a fraud, though—he's such an *entertaining* fraud.''

"I can't agree," said Kipling. "I don't find this fellow quite as enchanting as you appear to, Clemens. I'll grant you he knows how to spin an enjoyable tale. But that hardly excuses his imposing on everyone with the claim of being royalty.''

"That still isn't a crime in America," said Mr. Clemens, raising a protesting hand. "In fact, we don't know that he's up to anything criminal or even dishonest, besides giving himself airs. That's no cause for siccing the cops on him. I think the best thing we can do is simply to avoid him, so nobody will think we're endorsing his claims.''

"It would be a pity to have to cut him," said Mrs. Kipling, looking up from her reading. "He dances rather well, and he does tell such amusing stories. But Ruddy is right; we shouldn't allow him to continue this pretense.''

"We need to do more than just avoid him," said Mr. Kipling. "What if he's a burglar? Or what if he's looking for a rich widow to marry? Shouldn't she be warned she isn't getting the prince she expected?''

"I get your point," said Mr. Clemens, frowning. "But

I hate to malign a fellow who hasn't hurt anyone.''

"I'm afraid that if we wait for proof of bad faith on his part," Mr. Kipling argued, "it'll only come when we're docked in Southampton, with some unfortunate woman's jewelry gone missing, and Ruckgarten nowhere to be found. Do we want to be responsible for that?''

"You're right, Kipling. We can't take that chance," said Mr. Clemens. He looked out the porthole for a moment, gave a sigh, then turned to face us again. "Frankly, I don't think they can do much besides take the man aside and let him know they've spotted him as an impostor. I doubt they'll do even that—though it might make him think twice about any larcenous ideas he has. And then, if a passenger did complain about valuables missing, the authorities would have all the excuse they needed to search Ruckgarten's cabin. I guess we might as well take care of this without any more fooling around. Who do you think we ought to tell first?''

Mr. Kipling stood a moment in thought, then said, "I'd think the master-at-arms would be best. He'd be the one to investigate any crime on board, so he'd want to know of a passenger traveling under an assumed identity. If he feels it's important enough, he can investigate, or pass the matter on to the captain.''

"Good, that's who we'll go to," said Mr. Clemens. "Where do you think we'll find him?''

"Excuse me, gentlemen," said Mrs. Kipling. She put the manuscript page she was reading on the seat beside her, face down on a stack of other pages. Folding her hands in her lap—I noticed how small they were, almost as tiny as a child's hands—she looked up at her husband. "I think you're overlooking the simplest way to deal with the question.''

Mr. Kipling looked surprised. "Why, what would that be, Carrie? I'm sure Clemens would agree that we don't want to miss something obvious, if it's really the best approach.''

"Why not begin by confronting Prinz Karl directly?''

she said. ''He has been generous—to both of you, and it seems only fair to allow him to explain his actions before you summarily expose him. Tell him you believe he's given you a false identity, and ask for an explanation—in private. If you don't like his answer, you may still tell your suspicions to the master-at-arms, or the captain. The gentleman must know that his story can be checked by anyone who cares to do a little research. Perhaps he has a legitimate reason for concealing his identity.''

''Astonishing,'' said Kipling. ''Why didn't we think of that?'' I was equally surprised. While I had no idea what justification the prince might offer for his imposture, it was only common decency to give him a hearing before we turned him in to the authorities.

''Yes, we should have considered that ourselves,'' said Mr. Clemens. ''Thank you, Mrs. Kipling, it was the woman's touch we needed. I think it's exactly what we ought to do. Wentworth, why don't you come with us? I reckon it's a sensible precaution to have a big football player along when you're about to accuse somebody of being a liar.''

I nodded my assent, and followed Mr. Kipling and Mr. Clemens out the door.

10 〜

We came out of Mr. Kipling's cabin and looked both ways down the corridor. Suddenly, I remembered just how large the ship was. Prinz Karl could be almost anywhere; we had not known him long enough to have a notion of his habits. "Where shall we begin our search?" I asked.

"We last saw him on deck, so that would seem a logical place to begin," said Mr. Kipling. "Why don't the three of us walk a lap around the main deck, and if we don't spot him there, we'll at least have gotten some fresh air. Then we can decide what to do next."

We walked a short way down the corridor to the nearest doorway, and stepped out onto the starboard deck. There was a pleasant breeze blowing, and the late morning sun sparkled off the waves; I could see a few birds off in the distance, high in the air. I wondered if they were some sort of ocean-going breed who spent their whole lives at sea, then thought that unlikely. Where would they lay their eggs? I knew almost nothing about birds, I realized. My father, a town-bred creature though he was, had always enjoyed watching birds, and often spent a Saturday afternoon puttering about a country lane with a pair of field glasses. He would have been able to tell me what kind they were, and something about their habits.

Prinz Karl was not in immediate view in either direction, so the three of us turned toward the bow and began a leisurely walk along the deck. As before, there were a number of passengers taking advantage of the fine weather. Dr. Gillman sat in a deck chair with a blanket over his lap, poring over a travel guide to Britain. In the chair next to him, his wife was knitting something large and (so far) shapeless. A bit further along we met Wilfred Smythe and his employer, Mr. Mercer, both dressed as if for a day in the bank, walking briskly together in the opposite direction from our little group. I overheard Mr. Mercer say something about conversion rates, and young Smythe nodded, his face reflecting deep absorption in the subject. They paid us little notice.

On the broader expanse of the deck by the bow a group of the young Philadelphians were gathered, playing a noisy game of shuffleboard. There was a good deal of joking and horseplay—the fellows shooting the wooden disks at high speed, and fencing with the sticks as they argued over the rules. A little distance away, an older group played a more sedate game, carefully aiming their disks at the target, and quietly congratulating each other on good shots. They occasionally sent disapproving glances at the high-spirited youngsters. I could see at a glance that they were skillful players. And in their own way, they were enjoying themselves as much as the more boisterous group—although given the opportunity to join either game, I thought I would cast my lot with the Philadelphians.

At the bow, leaning against the railing and looking up at the ship's superstructure, stood Angus Rennie, the Scottish engineer, wearing a greenish-brown tweed jacket and a red-and-green plaid bonnet I thought somewhat ostentatious. In his hands were a notebook and pencil. With him was a bearded man in the uniform of a ship's officer. Rennie pointed with his pencil to some piece of machinery, and the other fellow nodded and began what I assumed was an explanation of the equipment or its function, as Rennie began jotting down notes. Mr. Kipling, taking in the same scene, turned to us and quietly said, "There's a fellow who when he goes to Heaven will spend his first week examining the hinges on the Pearly Gates.''

Mr. Clemens chuckled. ''Or trying to improve the furnaces, if he ends up in the other place.'' Then, after a slight pause, he added, ''No, they wouldn't let him—otherwise, he'd think he was in Heaven, after all.''

''Well, I shall have to cultivate Rennie,'' said Mr. Kipling thoughtfully. ''You'd be surprised how much you can learn from an engineer.''

We stood for a moment looking down at the foredeck and beyond it to the open ocean ahead of the ship. Somewhere, some thousands of miles ahead of us, was Europe. But for now, only the sky and the open sea were visible. I wondered how far from land we had come; hundreds of miles by now, no doubt. Even on our Mississippi riverboat, the *Horace Greeley*, we had usually been in sight of both banks, close enough for a moderately strong swimmer to reach the shore. But it would be four more days before *City of Baltimore* saw dry land again.

There was still no sign of Prinz Karl, so we turned away from the prow of the ship and began to make our way aft along the portside deck. This side of the ship faced north, and therefore was less crowded than the starboard, where the late morning sun compensated for the autumn temperature. Still, a few passengers had sought it out—possibly because of the relative quiet it afforded.

We came to one of the large hornlike ventilators located around the deck, when I heard someone speaking in a low voice: ''I wish you wouldn't pay any attention to that fellow—he's only jealous.'' Just then we came around the ventilator, and I recognized the speaker: Robert Babson, who was standing with his fiancée, Theresa Mercer. Miss Mercer's back was toward us, and she was evidently startled by our sudden appearance—she turned quickly as she became aware of us. Her hands were clasped behind her back, and I thought I saw her face redden slightly. Babson's view had been blocked by the ventilator, and so our presence surprised him as well. He looked up with an angry expression for a brief moment, until he recognized my employer and managed a smile. "Good morning, Mr. Clemens," he said, with more graciousness than I would have given him credit for.

Mr. Clemens gave some conventional reply, while Mr. Kipling and I nodded and touched the brims of our hats as we went past, leaving Babson and Miss Mercer to continue their tête-a-tête uninterrupted. Our business was to find and question Prinz Karl, not to stop and talk with Babson. I was just as glad—although it occurred to me that if I were to become friends with Babson's sister, I would undoubtedly find myself in his company from time to time. Well, I would deal with that eventuality if it arose.

I wondered for a moment to whom he had been referring in the brief comment I had overheard, then decided it was none of my business, and put it out of my mind.

We completed our circuit of the deck without seeing our quarry, although we met several others whom I recognized: Mr. Richards and his sister, Mrs. Martin, walking briskly as if for exercise; Harrison, our cabin steward, hurrying down a stairway carrying a large bundle of some sort; and Signor Rubbia, a pad of paper in one hand and a pencil in the other, standing at the stern watching the wake of the ship reel out behind us. He shot a scowl in Mr. Clemens's direction, but we simply nodded and continued on our way.

When we reached the point at which we had started, we stopped, and Mr. Kipling said, "Our fellow's not on deck, it seems—not unless he's been walking in the same direction as we have the whole time we've been looking for him."

"That doesn't seem likely," I commented. "Where shall we look next?"

"I reckon our best move is to split up," said Mr. Clemens. "I'll go plant myself in the main smoking lounge and see if he shows up there—staying put and waiting is always a good bet when you're trying to find somebody."

Mr. Kipling laughed. "Yes, good show—lay an ambush for the fellow. I think I'll take a look in the barbershop, then peek into the library and the other smokers. If he's not in any of those places, I'll find my own spot to lie in wait for him."

"Better yet, why don't you come join me and wait?" said Mr. Clemens. "We aren't in any real rush—we'll catch the fellow in the dining room, if we don't spot him before then. He doesn't look like a man who skips meals, to me. Same for you, Wentworth. Explore the ship a little bit, see if you spot our purported prince, and if you don't find him, come meet us in the smoker before lunch time."

"And if I do?"

Mr. Clemens looked at me for a moment, as if deciding what sort of message he could trust me to deliver. Then he shrugged and said, "Ask him to meet us in my cabin, after lunch. That'll be easiest. If he can't meet us this afternoon, ask when he *can* come. And if he wants to know what it's all about, pretend you don't know—he can check with me at lunch, if he's curious. Think you can handle that?"

"I should think so," I said, somewhat annoyed that he would even question me.

Mr. Clemens must have sensed my feelings from my tone of voice, for he looked at me with a serious expression and said, "Oh, I trust you to do the job, Wentworth. But remember—this is a delicate spot we're in. The prince may be exactly what he says he is, in which case he's not used to being quizzed and he won't be happy when he realizes that's what we're doing. But if he's an impostor, he's got more brass than Sousa's Marine Band, and he'll probably put up one hell of a front to keep from being found out. So we have to be ready to push him hard enough to decide whether he's what he claims to be, and ready to back off at full steam if we decide he's the real article after all."

"I'll be discreet," I said, somewhat mollified by his explanation. "I'll meet you in the smoking room if I haven't found him by eleven-thirty or so.''

''Aye, now we've got a sensible plan,'' said Mr. Kipling. ''This way, we shan't run ourselves breathless trying to search the entire ship. It's not as if we're afraid he's about to murder someone, is it?''

Mr. Clemens grimaced. ''If I thought he was, I'd sit in my cabin and smoke cigars while somebody else went to search for him. Murder might be great fun to read about, but I can tell you, in the real world it doesn't do a bit of good for the digestion.''

Mr. Kipling and Mr. Clemens had laid claim to the most likely hunting grounds on the cabin deck. Since I was traveling on an ocean liner for the first time, I decided this would be a good excuse to explore the parts of the ship I hadn't seen. Thus, I went down the first stairway I encountered, for a look at the lower levels of the ship. I had seen them when we embarked on the liner, but only quickly—and before I had any real notion of the ship's layout. If I met up with Prinz Karl in my wanderings, so much the better. If not—well, as Mr. Clemens had pointed out, the prince would surely make his appearance for the noon meal. And after all, there was no great urgency to our search.

I took the stairs down one flight, and found myself in a long corridor lined with cabins. There was no one visible in either direction, other than a maid coming out of one of the doors with an armful of towels. This was not likely to be a fruitful area for my search—although it occurred to me that if I knew the prince's cabin number, it would be worthwhile to knock on his door, on the chance that he was within. But I didn't even know for certain which deck his cabin was on, so (for the moment, at least) that avenue of investigation would have to remain unexplored.

To either side, a door with a porthole led to the outside. I went through the one to my left and found myself on deck again. This deck was narrower than the one above, with a roof overhead. A good idea in wet weather, though on a sunny autumn day like this the shade made it somewhat less appealing than the open deck one flight up. Still, there were a few passengers here, taking advantage of the fair weather and wide ocean view. Perhaps the prince was among them.

As I stood for a moment deciding which way to turn, a familiar voice called my name. "There you are, Cabot—come join us!" I turned to see my Yale friends, Johnny DeWitt and Bertie Parsons, leaning against the rail a short distance aft of me.

"Hello, boys," I said. "How's life in the nether regions?"

"Not quite the lap of luxury," said Bertie. "But I've slept in worse beds, and the food is at least as edible as the stuff in the Yale dining hall. I guess we've all survived a few years of that."

"Ate it and gained weight," I said, remembering how hungry I'd often been after football practice. More than once I'd gone back for seconds and thirds.

"You feel the motion of the ship a lot more down below," said Johnny. "My poor brother's seasick this morning. We tried to get him to come and get a breath of air, but all he wanted was to stay in his bunk. I guess it won't kill him, but the poor kid seems rather miserable just now."

"At least it's not catching," said Bertie. "I've never felt fitter in my life, thank God."

"Don't tempt fate," I warned. "Mr. Clemens thinks we're going to see some weather this trip, and he's made the crossing enough times to know. That could test the strongest stomach."

"Oh, I'll be all right," said Bertie, with a dismissive wave of his hand. Then he grinned at me. "I smuggled along a bottle of good old rye whisky for medicinal purposes. I've heard that if the weather gets rough, your best bet is to have a few stiff drinks and just sleep through it. That'll suit me just fine."

"Maybe it will," I said, somewhat skeptically. I remembered Prinz Karl's tale about his drunken English Channel crossing—evidently a full load of drink hadn't prevented him from feeling the effects of the waves and weather. "I'll let you try the experiment and tell me the results." I winked at him.

"Have no fear," said Johnny Dewitt, grinning. "If he can spare a sip or two for a fellow Christian in need, I'll try to duplicate the experiment." He laughed; then his expression changed as he looked over my shoulder and said, "Oh, hell—here comes that bothersome fellow again!"

"Which bothersome fellow?" I asked apprehensively; my friends' expressions were unreadable.

But before they could answer, a firm hand landed on my shoulder and a voice bellowed: "Now, haven't I told you imps to stay in your own part of the ship? You're paying for steerage and nothing more, and I'll be blasted if I let you walk all over the ship as if you owned it. Back down below decks with you, now!"

I turned to see a little dark-bearded man in a ship's uniform glaring up at me. I vaguely remembered seeing him the previous day when Prinz Karl and Robert Babson had squabbled about which of them would board the ship first. I stood perhaps eight inches taller than he, but there was something about him that suggested he would not be afraid to take on a bigger man in a test of strength.

"Excuse me, sir, but I am a first-class passenger," I said. "These fellows are my friends. They certainly weren't causing any disturbance . . ."

"Sure, and did I ask for any of your mouth?" he said. The hand gripping my shoulder was remarkably strong. "I've seen the three of you together before, and I know your tricks and dodges better than your own mothers do. You conniving college boys think you can pay for steerage and then sneak upstairs to socialize with the quality. Well, you'll not put anything over on Patrick Gallagher, I'll have you know."

"Easy, now, old fellow," Bertie began, but Gallagher cut him off.

"You want easy? I'll tell you easy. Easy would be if all the passengers stayed on their own deck. Every damned crossing there's somebody who tries to play fast and loose with the regulations—slick-talking rabble trying to make love to the women in steerage, or crooked gamblers trying to get the crew into card games, or smart alecks like you three who don't know their proper place. Back down below with you, before I kick the three of you downstairs all by myself!''

Small as he was, I had very little doubt that he could do as he threatened; in any case, I was reluctant to put him to the test. Johnny and Bertie hurried for the nearest stairway down, and I went with them—I'm sure my expression was every bit as sheepish as theirs. Gallagher followed close behind us, making certain we didn't dodge back up to the first-class decks. Then, when we were well away from first-class passengers who might be disturbed, he gave us a profanity-laden description of exactly what lay in store for us if he found us out of our proper place again.

I tried to interrupt. ''I beg your pardon, Mr. Gallagher, but I really am traveling in first class. I am Mr. Samuel Clemens's secretary. I have to meet my employer in the smoking lounge . . .''

''Aye, and I'm going directly there myself to borrow a pinch of snuff from the bloody Duke of York,'' the crewman growled. He reached up and grabbed me by the lapels and pulled my face down close to his, barking out, ''If you fast-talking college boys think you can outsmart me, you're in for a rude awakening. I'll tell you one last time, if I see hide nor hair of you three above this deck again, I'll lock your arses in the brig and feed you nothing but bread and water for the rest of the way across. And that goes double for anybody I find trying to bribe my crewmen. That's your last warning.''

Gallagher let go my lapels, turned on his heel, and stalked off to a stairway leading up to the region we had just left. Partway up the stair, he turned and favored us with one final glare, and from his expression I had little doubt that he would not hesitate to carry out his threats. While I knew that Mr. Clemens would promptly get me out of the brig should I end up there, I had no desire to be locked up even briefly. And I had begun to understand exactly how it felt to be accused of being an impostor. Of course, in my case the accusation was unjust. Inevitably, I wondered whether the same was true of Prinz Karl von Ruckgarten.

11 ~

"Well, that's a nuisance," said Johnny DeWitt, after Mr. Gallagher had left us. "There's a young lady I know on board—she's from Smith College. I saw her with her family on the dock, yesterday before we boarded, and I thought it would be fun to look her up again. It'll be a rotten bore if we have to stay down here the whole journey."

"Oh, don't let that ignorant little lout spoil all the fun," said Bertie Parsons. "Give him twenty minutes, and he'll be off somewhere splicing rope or whatever it is these fellows do aboard ship, and forget all about us. Then we'll stroll back upstairs, and get Cabot to his meeting, and you can look up your Smith girl. Perhaps she'll have a friend along."

We passed the next half-hour in catching up on the news of our old Yale friends, then sneaked up a different stairway to the first-class decks. Every step of the way, I had to fight the impulse to keep looking over my shoulder to see if Gallagher was following us, but we reached the cabin deck unchallenged by any of the crew. By my watch, it was time for me to join Mr. Clemens and Mr. Kipling in the smoking lounge, and so my friends and I congratulated ourselves on giving Gallagher the slip, and went our separate ways.

I walked into the lounge, with an involuntary wince as I nearly collided with a man in uniform—but it was merely a harried-looking waiter, taking out a tray of empty glasses. "I beg your pardon, sir," he said deferentially, and held the door as I went through. I nodded to him and stepped inside, looking for my employer. A burst of laughter revealed his presence at the center of a group of passengers, undoubtedly regaling them with one or another of his preposterous stories.

I moved quickly to join the group, perhaps still worried that Mr. Gallagher would appear and challenge my right to mingle with the first-class passengers. Too quickly: Before I was aware of any obstacle, I had collided with another passenger, knocking him off balance and jostling a glass of wine he was carrying. I grabbed his shoulder to steady him, and for the first time I caught a look at the fellow. It was Robert Babson.

"I'm sorry . . ." I began.

"You clumsy ape, why don't you watch where you're going? You've spilled wine all over my trousers," Babson said, his eyes narrowed. It was true; the red wine had spattered the leg of his trousers; almost as much had landed on the cuffs of mine, as well. I was uncomfortably aware that the conversation had stopped, and everyone in the lounge was looking at me and Babson.

"I am very sorry," I said again. "I'm afraid I wasn't paying attention. Here, let me buy you another glass of wine." I reached for my wallet.

"I've a good mind to teach you proper manners," said Babson, not at all appeased. He set the wineglass down on a nearby table and turned to face me, hands on hips. "I know who you are, and I'm surprised they let the likes of you in a private lounge with your betters. You don't see any other servants here, do you?"

"Mr. Babson, I will excuse your last remark on account of your ignorance of the facts," I said, as coolly as I could manage. "I have no desire to offend you. If you will remember, I offered to replace the drink I spilled. Will you accept that, with my sincere apologies?"

"Damn you, will you call me ignorant?" he said, his face turning bright red. "I've a good mind to call you outside and give you a thrashing despite your size.'' He raised his fist, and I feared he was going to try to strike me. I had no doubt I could defend myself, but I thought it stupid to allow such a trivial matter to lead to blows.

''Robert, that'll be enough!'' It was Mr. Babson senior. He strode over to us, interposing a shoulder between me and his son, his back to me. ''It is not your place to question Mr. Clemens's reasons for asking his secretary to attend him here. And it does you no credit to issue challenges to another gentleman's retainers. He has tried to apologize, and what's more he has offered to replace the drink he spilled. I am sure Mr. Clemens will stand behind the offer.''

Robert Babson glared at me, then looked away and shrugged. ''Oh, very well, Father. I suppose the fellow's not worth losing my temper over. Besides, I need to change my trousers before lunch. Excuse me.'' He walked past me as if I had ceased to exist, and left the lounge. Around me, I heard the buzz of conversation begin again.

''I am sorry, Mr. Babson,'' I said, but the lawyer had already turned away. I was left with no other choice but to continue on my way to join Mr. Clemens, who had risen to his feet when the disturbance began but was evidently satisfied that it would not require his intervention.

''Damnation, Wentworth, I thought you were going to get into another duel for a minute there,'' he said as I joined him and Mr. Kipling. ''Have a seat. I reckon you ought to have a drink to settle you down.'' I am not in the habit of imbibing before noon, but for once I decided to take him up on his offer.

Mr. Clemens ordered me a whisky and soda, then asked the group of onlookers to excuse us, since we had business to discuss, and they were quick to take the hint. While we were waiting for my drink to arrive, we compared the results of our search for Prinz Karl. Neither Mr. Clemens nor Mr. Kipling had had any more success than I in finding him. Either he was in his cabin, or he was somewhere else we didn't think to look. When I told

Mr. Clemens of my encounter with Mr. Gallagher, and my Yale friends in steerage, he laughed. "If I'd known you Yale men were so unwelcome in polite company, I'd have hired a couple more of you. Remind me to send a bottle of champagne down to those poor rascals, so they don't have to suffer the whole way over."

"Well, they already have a bottle of rye whisky," I told him. "My friend Bertie claims it's for seasickness."

"No doubt," said Mr. Clemens. "Snakebite's the usual justification, though it's uncommon in mid-ocean. Still, in my opinion you can never be too careful about such things. Has it worked so far?"

"Bertie seems well enough," I said, "but Tom DeWitt has had a bit of seasickness, poor fellow."

"He won't be the only one aboard, if I know the sea," said Mr. Kipling. "I spoke to Mr. Leslie, the purser, and he thinks we're in for a real blow by tonight."

"Well, then, this fellow's brought Wentworth's medicine just in time," said Mr. Clemens, as the waiter arrived with my whisky and soda. He glanced at his watch. "Drink up, boys. It's almost time for lunch. I reckon we'll need a good meal as well as a stiff drink under our belts when we put the prince to the inquisition."

As we had expected, Prinz Karl made his appearance for lunch at the usual time. Mr. Clemens went over to his table and quietly made the appointment to speak with him in our cabin afterwards; I saw the prince nod in agreement. Knowing we would need our wits about us for the delicate task of questioning the prince without giving offense should his credentials turn out to be genuine, I limited myself to a single glass of wine at lunch, and I noticed that Mr. Kipling did the same.

Robert Babson arrived several minutes late, wearing clean trousers, and shot a menacing look in my direction as he took his seat. That did not especially disturb me; I had apologized for my clumsiness, and his refusal to accept it in good faith reflected on him, rather than on me. What did bother me was that he promptly began grousing about the incident to his tablemates. I did not hear his exact words, but the general thrust of what he was saying was abundantly clear when several of them—including (to my distress) his sister Rebecca—turned to look in my direction. Well, perhaps I would have an opportunity to explain myself to her.

Despite my annoyance at being the object of Babson's slander, luncheon passed quickly and pleasantly. During the meal announcement was made of various activities and entertainments planned for the afternoon and evening. These included a band concert on the open deck, a tug of war, a shuffleboard tournament, a lecture on art by Signor Rubbia, and (to my puzzlement) horse racing on the foredeck. I had not seen any horses being brought on board, and I was almost certain that there was no place on the deck with sufficient room for even one horse to run freely. But when I asked my tablemates about it, Colonel Fitzwilliam and Mr. Kipling laughed, and told me I would have to find out for myself. My curiosity was piqued, and I promised myself that I would do exactly that.

Also, Mr. Leslie, the purser, announced the winner and runner-up in the "mileage pool" for the previous day. This was a bet on the distance the ship would cover in a given time. The *City of Baltimore* was hardly a competitor for the Blue Riband, the prize for the quickest Atlantic crossing, currently held by the Cunard liner *Campania*. Still, our ship could put on a respectable turn of speed: She had managed over 260 miles in her first "day," at a speed in excess of eighteen knots. Mr. Leslie encouraged interested passengers to place their wagers with him immediately after the meal, when the betting on today's run would be closing. To judge by the excited babble of conversation that followed his announcement, there was considerable interest in the pool among the seasoned travelers in our midst.

But the meal was soon over. As Mr. Kipling rose from the table, he said, "I'll just take Carrie back to our cabin, and I'll see you and Clemens directly after."

"Very well," I said, and turned to make my way back to Mr. Clemens's cabin, already thinking whether I might be able to contribute anything useful to the task ahead, or whether to let the two older and presumably wiser men ask the question, and confine my role to careful listening.

I had gone only a few steps when a light hand fell on my elbow, and a quiet voice said, "Excuse me, Mr. Cabot." I turned to see Rebecca Babson standing by my side.

"Good afternoon, Miss Babson," I said, somewhat apprehensively. If her brother had sufficiently exaggerated his story of my bumping into him and spilling his wine, she might have arrived at a low opinion of me. But then, why would she have sought me out?

She looked up at me with concern on her face, and said, "I think you should know that my brother has been painting a very unflattering picture of you." She nodded in the direction of the doorway, where I could see Robert Babson's back as he filed out with the rest of the lunchtime crowd.

"I feared as much," I said. "I realize that we are barely acquainted, but I hope you will credit me with better behavior than I suspect he has ascribed to me."

"Some of our friends are ready to believe him, but I know Bobby too well," she said, looking directly into my eyes. "Alan Mercer, Tess's brother, said that you tried to apologize, and I believe him, although Bobby claimed it was insufficient."

"I did try to apologize," I said. "It was an unfortunate accident, and I'm sorry to have caused it. I hope he doesn't hold it against me." In fact, it little mattered to me whether Robert Babson held it against me, as long as his sister was willing to be reasonable.

"I'm afraid my brother does not easily forget what he perceives as slights or injuries, Mr. Cabot," she said. She glanced around, as if to make certain no one was listening, then continued. "From what Bobby was saying at the table, I think he might try to play some sort of prank on you by way of revenge. I tried to dissuade him from going through with it, although he did not pay me much attention. If I learn what he plans, I will warn you. For now, at least I can tell you to be on your guard.''

"Thank you for the warning," I said. "I appreciate it. If something happens, I shall do my best to ignore it. The ship is too small to make an enemy over spilled wine, and in any case I should hope not to make an enemy of someone to whom you are closely related." I gave her my best smile.

"Why, Mr. Cabot," she said, blushing slightly. "I shall take that as a compliment, though I don't think I have done anything beyond returning your favor this morning, when you helped me in the library. But I should not stay here any longer. Bobby will certainly not tell me anything he plans if he learns that I have been talking to you. Take care, Mr. Cabot.''

"Thank you again, Miss Babson," I said. She gave a little curtsy and turned away. I watched her go for a moment, then looked around the room and realized that both Prinz Karl and Mr. Clemens had already left their tables, and so I hastened my steps in the direction of our cabin.

I had gone only a short distance down the passageway when a trio of uniformed men emerged from a side corridor ahead of me: Mr. Gallagher and two burly crew members. Gallagher saw me at once, and pointed directly at me, crying out: "There's the scurvy rascal—get him, lads!''

The two sailors began moving purposefully toward me. There were several other passengers between us, looking around in puzzlement at Gallagher's shout. Understandably, the crewmen were reluctant to charge forcefully through a crowd of well-dressed gentlemen and ladies to apprehend me, so I had a moment to decide whether to stand my ground or try to escape and go to Mr. Clemens's cabin by an indirect route. I glanced behind me, only to see the passageway blocked by an elderly couple, the woman leaning heavily on her husband's arm as they made their slow progress toward me. At the noise, the couple had come to an uncertain halt, and I suddenly realized that the wife was blind. To run in that direction would be to risk knocking her down. I turned to face Gallagher and his crewmen.

The seamen grabbed me roughly, and I was uncomfortably aware of the passengers in the corridor staring at me. Gallagher swaggered up to look me in the face. "Well, some fellows never learn their lesson," he said smugly. "Your partners gave us the slip, but that's all right. We'll make you an example, and maybe that'll teach them to stay in their place."

I mustered what dignity I could, and said, "Mr. Gallagher, I am a first-class passenger, and I can prove it. If you will only allow me to go to my employer's cabin, just a short way down this corridor, he is there right now and he will vouch for me."

"Aye, a likely story," said Gallagher, sneering. "But I'll not have anyone claiming Patrick Gallagher clapped him in the brig without a fair show. Let's go see this employer of yours. Keep a firm grip on him, Watts."

We made our way down the corridor past staring passengers, and soon arrived at the door to the cabin I shared with Mr. Clemens. Gallagher knocked on the dark mahogany door, while the two crewmen held my arms and I held my breath. To my dismay, there was no answer to the knock. "Try again," I said after a moment that seemed to last several hours. Where could Mr. Clemens be? Had he changed his plans without notifying me?

Gallagher favored me with a smirk, then turned and knocked again, more loudly. Still no answer within. "Well," he said, "I think we know how much this fellow's story's worth. Watts, Jones, bring him along."

"Wait just a little longer," I pleaded. "He was supposed to come here directly from lunch—he must have been detained."

"Aye, and so will you be," said Gallagher. "You'll have a chance to send a message, but we've got better things to do with our time than wait around for someone who might not show up for hours. We've already spent long enough chasing you. Let's go, lads.''

''Aha, I see you've finally captured that dreadful upstart,'' said a nearby voice. I turned to see Robert Babson, with two of his gambling companions, standing in the corridor with smug expressions. ''He's been sneaking into the lounge and pestering the passengers. I was going to report the fellow, but I see you've caught up with him.''

''He's lying,'' I shouted. ''Mr. Babson, this is a shabby trick!''

''Do you call me a liar?'' said Babson, with an angry expression. ''Have a care how you speak to your betters, you impudent rascal. If you persist in your misbehavior, you will find yourself in even more serious trouble.''

I was dumbfounded at Babson's false accusation, but I had no ready defense other than to call him a liar back. That seemed unlikely to accomplish anything useful. His sister had warned me that he might take some kind of petty revenge for my accidental spilling of his drink, but I had hardly imagined anything of this sort. Before I could think of any reply, Gallagher nodded to Babson and said, ''I guess that's all we need to know, mister. If you have any specific complaints against him, let us know—we'll see that he gets what he deserves.''

Babson had opened his mouth, undoubtedly to spout some other malicious falsehood, when Prinz Karl came into view down the corridor. He took in the scene and his eyebrows rose. He pushed past Babson and asked, ''What is the matter, Mr. Cabot? What has been going on?''

Suddenly I realized that Prinz Karl could corroborate my story. My captors might well have second thoughts if a respectable-looking older gentleman vouched for me. I knew that even if I were taken off to detention, Mr. Clemens would soon obtain my release. But I was angry at Babson, and did not want to give him the satisfaction of seeing me hauled away, and so I said, ''Prinz Karl, Mr. Gallagher here is under the false impression that I am an impostor. And this other fellow has been slandering me, claiming I am a steerage passenger who has been sneaking onto the first-class decks, when he knows perfectly well that I have as much right to be here as he does.'' I nodded at Babson, who had been edging away as he realized that his lie was about to be exposed. Gallagher and his men now looked confused, although Watts and Jones did not loosen their grip on my arms.

"This is an outrage," said the prince. "I know both these young men, and I will vouch for Mr. Cabot without hesitation. As for this other one"—he gestured toward the scowling Robert Babson, whose two companions had begun to shrink back from him—"he is a liar and a scoundrel and I say so to his face!" He rapped his cane loudly on the deck, and stood defiantly.

"Begging your pardon, sir," said Gallagher, suddenly deferential. "This young man told us his employer was staying in this very cabin. I knocked twice, and nobody has answered. Then the other gentleman came, and told us he was bothering the passengers. I don't want to contradict you, sir, but right now I'm not sure which story to believe."

"Well, I am here to meet this young man's patron, Mr. Mark Twain," said the prince. "He will come here in a few minutes, I think. But we should be able to settle the matter before then. Mr. Cabot, do you not have a key to this door?"

Of course I did. I felt like an idiot for not having thought of it myself. "Yes, right here in my pocket."

"Why do you not let go his arms so he may show you?" suggested the prince. The two crewmen looked at Gallagher, who nodded, and they released my arms. I took the key from my pocket, and slipped it into the brass lock. It turned easily, and the door opened. "So!" said the prince. "It looks as if this other fellow has not been telling you the truth."

All of us turned together to see what Robert Babson would have to say now that his accusations were proven false; but while I had been getting out the key, he had evidently made his escape. I looked both ways down the corridor, and saw neither him nor his companions.

Now that he was convinced that I was a legitimate first-class passenger, Mr. Gallagher (who I now learned was first mate of the *City of Baltimore*) was quick to apologize to me for offering to lock me in the brig. "I hope there's no hard feelings, young fellow—you'll have no more trouble from me, now that I know you. But that lying rogue who told us you were sneaking into the smoker and bothering people had best steer clear of me," he added with a significant grimace. "If he thinks he can play Patrick Gallagher for a fool, he's asking to learn a hard lesson."

"Perhaps he's already learned it," I said. "I feel foolish for not remembering I had a key to the stateroom, to tell you the truth. But all's well that ends well." I shook hands with Gallagher and his two crewmen, and they went off to resume whatever their normal duties were. The half-dozen passengers who had stood around watching began to disperse, as well.

Mr. Clemens and Mr. Kipling strolled up to the door just as the first mate was leaving. My employer looked at the departing seamen and the remaining onlookers and raised his eyebrows. "It looks as if we've missed the whole circus," he said. "What's been going on, Wentworth?"

"You'd have saved me a good deal of worry if you'd been in the room when I got here," I said. I held the door open and let him and Mr. Kipling in, and they sat down on the couch.

Mr. Clemens took out his pipe and tobacco pouch, then looked up at me. "Well, I'm sorry for the worry. I'd have been here a while ago, except the ship's librarian grabbed me as I was on my way down, and talked me into giving a lecture on the weekend. Then she took me down to the library to autograph three of my books, and while I was there I took a moment to look over that map you were telling me about," he said. "I ran into Kipling on the way up, and here we are. What were those crewmen doing here? Did you forget your key to the cabin?''

"In a manner of speaking," I replied, and began to relate the entire incident. At first, Mr. Clemens reacted with amusement. "I'm not surprised they took you for some sort of stowaway, Wentworth," he said, grinning broadly. "There's mischief written all over that face. Don't you think so, Kipling?" But when I told him of Prinz Karl's role in helping me refute Robert Babson's lies, his expression turned serious.

"Well, I'll be damned," he remarked. "The fellow's *acted* like a prince, whatever he really is. Where is he, by the way?"

"Why, that's odd—he was right here, a moment ago," I said, surprised that I hadn't noticed his absence. I went to the door and looked around in the now nearly-empty hallway. But like Robert Babson, the prince had evidently vanished. "He seems to have gone somewhere," I reported, feeling foolish at making such an obvious comment. "I distinctly heard him tell Gallagher that he was here to meet Mark Twain. What could have made him change his mind?"

"I suppose he divined what we were going to ask him, and dodged out," said Mr. Kipling, with a stern expression. "I think we shall have to report Prinz Karl to the master-at-arms, and let him decide how to proceed."

Mr. Clemens put down his half-filled pipe and tobacco pouch on the table in front of him, frowning. He stood up and paced a few steps, then turned and said, "Maybe you're right, Kipling, but I'm confused. The fellow just got Wentworth out of a pickle, and I feel that puts me in his debt. We still don't have anything crooked to pin on him, except maybe using a false name. But I'm confounded if I know what to make of him skipping out of the meeting."

"Perhaps he went to try to find Babson," I suggested, feeling indebted to Prinz Karl myself. "He isn't that late, yet. Why don't we give him a few minutes to keep the appointment?"

"That's a good point," agreed Mr. Clemens. "Maybe

he just had to talk to a man about a horse. We'll give him a chance to show up and explain himself before we turn him in to the management. Hell, I feel like a school-boy telling tales on his classmates.''

"We haven't told any tales yet," said Mr. Kipling. "In any case, we'll just be reporting our suspicions to the authorities, who will make their own decision what to do. How would you feel if we kept mum, and then he swindled someone?''

"Terrible, of course," said Mr. Clemens, shaking his head. "Still, I think we owe him a few minutes to show up and answer our questions." He walked over to the table and picked up the corncob pipe again, and resumed the task of filling it with tobacco.

"I wonder if the fellow's some sort of remittance man," said Kipling, rubbing his chin. "Perfectly respect-able origins, perhaps, but with no title and no inheritance to speak of. So he covers it up by playing the prince.''

"Remittance man?" I said, puzzled. "I'm afraid I've never heard the term.''

"A sort of involuntary exile," Kipling explained. "Usually a man who's caused some scandal at home, and who can't handle large sums of money. The family sends him a regular remittance to live on from one month to the next, on condition that he stays abroad and keeps out of serious trouble. I knew of quite a few fellows on that regime in India.''

"Ah, that might explain the business with the bad check that I saw at the dock," I said. Mr. Kipling looked puzzled, so I told him the story of my first encounter with Prinz Karl.

"That fits the pattern exactly," he said, nodding slowly. "He'd probably gone through one payment, and had to live as cheaply as possible till the next one arrived. He must have been gambling that the shipping line wouldn't try to cash his check until he'd gotten his next payment. It looks as if he lost that gamble, but when his remittance finally came in, he went down to the dock to try to put the best face he could on the situation.''

"Yes, I suppose that would explain it," I said. "But I still think we should wait for him to answer our questions."

But though we waited close to an hour, the prince never did come back.

12 ⌒

After Prinz Karl's failure to appear for the meeting, Mr. Clemens and Mr. Kipling came to the conclusion that the only way to resolve their suspicions of Prinz Karl was to turn the matter over to the master-at-arms and let him decide whether there was any ground for action. I would have joined them, but after a moment's consultation, they decided that if the two of them could not convince the authorities to look into the prince's identity, my testimony was unlikely to tip the balance. And so I was left on my own for the rest of the afternoon. I promised to join the other two gentlemen in time for a drink before dinner, and went out on deck to see the horse races that had been announced at lunch.

As I approached the foredeck, where the races were to be held, I became aware of an enthusiastic crowd of my fellow-passengers gathered in anticipation of the event. I made my way close enough to see over the front ranks of spectators, my curiosity considerably heightened. Bringing horses on deck was obviously an absurd notion; on the other hand, something exciting was clearly taking place.

I could see a booth set up to take bets on the first race, and a good number of passengers eagerly offering their money to Mr. Leslie, the purser, who was acting as bookmaker. Not surprisingly, Robert Babson and his companions were prominent among the bettors. Their wagers were surprisingly high; I saw Babson peel a twenty-dollar bill out of his wallet and place it on "Number five."

Then came the announcement, "The horses are at the starting gate. Ladies and gentlemen, place your final bets. *Pl-l-lace* your bets!" At this, I saw an open space on the deck, marked off in a sort of elongated gridiron. At the far end of the deck there were six wooden stands, of the sort that might support a small signboard, topped with carved wooden hobby-horse's heads, each bearing a number. So these must be the contestants! But how were they going to run?

After a final flurry of betting, the spectators lined both sides of the "track," and Mr. Leslie signaled to an assistant, who stepped over to a stand supporting something that resembled a birdcage, with an attached crank. He gave the crank a couple of spins, and I realized that the cage contained a number of dice. The cage stopped, and the assistant cried, "And they're off! Number one breaks cleanly with two lengths. Number three steps out one length!" As he called out the results, a second assistant moved the wooden horses. Now I understood it; it was no more than a dice game, with the hobby-horses representing the rolls of the dice in the cage. One might as well bet on Pachisi, a simple board game with which I and my childhood friends had sometimes whiled away a rainy afternoon.

In spite of myself, I burst out laughing. It was one of the silliest sights I had seen in a long time: grown men and women standing on the deck of an ocean liner, miles from land, all playing a children's game! I had no desire to bet on the races, but I had to admit I found the sight highly diverting.

The bettors were wildly enthusiastic, urging on their favorites with every turn of the cage. Robert Babson let out a whoop of glee each time "Number five" advanced a space, and his companions were equally vocal in support of their choices, as if the wooden horses could actually hear them and be inspired to run faster. The entire race took perhaps five minutes, with fanciful descriptions of the action from the assistant who twirled the dice-cage, and loud cheers from the crowd. At last "Number three" prevailed, coming from behind to nip "Number five" at the finish line, and the lucky bettors went to collect their winnings.

Robert Babson smacked his fist into his palm, then pulled out his wallet and went to bet another twenty on the second race. This time, "Number two" led the way from start to finish, and Colonel Fitzwilliam clapped his hands and went to collect his winnings. Babson had lost again. Finally I turned away, grinning and shaking my head at one of the most preposterous spectacles I had ever witnessed.

As I headed back aft, away from the "races," I noticed that the western sky had begun to cloud over, while the waves were noticeably rougher than they had been in the morning. The seasoned travelers' predictions of bad weather were evidently about to come true. I decided that if the weather was going to deteriorate, I might as well enjoy the sun while it shone, and so I spent most of the afternoon strolling the deck or leaning against the rail to scan the horizon. From time to time I would exchange a few words with one of the other passengers, but for the most part everyone on deck was more interested in the vast reaches of the ocean than in small talk.

Late in the day we overtook an eastbound clipper ship, flying American colors; when we came close, I saw she was the *Mary Grace*, out of Boston. She was making fine headway under full sail, taking advantage of a brisk tail wind. I doffed my hat and waved it to her as we came abreast her mainmast, and several of the men on her deck returned my salute. I heard them cheer us, and (straining my ears) I thought I could even detect the snap of the clipper's canvas and the steady lapping of the waves against her handsomely raked bow. I wondered what cargo the *Mary Grace* carried, and to what ports she was bound. She and her kind were a dying breed, and I thought how romantic it would be to see the world from the deck of a clipper ship. For that sort of adventure, I would readily agree to give up first-class accommodations on a modern steamer. But that adventure would have to wait for another time. At the moment, I was thoroughly enjoying myself, and I saw no reason to regret my circumstances.

Having been aboard the *City of Baltimore* over twenty-four hours, I had already begun to fall into the routine of shipboard life. There was little opportunity for boredom. Some activity or another was going on at almost every hour of the day, and there were enough choices to fit almost any taste. Those who were not inclined to watch and wager on the horse races could try their skill at shuffleboard, sign up for a tug of war, or merely watch the waves and sky. In the evening, there was a schedule of lectures, musicales, and other cultural events varied enough to make the ship a veritable floating Chautauqua. Of course, there was a constant succession of card games and plenty of stimulating conversation to be had in the smoking lounges—and, I assumed, in the ladies' lounges as well. And for those content to sit and lose themselves in the pages of a book, the library served the purpose admirably.

Meals—especially the formal dinners—were the only occasions when the entire company sat down together at once. There was music from the ship's little orchestra, a spirited round of toasts, and uniformly excellent food. Mr. Clemens was especially pleased with the cuisine on board, comparing it to his early voyages when even the richest passengers had to sit on long wooden benches, contenting themselves with such uninspiring fare as boiled beef, codfish, potatoes, "dog in a blanket," and plum duff. I, for one, had no complaints about the food aboard this ship—and I had tasted New Orleans cooking at its finest.

I was somewhat surprised to learn that many of my fellow passengers were quite familiar with the writings of Mr. Kipling. I had read one of his books a few months earlier, at the recommendation of Mr. Clemens, and found his tales of life in the British military barracks of

India colorful and well-told, if perhaps too exotic for the general American public. But Colonel Fitzwilliam was far from the only passenger who recognized Kipling, and showed some awareness of his work. In contrast to Mr. Clemens, who very much enjoyed life in the public view, Mr. Kipling seemed jealous of his privacy. He was clearly uncomfortable at the extent to which he was recognized and sought out by others on board, and Mrs. Kipling often took it upon herself to bluntly inform those she saw as intrusive that their attentions were unwelcome. By our second day aboard I noticed that the couple had begun spending more time in their cabin—presumably so that Mr. Kipling could write or read—than in the public areas, at least during daylight hours.

Prinz Karl seemed to be making himself scarce, as well. He did not appear for the evening meal, and I wondered whether something had come of my employer's visit to the master-at-arms—although I could not imagine what it might be. Mr. Clemens had reported that the officer had listened with interest and promised to look into the matter, without promising anything in particular. Perhaps, despite his claim that the ocean did not affect him, the prince was suffering from seasickness.

Another who appeared to be staying in her cabin was Rebecca Babson. I did see her at dinner, although we were seated at different tables and thus unable to talk. But she did not appear on deck, nor did I encounter her in the ship's corridors. Once I even peeked into the library, thinking that she might be there, but I saw only Mrs. Tremont, busily arranging books on the shelves. Miss Babson did not seem to be avoiding me; she smiled and said "Hello" as we were leaving the dining room after dinner. But she was with her parents, and as they did not stop to speak, neither did she.

I saw far more of her brother, since he was a frequent habitué of the smoking lounge—almost always drinking and playing cards with a constantly shifting cast of opponents. As far as I could tell without paying close attention, Robert Babson was more often the loser than a winner. For the moment, at least, he had apparently forgotten his petty quarrel with me over the spilled wine. Perhaps, after the failure of his attempt to get me in trouble with Gallagher, he'd decided to pretend that the episode had never occurred. Whatever the reason, I was just as glad not to be the object of his notice.

Equally, I was relieved to no longer be the object of Mr. Gallagher's particular notice, although I did see him once or twice on deck. We said nothing to one another, though he favored me with a wry half-grin as we passed. As for my Yale friends, Bertie and the DeWitt brothers, whom he was presumably still trying to prevent trespassing on the first-class deck, I saw nothing of them, though I kept hoping to. Having met them, I realized that however much I enjoyed my employer's company, I missed talking to friends of my own age. I would have to make another sally below decks and seek them out. Bertie would be infinitely amused by the tale of my encounter with Gallagher, not to mention my near-jailing.

And so I adapted comfortably to the life of the ship. Even Mr. Clemens was less demanding than usual, although my work for him had never been onerous. With no telephone office and no daily mail delivery, no constant changing of hotels and restaurants, my duties boiled down to a bit of filing and taking dictation, and running an occasional errand to the library. I began to think I could very easily come to appreciate this sort of travel—especially with someone else footing the bills.

Not that everything went smoothly or without incident. Far from it. As predicted, the weather continued to grow stormy. At the evening meal, the soup in my bowl and the wine in my glass sloshed visibly back and forth, and at a nearby table one unfortunate waiter was caught off-balance by a sudden movement of the ship, spilling gravy onto the sleeve of a gentleman he was serving. Of course, the head steward came rushing up and promised to have the garment cleaned in time for the next meal. The gentleman took it all good-naturedly, especially after the steward brought an especially fine bottle of red wine to the table "compliments of the captain." But it was an unmistakable sign that we were in for a bout of rough sailing.

Not all the passengers responded to the heavy seas with the same equanimity as the gentleman whose sleeve was stained. At my dinner table, Lady Fitzwilliam and Dr. Gillman were both "off their feed," and attendance was noticeably down at the next morning's breakfast table. It became something of an exercise in navigation to move from one side of a room to the other, since the path might begin as an uphill climb and switch midway to a downhill slide. While I managed easily enough, it was clearly a bit of a hazard to some of the older passengers, who were less steady on their feet, even when the deck was fairly level. I began to discern the full meaning of the expression "getting one's sea legs."

Inevitably, the more difficult conditions took a toll on the passengers' dispositions. Mr. Clemens could be irascible in the best of circumstances, particularly first thing in the morning. Shaving was a great trial for his temper, and I had grown accustomed to hearing him fire off a reverberating volley of red-hot curses every time he nicked himself. But with the ship pitching every which way, it became worrisome to be in the same room with him as he shaved. I began to fear that the Deity would decide to put an end to my employer's blasphemies with a bolt of lightning, and blow me to flinders along with him, innocent bystander though I was. It took a heavy weight off my mind when, on the second morning of rough weather, he went to the barbershop for his shave.

I had learned that Mr. Clemens's temper was like New England weather, apt to change every five minutes. I did not take it any more personally than I would a sudden shower on a summer day. Besides, his spurts of anger were far less frequent than his usual good humor and joking. But when half the passengers seemed out of sorts, it was never quite certain whether a social occasion would proceed as planned or degenerate into a petty spat.

That became apparent on the first night of bad weather.

I had gone to hear Signor Rubbia lecture on modern French art. Despite Mr. Clemens's mockery of the artist-turned-tour-guide, I was intrigued by some of the Italian's comments on art that I had overheard. While I would not be able to accompany him and the Philadelphians on their tour of European museums, I expected some day to visit many of the same galleries on my own. It made sense to learn from Rubbia's knowledge and experience.

The lecture was held in the Grand Saloon, and the room was packed. All the Philadelphians had come to hear the lecture, most of them crowding into the front row chairs and saving them for their friends and family members. I had a seat to begin with, but gave it up to Mrs. Gillman when she arrived to find all the chairs taken. By the time the talk began, half a dozen other men had joined me where I stood in the back. Signor Rubbia's smile grew broader by the minute as he saw the seats filling up, and when at last Mrs. Tremont introduced him as "Maestro Giorgio Rubbia, the celebrated Italian authority on the fine arts," he stepped up to the podium almost visibly swelling with pride.

Robert Babson, who sat toward the back of the room with a pack of his cronies, was highly amused by Signor Rubbia's self-important mien. I could hear him laughing and making rude comments from where I stood. From the front of the room, Signor Rubbia was aware of the noise, but not of its origin or substance. He stood at the podium staring around the audience, waiting for quiet, and growing increasingly impatient. He was not the only one impatient with the delay; Mr. Mercer, who was *de facto* leader of the Philadelphia contingent, turned and glared directly at young Babson, then uttered a loud "Shhhh!" that quieted the disturbance momentarily.

I wondered why Robert Babson had even bothered to attend the lecture; he had made it amply clear he had little interest in art, and no respect at all for Signor Rubbia. Perhaps Babson's parents had insisted on his attendance, hoping he would learn something. That outcome did not seem very likely to me; I remembered all too well the reception some of my Yale classmates had given unpopular speakers whose lectures they were compelled to attend. I had hissed at a few dull speakers in my own days as an undergraduate, emboldened by the example of my peers and the anonymity a large audience provides.

With quiet established, Signor Rubbia began his talk. "Some people say that painting is dead," he said, with a sweeping gesture. "The cameras are supposed to have killed it. I tell you that is not so. No, because now that we have the cameras, we can understand better than ever before what painting is truly about. To paint is not to make copies of what we see, but to make us see something new. And the best way to learn this is to go to Paris."

"We're certainly never going to understand it listening to you," came a voice from the back of the room. It was Robert Babson, of course.

Rubbia glared—he knew perfectly well who had made the remark—then decided to ignore the interruption. "The new painters who create the most exciting art are exhibiting in Paris," he went on. "You will not yet see them very much in the salons and galleries, but on the streets and in the cafés and restaurants, they are easy to spot."

"Dead drunk on the floor, no doubt," came Babson's heckling voice again, followed by a chorus of scattered giggles.

"I think the drunk person is here, not in Paris," said Rubbia, his face turning red. He came around to the front of the lectern, pointing in Babson's direction. "I do not come here to have you make a fool of me."

Several people in the audience had turned around to shush the interruption, and Mr. Mercer had stood up to glower at the younger Babson. In the front row, Rebecca Babson seemed to sink lower in her chair, as if to avoid association with her brother.

Evidently Robert Babson *was* drunk, because he

laughed out loud and said, "I can't make you any bigger fool than you already are, old fellow."

At this, Rubbia let loose a volley of rapid Italian, which it was probably just as well none of the audience understood. But his meaning was clear, as he began to stalk determinedly toward his tormentor. "I show you who the fool is," he muttered, his fists clenched.

Robert Babson slouched back in his seat, grinning at his friends. "Good, this'll be amusing for a change," he said. "What do you think you're going to do with me, eh?"

"Robert, that will be quite enough," said Mrs. Babson, in a high-pitched voice that wavered on the edge of panic. She had risen to her feet along with half the front-row audience. "You are embarrassing your mother."

By this time Signor Rubbia had come almost to the back of the room. Vincent Mercer had followed close behind him, and when Rubbia stopped opposite Babson's seat, the banker put a hand on his arm, speaking quietly into his ear. Rubbia nodded and drew back a step. Still, there was mayhem in his eyes. "Robert," said Mr. Mercer, " I believe it would be better if you sought your diversion elsewhere."

"Oh, bother," said Robert Babson, but then he sat up straight and looked at his cronies. "I guess Mercer's right, fellows. Who's up for whist?"

Two of his friends nodded their assent, and together they stood up and made their exit, with Rubbia glaring at them the whole way out. His anger was dampened for the moment, but I wondered how long it would be before another incident set it blazing again.

13 ⤳

After Robert Babson's ejection, Signor Rubbia's art lecture went rather well, although it took a while for the artist to regain his composure. At the conclusion, I went to the smoking lounge to join Mr. Clemens, who had wisely decided to spend his evening swapping stories with Mr. Kipling, Colonel Fitzwilliam, and some of the other passengers rather than sitting through a lecture. "Wisely" in contrast to Robert Babson, who after his departure from the Grand Saloon sat with a group of his fellows playing whist—without much luck on his side, to judge from his expression.

I gave Babson a wide berth when I entered the lounge, not wanting to provide him a fresh target, but he still took no notice of me. Two or three other gentlemen who had been present at the lecture also steered clear of him as they entered the room. It reminded me of pedestrians crossing the street to avoid passing a yard that housed an ill-tempered dog. For my part, I found a seat near Mr. Clemens, who was in the midst of a harrowing story of a mining cabin infested with huge spiders.

The other veteran travelers chimed in with their own tales of the vermin that inhabit strange countries—Colonel Fitzwilliam with a tale of a man who fell into a nest of the beautiful but deadly cobras of India, and somehow survived to tell about it. But Mr. Kipling took the prize for sheer terror with a tale of a man pursued by a pack of wild dogs who escaped by leaping over a cliff into deep water—the cliff being home to huge colonies of bees, which forced the poor fellow to keep ducking under water to escape their enraged stings. It was a gripping story, and I told him he ought to put it in a book. "Oh, I already have," he said, smiling quietly.

Just about that time, I looked up to see Mr. Mercer and Mr. Babson enter the room, their faces grim. They made straight for Robert Babson's group of card players, and I saw Mr. Mercer lay a peremptory hand on his shoulder. Young Babson looked up in annoyance, but a worried look crossed his face when he saw that it was his father and his prospective father-in-law who summoned him. Then he turned back to his whist partners, with a blasé expression, and excused himself. Pushing his chair back, he rose from the card table and followed his apprehensive father and the stern-faced Mr. Mercer out of the room. *That fellow's in for a scolding he won't soon forget,* I thought. In spite of all he had done, I felt a twinge of sympathy for him. Nonetheless, I was pleased to note that he did not return to the smoking lounge that evening.

Mr. Clemens also saw the incident, and shot a questioning glance in my direction as he watched the three men leave the room. But he said nothing about it until the end of the evening. Back in our cabin, he kicked his shoes off, loosened his tie, and plopped himself in a chair to sip on a nightcap. Seeing him settled for the evening, I was about to retire to my bunk when he stopped me with a raised hand. "One last question before you turn in, Wentworth. What's the story behind Mercer and Babson coming in like bailiffs and hauling off that young scamp? You looked as if you knew what was going on."

I briefly described Babson's expulsion from the lecture, and my employer nodded. "Now I'm even gladder I decided to spend the evening with a good cigar instead of going to hear that silly artist," he said. "I'd have been tempted to take a few potshots at Rubbia myself, and like as not I'd have ruined my digestion trying to keep from doing it. A man like Mercer doesn't like to hear that his pet artist is a humbug, especially in front of an audience. I reckon he'll give the Babson boy a first-class cussing-out.''

"A well-earned one, in my opinion," I commented. "Perhaps it'll teach Babson to think a little more before he speaks."

"Oh, I doubt it," said Mr. Clemens. "More likely it'll just teach him to pick his targets more carefully. If Bobby Babson had been slanging socialism and free silver instead of poking fun at Rubbia, the banker would think he was a prime wit. It ain't what you say that makes most people think you're smart, it's how well you agree with their opinions." He sighed. "I think Rubbia's a pompous fool, though a harmless one. But that Babson boy's a bully, and that's a damn shame."

"Well, I certainly hope he won't decide that I'm a safer target than Rubbia," I said. "I've had all the unpleasantness I need from that quarter."

"If that young fellow thinks you're a safe target, he'll learn better pretty fast," said Mr. Clemens, with a wicked grin. "The cussing-out he got from old Mercer is just a homeopathic dose compared to what he'll get if he crosses Sam Clemens. Normally, I'd be ashamed to waste my time on such a pitiful opponent. But if he tries to play any more games with you, I'll put aside what few scruples I have and fry him good and crisp."

"I appreciate your concern," I said, somewhat testily. "But I can take care of my own problems."

"I guess you can," said Mr. Clemens, looking me up and down. "But if you decide that pitching the no-good son of a lawyer overboard is too much work, I'll be glad to skewer him for you. In fact, I'll positively enjoy it."

The ship's rolling and pitching had noticeably increased by the next morning, and a glance out the port-hole showed a hard driving rain washing down the decks. It was something of a challenge to keep one's balance while performing such ordinary tasks as putting on trousers. And on the way to the dining room, both Mr. Clemens and I had to keep one hand against the wall to guard against being thrown about by sudden movements of the ship. I saw one poor woman take a heavy fall when she was caught off-guard by the ship's rolling.

There were quite a few empty seats at breakfast. Rebecca Babson was among those who did not appear, and I feared that her absence was due to seasickness. Her brother Robert was also among the missing. It struck me that if Bertie Parsons's theory that drinking was the best way to avoid seasickness, Babson had surely taken on enough liquor to realize whatever preventative effect it might have. Perhaps his sister would know; if I had the chance to speak to Rebecca Babson, I would make it a point to inquire after her brother's health.

Because of the weather, many of the activities that would ordinarily take place on-deck were either moved inside or canceled entirely. The shuffleboard tournament was postponed, and the horse races were held in the dining room after lunch. Robert Babson had made his appearance by then, and while he looked a bit peaked, he ate his lunch with a good enough appetite, although he was drinking his wine diluted with soda water. Whether he chose this beverage because of a delicate stomach or because his father and Mr. Mercer had warned him to moderate his consumption of alcohol, I hoped it would make him a more congenial traveling companion. I should not have been so optimistic.

I spent much of the day helping Mr. Clemens proofread the manuscript he was delivering to England, a task that sent me to the library two or three times to verify spellings or matters of fact. I kept hoping that Rebecca Babson might be there, but she was evidently occupied elsewhere. Of course, my work would not have left me much time for conversation. Still, every time I saw a young woman with blond hair, I felt an undeniable anticipation, until closer examination proved me wrong. I finally admonished myself not to build up my expectations, but to let things work out however the fates decreed. I had no evidence that her interest in me was motivated by anything other than a desire to warn an innocent person of her brother's malice.

Late in the afternoon, Mr. Clemens declared the day's work at an end, and we made our way to the smoking lounge, which had become our regular place to meet with Kipling and a few other fellow passengers with whom my employer enjoyed talking.

The minute we entered the room, we could hear Robert Babson's voice from the card table. "Leon, you dog, you dealt me this trash on purpose. How's a fellow supposed to play a hand like this? Well, I guess I have to lead *something*—here, put that in your pipe and smoke it." His belligerent tone and slurred speech were all the indication anyone needed that, if diluting his wine was intended to keep him sober, the stratagem was ineffective. A glance at his red face confirmed my diagnosis.

We went to the far corner of the smoking room, where Babson's noisy attempts at witticisms were less intrusive. Kipling and Colonel Fitzwilliam arrived a short while later, and we ordered up a round of drinks and soon were carrying on a lively controversy about Shakespeare. Somewhat to my surprise, Mr. Clemens took the position that Shakespeare was a semiliterate tradesman, whose plays were actually written by someone else—probably Sir Francis Bacon. "There's only one uncontested poem from his hand, and that's a wretched bit of doggerel," my employer said, referring to the inscription on the Bard's tombstone. "You know something about poetry, Kipling. Do you really think the same man who wrote *Hamlet* could write 'Good friend, for Jesu's sake forbear'? Would he allow those godawful lines to be carved on his monument for the ages to read? Would you want a stranger to come to your grave and read that, when you know you could do better?"

"Hum—I shan't care much what's written on my grave, if I'm content with what I've done before I reach it," said Kipling. "As for Shakespeare, I'm perfectly content to believe he wrote every word of the plays. The common man can learn to mimic the speech of kings and generals, but no aristocrat can capture the speech of the common man as well as Shakespeare has.''

"Shakespeare is a fraud," said Mr. Clemens, in a drawling tone that challenged the listener to guess whether he was jesting or in earnest. "None of his contemporaries took any notice of him. You'd think he'd have been the toast of London, even in that miserable era.''

"Ah, Clemens, the time of Elizabeth was hardly a 'miserable' era," said Kipling. "It's easy for us to sit at the summit of nineteenth-century civilization and mock the past, but I'll have you remember that three centuries of playwrights haven't topped the common fare of Elizabeth's time. As for the obscurity of Shakespeare's life, I count that rather to his advantage. You may think it easy to be a public figure and write well; I should find it an immense distraction.''

"I wouldn't be surprised if he were a little mousy fellow who sat in the corner of the tavern listening, then went home and wrote it all down," said Colonel Fitzwilliam, leaning forward eagerly. "His picture has that look, don't you think?''

"Ben Jonson considered him a superlative wit, and said so in print," declared Mr. Kipling. He swirled the whisky in his glass and looked at my employer. "By Allah, I'd think that would be all the testimony even you need, Clemens. What better endorsement can you ask than the recognition of his peers? That counts for everything.''

Mr. Clemens gleefully pounced on this point. "Sure it does, and that's exactly the problem. Look at what happens when you or I publish a book, Kipling. Every damn fool on three or four continents has something to say about it, usually pure drivel, but that's not the point. The damn fools in Shakespeare's time can't have been any different. Why aren't there reams of letters and articles about Shakespeare? *Went to see* Hamlet *last night; full of the veriest nonsense, but a good sword fight at the end. To the Mermaid Tavern afterwards for a cup of sack. Shakespeare and Jonson were there, with a rabble of players, all mightily drunk and making lewd japes.* There's nothing like that.''

''And if he was like that, why would his contemporaries pay it any more attention than we do that young jackanapes over there?'' said Colonel Fitzwilliam, gesturing in the direction of the card table. ''It's what he wrote that we care about, not how drunk he got.''

At the colonel's gesture, I glanced in the direction of the card table, and perforce at the door beyond it. As it happened, Robert Babson was also seated facing the door. And at precisely this moment, it opened to admit Prinz Karl, who glanced around the room. It seemed to me that his eyes lit on our little group, and that when he saw Mr. Clemens and Mr. Kipling, his face fell. After a moment of hesitation on the threshold, he turned and went out the door. ''Did you see that?'' I whispered to Mr. Clemens.

''What, Wentworth?'' said Mr. Clemens, looking at me; he obviously had no idea what I was referring to.

But Robert Babson had seen the prince's entrance and abrupt exit, as well. His crowing voice came to us loud and clear. ''Did you see that, Jack?'' he said to the fellow on his right, echoing my exact words. ''That pompous foreigner must have learned his lesson after all. He slunk right out the minute he laid eyes on me. You know, he tried to give me some of his lip the other day, but I stood up to him. That's all you have to do with his sort. He's not looking to tangle with Bobby Babson any more, no sirree.''

''Why, that fellow's an outright liar,'' I said to Mr. Clemens. ''He's the one who ran away, when the prince showed up to contradict his stories.''

''Yes, I doubt the prince was dodging Babson, whatever the young fellow wants to think of himself,'' said Mr. Kipling, looking at Mr. Clemens. Mr. Clemens nodded. After a moment's thought, I realized what Kipling meant; the prince had most likely been quizzed by the authorities, and unless he was an utter fool, he must have guessed who had raised the question as to his *bona fides*. It was my employer the prince had looked directly at before making his abrupt departure.

I myself had had nothing to do with exposing him to the master-at-arms, of course. But I could not help feeling guilty at the sad expression he had turned our way before walking out of the convivial milieu of the smoking lounge. It made me feel like a traitor to a man who had helped me, and I did not like the feeling one bit. Neither did I want to be a possible accessory to fraud, however. It was an awkward dilemma, not likely to be resolved until we reached England.

14 ≈

That same evening, there was a musicale scheduled for the Grand Saloon, and despite the rough seas, a majority of the passengers turned out for what promised to be one of the highlights of the voyage. The ship's little orchestra had shown itself to be remarkably versatile, expertly performing every style of music from symphonic selections and soothing chamber music to rousing patriotic airs, popular dances, and solemn hymns. Even Mr. Clemens decided to postpone the conversational pleasures of the smoking lounge in favor of the concert.

The occasion was remarkable in that both Robert Babson and Prinz Karl were in the audience, standing some distance apart from one another; the prince had made some effort to avoid any unnecessary meetings with the younger Babson. For his part, Babson had grown progressively boisterous at dinner, drinking and laughing at a great rate. While I was not close enough to overhear what he said, it was funny enough to send his friends into gales of laughter so loud that several of those at nearby tables turned to shush them during the meal. And tonight, Mr. and Mrs. Kipling had been invited to sit with Mr. Clemens at the captain's table, so the contrast between the low-key conversation around me and the high spirits at Babson's was particularly obvious. As disgusted as I was at Babson's drunken antics, I could not help feeling a certain attraction for the young, lively crowd around him—especially since it included his sister Rebecca. While she seemed to do no more than peck at her dinner, she seemed to be in fair spirits. Her face was a bit pale, but at least she was managing to keep a smile upon her lips.

Prinz Karl, for his part, had arrived at dinner several minutes late, attired in his dress uniform and looking neither to the right nor to the left as he took his customary seat. And while he seemed to eat his meal and drink his wine with no lack of relish, he was quieter than I had seen him before. Our eyes met once as I looked in his direction, and then I quickly averted my gaze. I still felt guilty about his having been quizzed by the authorities aboard ship, especially after he had taken my side against Babson.

The music was scheduled to begin half an hour after dinner. Mr. Clemens and I went back to the cabin for a few minutes to refresh ourselves, then strolled down a still-unsteady corridor to the Grand Saloon. Some of our fellow passengers seemed themselves unsteady, whether from seasickness or a surfeit of drink with dinner, I could not tell. My employer took a seat on the side aisle, but I (remembering the crowd at Signor Rubbia's lecture) decided to stand along the wall a short distance away so as to allow for the ladies who would undoubtedly make up a large part of the audience.

I was pleased to see Rebecca Babson enter a short while later, with her mother and brother. Robert Babson escorted them to a pair of seats up front, then strolled over to join a couple of his usual companions standing in the far rear corner. I saw sly grins on their faces, and then one reached into his jacket pocket and extracted a small flask, which he passed to his companions. Babson appeared to have gotten over his hangover—but it was clear that he was working on another one for the morrow.

The saloon rapidly filled up, and at the appointed hour, the musicians made their entrance, dressed in formal evening wear instead of the uniforms in which they had played their little concert on deck the day of our departure. There was a flurry of rustling as the late arrivals settled into their places, accompanied by shushing from those already seated.

The conductor, whose exemplary posture set off evening attire as effectively as a uniform, took a seat at the grand piano, placed some sheets of music on the rack, and waited for his men to adjust their instruments and music stands. When he was satisfied, he nodded to the front row of the audience, and Captain Mortimer stood up and turned to face us. "Good evening, ladies and gentlemen," he said. "We have all had the pleasure of listening to our ship's orchestra, led by Professor Isaac Goldberg, throughout the voyage, and I am sure you have enjoyed their playing as much as I have. Tonight, we give these fine musicians a chance to show their talents individually as well as in a group. We have also prevailed upon several of the passengers, who are gifted musical amateurs in their own right, to join in an evening of music and song. So without further preamble, let me turn the proceedings over to Professor Goldberg and his musicians."

The orchestra conductor rose to acknowledge the applause, bowed to the audience, and then resumed his seat at the piano as the room fell silent in anticipation. He nodded to his musicians, counted softly to four, and they began to play one of Mozart's instrumental pieces. I am afraid my taste runs more to popular dance music—or to Buddy Bolden's band, which I heard in New Orleans— than to the classical repertory. But it would have been difficult not to admire the superlative musicianship. Conducting from the piano bench, Professor Goldberg varied the program skillfully, changing moods and styles frequently. Of the soloists, I was especially impressed by the first violinist, who played a devilishly complicated number by Paganini, and by the professor himself, whose keyboard virtuosity sometimes gave the impression that he had more than the usual number of fingers.

After an hour or so, there was a brief intermission, followed by the amateur portion of the musicale. While the level of musicianship did noticeably decline with the arrival onstage of my fellow passengers, several of the young ladies sang very prettily, and Michael Richards, who as a small boy had known Mr. Clemens in his California days, turned out to have a fine clear tenor voice, gaining an enthusiastic round of applause for his rendition of "Willow, Tit-Willow," from *The Mikado*.

But there were moments best forgotten. Mme. Trappeaux, a sturdy woman of the contralto persuasion, favored us with a wobbling version of "O Promise Me," that reminded me of nothing so much as an ailing steamwhistle. Mr. Clemens looked around as if to locate an escape route; had the performance gone on much longer, I think I would have raced him to the exit, and knocked him down if he hindered my getting through the door. Professor Goldberg managed to display a polite smile despite the singer's misguided attempts at some of the high notes. Accompanied by polite applause—probably for not offering an encore—Mme. Trappeaux returned to her seat.

Then the professor yielded up his seat at the piano, and Theresa Mercer sat down to play. Her selection was a folklike melody in a strange minor key, by a Norwegian composer of whom I had never heard—Edvard Grieg. I am not certain whether it was the piece itself or Miss Mercer's rendition that most affected me, but while I listened, I was convinced that I had never heard anything so haunting. Her movements were remarkably graceful, and her face made it clear that she was not simply regurgitating some hard-learned lesson, but playing music that she loved. Possibly because she was Robert Babson's fiancée, I had not paid Theresa Mercer any particular attention before this evening, but by the time she had finished playing, I knew that she was a very accomplished young woman. As the last notes rang out, the room burst into applause; she had clearly won the hearts of all the listeners.

Somewhat to my surprise, Prinz Karl stepped forward as Miss Mercer stood up from the piano. "Young lady, you have a rare talent,'' he said, with a formal bow. ''Your playing has lightened my heart, and I would be much pleased if you would offer another selection.''

Miss Mercer blushed very charmingly, and made a curtsy to the prince. ''Oh, thank you so much, but I really couldn't,'' she said. ''I only have the one piece really prepared for tonight.'' And she returned to her seat as the applause continued, smiling and blushing. I was sorry she had not been willing to play again, especially since the next performer—Miss Mabel Archer, another of the young Philadelphians—sang ''Ben Bolt'' with a tuneless voice and affected diction that even her undeniably pretty face could not outweigh. While she was hardly the worst singer we were subjected to that evening, the contrast with Miss Mercer's musicianship made her seem a lifeless puppet. She returned to her seat with a smattering of applause, led mainly by her parents.

Finally, the supply of musical amateurs was exhausted, and the orchestra returned to play a last gay piece as finale to the evening's entertainment. The audience rose to its feet, and began to thread its way out the door to its various destinations. I made my way to Mr. Clemens's side, intending to go with him to the smoking lounge, where Mr. Kipling and Colonel Fitzwilliam had elected to spend the evening.

But before we had gone more than a short distance, the crowd stopped its forward motion, and I became aware of a disturbance near the door. I stood on tiptoe to peer over the heads in front of me, but believed I already recognized the two raised voices. Sure enough, Robert Babson and Prinz Karl stood blocking the exit, neither willing to yield to the other. *What childish behavior,* I thought. Several others in the crowd muttered similar criticisms, and to my right I saw Captain Mortimer pressing forward to break the jam.

Robert Babson drew back his fist and cursed at Prinz Karl. ''Damn you, you've been in my way the whole voyage, you arrogant Kraut. You act as if you expect us to give you the road, as if we were peasants and you the master. Well, I don't give a damn what kind of prince you claim to be. I'll show you what a Yankee thinks of your nose in the air.'' And before anyone could stop him, he struck the prince directly in the face.

Prinz Karl fell back a step, and I could see blood running from his nose. He reached up to his face, then gave a guttural cry in German, and leapt upon his attacker, swinging both fists. The next moment, both of them were rolling on the floor. The ladies nearby drew back in horror, but I stepped forward and, with the help of two or three other men, managed to separate the combatants and pull them to their feet just as Captain Mortimer arrived.

''You two should be ashamed of yourselves,'' said the captain, his hands on his hips. He looked first at Babson, then at the prince, shaking his head. ''How dare you spoil such a lovely evening of music with your petty squabbling?'' he demanded. ''I might expect such clownish behavior from the steerage passengers, but from two supposed *gentlemen* . . .'' He let the thought trail off, and I saw Prinz Karl hang his head as if to acknowledge the justice of the captain's accusation.

Babson was by no means chastened, however. ''Gentlemen, you say?'' he sneered. ''Unless you're judging him by his suit, this tub of lard is no more a gentleman than the micks who stoke the boilers. People all over the ship are talking about him behind his back, but I'll say it to his face—he's as phony as a wooden nickel.''

''Accusations you cannot back, you should not make,'' said Prinz Karl, now glaring angrily at the young man. ''If you did not learn that lesson from yesterday, then in church you should have been taught it: *Do not bear false witness.*''

''You call me a liar, do you?'' shouted Babson, and lunged suddenly at the prince. The men holding Babson back must have been caught off guard, for he managed to break free and take another swing at Prinz Karl, who was unprepared to defend himself. The blow caught him in the side of the neck, and he went down heavily. In an instant, Babson's guards had pulled him back again, but not before he aimed a kick at the fallen man's ribs. "No damned foreign snob is going to call me a liar," he shouted.

Prinz Karl rose slowly to his feet, his face a frightening mask of anger as he dusted off his clothes. "You will pay for this, young man," he said in a chillingly quiet voice. "I will say no more for now, but I do not make idle threats."

"That will be sufficient," said the captain, in a voice that exuded authority. "If either of you misbehaves further, I will confine the offender to his cabin until we dock in England. Sir, I suggest you take advantage of the opportunity to leave the room while this young man is still under restraint."

The prince looked at the captain and nodded. "Very well, Captain. I know how to bide my time," he said, then turned on his heel and stalked out of the room.

"Oh, I'm so frightened," said Babson, smirking. "Bide your time, mister. I'll be ready whenever you are."

"Robert, I would advise holding your tongue," said Mr. Mercer, who had at last come up beside him. "You are already in more trouble than you appreciate."

"Don't you worry, Mr. Mercer, I can handle myself," said young Babson. He looked a bit less defiant, face to face with his intended father-in-law. At the captain's gesture, the rest of the audience had begun to file out the door, with the ladies casting sidelong glances at the truculent young man. He grinned at them as if he had won a solid victory over a brave opponent, instead of launching two cowardly attacks on an older man who was not expecting violence—who, in fact, had not long before given his fiancée a compliment on her musicianship. Seeing Babson in that stance, I found it hard to understand what Miss Mercer saw in him.

The heavy seas seemed to have abated during the concert—or perhaps it was the audience's absorption in the music that made the weather less noticeable—but almost as soon as we left the Grand Saloon, the ship began to roll and pitch even more disturbingly than earlier. Mr. Clemens and I adjourned to the smoking lounge for a nightcap with Mr. Kipling and Colonel Fitzwilliam, and found the place half-empty. Even the two veteran cribbage players, who had hardly moved from their table except for meals since we had left New York, were absent tonight.

The weather was certainly the roughest I had felt on our trip so far. After the short trip down the corridor from the Grand Saloon, I was glad to find a good firm seat and plant myself securely in it. The waiter who negotiated the tilting deck without spilling a trayful of brimming glasses must have been a preternaturally skilled acrobat: I found it hard to keep my drink from sloshing out of my glass while holding it in my hand. As for setting down the glass, that was next to pointless, unless one saw some benefit to irrigating the carpet with whisky.

Despite the wretched weather, Mr. Clemens seemed to be in high spirits—at least, once he had a drink in his hand and a cigar in his mouth. He began swapping tales of storms at sea with Colonel Fitzwilliam, who had sailed at one time or another to almost every place Her Majesty's army had troops stationed. Mr. Kipling had done his share of sailing, as well, between England, India, Australia, and America. Compared to these three veterans of the high seas, I felt a veritable tadpole—though I had grown up with the Atlantic practically in my backyard.

After several progressively more colorful stories from Mr. Kipling and the colonel, Mr. Clemens said, "Well, the Atlantic can be rough, I'll grant you. I've crossed it often enough to know. But the damnedest voyage I ever had was on the Pacific—the first voyage I ever took, in fact. She was a three-masted sailing ship, and there were quite a few young people aboard besides me—I was young then, believe it or not, Wentworth. We left San Francisco for the Sandwich Islands. It must have been near thirty years ago, just this time of year, too. And at first, everything went pretty well, all things considered.

But halfway to the islands, two thousand miles from any shore, we were becalmed.''

"Ah, that must have been dreary," I said. "How long were you without wind?"

"Well, it must have been two weeks," said Mr. Clemens. He carefully reached out to tap the inch-long ash off his cigar. "We kept our spirits up by singing songs every evening. It struck me as very funny that one of the favorite songs was 'Homeward Bound'—we sang it every blessed night, though of course we weren't bound anywhere at all, being becalmed. We sat the entire fortnight in that one single spot, in sweltering heat, but it was pleasant enough, singing under the stars with that group of young people. Lord knows what's happened to most of them.'' He paused a moment, seemingly immersed in reverie over his lost youth.

The door to the smoking lounge came open, and I saw Prinz Karl stick his head in for a moment. He had evidently been out on deck—his hair was damp, and windblown. His expression was unreadable, but after glancing around the room a moment, he withdrew as he had earlier in the day, closing the door behind him.

"It's not much of a night for singing under the stars tonight, is it?" said Mr. Kipling, shaking his head. I thought at first that he was referring to Prinz Karl's appearance, but then I realized that he and Mr. Clemens were facing away from the door and could not have seen the prince.

"Well, I'm not much of a singer in any case," said Mr. Clemens. He took a sip of his whisky and wiped his mouth. "You know, I'd almost forgotten that voyage. The most curious thing happened. After two weeks of sitting in the same place, a breeze sprang up, and we thought we were on our way at last—homeward bound, after all our wishing for it in song. The sails filled, the ropes strained, and all our hearts were lighter. And yet, the ship didn't seem to be moving at all.''

"I've never heard the like," said Colonel Fitzwilliam, a skeptical look on his face.

"Well, it certainly surprised the captain," said Mr. Clemens. "It took us the better part of the day to figure out what was wrong." He paused, taking another long sip of his whisky.

Mr. Kipling had a little smile on his face. "I assume you're going to tell us what the problem was," he prompted.

"Why, of course," said Mr. Clemens, with a hurt look. "It was completely unprecedented. The captain had been sailing the Pacific for years and years, and his first mate was even more experienced, and neither of them had ever seen the like."

"The like of what?" asked the colonel.

"The barnacles, of course," said Mr. Clemens. He glanced around at his listeners, and experience told me that he was preparing one of his leg-pulls. "While the ship was sitting becalmed on that one spot for two weeks, the barnacles had been fastening themselves to the bottom of the ship. They grow very quickly in warm climates, you know. And then more barnacles had attached themselves below, and then another layer still."

"By Allah, I think I see what's coming," said Mr. Kipling.

"Yes," said Mr. Clemens. "The barnacles grew so thick that they formed a solid column all the way to the bottom of the ocean, and the ship was anchored fast to the floor of the Pacific—five miles deep."

"Why, I never heard of anything like it," said Dr. Gillman, who had joined our little circle for the evening. "How on earth did you get the ship loose?"

Mr. Clemens tapped the ash off his cigar again. "You know, I've entirely forgotten how we got free. It's curious, because we must have gotten free, somehow. After all, here I am. So it must be the truth, mustn't it?"

"Every word of it, I'm sure," said Mr. Kipling, chuckling deeply.

"I'm glad to hear that, Kipling," said Mr. Clemens, still keeping a grave expression. "I'd be very disappointed in myself if I'd made up something so improbable.''

At this, there was a general round of laughter, in which even Dr. Gillman joined. I felt relieved that he had finally caught on to the joke; it was not that long since I myself had listened to my employer's tall tales, believing every word until he finally pulled the rug out from under me.

Next morning, the sea was still choppy, but the sky had begun to clear, and I thought the worst of the storm might be over. It was again possible to put on one's trousers in a standing position, rather than safely seated. Mr. Clemens even managed to shave himself without an explosion of profanity. I looked forward to being able to go out on the open decks again.

But at luncheon, it was impossible to ignore the whisper that went around the dining room: *Robert Babson is missing*. I had noticed his absence at breakfast, but had drawn the obvious conclusion that he was paying for his overindulgence in liquor the night before. I had not thought it significant at the time, but now I remembered seeing his father striding along the corridor outside our cabin before breakfast, an anxious look on his face.

"One of the officers saw young Babson on deck last night," said Dr. Gillman, with the smug expression of one who retails a choice morsel of gossip. The doctor had been one of the winners of the mileage pool the day before, and had learned the news when he went to the purser's office to collect. "The sea was still very rough, and the deck was slippery, of course. The officer warned him of the danger, but Babson told him to mind his own business."

"That sounds just like the blighter," said Colonel Fitzwilliam, gruffly. "No respect for authority. No great loss, I say."

Lady Fitzwilliam put down her soup spoon. "Henry!" she said in an imperative whisper. "I'm sure none of us were fond of the young man, but you should have some consideration for his parents' feelings." I noted that she already spoke of Babson in the past tense.

"Yes, of course. Still, the fellow might have had some consideration for everyone else's feelings," muttered the colonel, in a more conciliatory tone.

Dr. Gillman leaned forward and continued in a low voice. "The officer went on his rounds, and the next time he came by, the boy was gone. Of course, the officer thought young Babson had taken his advice after all—it was not a night most people would want to be out in the weather. His mother went to look for him this morning and found his bed hadn't been slept in. They're searching the ship now, but odds are he's fallen overboard."

"I wouldn't be so certain," said Mr. Kipling. "There's still a chance he'll turn up somewhere below decks. He could have gone looking for mischief somewhere—a card game, or a bottle of something to drink. If I were in charge of the search, I'd look for him down in steerage—most likely in a vacant bunk, sleeping off the liquor."

"Yes, that would be like him," I said. I thought of my Yale friends in steerage, and wondered if he'd ended up in their company. I suspected the DeWitt brothers would find Robert Babson as uncongenial as I did, but even so, they would have helped him find a bed if he'd gotten too drunk or sick to return to his own cabin by himself. If that had happened, they might even conceal his whereabouts from any of the crew who came looking for him, adopting him as a fellow rebel against the authority of First Mate Gallagher. But they would tell me. And while I had no affection for Robert Babson, it would be a kindness to relieve his family's anxiety if it was in my power. I decided to pay my friends a visit.

After lunch, I went to the stern and made my way down a series of increasingly narrow stairways to the lower decks. Johnny Dewitt and his brother Tom were in the steerage dining room, the only public area other than the open deck for steerage passengers. The steerage dining room was in stark contrast to the richly decorated first-class areas. Instead of polished wood and fine art, there were plain metal walls, painted a drab gray color, with bare electric bulbs for illumination and exposed pipes running across the ceiling. A first-class passenger would meet with only the occasional reminder that the *City of Baltimore* was a huge machine instead of a luxurious hotel. Here, there was no illusion. But my friends had found a backgammon set somewhere, and were playing a lively game. "Hallo, Cabot, what brings you to the nether regions?" said Johnny. "Sit down, and you can play the winner."

"I'm not much good at backgammon," I confessed, plopping myself on the bench next to him.

"Good. We'll play for money, then," said Johnny, grinning. "Maybe it'll pay me back for all those times you murdered me at the billiard tables. You owe me a chance to get my money back, now that you're one of the privileged few, hobnobbing with the first-class passengers."

"I'll have you know I work for a living," I said, giving him a playful punch in the shoulder. "While you loaf your way across the ocean, playing backgammon and chasing pretty Smith girls, I'm earning my passage to Europe. That first-class ticket is the fruit of honest labor. Let that be a lesson to you, Master DeWitt."

"I'd rather learn how to get money without honest labor," said Tom DeWitt, idly toying with the dice. He seemed to be over his seasickness, at last. "Half the boys up at Yale seem to come from families where nobody's worked since the school was founded, and they never seem short of money. But they won't tell me the secret, whatever it is. You'd think they'd do as much for a classmate, wouldn't you?"

"Oh, if everyone knew how to make money without work, it wouldn't be a secret worth keeping," said Bertie Parsons, strolling through the door. "Speaking of secrets, have you any idea what that weasely Gallagher fellow is up to? He just now stopped and quizzed me about some passenger they can't find, but he wouldn't say what it was about. So of course I kept mum. I don't know what the poor devil's done to get the crew after him, but I'm certainly not going to help old man Gallagher find him.''

''Well, as it happens, I came down here to ask you fellows about that exact same thing,'' I told Bertie, and I saw him raise his eyebrows. I outlined what I knew about Babson's disappearance, including his drunkenness and the fight with Prinz Karl the evening before. ''So either he's hiding somewhere they haven't thought to look yet, or he fell overboard in the storm last night,'' I concluded.

''I'll be damned,'' said Johnny, sitting upright in his seat. ''What did this Babson look like again?''

''About your size, light brown hair, sort of a round face with a smug expression,'' I said. ''Pretty well dressed, and probably half-drunk or worse, at least last night.''

''Bobby Babson—yes, that's the same fellow,'' said Bertie, nodding. ''He was down here, all right, but not last night, as far as I know. We saw him the night before. He came looking for a card game.''

''And by any chance did he find one?'' I asked.

Johnny gave a sheepish grin. ''Well, Bertie and I took a poll, and determined that we had enough money to risk finding out whether he was a good enough player to beat us despite being thoroughly sloshed. As it turned out, he wasn't. After a couple of hours of losing, he gave up and went to look for something else to do. Not before we got a good bit of his money, of course.''

''We paid a terrible price, though,'' said Bertie, a rueful look in his eye. ''While we were taking the rascal's money, he drank up all Johnny's rye whisky. And there doesn't seem to be an open bar down on this deck—very shortsighted of the steamship line, I must say. Surely the steerage passengers want something to drink as often as their betters—maybe even more often.''

"So we'll have to be strict teetotalers until we land in England. Unless, of course, you know somebody who could help three Christian gentlemen in their hour of need," added Johnny, turning a speculative look in my direction.

"I would be glad to look into the possibilities for you," I said, thinking that Mr. Clemens might be persuaded to part with some of his supply of Scotch whisky. That reminded me of the subject I was more directly concerned with. "Are you sure that was the only time you saw Babson here in steerage?"

"We didn't know we were supposed to be keeping track of him," said Bertie. "Say, old boy, is this Babson fellow a particular friend of yours, or are you taking up police work in case the literary game doesn't play out?"

I laughed. "Neither one, thank you. As it happens, he has a very pretty sister. Very good-natured, too—quite unlike her brother, who was a rotten apple if ever I saw one."

"*Was?*" asked Johnny DeWitt. His expression turned serious. "You talk as if he's dead and gone. How do you know he didn't crawl inside a lifeboat and fall asleep? There's hundreds of places to hide on a big ship like this. Half an hour from now he'll come crawling out from somewhere, with a world-record hangover, and you'll feel foolish for ever wasting time looking for him."

"I guess you're right," I said. "I'm probably worrying too much. I've been involved in two murder cases since I became Mr. Clemens's secretary, and I suppose I've become suspicious. Of course there's no reason to think he's dead—and even if he is, no reason to suspect anything but an accident."

"That's right," said Bertie. "Now, if you want to play detective, why not see if you can track down another bottle for some friends in need?"

"I'll get on the case immediately," I promised, and shook hands with all three of them before climbing upstairs to the first-class decks again, whistling a little tune. Talking with my Yale friends had cheered me up immensely; I had far better things to do than to worry about Robert Babson. And besides, it was not really any of my concern, though I felt sorry for his family, especially Rebecca, if he really had fallen overboard in the night.

Mr. Clemens and I spent the afternoon in our cabin, proofreading his manuscript. We were interrupted briefly by one of the stewards knocking on the door: Harrison, who'd shown us to our cabin when we'd first boarded. "Beggin' your pardon, gentlemen," he said. "There's a young gentleman gone missing, and we're searching the ship for him. Captain's orders. Have either of you by any chance seen Mr. Robert Babson?"

"Not since last night," said Mr. Clemens. "Come in and look around, if you want to."

"If you gentlemen don't mind. Pardon the interruption."

"No trouble at all," said Mr. Clemens. "There's no news, then."

"Well, no news is good news, so they say," said the steward, opening the door to Mr. Clemens's bedroom and peering in. "But I guess that don't apply to a man missing at sea. If he hasn't turned up by now, I wouldn't be too sure he's going to. Terrible shame—I hear his mama's taking it awful hard."

"Yes, these things are always hardest on the poor women," said Mr. Clemens, shaking his head. "Young Babson was as sorry a specimen as I've seen, yet even he had a mother to grieve for him. Well, maybe he'll turn up yet, though I wouldn't bet on it."

"I'm not a betting man, but I'll agree with you on that, sir," said Harrison. He looked in my bedroom; then, satisfied that we were not concealing Robert Babson, he went on his way to search another cabin.

When we finished our day's work and went to the smoking lounge before dinner, there was still no word of Babson. The crew had reportedly searched every inch of the ship without finding him. The prevailing opinion was that he had gone on deck and fallen overboard in the night; given his intoxication at the concert, it was easy to believe. He could not have survived very long in such rough seas. The gentlemen in the lounge shook their heads and tut-tutted over their drinks, but I saw very little evidence that any of them particularly regretted the loss of Babson's company.

Not surprisingly, neither the mother nor the sister of the missing man were at dinner that evening, although his father was present, sitting next to Mr. Mercer at the Philadelphians' table. Robert Babson's usual table was quiet as a church, and the somber mood was contagious; conversation all around the dining room was conducted in respectful whispers. The wine seemed to flow less freely, too. Even Mr. Clemens kept his witticisms under wraps for an evening, speaking in a calm voice and limiting himself to subjects calculated to give as little offense as possible.

At the end of the meal, the captain rose to his feet and announced that the evening's scheduled entertainment—a comic skit put on by the ship's officers and crew—had been canceled. Instead, the Reverend Mr. Smythe would preside at a memorial service for poor Robert Babson, now officially "missing and presumed lost at sea." All passengers were urged to pay their last respects.

"I would think it's rather premature to hold services," said Mrs. Kipling, a skeptical look on her face. "It would serve them right if he stumbled in, half drunk, right in the middle of the eulogy."

"Yes, wouldn't it?" said Mr. Kipling, grinning. "If it really happened, it would make it worthwhile to go to the service just to see everyone's faces. It would make a first-rate story—though Clemens has already put his stamp on it, I fear. Even if I told it as true, nobody would believe I hadn't stolen it from *Tom Sawyer*."

"Truth is stranger than fiction," commented Colonel Fitzwilliam. "I can't say I had much use for the Babson boy, but I suppose I will go to the services. They're not so much for him as for the family, and they seem a decent lot.''

The rest of the passengers evidently shared the colonel's feelings; the Grand Saloon was full. Even Signor Rubbia, who might have considered himself well delivered of an affliction, was present. Perhaps the tour guide thought that Mr. Mercer, in whose good graces it was to his advantage to remain, would take offense at his absence from the service. In any case, Rubbia did his best to keep an appropriately mournful expression, whatever his personal sentiments regarding Robert Babson. Except for the Kiplings, who evidently made it a habit to avoid such large public gatherings, the only person conspicuously not in attendance was Prinz Karl von Ruckgarten, and I for one was not surprised, considering how obnoxiously the young man had treated him. Indeed, his presence might have caused more comment than his discreet absence.

The service was neither unseemly brief nor oppressively long. The Reverend Mr. Smythe did not go on at length about Robert Babson's merits, whatever they might have been. Instead, he directed our attention to the untimely loss sustained by his family and friends and to the hope of a reunion in a better world. We sang two or three appropriate hymns, recited the 23rd Psalm, and all in all gave the deceased a valediction far more tasteful than most of his living actions that had come to my attention. I arose from my seat at the service's end with a certain sense of completion; while I might not feel much genuine grief at Babson's demise, it surely did no harm to mark his departure from the Earth in a dignified manner.

Babson's family sat in the front row. His mother wept constantly, poor woman. It was touching to see Rebecca Babson lean over to whisper words of consolation in her mother's ear, or to help her wipe away the tears. For his part, Mr. Babson sat stiff as a rod, his posture conveying stoic determination—and perhaps a certain degree of anger at the injustice of his son's premature demise. Next to the Babsons sat Mr. Mercer and his family—including his daughter Theresa, the deceased's betrothed, who was clearly devastated by his disappearance. She was the most visibly distraught of anyone other than the mother of the departed. I could not help feeling sorry for her, or for young Babson's other friends, who sat in a row directly behind the family. It was the quietest I had ever seen them.

At the end of the service, everyone lined up to pay their respects to the bereaved family. This process did not take long, considering that few of us knew Robert Babson well, and fewer still were likely to have much good to say of him. (I would not have been surprised if Signor Rubbia's first impulse upon hearing of the death had been to dance a jig upon the foredeck.) I mumbled a few words of dubious solace to Rebecca Babson, feeling like a great hypocrite. But her brave little smile more than repaid me for the effort, and I left the memorial service with a sense that something had been accomplished after all.

Coming out, Mr. Clemens turned to me with raised eyebrows. ''Trouble's brewing, or I don't know the smell of it,'' he muttered, cocking his head to the right. I followed his gesture and saw Mr. Mercer and Mr. Babson over to the side, locked in deep conversation with the captain. All three had very grave looks on their faces, and I wondered what they might be discussing that seemed so important. Were there complications following young Babson's presumed death—some sort of paperwork or other formalities? Or did Mr. Babson have some notion of holding the steamship line liable for the young man's accident? If the latter, I doubted he had much of a case, considering his evident intoxication on the night of his disappearance. In any case, I doubted it would have much effect on either me or my employer.

It did not take long for me to find out how wrong I was.

16 ~

After the memorial service for Robert Babson, Mr. Clemens and I headed for the smoking lounge. Since many of the passengers had been to the service, the lounge was less crowded than usual as we arrived. But Prinz Karl sat there calmly, reading a book and puffing on an old meerschaum pipe. He had placed himself next to Mr. Clemens's favorite corner seat—almost certainly by design, I thought. He looked up as we entered, an eager expression on his face.

Mr. Clemens glanced at me, and I shrugged, not knowing what to make of the situation. We had not spoken to the prince since he had disappeared just before the meeting we'd invited him to, hoping to resolve the question of his origins. Not that we had gone out of our way to avoid him; rather, it was he who had seemed to dodge us at every chance encounter. Something must have changed.

Mr. Clemens was not one to evade such an obvious effort to meet him. "Hello, Prinz Karl," he said, walking over and plopping himself on the couch. I followed, taking a chair adjacent to my employer.

"I am glad to see you, Mark Twain," said the prince, putting his book facedown on his lap. The title, I saw, was in German, embossed in old fashioned Black-letter script: *Also Sprach Zarathustra*, followed by *F. Nietzsche*, which I presumed was the author's name. "I am sorry to have missed our meeting two days ago," the prince continued. "Is it possible we can make the opportunity for a meeting tonight?"

"Well, I don't see why not," said Mr. Clemens. He somehow managed to look as if the prince's overture was exactly what he had expected; I am not certain I was as successful at concealing my surprise. "I'd like Kipling to join us, though. Why don't we wait a few minutes for him? He decided to skip the shindig tonight, but I reckon he'll come out for a smoke before it gets too late. If he doesn't come, I'll send Wentworth to get him. Then we can all go to my cabin for a little more privacy."

"Yes, of course," said the prince, looking somewhat relieved at the reception he had gotten. "He should be included in the group, by all means."

"Good, then we'll wait for him," said Mr. Clemens. He took his own pipe out of his pocket, an old-fashioned corncob with a simple stem. I could not help thinking how sharply it contrasted with Prinz Karl's meerschaum, the bowl of which was elaborately carved into a turbaned Moor's head, slowly turning a rich golden color with long years of use. It was almost the same color as the amber stem. If such a pipe tasted as good as it looked, I could almost be tempted to take up smoking. But though I took no exception to others smoking, I had long ago learned that tobacco agreed with neither my palate nor my stomach.

We sat in a silence that might have been awkward, but Mr. Clemens temporized by fiddling with his pipe, and Prinz Karl was sufficiently master of his composure not to show any sign of impatience. I wondered what the prince expected to accomplish by talking to us now; perhaps after explaining himself to the ship's officers, he hoped to return himself to Mr. Clemens's good graces. But what could explain his claim to come from a nonexistent place? It would have to be a good story to satisfy my employer; in my experience, he was not easily misled by impostors.

Mr. Clemens had just finished packing his pipe with tobacco, and was reaching for a match, when the door to the smoking lounge opened to admit Mr. Babson, Captain Mortimer, and another officer I did not recognize: a tall, athletic-looking man with cool gray eyes. The three of them strode briskly in our direction, determination on their faces. "Damnation," said Mr. Clemens, although his voice gave no particular sign of annoyance. "That's the master-at-arms. I reckon we're about to be interrupted."

"Excuse me, gentlemen," said the captain, stopping directly in front of Mr. Clemens and the prince. "Prinz von Ruckgarten, I must ask you to come with me. Mr. Jennings and I have some important questions we would like you to answer." He kept his voice low, but every ear in the room was cocked to hear him.

"What sort of questions?" said the prince, looking up with a calm expression. "I will answer you right here, if you do not mind."

"I think you may prefer to talk to us in private—" began the captain, but Julius Babson cut him short.

"Questions concerning your whereabouts and activities last night," said Mr. Babson in a harsh voice. "I should warn you that anything you say may be held against you."

"Held against me?" said the prince, rising to his feet. "What you refer to, I do not understand. What do you have to hold against me?"

The captain's face was grim. "As you probably know, Mr. Babson's son disappeared last night, and we believe he fell overboard . . ."

"Not fell, but was pushed!" said Mr. Babson, in a voice that echoed in the smoking lounge. If anyone had not been looking in our direction before, they certainly were now. "And you are the one who did it, Ruckgarten—or whatever your name is: I expect we will learn that soon enough. Last night, you fought with my son. He bested you, and you threatened, in everyone's hearing, that you would take your revenge in due time. You did not wait very long; you found him on the deck not long afterwards, and pushed him overboard. Captain, I accuse this man of premeditated murder!''

The effect of Babson's accusation was like a thunder-bolt. The prince stood transfixed, shaking his head as if in disbelief. The lounge was dead silent as Captain Mortimer signaled the master-at-arms to escort Prinz Karl out of the room.

''It'll be best if you come along quietly, sir,'' said Mr. Jennings, in a matter-of-fact tone.

''I had nothing to do with young Babson's disappearance,'' said Prinz Karl, looking at the captain. ''It has to have been an accident, nothing more. But I will give you no trouble. An innocent man has nothing to fear from a few questions.'' He stepped forward, and Mr. Jennings put his hand lightly on his shoulder, although the intention was as clear as if he had placed him in handcuffs.

Then, before anyone else moved, Mr. Clemens rose to his feet, and put his hand on the officer's shoulder. ''One moment, if you don't mind. I'd like to ask this fellow just one question.''

''The man is a murder suspect,'' said Mr. Babson, his voice rising in pitch. ''If anyone's to question him, it should be the proper authorities.'' He had turned to face Mr. Clemens; his face was red, and his posture belligerent. For the first time, I realized that Robert Babson might have learned his hostility from his father—if he had not in fact inherited it directly.

''Looks to me as if the authorities are right here, and last I heard, you were just another passenger,'' said Mr. Clemens, giving Babson an annoyed look. Then he turned slightly, facing the captain. ''I'm going to ask my question, and Prinz Karl can answer it—or not—however he sees fit, and the authorities are here to take notes, if they want to. They can make whatever they damn well please of the answer. I'm not about to stop them from listening.''

''Ask away, Mr. Clemens,'' said the captain. ''Prinz Karl has the right to remain silent, of course.''

''A useful right,'' said Mr. Clemens. ''We'd all be

better off if more people would make use of it. But I
only have one question, and then the authorities can go
wherever they want and ask their own questions.'' He
turned to the prince. Silence reigned in the lounge; games
and conversations were forgotten as everyone turned to
stare in fascination at the scene unfolding in the bright
glare of the electric lights. Seeing a fellow passenger accused of murder could hardly be a commonplace occur-
rence in the first-class lounge, I thought.

Mr. Clemens stroked his mustache a moment before
speaking. ''Prinz Karl, we were going to reschedule our
meeting, and I guess we won't have a chance to, now.
So here's what I wanted to find out. You say you're from
Ruckgarten, in Germany. Well, I've been to Germany; I
lived a few months in Heidelberg, and in Munich, and in
Berlin. I even spent the better part of a month in Bohemia, and never in all that time heard of a place called
Ruckgarten. Neither has Kipling, whom I consider a
pretty well-informed man. When I asked you about it the
other morning, I thought you were trying to dodge the
question. So I had my secretary look for it on a map of
Germany.''

''I see,'' said the prince thoughtfully. He smiled at me,
almost apologetically. ''I think I know what you found,
young man.''

''I could not find Ruckgarten on the map,'' I said,
conscious of everyone in the lounge listening to my implied accusation. ''Does it have some other name?''

''No, because there is no such place,'' said the prince,
still smiling. Then he straightened his back and raised his
chin. ''Nonetheless, I am a prince of the royal blood.''

''He's lying!'' said Mr. Babson triumphantly. ''The
fellow is an impostor, from start to finish! Take him
away, before he insults us with any more of his nonsense.''

''We were going to do that in any case, Mr. Babson,''
said the captain coldly. ''But I'll ask you to remember
who's giving the orders here. You may be an important
man in Philadelphia, and I am aware that you have just

lost your son. But as Mr. Clemens pointed out, aboard my ship you are just another passenger. Mr. Jennings, would you escort Herr von Ruckgarten to my office, so we may continue in private?''

''Aye aye, sir,'' said the master-at-arms, and without another word, the two officers marched the prisoner out of the room, with Mr. Babson trailing behind them like a boy intent on following a parade despite being forbidden to do so by his parents.

There was dead silence in the room for a moment as the prince was taken away for questioning. Then everyone seemed to begin talking at once. ''My God, did you ever see the like of that?'' said one of the cribbage players. ''Who'd believe a murder on the high seas?''

''Murder, my eye,'' said the other. ''That boy was drunk as a lord ever since we sailed. I'm surprised he didn't fall overboard a lot sooner.''

''I wonder if he's even dead,'' said the first player, a gap-toothed fellow in an appalling checked blazer. ''In my opinion, it was premature to hold a memorial service. They've hardly had time to do a proper search. I'll wager the rascal's still sleeping it off somewhere. Won't they be embarrassed if he turns up tomorrow morning?''

''Well, they searched *my* cabin pretty thoroughly,'' said the other cribbage player, a balding man with half-glasses. ''The steward even opened up my steamer trunk. I don't see how he could have crawled in there, no matter how drunk he was.''

The buzz of excited conversation continued, but even now some of the passengers were starting to return to their card games or picking up their magazines again. Apparently not even the shock of a murder accusation could ruffle the atmosphere of the smoking lounge for very long. Mr. Clemens and I sat back down, glad that we were no longer the focus of attention. ''I suppose Mr. Babson has the right of it,'' I said quietly. ''The prince has been lying to us from the beginning.''

Mr. Clemens picked up his still-unlit pipe and found

another match. There was a moment's pause while he lit it; when he finally had the pipe going to his satisfaction, he looked up at me and said, "Well, he didn't try to bluff when I asked him about Ruckgarten, and he had as good an excuse to lie as he'll ever need." He looked around the room, as if to make sure nobody was listening too closely to our conversation, then continued in a lower voice. "I reckon a lot of the passengers are ready to believe he threw that boy overboard, and most of the rest of the ship will believe it by morning. He might have averted some of the suspicion by dodging my question about Ruckgarten, even if he knew he'd be found out later. The man has his share of courage, even if he's short on common sense."

"I'd question whether he has either courage or common sense, if he really did murder Babson," I said.

Mr. Clemens gave me a look that made me wish I'd held my tongue. "I don't know a damn thing about the murder, yet. I don't even know whether there *was* a murder, and unless you're letting that Philadelphia lawyer do your thinking for you, neither do you. At least the father has a reason to be upset. It's natural for him to look for somebody to blame for his loss. Grief will cloud a man's judgment, especially grief at the sudden death of a family member." He paused, and I recalled that he had lost his own brother in a steamboat explosion.

I felt as if I ought to shrink through the deck, but Mr. Clemens kept talking, in a voice that stung without ever getting loud enough for anyone to overhear. "I do know what I saw last night, which was a drunken bully throwing punches at an older man. Robert Babson picked the fight, and he threw the first punch at a man who wasn't expecting it. He probably figured he could do it with impunity. After all, he had what every bully dreams of— a high-powered lawyer for a father, to defend him against anybody who tries to hold him accountable for the harm he does."

"You're right, of course," I said. "But the lawyer must have convinced the captain to take his accusation seriously. It does look bad for Prinz Karl. But they would need something beyond the fight last night to incriminate the prince, don't you think? He was hardly the only one who tangled with Robert Babson. The fellow picked fights with everyone. Why, I had a run-in with him myself, and so did Signor Rubbia. Do you think we all joined up to push him overboard?''

''Maybe you did,'' said Mr. Clemens, leaning back on the sofa. ''I wouldn't put it past the bunch of you to heave his drunken carcass over the rail, then shake hands on a job well done.'' He chuckled at his own gallows humor; then his manner turned serious again. ''I reckon the father knows how to argue a case against somebody—that's a prosecutor's bread and butter. And you have to remember, the captain isn't an expert on the law—he might hold a man on grounds a regular judge would throw out like last night's dishwater.''

''I suppose so,'' I said. ''But once he gets to England, the captain will just turn things over to the regular police, won't he? Then a real judge will decide whether there's been a murder, and who the likely suspect is.''

''That makes sense to me,'' said Mr. Clemens. ''Can't say I've ever been on board an ocean liner where someone's been murdered on the high seas. Not that I haven't been tempted to pitch a few people over the rail, myself. I might even have done it, if I hadn't been afraid of getting caught.''

''Hallo, who are we throwing overboard?'' said Mr. Kipling, who had come in while we were talking. He took a seat on the couch next to Mr. Clemens. ''I could name a few candidates, if nominations are still open.''

''The prime candidate's already gone into the drink,'' said Mr. Clemens. ''That's old news. The part you haven't heard is that our friend Prinz Karl has been accused of helping him over the rail. They're questioning the prince right now.''

''You don't say! I'd never have made him out a killer,'' said Kipling. He took out a cigar and clipped off the end.

"Nor would I," Mr. Clemens agreed, frowning. "That young bully rode him pretty hard, though. Not everybody could have taken as much as he did without trying to get back. But I wouldn't have expected him to shove the boy into the ocean. It doesn't seem much like the prince's style, to me."

"You never know what'll drive a fellow to murder," said Mr. Kipling. "We used to see things in India—some little mouse of a clerk would take years of abuse from his supervisor, never saying a word, until one morning he'd pull out a razor and slit the fellow's throat. Or a silly incident no sane man would remember for five minutes would turn into a shooting match. The sahibs would blame it on the heat, or on being so far from home and civilization. But that's another story."

"Sounds like the mining camps in Nevada," said Mr. Clemens. "We didn't blink an eye at half a dozen killings a week in Virginia City. But that's not my point. If Babson was murdered—and from what I've heard, I'm not convinced he was—there's no proof it was the prince who did it. I don't think he's strong enough to have overpowered the boy, no matter how drunk he was. And it doesn't jibe with his character."

"Why not?" said Kipling. "The fellow is a patent fraud. We gave him a chance to lay his cards on the table, and he didn't bother to come to the meeting. That's as good as admitting he wasn't what he claimed to be. More to the point, young Babson tormented him mercilessly. Better men than he have snapped under that sort of abuse."

Mr. Clemens sat silently for a moment, puffing on his pipe. At last he said, "He may be a fraud—he as much as admitted it, just before the captain hauled him off. But if being a fraud makes a man a murderer, we're all destined for the gallows, Kipling. I make my living by telling lies, and so do you. That Signor Rubbia gets people to pay him for showing them how to see things they can't see for themselves. Come to think of it, Babson took a few verbal potshots at Rubbia, too. Why isn't *he* being put to the question?''

"The short answer is that he's one of the Philadelphia party, and our so-called prince isn't," said Mr. Kipling. "But I take your point, Clemens. I wouldn't lose any sleep about it, if I were in your shoes. If the fellow didn't kill Babson, the captain will let him go for lack of evidence. And if he can't prove his innocence to the captain, he'll still have his day in court when we dock in England." He blew a cloud of cigar smoke and looked around the room. "Are all the waiters helping out with the inquisition, or can a fellow get a drink this time of night?"

"Sure, a fellow can get a drink," said Mr. Clemens. He stood up. "In fact, if you'll come down to my cabin, I've got a bottle of better stuff than they give you here. Better yet, we'll be away from people who don't need to hear what we're talking about."

"Why should we worry about that?" said Kipling, looking up at Mr. Clemens in surprise. "I've barely started this cigar."

"Stub it out; you can relight it in my cabin," said Mr. Clemens. "I don't think there's been any murder here, just a young fellow who got drunk and fell overboard in a storm. But because Babson was a hothead who rubbed everybody the wrong way, and because his lawyer father wants to hold somebody accountable for his loss, people have lost sight of the facts. Well, I know the difference between an accident and a murder, if nobody else does. I'm going to find out the truth, and you two are going to help me. Come along, Wentworth. What are you waiting for, Kipling?" I had to jump to my feet and scurry to catch up with him before he reached the door.

17

The door of the smoking lounge had barely closed behind us when Mr. Kipling called out to my employer, who was forging ahead with a determined air. "I say, Clemens! Wait a moment, will you?"

"What the hell for?" said Mr. Clemens, but he stopped and turned around.

"I think we'd best hold this little conference in my cabin," said Mr. Kipling. "If we're really going to try to help this fellow, I want Carrie to be in on the planning. She's got as good a head on her shoulders as any man aboard, and better than most."

"Hmm—you're right, Kipling. She gave us good advice the last time we were about to go off half-cocked. Tell you what—Wentworth can fetch that whisky for us, and we'll go spring the news on your wife."

I thought this a good plan, having been impressed with Mrs. Kipling's common sense. So I went to our cabin, fetched the whisky bottle, and took it to the Kiplings' cabin. There I found Mr. Kipling sitting on a couch next to his wife and puffing on his cigar. Mr. Clemens poured whisky and soda for us three men. When he handed out the glasses, Mr. Kipling raised his in salute. "Here's mud in your eye," he said, and we all took a sip. "Now, Clemens, why don't you explain to me why Prinz Karl needs our help—or anybody's—to prove he didn't murder young Babson? Captain Mortimer's no fool. And if he doesn't know how to weigh the evidence, the master-at-arms surely does—it's his job. It won't take them long to learn whether or not there's reason to believe the father's accusation.''

"Yes, please do," said Mrs. Kipling. "I don't think the captain would hold a fellow without proof of foul play. Even Mr. Babson will have to relent if he can't get real proof. No prosecutor wants to go to trial without a sound case. And if he *does* have a sound case against Prinz Karl, why should we want to take the man's side?''

Mr. Clemens set down his glass, clasped his hands behind him, and paced few steps before answering. "You two weren't there to see them haul the prince off for questioning. Babson was busy stacking the deck against him—he *wants* to hold the prince responsible for his son's death. Some of the passengers were already judging him guilty. If that lawyer has his way, the whole ship will believe the prince killed that boy. Well, that ain't my idea of fair, Kipling. Prinz Karl deserves a better show than that, and I mean to see that he gets it.''

"And how do you intend to do that?" said Mr. Kipling, wrinkling his high forehead. "Do you have some reasonable plan, or are you just going to rush in half-cocked? You're a man of many talents, but you're certainly not a barrister.''

"Thank God for that!" said Mr. Clemens. "Why, if the prince went to trial in England, I'd have to put on one of those silly wigs, and nobody would ever take me seriously again." He struck a pose, with his arms crossed and a stern look on his face, and for a moment I could imagine him as a pompous barrister in robes and full-bottomed wig.

"I'm rarely sure whether to take you seriously as it is," said Mrs. Kipling, smiling at Mr. Clemens's antics. "The fact remains that Prinz Karl hasn't been formally charged with anything, and hasn't even asked you to help him. You have no standing—you're just one passenger among several hundred, even if you are the most famous person aboard.''

Mr. Clemens cocked a finger at the Kiplings. "Ah, but

I've got a few advantages not every passenger has. Because I'm a famous writer, people will talk to me. You know as well as I do, Kipling: People are flattered when a famous writer takes an interest in them. You've got to make an active effort to *keep* them from talking to you.''

"I know it all too well," said Mr. Kipling, with a shudder. "Not all of us enjoy living on center stage as thoroughly as you do, Clemens. But I take your point."

Mr. Clemens rubbed his hands together, warming to his subject. "Now, I reckon Robert Babson's disappearance is going to be the talk of the ship, all the rest of the way to England. So it'll seem natural enough for me to draw people into conversation about it. And because I've got a reputation as a funny fellow, they won't guard their tongues around me, because they won't realize I've got a serious purpose in talking to them. They'll tell me stuff they certainly wouldn't tell a ship's officer or a prosecutor—some of them will tell me things they wouldn't tell their own mothers."

"The bulk of it lies, most likely," said Kipling. "You'll be lucky to get any two to tell you the same story. Even if they do, you'll never know how much of it to believe."

"Don't be so sure of that," said Mr. Clemens. "I've met most of the foremost liars of the century: mediums and millionaires, congressmen and card sharks, inventors and phrenologists, jackleg preachers, snake-oil salesmen, stagecoach drivers, riverboat pilots—and my share of murderers, as you might recall. There's not a lie worth hearing that I haven't heard, usually in five or six dozen dialects and local variations. By now, I can usually tell the difference between the straight truth and a shameless lie—and most of the fine gradations between the two, as well. Why, if I thought I could make money at it, I'd consider setting up as a detective."

"You and half the boys in England and America," said Mr. Kipling, with an indulgent smile. "But I guess if anyone could make a go of it, you could—at least, to judge from those two cases you told me about."

"That's all very well," said his wife. "But what if nobody's seen anything worth talking about? Robert Babson disappeared at night. A dark and stormy night, at that—he and the officer who reported seeing him may have been the only ones on deck."

Mr. Kipling had taken off his glasses and wiped them on his pocket handkerchief. He held them up to the light, then, evidently satisfied with his inspection, put them on and looked at Mr. Clemens, then back at his wife. "If that's the sum of the evidence, the captain will surely let Prinz Karl go free. The father can make all the accusations he wants, but with no witnesses and no proof, there's really no case against the prince."

Mr. Clemens nodded. "True enough," he agreed. "But the suspicion remains. Even if the captain lets him go for lack of evidence, unrefuted accusations can hurt a man as much as a conviction. Half the passengers will look at him and see the mark of Cain on his brow. That's why I want to see if we can clear the prince entirely. I got the idea he was about to come clean with us about the Ruckgarten business—and I suspect the story of why he wouldn't name his real home country is mighty interesting in its own right. What's worse, I think we have jumped the gun when we reported our suspicions that he's an impostor. That probably made the captain more willing to take Babson's accusations seriously. That's why we owe it to the prince to find out the truth—and make sure everybody knows it."

"I wonder why the captain called him away in front of a whole room full of passengers?" mused Mr. Kipling. "You'd think he'd want to keep it discreet, if he doesn't have anything solid."

Mr. Clemens nodded, swirling his drink. "I think he did want to keep it quiet, but Babson's father blasted out his accusation for the whole ship to hear. Now that I think about it, I wouldn't be surprised if he *wanted* them to hear. The master-at-arms looked mighty uncomfortable. He knows it's worth his skin to bring a false accusation against an important passenger—if that's what the prince turns out to be.''

"And if it turns out he's guilty after all?'' said Mrs. Kipling. Mr. Clemens stopped in his pacing and looked down at the other writer's wife where she sat on the couch.

"Carrie's right, you know,'' said Mr. Kipling, sitting up straight. "We can't shy away from that possibility, whatever we want to believe.'' The challenge in his voice was unmistakable.

"If we find evidence that says he's guilty, I'll deliver it to the captain myself,'' said Mr. Clemens. He turned and looked out the porthole for a moment, then continued. "What I bet we'll find is that Robert Babson fell over the rail with no help from anybody—if he could hold his liquor, I never saw any evidence of it. He was a damned nuisance at best, and not many except his family are going to miss him. But if the prince is a killer, none of us are safe. I'll turn him in, no question about it. And if somebody else murdered the brat, I want to find *him* and turn him in, as well.''

"Good,'' said Mr. Kipling, slapping his hand on the arm of the couch. "Then we're with you. Let's get down to work.''

After talking it over, we arrived at a strategy. Our goals were to find anyone who had seen Robert Babson after the fight with Prinz Karl, and to learn how many people other than the prince might have had grudges against Babson. Mr. Kipling was to make inquiries of the officers and crew of the *City of Baltimore*; his wife would see what she could glean from the ladies' conversations in the Grand Saloon; I was to talk to the younger passengers, who were likely to be most comfortable with me; and Mr. Clemens would turn his attention to the rest of the passengers. We decided to meet briefly to exchange information three times a day: just before the lunch hour, before dinner, and before retiring in the evening. This way each of us would know whatever the others had learned during the day, and possibly use the information to direct our own inquiries more effectively. If the storm had not delayed our passage, we had a little more than two days to find the murderer—or prove the death an accident.

I told my employer and the Kiplings the one bit of news I had learned earlier today, that being my friends' report of Robert Babson's visit to steerage in search of a card game and drinks. "Bertie told me the fellow drank up all their whiskey, but he made up for it by losing a good amount of money to them."

"Now, there's something worth knowing," said Mr. Clemens, smiling broadly. "For all we know, Babson's gambling was what made somebody do him in."

I had my doubts as to that theory. "Every time I saw him, he was losing money," I said. "That's not a reason for anyone to kill him. More likely, they'd keep him alive so he could lose more money to them."

Mr. Clemens waved away my objection. "Maybe he was cheating, to try to get his losses back. If he was playing crooked and somebody caught him, there's no telling what they might have done. The same thing if he accused somebody else of cheating—I've seen Bowie-knife fights because some miner thought he saw a city fellow stacking the deck against him."

"We certainly can't rule it out, but I doubt any of those Philadelphia society lads he's been playing with are going to pull out a Bowie knife," said Mr. Kipling. "If they thought a fellow was cheating, they'd likely take him aside and give him a good talking to, or at worst banish him from their games. Besides, as much as Babson usually drank, I doubt his hands were sure enough to hold his cards properly—let alone do anything very clever with them."

"Still, that doesn't rule out his accusing somebody else of trying to cheat, rightly or wrongly," said Mr. Clemens. He looked my way. "Just keep it in mind as a possibility when you talk to his gambling friends, Wentworth. Be ready to follow up any hints that there was something funny about one of the games, or that Babson thought there was.''

''I'll keep my eyes open, but I doubt it's a very strong possibility,'' I said. ''To my mind, Signor Rubbia would be a more likely suspect than any of the card players. Babson insulted him at every opportunity.'' I didn't think my old friends were likely to be cheats (let alone murderers), although I had to admit that I hadn't spent much time at the card table with them. It would be bad practice to exclude my friends as suspects just because I'd known them in college.

''Speaking of Rubbia, who's going to talk to him?'' asked Mr. Kipling. ''It can't be you, Clemens—you've sent as many barbs his way as poor Babson did. He'll suspect something if you have a sudden change of heart.''

Mr. Clemens nodded. ''You're right, Kipling. He'd smoke me out right away, especially if he's trying to hide something. What about you, Wentworth? You ought to be able to talk to him and keep a straight face. Just don't let the old fraud get started on art, or he'll have your eyes glazing over within ten minutes.''

''Well, that's no problem. I actually enjoy talking about art,'' I said. ''I'm sure he won't mind telling me about paintings to see in Europe.''

''Don't let him go on too long, then,'' said Mr. Clemens, with a malicious grin. ''That fellow could have you pinned in a corner listening to his half-baked opinions about painting the rest of the way to England. You've got to talk to a few of the other passengers, as well.''

''Never fear, I won't let him monopolize my time.''

''Good. Mrs. Kipling, I especially want you to listen for any gossip about Babson's fiancée, Theresa Mercer. Find out if she rejected any other suitors for him, and whether they're on board. Or if she might have been getting tired of seeing him make an ass of himself in public. I can't see the Mercer girl pushing him overboard herself, but if she had another beau, she might have gotten *him* to do it for her. For all I know, there are five or six jilted suitors on board, and they all ganged up to feed Babson to the fish.''

We all laughed at Mr. Clemens's absurd suggestion, though his comment about the jilted suitor seemed to remind me of something I'd heard. I couldn't quite remember what it was, though I was sure it would come back to me.

"Not a very probable conspiracy," said Mr. Kipling. He took one last swig of his whisky and set down the empty glass. "I'd say Rubbia is a better bet. And an accident the best bet of all."

"I'd agree with you," said Mr. Clemens, "but we have to look at all the possibilities." He took out his watch to check the hour. "We've still got time before most of the passengers go to bed. What say we three men go back to the smoking lounge and begin our fishing expedition?"

Mr. Kipling stood. "Yes, unless we hurry, we'll be in England before we've learned anything at all. Tell you what, though—instead of going to the smoker, I think I'll go out on deck and talk to the watch. If it's the same man who was on duty last night, he may be able to give me more useful information than anyone inside, and my talking to him won't attract half as much notice as all three of us arriving at once and starting to quiz people about the Babson boy. If someone has something to hide, that's the surest way to alert them."

"Good point, Kipling," said Mr. Clemens. "In fact, now that you mention it, it makes sense for all three of us to split up. Wentworth, why don't you visit your Yale friends down in steerage again? Now that Babson's officially lost, they may think of something that slipped their minds before. Or maybe some of the other passengers down there saw him; if he spent much time down in steerage, it's a good bet he made as many enemies there as he did among the first-class passengers."

"If he went there, I'm sure he made enemies," I said. "It seems to have been his greatest talent."

Mr. Kipling nodded vigorously. "Precisely. And like

most snobs, he chose his targets from outside his own class. Can you imagine if he'd insulted a few Irish stokers who didn't get out of his way fast enough to please him?—although he'd have to go a good bit out of his way to get into their territory.''

"I'd be surprised if he got that far afield," said Mr. Clemens. "The way these modern ships are set up, not many passengers ever lay eyes on the black gang, let alone find their way into the crew quarters.''

"Black gang?" I asked. "Are there Negroes in the crew?''

Mrs. Kipling laughed. "No, mostly they're Irish," her husband said, smiling at her. "Shovel coal into a boiler for eight hours, and see what *you* look like in the mirror. Anyway, those fellows down in the hold know it's worth their jobs to tangle with a first-class passenger, no matter how much he provokes them. But we can't take the crew completely for granted—if any passenger could've made a stoker mad enough to step out of line, it would've been Robert Babson.''

"I'll see if my friends have heard anything," I said. "But I suspect they're more interested in sneaking up to first class to meet girls than in knowing what's going on further below decks. Babson might have blundered into the wrong part of the ship if he was drunk enough. But I doubt they'd have heard anything about it, if he did.''

"Not necessarily. He might have told them about it afterwards," said Mrs. Kipling.

"But then they'd have told me, when I saw them this afternoon," I pointed out.

"Well, we could jaw about it all night, and never learn anything we don't already know," said Mr. Clemens, holding up his hands and frowning impatiently. "Let's go talk to people. We'll all meet again tomorrow morning, unless one of you uncovers something urgent before then. You know where I'll be, if you do.''

I went down the stairways to the lower decks again, and found my friends in the dining room again, in the midst of a lively crowd. I hadn't realized before how many people were traveling in steerage. Coming from Europe, of course, the ship would easily have filled its cheap berths with immigrants hoping to find a new life in America. But there was clearly no lack of passengers for the eastward voyage, either.

I would have thought that most Americans who planned to travel to Europe were likely to be of the wealthier classes. A glance around the crowd in steerage convinced me otherwise. A fair number were clearly students or recent graduates, like my friends from Yale. There were others, as well—respectably, if not expensively dressed business men, who I guessed must be traveling either to sell American goods abroad or to establish contacts with European suppliers. Some may have been recent immigrants themselves, who had already found success in the New World, and who were returning to visit loved ones in the old country. I heard conversations in a variety of unfamiliar languages and dialects—here, even more than in the Grand Saloon, was a truly cosmopolitan assemblage.

In the center of the room, a pair of musicians played a lively dance tune—one a somber-faced violinist with long, nimble fingers, the other grinning broadly between muttonchop whiskers as he played a concertina. The pair seemed to know the same tunes; I wondered if they had played together before, or if the impromptu concert was the result of a chance meeting. In any case, a smiling circle of passengers sat around them, clapping in time to the music. Someone had brought a large jug aboard, from which passengers were taking sips before passing it on around the circle. It would have been a dour individual who could resist joining in the celebration.

Bertie Parsons and Johnny DeWitt were standing on the fringe of the circle around the musicians. "Hello, Cabot," said Johnny as he saw me approach. "Have they run out of champagne upstairs?"

"I doubt there's much champagne being drunk up there tonight," I said. "They just held a memorial service for that fellow who's been missing. And the ship's officers are questioning someone they think may have pushed him overboard.''

''Really?'' said Johnny, raising his eyebrows. Bertie turned to look at me, as well. ''Now, there's a story I'd like to hear. Let's go sit where it's not so noisy, and you can tell us about it.''

We moved to a table away from the music, and I told them about the confrontations between Prinz Karl and Robert Babson, our suspicions concerning the prince's origins, Babson's disappearance, and how the captain and master-at-arms had come tonight to apprehend the prince. The fellows listened intently as I described the scene, interrupting occasionally with a question. At last, when I was finished, Bertie gave a low whistle. ''Do you really think the prince did it?''

''Mr. Clemens doesn't think so,'' I said. ''I'm not certain why not, to tell the truth.''

''It's a hell of a story, either way,'' said Johnny. ''Damn shame about the Babson fellow. He didn't seem a very pleasant sort when we met him, but that hardly excuses shoving him overboard.''

''*If* that's what happened,'' I pointed out. ''Babson had had plenty to drink. He could have fallen overboard without any help, in my opinion. You don't know what it was like on deck that night.''

''We're on the same boat as you, old boy,'' said Bertie. ''It was plenty rough down here, as well. Had the devil's own time just staying in my bunk.''

''And our decks get just as much weather as yours,'' added Johnny. ''Not that we were out dancing the polka on deck, you understand.''

''It would be the first I'd ever heard of you dancing the polka anyplace,'' I said, grinning at him. ''But anyhow, Mr. Clemens isn't convinced that Babson was murdered—or if he was, that the prince did it. He sent me down here to find out if you fellows had seen Babson any time other than when he came looking for the card game.''

"Not that I remember," said Bertie. At my urging, he and Johnny went over the details of their meeting with Babson again, covering much the same ground as before. While they did come up with a few details they'd omitted the first time, nothing that they recalled seemed to shed new light on Babson's disappearance. And neither one of the fellows claimed to have seen him after their card game. "We had better things to do than look out for him." said Bertie. "Unless he wanted to lose more money at cards, y'know."

"From what I saw of him, that was his main occupation—that and making enemies," I said.

"Well, if he lost money regularly enough, I suppose there must have been a few fellows who wanted to keep him alive," said Johnny, with a shrug. "It would've been like killing the goose that lays the golden egg. Of course, it doesn't mean they had to be his best friends, either."

"No," I agreed. It looked as if I'd come below decks for nothing. Then a thought struck me. "I wonder who his best friends were? Did he mention any names when you were playing cards with him?"

Bertie frowned, trying to remember. "He might have, but damn me if I can remember. The only times he talked about anybody but himself were to complain about his tight-fisted father, and about his fiancée's father, who's apparently a stiff-necked old fellow with no sense of humor. The girl must be something special if he was willing to put up with the old man. What's her name—is it Tess?"

"Theresa Mercer," I said. "She *is* very pretty, though not really my sort."

"Mercer, that's it," said Johnny Dewitt, nodding. "Well, she may be pretty as a picture, but I'm not at all sure that was her main appeal for him."

"What do you mean?" I asked.

"Why, don't you know? Her father's a banker, and he's rich as Croesus," said Johnny. "Pretty girls are all very nice—don't get me wrong. But a fellow with Babson's luck at cards is ten times better off with a rich one.

She could have a face like a spaniel and a voice to match, as long as the dowry's big enough to cover his debts.''

''Even less reason for his cronies to kill him, then,'' I said. ''So I guess we're back to figuring out who his enemies were.''

''Well, it sounds like you've spotted enough of them,'' said Bertie. He thought a second, then a mischievous smile came to his lips. ''I say, Cabot, if I were you, I'd find out what that old First Mate Gallagher was doing that night. From what you told us, Babson made a monkey of him just the day before. It'd be just like the nasty fellow to push him over the side, out of pure spite.''

''Oh, be serious, Bertie,'' I said, and all three of us laughed at the preposterous suggestion. But in the back of my mind I thought that even his humorous notion might have some truth to it. Robert Babson had no shortage of enemies. The only question was whether one of them had gotten angry enough to push him into the stormy seas—and if so, which one. Thinking about the question got me nowhere, and despite another hour joking with my friends and listening to the music, I went to bed in a decidedly grumpy state of mind.

≈ 18

Next morning was Friday, our fifth day at sea. At breakfast, the passengers learned that the storm had forced the captain to cut speed; our arrival in England would be delayed by a day. There was considerable grumbling in the dining room when this announcement was made. At a nearby table, I overheard Mr. Mercer and Signor Rubbia discussing their group's itinerary in England, and which of their planned sightseeing excursions could be dropped from the schedule without disappointing too many of those on the tour. Among our usual dining companions, Dr. Gillman was annoyed as well. "I have only a limited time in England, and here I am losing a whole day at the outset. I shall send a very harsh letter to the director of the steamship line, believe me," he said heatedly.

"The director can hardly be held responsible for the bad weather," said Mr. Kipling, peering through his thick glasses. "The passengers' safety comes first. That's always been Cunard's policy, and I'm glad to see the American Steamship Line adopting it."

Dr. Gillman put down his coffee cup firmly. "If I'd wanted Cunard's policy, I'd have booked with Cunard," he said. "I chose the American Line because it has the faster ships, and I'm very disappointed with the delay."

I was tempted to agree with him—there was something grand about the notion of racing the elements across the open sea. On the other hand, Mr. Clemens and I would be very little inconvenienced by a late arrival. My employer had allowed himself a whole week in London before the start of his lecture series, so as to enjoy his reunion with his wife and daughters. Of course he would be unhappy to lose time with his family, but it was only one day, after all. I was glad that I would not have to spend my first days ashore trying to juggle appointments and reschedule lecture bookings. Besides, we might need the extra time at sea to uncover the truth behind Robert Babson's disappearance.

"I agree with Kipling," said Colonel Fitzwilliam. "We aren't on such an urgent mission that we have to make speed at all costs. Give Captain Mortimer credit for good sense. Easier to change a few missed appointments than to explain to a board of inquiry why you lost half your passengers in a storm."

"Well, we've lost one passenger already," muttered the doctor. "If the captain was so solicitous of his passengers' safety, why'd he let that fool boy wander out on deck that night?"

Mr. Kipling finished spreading marmalade on his toast, then looked at Dr. Gillman. "The captain did what he reasonably could," he said. "The officer on watch warned young Babson that it was dangerous on deck; the boy didn't listen. I talked to that same officer last night, and I'm satisfied that he did what *he* could, short of laying hands on the boy and forcing him back inside. You can be sure there'll be some hard questions for him to answer, when he has to explain himself to the owners. But I doubt they'll punish him, when all's said and done. You can't order first-class passengers around like coolies, you know."

Colonel Fitzwilliam leaned forward and lowered his voice. "That's not half the story," he said. "There's good reason to think it wasn't any accident. I saw them take that German fellow, Prinz Karl, off for questioning last night, and this morning, there was a man standing guard outside his cabin. They've got him confined on suspicion of murder."

The doctor snorted. "I'm not surprised. I never did think much of that so-called prince, with his foreign airs. Could you pass the butter, my dear?"

"Now, Lloyd, don't be so quick to judge," said Mrs. Gillman, handing him the butter. "He always seemed a perfect gentleman to me, not that I've known him very long, of course."

"Yes, I'd be very surprised if the fellow is a murderer," said Mrs. Kipling, in a manner that brooked no opposition. "He is quick-tempered, but I think you can ascribe that to the natural pride of an aristocrat. And the Babson boy was very difficult, you must admit." I followed her glance toward the adjacent table, where Babson senior still sat drinking his coffee, but he seemed to have taken no notice of our discussion. It struck me that the only way for Mr. Babson to avoid hearing people talk about his son would be to confine himself in his cabin. Robert Babson's presumed death was undoubtedly the main topic of conversation at every table in the dining room.

I felt sorry for the bereaved father. But I had promised Mr. Clemens that I would help him find the truth about Robert Babson's death, and I meant to do exactly that— no matter whose feelings were hurt by the answers we found. Privately, I thought that the most likely thing for us to discover was the age-old story of a storm at sea and a passenger who thought himself immune to danger.

Walking out of the dining room after breakfast, I found myself side by side with Wilfred Smythe, Mr. Mercer's assistant at the bank. I had gotten the impression that he was a melancholy sort, not quite comfortable in the merry routine of shipboard society. It was a trait I had observed in other children of ministers. Much to my surprise, he seemed far more lighthearted than I recalled having seen him before. I nodded to him and said "Good morning" as we came out into the corridor.

"Hello, Mr. Cabot," he said, smiling. "We seem to have some fine weather at last."

"Yes," I agreed. "I think we're entitled to it, after the storm we had. I've missed getting out on deck and looking at the ocean."

"I haven't been much in the mood for that," he said, his expression serious again. He paused at the end of the foyer, where one corridor led to a series of staterooms and another to the door leading out on deck. "For some reason, it made me very lonely to look out on all that vast expanse with not another living soul in sight. But you know, I don't feel at all like that now. The change in weather must have been good for me."

I followed his gesture and saw blue sky through the porthole, with fleecy clouds over the blue ocean waves. Someone who hadn't been with us the entire voyage would have had a hard time guessing how fiercely the tempest had raged less than two days ago. I nodded my agreement and said, "I doubt anyone would argue with you—although the rough weather didn't bother me as much as it did some. At least I haven't been seasick. Or worse yet, swept overboard like that poor fellow night before last."

"Ah, yes, Bobby Babson," said Smythe in a calm voice. "Well, I'm sad for his parents, and poor dear Tess, of course, but I can't help feeling that he brought it on himself."

I looked in both directions as if to see whether anyone was paying attention to us, then said in a lower voice. "Maybe not. I've heard talk that Babson didn't fall overboard by himself. Some say he was pushed—in fact, they're questioning that German prince about it. Though I can't see why they think *he* would have done it."

"Any more than another person, hey?" said Smythe. The smile he turned my way was smug. "I've heard you had a brush with him yourself."

"Well, I can't deny that I did," I said. "But I certainly don't like your implication." Involuntarily I straightened up before I realized what I was doing and relaxed, at least mentally. Being an amateur detective did have that unpleasant side to it—if one goes around casting suspicion, one must be prepared to be accused in one's own turn.

Smythe waved his hand dismissively. "Nothing personal intended, Mr. Cabot. All I meant is that Bobby wasn't a pleasant person. I've never understood what Tess saw in him."

He turned toward the door leading out onto the deck, and I moved to follow him. "I suppose you had your quarrels with him as well," I said. "Or did you manage to avoid his notice?"

Smythe gave me an appraising look, then shrugged. "Half of Philadelphia knows my story, so there's no reason you shouldn't. Why don't we talk about it out in the air, at least?" he suggested. I nodded, and followed him out the door.

There was a touch of chill in the air, but the sun was bright on the wave-tops. We walked forward a bit, so as to be out of the immediate vicinity of the doorway, and then Wilfred Smythe turned and put both hands on the polished brass rail, peering out into the ocean. I stopped beside him and looked over the water. There must have been another steamboat off to the south, for I could just make out a wisp of smoke at the farthest reach of my vision, though no vessel was in sight.

After a moment Smythe turned to me and said, "It's funny you should ask whether I managed to avoid Bobby's notice. In a sense, that describes the whole of our relation. Rather, I should say that he invariably treated me as beneath his notice."

"I can understand that," I said. I moved to the rail next to him, and leaned my back against it. "Once he learned I work for Mr. Clemens, he insisted on treating me as if I were a servant."

"Yes, that's Bobby's style precisely," agreed Smythe, with a wry smile. "Bobby treated me as just another worker in the bank, no better than one of the tellers. It doesn't matter that Mr. Mercer takes me into his confidence on many important matters, or that he has twice promoted me in just under two years. It doesn't matter that the Babsons and Mercers all worship in my father's church, and that Father has been a guest in both their homes. No, to Bobby I was an underling to be snubbed. It would have been almost a sign of favor if he'd taken an actual personal dislike to me.'' His lips quirked again in that wry smile, and I began to think I could grow to like this minister's son.

I listened sympathetically. The description of Babson tallied with my experience. Yet there had to be more to the story, I thought. ''I guess I'm one of the favored few, then,'' I said. ''He *did* go out of his way to make trouble for me. But that's water under the bridge. You said half Philadelphia knows your story, and what you've said so far is hardly a story at all. There's something more, isn't there? Some actual incident you were referring to.'' I might like Wilfred Smythe personally, but it was still my business to find out the facts.

He turned to look at me, suspicion written on his face. For a moment I feared that I'd exhausted his supply of frankness. But then he shrugged and said, ''What difference does it make now? Bobby's gone, and I have a chance at a fresh start with Tess. She and I were sweethearts for a while—I had dared hope that it would blossom into something more. Mr. Mercer knew from my work in the bank that I was a steady, reliable person. And he certainly knew the family I come from. I think he would have looked favorably upon a proposal from me. But Bobby had money, and fine clothes, and an air of excitement about him, and all that turned Tess's head. I saw it happening, and I didn't know what to do. The next thing I knew, he'd asked for her hand, and I was out in the cold. I think I could have killed myself the day I realized what had happened.''

Suddenly I found myself paying very close attention. Mr. Clemens had speculated about a jilted suitor having killed Babson, and here I was, face to face with someone who admitted that he and Babson had been rivals for Theresa Mercer's affections. Could Wilfred Smythe have taken matters in his own hands, hoping to regain his lost love by removing a hated rival from the field? It didn't seem quite in character, but who could tell what might be seething underneath the surface? Even more to the point: If Miss Mercer stood to inherit a large sum of money, Smythe had another strong motive in addition to jealousy. A minister's son, even one working in a bank, was unlikely to have many prospects of wealth. But although standing next to him and looking at a beautiful seascape made it hard to think ill of him, I knew full well that my feelings had little to do with the question of his innocence or guilt.

"I'm sorry to hear that," I told him. "As you say, Robert Babson didn't give anyone many reasons to like him, but you seem to have gotten a worse deal than most."

"Perhaps I did," said Smythe. He turned and looked out toward the distant plume of smoke, then fixed his gaze on me again. His face was grave as he continued. "But we should find another topic. Nothing's to be gained by holding grudges, now that he's gone to meet his maker—as my father tells me."

"A good policy, I think," I said, although I'd hoped that playing on his feeling of being wronged would prompt him to tell me more. I couldn't tell whether he was genuinely unwilling to speak ill of the dead, or whether my prompting had made him wary of saying too much. We stood at the rail a while longer, looking out over the ocean. We chatted about our plans for London; it turned out that Smythe was as interested in art as I was, and enthusiastic about visiting the museums and galleries. After a while, a comfortable silence fell, and we stood watching the waves until he looked at his watch, claimed an appointment with Mr. Mercer, and went on his way.

After my conversation with Smythe, I looked into the smoking lounge, expecting to find Mr. Clemens there, but he was not in his usual place. However, several of the young fellows who used to gamble with Robert Babson were on hand, for once not sitting at the card table, but gathered in a small group and conversing. Mr. Clemens had asked me to scout them out and see whether any of them might have seen Babson the night of his death—or, possibly, have had a motive for doing him in. There was no better time than the present, so I walked over to join the group.

"Good morning," I said. "I'm Wentworth Cabot. Seeing that we're shipmates, I thought I'd take the opportunity to get acquainted with you fellows before we land in England." I smiled and held out my hand to the nearest of the group.

"Hullo, Cabot," he said, reaching up to shake hands. He was a lanky fellow with stringy blond hair falling in his eyes. "I'm Alan Mercer—glad to meet you. Why don't you pull up a seat?"

"Ah, your father must be the banker," I said, taking a chair from one of the card tables and joining the circle. "I saw you on deck before, but didn't make the connection between you two."

"I'm not surprised," said Mercer, grinning sheepishly. "I do my best to keep my distance from Papa."

I chuckled softly, and said, "You should try traveling without your parents—it makes it a lot easier to do as you please without accounting to anyone."

"Al's afraid the old man will put him to work," said one of his companions. This was a sandy-haired young man with a round face and a budding mustache that looked as if it meant to be red when it finally came in. "I'm Harry Williams," he added, almost as an afterthought. At this, the rest of the group introduced themselves and shook hands, as well: Jimmy Archer and Leon Trombauer, both from Philadelphia, and Jack Holtzman, who turned out to be a Princeton man.

"You played football at Yale, didn't you?" asked Holtzman, looking at me with evident curiosity. He had bushy brown hair that made his forehead look unusually low. "I spent one of the coldest afternoons I can remember watching you fellows beat the stuffing out of our team three years ago, when I was a freshman.''

I remembered the game rather well, because I'd blocked a punt, and one of our boys had run the ball in for our fifth touchdown of the game. It had been one of the highlights of my football career. ''Yes, it was a nasty day. I suspect it was a bit colder on the loser's side of the field, though.'' I smiled again and shook his hand, and he laughed.

''Well, you can't have lost too often with *that* team,'' said Holtzman. ''You were a damn fine football player, and I ought to buy you a drink even if you did go to Yale.''

''Well, thanks for the compliment,'' I said, dodging the offer of a drink. It was barely ten in the morning, but there were half-empty wineglasses on the low table in front of them. If this was the crowd Robert Babson associated with, his heavy drinking must not have seemed unusual to them. ''I'm surprised you fellows aren't at the card table,'' I remarked, hoping to steer the conversation around to the subject I was interested in. ''The main reason I didn't introduce myself before now is not wanting to interrupt the games.''

''Well, I guess the games are broken up for good now,'' said Trombauer, shaking his head. He was a big, complacent-looking fellow, wearing an expensively cut woolen suit in a checked pattern that made him look even bigger than he was. ''It's not the same without Bobby taking a hand.'' He turned to look at me and asked, ''Did you know him?''

I saw Archer elbow him in the ribs, but I smiled and said, ''Not really well. I guess we got off on the wrong foot, and I never got the chance to make up with him, more's the pity. He didn't seem a bad sort, all in all.''

''Best fellow in the world,'' said Trombauer. ''He was always looking for some sort of fun—just the kind of fellow for an ocean voyage like this, you know. Damn shame about him going overboard—terrible accident.''

''Well, that's not the story old man Babson's telling,'' said Harry Williams. He picked up his wineglass and drained it, then glanced around the circle of young men. "You saw how hot under the collar Bobby got when that old charlatan, Prince what's-his-name, started flirting with Tess after the music. Bobby gave the rascal a good licking, and the fellow swore he'd get back. They think the prince waylaid him on deck after the fight and forced him overboard."

"I'll bet poor Bobby was leaning over the rail, then," said Trombauer. "Lord knows, he'd had enough to drink."

"Hardly gave him a sporting chance, if that's how it went," said Holtzman, picking up the wine bottle. "I hope they hang that damned prince, if it's true. Here, Harry, give me your glass." He filled Williams's glass, and then his own. He seemed to have forgotten his offer of a drink to me.

"You'd think a sturdy fellow like Babson could defend himself against a fat old man, drunk or sober," I remarked. "You boys must have talked to him after the fight. Did he take the prince's threats seriously?"

"Not a bit," said Williams. "If you'd known Bobby, you wouldn't have to ask. He was laughing about it, not ten minutes later. Said he'd lick the prince and his whole army, if they had the guts to face him."

"That was Bobby's style, for sure," said Trombauer, nodding vigorously. "Same as at the card table—I never saw him back down from anybody, whether he had the cards in his hand or not."

"He'd have been better off if he had backed off, sometimes," said Holtzman, fingering his wineglass. "Poor Bobby owed me close to four hundred dollars, not that I'll ever see it."

"Nor will any of us," said Jimmy Archer, with a shrug. "He owed me more than that. But I'd forgive every penny Bobby owes me just to see him come through that door and sit down at the card table again. He was a damn fine fellow, as good a friend as you'll ever see. Sooner or later, he'd have paid us every cent without one cross word. Bad luck, and no two ways about it.''

I was frankly surprised to hear these glowing testimonials to Robert Babson's character. I found them hard to reconcile with Wilfred Smythe's bitter allusions to his snobbery, or with my own experience of him, for that matter. But I supposed that few of us would recognize our own portraits if they were painted from descriptions provided by our enemies. Then I remembered something else that Wilfred Smythe had said. ''What, did Babson owe you all money? I thought his father was quite well off.''

The group was quiet for a moment, evidently embarrassed by the mention of money. Then Harry Williams cleared his throat, and looked around as if to see whether anyone objected, and said, ''Bobby's father had been pulling on the reins lately—not giving him everything he asked for. I don't think he was really short of money— Bobby would have told us if he was. I think he was just trying to make Bobby pay attention to how much he spent. When Bobby was flush, he'd never let anyone buy him a drink without standing the next round. If he was a little short these last few days, we all knew he'd be good for it in due time.''

Alan Mercer sneered. ''You don't know half the story, Harry. Old man Babson's up for re-election as District Attorney in the spring, and that's why he's been keeping a death grip on the purse strings. He needs every red cent he can scrape together.'' Young Mercer rubbed his hands together and leaned forward, drawing the group in to listen closely as he continued in a conspiratorial whisper. ''Papa says Babson's in a real scrap this time, and spending like a drunken sailor, trying to get votes. He's borrowed a fair amount from the bank, I think. Some of the party regulars are backing the other fellow—that old stick Martin Fleetwood, who's been raising hell about graft and corruption. From what I hear, the old man was ready to cancel this trip to Europe, until he found out he couldn't get a refund. That changed his mind pretty quickly.''

"Really," said Trombauer. "Even so, Bobby would have been good for what he owed us, once he'd married your sister. That would have solved all his problems— all his money problems, anyway.''

"I guess you're right," said Alan Mercer. "Papa would've taken good care of Tess's husband, even if he thought Bobby was a bit too easygoing. Papa's got old-fashioned notions—*early to bed and early to rise; a penny saved is a penny earned*, and all that silly cant from old Colonial times. I suppose that's fine advice for a fellow who doesn't have anything and wants to make some money. What Papa doesn't grasp is that a fellow who's already got his money doesn't have to live that way.''

"I hope to God not," said Trombauer, with a loud laugh. "We'd be in a sorry state then, wouldn't we?''

"They'd be in mourning at Princeton," said Jack Holtzman, grinning. "At Yale too, I guess—what d'you say, Cabot?" His voice was slurred, and I thought he'd already had enough to drink for the middle of the morning.

"Well, there's the difference between Yale and Princeton," I said, returning the grin. "We figure that a fellow's got to decide what he wants, then do whatever it takes to get it. I'd never have set foot on this boat if I'd had to depend on my parents to pay for my passage. But here I am, going to Europe all the same.''

"Good old New England self-reliance," said Mercer, looking at me through narrowed eyes. "Well, if it works for you, I guess it's all right. I don't mind work, as long as somebody else does it.''

Everyone laughed at Mercer's joke, and I joined in, although I wasn't sure whether he was making fun of me or not. But before the laughter had fairly died away, a different voice from behind me said, in a sharp tone, "That's what's wrong with the lot of you, if you ask me.''

I turned to see Julius Babson, Robert's father. He had a thin leather briefcase under one arm, and a frown on his face. "If you boys had set a better example for Robert, there's a good chance he'd still be here today," the attorney said. He looked from face to face, and I could see all of them hanging their heads contritely.

"I'm sorry, Mr. Babson—" said Alan Mercer, but Babson cut him off.

"Well you should be," he said, shaking his finger like a scolding schoolmaster. "I know as well as anyone that Robert had a touch of mischief about him, but he was a good boy. If you hadn't egged him on, and laughed at his impertinent pranks, he might have settled down before now. I thought the responsibility of supporting a wife would give him a fresh start, a chance to show his true worth. Now he'll never have the chance, and every one of you will have to live with the knowledge that you kept him from being what he could have been."

"We're all sorry, Mr. Babson," said Harry Williams, in a quiet voice. "But nobody could have known what was going to happen. You can't blame us for an accident."

"Accident?" Babson drew himself up to his full height, and gave Williams a look that would have withered an oasis. "It was no accident, and I mean to prove it. The vicious monster that murdered my son will hang— and I will take the greatest of pleasure in bringing iron-clad proof of his crime before the court that condemns him."

He paused, looking around the circle of young men with a sneer, before turning his back and stalking off. Halfway to the door, he looked back over his shoulder and said in a scornful tone, "Enjoy your wine, gentlemen. I have *work* to do!"

19 ⌒

Shortly after Mr. Babson concluded his tirade, I left the group in the smoking lounge to join Mr. Clemens and the Kiplings in our cabin, to share whatever we had managed to learn since our meeting the night before. Although Alan Mercer had attempted to make light of Babson's obsession with convicting the man he believed to have caused his son's death, none of the rest of the crowd seemed inclined to join him. With such a wet blanket thrown over their levity, I doubt most of them even noticed when I took my departure.

Mr. Clemens was already in the cabin, puffing on one of his corncob pipes while he paced the floor—or was it properly called the deck, here inside the cabin? He nodded absently at me as I entered and made a vague motion toward one of the seats. I sat down without speaking, pulling in my legs so as to take up as little as possible of my employer's constricted pathway. There was no point in my breaking his concentration, since we would simply have to repeat anything of interest once Mr. and Mrs. Kipling arrived. So I sat and waited, trying to make sense of what I had learned in my investigations so far.

The opinion I had formed of Robert Babson was that he was spoiled, arrogant, and quite capable of gratuitous cruelty under the pretext of humor. The reports of my Yale friends and of Wilfred Smythe more or less supported my judgment. But young Babson's usual companions painted a different picture. Had I known him only by their accounts, I should have thought him quite a capital fellow. And while it might be tempting to dismiss his friends as a frivolous bunch whose opinions were colored by camaraderie, I could see myself, in other circumstances, fitting comfortably into their circle. Except for the small matter of their parents' paying their passage to Europe, they were not much different from me, or my classmates traveling in steerage.

A knock on the cabin door interrupted my train of thought. "That'll be Kipling and his wife," said Mr. Clemens, striding over and opening the door.

"Mr. Clemens, pardon the intrusion." It was the officer we'd seen last night in the lounge, who'd come with the captain and Mr. Babson to take away the prince. Mr. Jennings, the master-at-arms, I remembered. "I'd like to speak to your secretary, Mr. Cabot. Is he here?"

"I'm here," I said, standing and turning to face the door. "What can I do for you?" I now saw that Mr. Jennings was accompanied by Patrick Gallagher, the first mate, who'd been stalking my friends in steerage. I wondered if they'd finally been caught, and had claimed an invitation from me as their defense.

"We need to ask you a few questions," said Mr. Jennings, stepping partway into the cabin. "Would you mind coming down to my office?"

I was about to answer when Mr. Clemens held up his hand as if to block the officer's entry. "Cabot doesn't mind answering your questions," he said, giving me a look that I understood to mean that I should be on my guard. "But what's wrong with right here? We were expecting visitors this very minute, and we might have some questions to ask you when they get here."

Mr. Jennings took a step backward, evidently surprised at Mr. Clemens's request. "To tell the truth, Mr. Clemens, we're in the process of questioning possible witnesses to a serious crime that may have been committed aboard ship. I believe you know what I'm referring to."

Mr. Clemens nodded and moved forward to block the door even more definitely. "Yes, I saw you take away

Prinz Karl last night. Do you consider Cabot a witness? Or has someone accused him of killing that young fellow?''

"Neither one, to tell the truth," said Jennings. He was about to continue, when Mr. Kipling arrived, alone.

"Hullo, Carrie asked me to give her regrets," said Kipling. Then he looked at the two men in uniform. "I say, I didn't expect such a large party. Should I come back another time?"

"Not at all," said Mr. Clemens. "Why don't you all come inside and have a seat—it's plenty private here. We'll get this straightened out in no time at all, and maybe everyone can learn something to his advantage, while we're at it." He stepped back, and made a sweeping gesture of invitation.

Mr. Jennings paused a moment, then nodded and said, "Very well. Come along, Gallagher." He stepped into the room; Gallagher stood back to let Mr. Kipling enter, then came through the door himself, and stood to one side while Mr. Clemens closed it. Mr. Kipling and Mr. Jennings went to the couch, and (on Mr. Clemens's signal) I planted myself in the adjacent armchair. Gallagher moved in behind the couch, standing with his legs apart and his hands clasped behind him, while my employer moved to the front of the little group, unobtrusively but unmistakably taking up the commanding position.

"Well, Mr. Jennings, you have some questions for Cabot," said Mr. Clemens. "Why don't you start off by asking him whatever you need to know, and then we'll see what else the rest of us have to say."

"Very well," said the master-at-arms. "But I'll request that you allow Mr. Cabot to answer without prompting, if you please. I don't think Mr. Cabot has anything to conceal, but it would make things easier if I could be certain of that."

"Of course, of course, ask away," said Mr. Clemens, waving his hand nonchalantly. He picked up his corncob pipe from the ashtray where he'd set it down, and began poking at it with some sort of pipe tool he pulled out of his pocket. But I saw that his attention was focused on the two crew members, rather than on the pipe.

Mr. Jennings looked at Mr. Clemens a moment, then turned to me. "Mr. Cabot, you had a bit of a run-in with Robert Babson, the missing passenger, the day before he disappeared. Is that correct?"

Once I had realized that the two officers were here about Babson, rather than my Yale friends, I had been expecting this question. I nodded and said, "Yes, you could describe it as that. Mr. Gallagher was there, and I'm sure he can tell you what happened."

"I've already talked to Gallagher, thank you," said Mr. Jennings. "We've served together on *City of Baltimore* for a number of years, so I have a great deal of confidence in his reports. But could you please tell me in your own words what went on between you and Robert Babson that day?" He had taken a notebook out of his pocket, and held a pencil ready.

"It wasn't much, really," I said. "I accidentally bumped him in the smoking lounge, and spilled his drink. I tried to apologize, but he didn't want to hear it. Then, after lunch, Mr. Gallagher apprehended me under the false impression that I was a steerage passenger trying to sneak into first-class. Babson came along just then, and told Mr. Gallagher that I had been annoying the first-class passengers for some time. Luckily for me, Prinz Karl happened to come by at just that time, and reminded me that I had a key to this room—so I could prove that I belonged here. Babson must have realized that his lie was refuted, because when we turned to look for him, he was nowhere to be seen."

Mr. Jennings nodded. "Well, that jibes with what Gallagher has said, except for the parts he didn't see. And one of the smoking lounge waiters told us about the earlier part."

"There, you see?" said Mr. Clemens. "It's all explained. No reason at all to suspect Cabot."

"Apparently so," said Mr. Jennings. "You understand, I have to verify all the possible suspects' stories, and your run-in with Babson makes you a suspect, Mr. Cabot. I assume you can account for your whereabouts on the night Babson disappeared?''

"He was with me the whole evening, first at the concert and afterwards in the lounge," said Mr. Clemens. "Here's a question for you. Can Gallagher account for his whereabouts that night?"

"If you please, I'd like to hear what Mr. Cabot has to—" Jennings began, but he was interrupted by the mate.

"What the bloody hell is that about?" demanded Gallagher, with some vehemence. "Mr. Jennings knows I didn't have a thing to do with it."

"But I don't know it," said Mr. Clemens, still speaking to Jennings. "Babson made a monkey out of Gallagher with his lie about my secretary sneaking up here from steerage. Gallagher might be the kind of man who holds a grudge. If he was on deck that evening and saw Babson, he might have decided to give the boy a piece of his mind. Drunk as Babson was, he might have gotten his back up about it. Maybe he shoved Gallagher, and Gallagher shoved him back, and Babson lost his balance and went over the side."

"That's too damned many *mights* and *maybes*," said Gallagher, turning red. "I bloody well didn't do it, and that's all."

Mr. Jennings turned to face the mate. "Easy now, Gallagher, I see Mr. Clemens's point," he said, shaking his pencil in mild reproof of the man's intemperate language in front of passengers. "He has every right to be suspicious of the crew, especially since he doesn't know what I know." He faced Mr. Clemens again. "We don't leave anything to chance in a matter this serious, Mr. Clemens. I've already checked on Gallagher's whereabouts that night. Two men have told me that he was in his bunk early, and stayed there the whole night. I'm satisfied that he had nothing to do with Babson's death."

"Good," said Mr. Clemens. "I just wanted to make sure we were all on equal footing here. I reckon you're a good officer, but you might have had a blind spot about your own men. It's natural to get into the habit of taking your crew for granted—and I've learned just how bad a mistake that can be. Now I know you aren't making that mistake. Did you have anything else you wanted to ask my secretary?''

Mr. Jennings looked at his pad, as if to see where he'd left off his questions. ''Yes, just a few more points I'd like to verify. Mr. Cabot, you didn't mention Prinz Karl's response when he learned that Mr. Babson had run away. Did he say anything to that?''

''No,'' I replied. ''He seems to have disappeared almost at the same time. Mr. Clemens came up just then and asked what was going on, and when we looked for the prince, he'd gone away. It was rather an inconvenience, since we'd invited him here for a meeting.''

At this, Mr. Jennings looked up from his notebook. ''Hmm—I don't suppose you had any idea where he'd gone?''

I shrugged. ''No, we thought he might have gone after Babson, but that's just a guess, really.''

''Perhaps, but it's the same guess I'd have made—unless he changed his mind about the meeting. Do you gentlemen mind telling me why you'd called the prince here for a private meeting?—I assume that's why you had it in a cabin, instead of in the lounge, or on deck.''

Mr. Clemens answered. ''Kipling and I had become suspicious of the prince's origins—neither one of us had ever heard of the place he claimed to hail from. We were concerned that he might be some sort of swindler, but since we couldn't be sure, we were going to give him the chance to explain himself. When he didn't show for the meeting, we came and told you what we suspected. That was the last we spoke to him until just before he was arrested.''

''Yes, your report brought him to our attention,'' said Mr. Jennings, rubbing his chin. ''We did a little bit of research of our own, based on your information, and asked a few key people on the staff to tell us if they noticed anything curious about him, any sort of hint that he might be up to something. We got an earful every time he tangled with Babson, but other than that, there was nothing to single him out.''

Mr. Clemens thought for a moment, rubbing his chin. ''I don't suppose he's told you anything since last night, has he?'' he asked Jennings.

''Nothing except to insist that he's innocent,'' said the master-at-arms. ''And to demand that we set him free, of course. If we can't find anyone who saw him push the boy overboard, we'll have to do just that.''

''I wonder if he'd talk to me,'' said Mr. Clemens. He stared out the porthole for a moment, then turned and continued. ''Prinz Karl had come to the smoker looking for me in particular, just before you showed up to haul him off to the brig. I think he had something to tell me, and he didn't get the chance. Maybe it's something that could help us get to the bottom of things.''

''Well, I'd certainly like to get to the bottom of things,'' said Jennings. ''If the prince was playing some sort of confidence game, it was too subtle for us to spot. It's a complete enigma to me.''

''So why don't you let me go talk to him?'' said Mr. Clemens. ''Maybe I can find out something that makes your job easier. Wentworth forgot to pack my arsenal and burglar kit, so I can promise you I'm not about to smuggle in a Gatling gun or hacksaw. Besides, even if I did help him escape, it wouldn't do him much good in mid-ocean.''

Jennings laughed. ''We aren't much worried about that,'' he said. ''We haven't really locked him up—he's in his own stateroom, with a guard outside the door. If it were up to me, I'd let you talk to him, but I have to get the captain's approval before I can say yes or no. I've got a couple of other witnesses to interview before I see the captain—he'll want a full report before he makes any decisions. What say I give you an answer before dinner?''

''Fair enough,'' said Mr. Clemens. ''We're planning

on asking a few people some questions, ourselves.''

Jennings looked at my employer with a curious expression. ''Are you running your own investigation, Mr. Clemens? Frankly, I don't see the need for it. We've got the matter well in hand, and I can assure you we're not in the least inclined to prejudge the gentleman's guilt or innocence. We'll let the facts speak for themselves.''

Mr. Clemens pointed his pipe stem at Jennings. ''Answer me this, then. If you're not inclined to prejudge him, why the hell is there a guard outside his door?''

''Captain's orders,'' said the master-at-arms briskly.

''Is that so? And what reason did the captain give for putting a guard on him?''

''When the captain gives an order, it's my business to carry it out, not to ask his reasons,'' said Mr. Jennings. He had stiffened his posture, and I could see Gallagher scowling as he stood at attention behind him. ''Nor do I consider it necessary to defend his orders to passengers.''

''Well, I can see why you don't want to defend it,'' said Mr. Clemens, raising his voice and pointing the pipe. ''It's a damn-fool order, and any man with a nickel's worth of sense would be embarrassed to have to explain it. The prince can't go anywhere, he isn't likely to hurt anybody, and there's no goddamned reason to lock him up like a common crook. I've got a good mind to go give the captain a cussing-out he won't forget. Jesus H. Christ, this kind of idiocy makes me worry whether he's smart enough to trust with running the ship. Why, if there was another boat I could switch to, I'd do it in less than a minute—and I wouldn't care whether I got my feet wet doing it.''

Mr. Jennings said nothing, but his jaw was firmly clenched; Gallagher's eyes were open wide. I could see that my employer had a full head of steam up, and I feared he was about to continue. But Mr. Kipling interrupted him with a raised hand. ''Now, Clemens,'' he said, ''I know how you feel, but this is no time for tilting at windmills. I'm sure Mr. Jennings is as anxious as we are to see justice served, but he has to do things by the book. You know that—even on your Mississippi river-boats, there must have been a proper chain of command.''

Mr. Clemens brought himself under control—with a good bit of an effort, I thought. ''You're right, Kipling. I apologize, Mr. Jennings. I still think it's a pointless order, and I'll tell the captain as much when I see him. But I shouldn't hold your feet to the fire for it. Just tell the captain that if he'll let me speak to Prinz Karl, I think I can learn something useful. And I promise to pass along anything I learn from him that might clear things up.''

''I'll do that, Mr. Clemens,'' said Jennings, rising to his feet. His expression was neutral, but his eyes were cold and his posture was as stiff as ever. ''I shall certainly expect you to pass along anything you learn from anyone else, as well—as Mr. Kipling says, my aim is to see justice served. That puts us on the same side, I should hope. Now, if you'll pardon me, I have more people to interview. Thank you for your help, Mr. Cabot.'' He turned to me and nodded his head a fraction of an inch; then he and Gallagher left the cabin.

Mr. Clemens closed the door behind the two men, then returned to take a seat facing me and Kipling. ''Well, they may have locked the prince up, but at least they haven't stopped looking for other possibilities,'' he said. ''Maybe they'll turn up evidence to exonerate him, and save us the trouble.''

''Don't be so sure,'' said Mr. Kipling. ''Jennings's intentions seem good enough, but he was much too willing to take your word that Cabot was with you that night—he didn't follow up his questions at all, or try to catch you in a contradiction. If you two were hiding something, he'd never have twigged to it. I'll wager he was no more diligent in checking Gallagher's alibi. He may think he's conducting a full and open-minded investigation, but unless an anomaly jumps out of the brush and bites him on the ankle, he's going to march right past it.''

''Do you think he's already made up his mind, or is he just lazy?'' I asked.

"There ain't much difference, is there?" said Mr. Clemens. "What worries me more is the possibility that he's under orders not to ask embarrassing questions."

"What, from the captain? I can't believe it," I said. While I'd had almost no contact with Captain Mortimer, he hardly seemed a man who would impede a murder investigation on his ship.

"Not impossible, though I wouldn't think it likely," said Mr. Kipling. "Clemens, you've seen more of the captain than I have. Does he strike you as corruptible?"

"Hell, I've never met the man you couldn't corrupt if you knew what to offer him," said my employer. He sucked on his pipe; belatedly realizing it had gone out, he snatched it out of his mouth and gave it an irritated look before continuing. "Captain Mortimer seems pretty honest, in the regular line of things. I reckon losing a passenger overboard hasn't made him happy—not under these circumstances. There'll be a board of inquiry when he gets to port, and he can't be looking forward to that. It's in his best interest to have everything wrapped up like a Christmas present—nice and tight and pretty, so nobody can tell him he should have done anything different."

"So it's hardly to his benefit to see the prince falsely accused, is it?" I said.

"Not unless there's some sort of dirty business going on," Mr. Clemens replied. "Say, if somebody offered him a huge wad of greenbacks fresh from the Philadelphia mint."

"I have my doubts about that," said Mr. Kipling. "The captain of a ship like this can retire to a life of luxury, if he keeps his good reputation. He risks losing everything if it comes out that he's taken bribes to cover up a murder. You'd have to offer him a great deal of money to make him risk that."

"What about blackmail?" I suggested. "Suppose someone is threatening to reveal something that would cost the captain his command?"

"Possible," said Mr. Clemens. "Damned unlikely,

though. I think we're barking up the wrong tree, trying to involve the captain in some kind of conspiracy—I might change my mind if he refuses to let me talk to Prinz Karl, though. More likely, Jennings is just plain lazy. Or maybe he's doing the best he can, and we're expecting more than he can deliver.''

''Or maybe someone's bribing Mr. Jennings,'' said Kipling. ''He'd be easier to reach than the captain, and far cheaper.''

''True enough,'' agreed Mr. Clemens. ''So I reckon we'll just have to learn the truth without his help, won't we?''

''I guess so,'' I said. But I was far from certain we had any chance of doing that before the ship reached port.

O ur morning conference did not produce any great
surprises. Mrs. Kipling, having nothing to report,
had decided to spend her morning talking to the
ladies in the Grand Saloon, and would join us in the
afternoon if she learned anything of interest. I recounted
my conversations with my Yale friends, with Wilfred
Smythe, and with Robert Babson's circle of friends. I had
discovered that I had a knack for remembering the details
of a conversation, which made these summaries much
more useful to my employer.

Mr. Clemens was particularly interested in Smythe's
story. "A jilted suitor—I knew there'd be one—and right
here on board, too! Tell me, Wentworth, how do you size
him up? Could he have done it?"

I thought for a moment, leaning back on the comfortable sofa. "I saw him glaring at Babson and Miss Mercer
when we first came aboard, and thought I wouldn't want
to be the fellow he was angry at. He's moody. I suppose
he could have overcome Babson, especially considering
how drunk Babson was that night. But I'm not certain
he's the murdering type. After all, he is a minister's son,
and he's earned a position of trust in Mr. Mercer's
bank."

"Doesn't mean a damn thing," said Mr. Clemens,
waving his hand dismissively. "Some of the worst scoun-
drels I've ever seen were sons of preachers. And I'd
sooner trust a horse trader than a banker—though I'll

grant you they're more likely to pick your pockets than to stab you or shoot you.''

"Hum—I'll agree he bears watching," said Mr. Kipling. "But don't forget the gambling crowd, either. Cabot says he owed some of them a good bit of money."

"I don't think any of them would kill a man who owed him money," I said, somewhat surprised. "It hardly seems the way to collect on a debt."

"They needn't have had killing on their mind at the start," said Mr. Kipling. "Suppose one of them needed cash, and tried to get Babson to make good his IOUs. From what you say, his father had been holding the purse strings tighter than usual, so he'd have been hard-pressed to pay up. They might have argued, and the rest is easy to imagine. A couple of drunken fellows start shoving one another, one loses his balance on a slippery deck—that's all it takes."

"Seems likelier than the story old man Babson is peddling, in any case," said Mr. Clemens. "If the boy and Prinz Karl hadn't scuffled, everybody would have figured his disappearance was an accident, and left it alone."

"I think it unlikely the prince would have taken revenge so quickly," said Mr. Kipling. "He'd have known that everyone would instantly suspect him. He's got a quick trigger on his temper—we've seen proof of that—but that's another story from cold-blooded revenge."

I saw one difficulty with that analysis. "What if the prince had gone on deck and unexpectedly met Babson? If Babson had started slanging him again, he might have lost his temper again."

"Yes, of course it's possible," said Mr. Kipling. "If that's what actually happened, then we're chasing a phantom. But lacking a witness, I think we have to begin with a presumption of innocence."

"Bulls-eye, Kipling," said Mr. Clemens. "Prinz Karl's an easy target for the father to blame his son's death on. Easier to pin it on somebody you don't like than to admit it was probably the boy's own fault. If my daughters were as rotten as that Babson boy, I'd likely be trying to ignore it, too. But we don't have any love for the boy, so we see his faults clearly. I still don't think the prince did it, and I'm going to make damn sure he doesn't get railroaded.''

Mr. Kipling stood and walked over to the porthole, then said in a quiet voice, ''What we need are witnesses who can establish the prince's whereabouts that evening. If the captain agrees to let you interview him, we'll know his account of his movements. If we're lucky, he'll have been someplace where people will have seen him.''

''And if we're not lucky, he was in his cabin, reading,'' said Mr. Clemens.

''Good lord,'' I said, slapping my forehead. ''I just now remembered—I did see the prince that night. We were sitting in the smoker, and he stuck his head in just briefly, as if looking for someone he didn't find. His hair was wet and disheveled—as if he'd been out on deck, in the rain. I'd forgotten that entirely.''

''Damnation! That makes him look guilty as the devil,'' said Mr. Clemens. He stood up and paced several steps, nearly running into Mr. Kipling before he spun around to face me again. ''Well, I suppose it's better to know it before I go in to talk to him than to have you spring it on me later. Do you think anybody else saw him?''

''I can hardly say. Nobody's mentioned it to me, at least.''

''You can bet your last penny that if anyone did see him, they've told Jennings—or Babson,'' said Mr. Kipling. ''It'll make the case against him all the blacker.''

''Damn, damn,'' muttered Mr. Clemens. ''Well, if it turns out the prince did kill the boy, I'll go smoke my pipe and mope about misplaced faith in humanity. But I still don't think he's guilty, and if nobody else will make the case for him, I reckon I'll have to make it myself.''

He paced a little more, thinking, then stopped and pointed at me. ''Wentworth, I want you to follow up on the jilted suitor. Find out where Wilfred Smythe was when Babson disappeared. See if you can talk to Miss

Mercer, or some of her friends, whoever they are; try to learn whether their engagement was going well, or whether there were signs of trouble. Was she making eyes at young Smythe again? What did her father think of Babson? Mercer strikes me as a stiff old buzzard—he couldn't have liked the idea of his daughter marrying a wastrel.''

"I doubt any of us would," said Mr. Kipling dryly. "What would you like me to do?"

"I think you've got the right idea about finding witnesses. Try to find anyone who was on deck that night—there shouldn't be that many of them. I take it the watch officer didn't mention anybody else?"

Mr. Kipling shook his head. "No, but the only ones I asked him about were Babson and the prince. Someone could have thrown Babson overboard and run back inside in a matter of moments—if the watch was on the other side of the deck, a pock of thugees could have strangled Babson and thrown him overboard, with the watch none the wiser. I'll make it a point to find him this afternoon and ask him again. He was perfectly willing to talk about it.''

"Good," said Mr. Clemens, "and I'll see whether anybody else in the lounge noticed the prince when he stuck his head in—or any other time that night. I'll probably get a whole pack of contradictions, but at least it'll give me something to work with when I go talk to the prince.''

"That's assuming the captain will let you talk to him," I pointed out.

Mr. Clemens's eyes blazed as he looked at me. "He'll let me talk to the prince, all right. When Captain Mortimer invited me to sit at his table for supper, he figured he was just getting Mark Twain, the famous funny fellow, to entertain his other guests. He didn't figure on getting Mark Twain the hell-raising roughneck—but he's about to find out the two come in the same package. If he's got any notion of stopping me from seeing the prince, he'll change his mind right soon—and you can take that to the bank, Wentworth!''

I decided to approach Miss Mercer after luncheon. She had resumed taking her meals in the dining room with the rest of the passengers; Robert Babson's mother and sister were still conspicuous by their absence. While her somber dress acknowledged the recent loss of her fiancée, Miss Mercer seemed in good spirits when I turned to look at her. I saw her talking quietly with her friends, though she did not often smile. But when she and two other young ladies arose from their table and left the room before I had time to put down my dessert fork, I was left to my own devices to discover where she might be.

The weather had turned sunny again after our bout with the storm, and having no better notion where Miss Mercer might have gone, I decided that a turn around the decks would give me a chance of meeting up with her, or possibly with one of the young ladies I'd seen her talking with. If she was not on deck, at least I would get a welcome dose of fresh air and sunlight.

The first-class deck was as crowded as I had seen it. Half the ship appeared to be there, sitting with a book, leaning on the rail to look at the waves, or strolling with a group of friends. Most of those on deck seemed to have congregated on the starboard side of the ship, where the afternoon sun was warmest. I had taken only a few steps before I was glad of my decision; the salt air was invigorating, and the light off the wave-tops sparkled like a chest of jewels. The sound of excited voices came from the direction of the shuffleboard courts, and so I turned my steps that way, on the chance that Miss Mercer or some of her friends might be playing or watching the game.

I arrived to discover Alan Mercer and his friends in the midst of choosing teams for a shuffleboard match, while a small group of young ladies (including Miss Mercer) stood watching. As I walked into view, Jack Holtzman—who'd been so extravagant in his praise of my football prowess—spotted me and said, "Here's the very man I want on my team! Cabot, we're one short—be a good fellow and take one of these sticks, will you? The losers buy the drinks this afternoon."

"I doubt I'll be much use," I said, taking the pronged cue he thrust in my general direction. "I've never played this before, you know."

"Do you think the rest of us are trumps?" said Holtzman, laughing. "I never played this silly game before I came aboard ship. Besides, you're a football star—you'll pick it up in an instant."

"Well, I could use a bit of fun," I said, hefting the stick experimentally. "Just tell me what the rules are." Despite my disclaimer, I realized that the game might afford an excellent opportunity to make the acquaintance of Miss Mercer and her friends, after which it would be the most natural thing in the world to strike up a conversation with them.

Holtzman quickly explained the rules, with good-natured interruptions by Trombauer and Alan Mercer, who was the captain of the other team. We were playing four to a side; I was teamed with Holtzman, Trombauer, and Harry Williams, while Mercer had chosen Jimmy Archer and two other fellows I hadn't met before, Marty DuPont and Archer's brother Ted. After a good bit of laughter and flippant taunting of the opponents, we were agreed on the rules and the stakes, and the game began.

Holtzman was right—I seemed to get the knack of the game almost instantly, though it was more akin to billiards than to anything I'd ever done on the football field. There was a triangular target painted on the deck; we slid wooden disks at it with our sticks, aiming for the highest-scoring numbers and trying to knock away the opponents' disks. Once I got the touch, I found I could place my disks with gratifying accuracy. I had missed the camaraderie of a hard-fought sporting contest, and in the heat of the competition, I found myself almost forgetting my ulterior motive in entering into the game.

Mercer and his teammates began the match in a frivolous spirit, letting their disks fly with abandon. In fact, Jimmy Archer seemed at first to care nothing at all for the game, but sent his disks flying at the feet of any young lady who ventured too close to the field of play, laughing as they jumped and squealed. His brother adopted a different approach, sliding his disk like a cannonball at the other end of the court, trying to scatter the other disks (regardless of which side's they were) like bowling pins. But Holtzman and I took a more sporting attitude, playing for score, and soon we had a good lead.

Then Alan Mercer realized that he and his friends were about to buy a round of drinks for us. Jimmy Archer let loose another of his wild shots, making a pretty girl skip out of the way, and Mercer sneered. "Perfect shot, Jimmy. Now, if you can get as close to the target as to Alice, Jack and his boys will be buying *us* the drinks."

"Oh, can't a fellow have a bit of fun?" groaned Archer, but he looked chastened, and at that point, began to play in earnest. With a little luck on their side, Mercer's boys brought the score back to even. Jimmy Archer proved he could target the scoring surface as well as the ladies' shoes, and Ted Archer suddenly developed a better aim, though the velocity of his shots did not noticeably alter.

As the game became more competitive, the young women began cheering on their favorites, and soon we were having a merry time. Somewhat to my surprise, Miss Mercer began to take an active interest in the game. She sided against her brother, mocking him when his shots went awry, and clapping when his opponents played well. When I made the final shot—a tricky double carom that knocked away one of the other team's disks and at the same time nudged one of ours onto the highest scoring area—she cried out, "Well played, well played!"

"Beginner's luck," I said, with a mock-serious bow toward her and the laughing young ladies standing with her. "Although having such enthusiastic supporters certainly didn't hurt." I smiled directly at Theresa Mercer, to make certain she knew which of the supporters I was referring to, and I thought she smiled back at me.

Alan Mercer grimaced. "Well, sis, I suppose I shouldn't have expected you to root for my team, but I didn't think you'd be so glad to see me lose. It was bad enough when I used to play tennis with Bobby—at least I could usually beat him, in spite of your blatant partiality."

Any hint of a smile disappeared from Miss Mercer's face. "I won't have you making remarks about poor Bobby," she said, glowering at her brother. "He was a better man than you'll ever be, and you know it, Alan. You know it."

"Wait a minute, sis, I didn't mean anything . . ." Alan protested. There was genuine contrition on his face, I thought, but he might as well have been talking to the ocean.

"I thought that if I came out with my friends for a little while, it would divert my mind from what happened to Bobby," she said, stepping up to confront her brother. Her hands were on her hips, and she was the picture of defiance. "It's *hateful* of you to bring it up. I think you must have done it on purpose to make me miserable."

Alan Mercer backed up a couple of steps. "Sis, I didn't say anything about him . . ."

"You certainly did," she said, pursuing him. Her voice had gone up an octave, and suddenly she seemed far less attractive than I'd thought her just two minutes earlier. "You've never been able to forego any opportunity to make me miserable. You don't care at all about me. You don't care that I'll never see Bobby again. He was a good man and I loved him, and now he's gone forever." There were tears on her cheeks as she continued. "If you had a heart at all, you'd remember that. I think you're absolutely despicable!"

"Confound it, sis," said Alan, clearly distressed at the turn of events. But almost before the words were out of his mouth Theresa Mercer had turned on her heel, sobbing, and fled from the now-silent group. One of the other young women darted a hostile glance at the dumbfounded brother, then sped off in pursuit of the fleeing Theresa.

Alan Mercer stood speechless for a moment, then turned to his friends. "What could I have said, Harry? Was I that cruel?"

"She's your sister," said Harry Williams, trying to appear nonchalant. "How am I supposed to know what's going to upset her?"

"There's not much you can do about it, Alan," said Trombauer, his face serious. "She's upset about poor old Bobby, and I guess I don't blame her. I miss the old rascal myself—more than I'd have thought. I guess she'll get over it with time, but maybe you'd best tread lightly for now." Then his voice assumed a heartiness that didn't quite ring true, to my ears. "Do you want to shoot another round, or are you ready to pay the piper?"

Mercer tossed his shuffleboard stick to Jimmy Archer, who fortunately was paying attention and caught it before it hit him in the face. "Oh, hell, let's go have a drink," he said, an annoyed expression on his face. "I guess I'm buying, more's the rotten luck."

Mercer's good nature seemed to revive somewhat, once he had a glass in his hand. I had pegged him as a sore loser, but he was soon bragging about his team's dramatic recovery, after a bad beginning, to make the score close at the very last. "By George, if Jimmy hadn't been sniping at the girls, we'd have beaten you after all. That last shot of yours was damned clever, though, Cabot," he said, raising his glass.

"Thank you. We'll have to play a rematch some time," I said, more sincerely than I might have a short time before. I'd had a good time, almost forgetting that I was there as a spy, gathering information in hopes of exonerating Prinz Karl.

"A shame we broke up so soon," said Harry Williams, staring at his glass of wine. "We may not get as nice a day again before we reach England. There could be another storm tomorrow."

"Damn me if we didn't have enough of a storm today, thanks to Tess," said Mercer, shaking his head. He looked around the group as if for sympathy, but none of the others betrayed any emotion. "She and Bobby were a pretty good match, don't you think?" he asked, elbowing Williams. "I don't think I'd want to have lived downstairs from them once they married, though."

"Well, I never saw 'em argue much with each other, if that's what you mean," said Williams. "Bobby had a temper, sure, but he was mild as a minister around her."

"That's the truth," Jimmy Archer agreed. "But he'd get his Irish up right fast if he thought somebody was paying too much attention to her. You saw how he went after that silly old German who started flattering her piano playing."

Mercer gave a low whistle. "Wow, didn't I? But Bobby went a little too far there, I'd say. Of course, how was he to know the fellow was going to murder him because of it?"

"I still don't see how they can be so sure it's murder," I put in. "I got to know that German fellow a little bit, and he doesn't seem that bad to me. A bit of a stuffed shirt, but that's no proof he's a killer."

"Bobby's dad says it's murder, and he's the expert," said Mercer, shrugging. "He's seen scads of murderers since he's been a prosecuting attorney, and sent plenty of 'em to the gallows, too. I guess I'll take his word for it."

"I don't know," I said. "My father's an attorney, too. Every time I'd try to get him to speculate about a case in the news, he'd tell me 'Don't judge by the newspapers. Twelve good men and true will tell us who's guilty and who's not.' If the fight is the only evidence Mr. Babson has, I don't see how he'll get a conviction. Did anybody even see the German fellow out on deck? For all any of us know, he went back to his cabin and licked his wounds all night."

"Good question," said Trombauer. "I sure didn't see him—that wasn't a fit night to stick your head outside. I don't think Bobby would have gone out, if he hadn't been so drunk. I *wish* he hadn't gone, so help me God. If I'd known what was going to happen, I swear I'd have stopped him.'' Several of the others around the circle nodded and murmured their assent.

"No disrespect toward the deceased, but who's to say he didn't fall overboard by himself?'' said Holtzman, raising an eyebrow. He took a cigarette case out of his pocket and offered it around the group before taking one for himself and lighting it. Jimmy Archer and Trombauer joined him.

"Well, if I had to bet, that's what I'd bet on,'' I said, keeping my expression neutral. "Poor Bobby got caught by a lurch of the ship, slipped on the deck, and went over the side. If he hit his head, he couldn't even have called for help.''

"You'd lose that bet,'' said Alan Mercer, a smug expression on his face. "I can't tell you all the details, because I didn't hear them all, but I heard my papa and old Babson talking. And I can tell you for a fact, Babson's got an eyewitness.''

"A witness!'' said Harry Williams. Everyone in the group turned to look at Mercer. "Who is it?''

"Now, I'm not sure I ought to tell you,'' said Mercer, smirking. He picked up his wineglass and took a sip.

"Damn your eyes, Mercer, if you don't tell us, I'll throw *you* over the side, and every single man here will swear I'm innocent,'' said Williams. "There's not twelve Christians in the world that would vote to convict me. Who is it?''

Mercer looked around the silent group, grinning broadly. Then Williams raised his fist in a mock threat, and Trombauer said, "You're a dead man if you don't spill the beans.''

"Oh, very well,'' said Mercer, savoring his moment of power. He paused, milking the suspense for one more instant. Then he leaned forward and said, in a conspiratorial whisper, "It's that silly artist, Signor Rubbia. He saw it all.''

21 ⌒

"**R**ubbia!" said Mr. Clemens. I had gone directly to our cabin to tell him the news of a witness to the murder. He sat and listened to my report with an open mouth, shaking his head in disbelief. After I had finished, he leapt to his feet and demanded, "What the hell was he doing out on deck in a storm? It's crazy enough that Babson boy was out there. I can't believe that little peacock would risk getting his feathers wet on a night like that."

"Nonetheless, that's what Alan Mercer says he overheard Mr. Babson say," I said. "I can't vouch for it myself."

"Damnation!" said Mr. Clemens. He stalked over to the whisky decanter and sloshed some of the contents into a glass, then raised it in my direction with a questioning look on his face. I shook my head, and he stoppered the decanter again, then took a long sip of the whisky.

"I guess we've got our work cut out for us now," he said, after a moment. "I want to know what Rubbia's story is before I talk to the prince." He pulled his watch out of his pocket and inspected it. "We've still got an hour and a half until dinner. See if you can run Rubbia down and get him to talk, Wentworth. If he really did see Prinz Karl throw Babson overboard, there's nothing more we can do. And if he's lying, I damn well want to find *that* out—more important, I want to find out why."

He began to pace, by which I knew he was thinking furiously.

"Why would he be lying about something so serious?" I asked, taking the seat Mr. Clemens had vacated. "He's taking a man's life in his hands. If it comes out that he's lying, he'll get himself in hot water with the authorities—not to mention losing credibility with his patrons in Philadelphia."

"Damned if I can make any sense of it," said my employer. "I don't think Rubbia would blink an eye at telling an ordinary garden-variety stretcher, if it magnified his own importance. But why he'd lie about something that could send a fellow to the hangman is way too deep for me." He stared out the porthole, then took another drink and turned to face me with raised eyebrows. "Of course, there's a chance Rubbia did it himself. Maybe he's trying to shift suspicion."

"Excuse me? What makes you think he could be the murderer? He's even less likely than the prince, I'd think." This was an angle I hadn't expected; I looked up to see if Mr. Clemens was serious.

"You're not thinking with your whole brain, then," said Mr. Clemens. "Remember that lecture you told me about, where Babson and his cronies sat in the back and heckled Rubbia until he was ready to try and lick 'em all? Remember the time Babson baited Rubbia until he stomped out of the dining room? I thought Rubbia was ready to spit right in the boy's face—hell, I bet he *would* have, if the men who're paying for his ticket to Paris hadn't been sitting right there. Rubbia had plenty of reason to hold a grudge against the Babson boy, and it wouldn't surprise me one bit to find out he sneaked up behind the brat when he was leaning over the rail and gave him a shove." He picked up one of his pipes from the table and peered into the bowl, trying to decide whether there was anything left in it to light.

"I suppose you're right," I said. "But if he did murder Babson, he's not likely to reveal it to a near-stranger. I hardly know what to ask him."

Mr. Clemens grimaced. "Hell, he's even less likely to reveal anything to me—the son of a bitch stuck his nose in the air the minute he found out I was getting more attention from the other passengers than he was. He might talk to Kipling, but Kipling's off trying to learn whether the crew saw anything that night, and I don't have time to go run him down. And Kipling's wife is busy eavesdropping on the ladies. So the job's yours. Maybe you can just tell him you heard a rumor he'd seen the murder, and ask if it's true. Almost anything you learn will be better than what we have now. So go find Rubbia and pump him. If his story holds up, our whole goddamn case is a bust."

He knocked back the rest of his whisky, then stood in silence for a moment, the burned-out pipe in one hand and the empty glass in the other. "Jesus, Wentworth, do you suppose we've all three been fools—you, me, and Kipling? First we go snitching on the prince because we think he's some kind of phony. Then when he's accused of something really serious, we turn right around and try to get him cleared. Maybe I've let all this detective foolishness go to my head. Sure, I saved an innocent man from the gallows down in New Orleans, but that don't mean I'm right this time. Maybe the only one who can't see the plain facts is pig-headed Sam Clemens, who thinks he's a master detective."

He gave me a sharp look. "Well, Wentworth, what do you think? Are we chasing a wild goose, or is there still a chance Prinz Karl is innocent?"

I didn't know what I was going to say until I opened my mouth. "Well, sir, I suppose we could have been carried away by our successes. But where's the harm if we try to establish Prinz Karl's innocence? If the case against him is overwhelming, we'll know it soon enough. And if it's not, someone should point that out. I don't think Mr. Babson is in any mood to seek a fair verdict—he's made up his mind, and he's out for revenge. And Mr. Jennings may not be doing much more than going through the motions in his investigation. So I think we ought to keep looking for answers—because it's important that the truth be known, whether Prinz Karl is innocent or guilty. And I don't think anyone except us is making any attempt to find it out.''

Mr. Clemens nodded. ''You know, they did teach you a few things at Yale, Wentworth. Or maybe I should take the credit. Well, no matter—I've made up my mind. Go find Rubbia and see what that little poseur has to say for himself. We may not clear Prinz Karl, but we can try to find out the truth.'' He made an impatient motion, shooing me out the door. I quickly took the hint and went in search of Signor Rubbia.

I still found it hard to understand Mr. Clemens's low opinion of Signor Rubbia. I had noticed that my employer's interest in the visual arts was rather limited, and that his judgments were more often based on an accurate portrayal of the world as he saw it than on concerns of technique and composition. I could see that Signor Rubbia had an inflated sense of his own worth, and perhaps a certain resentment of Mr. Clemens's fame. And I could understand my employer's including the artist among our suspects. That did not invalidate the fact that the artist had sensible and interesting things to say about painting— even if there was a hint of vanity in his character.

I remembered having seen Signor Rubbia bringing his drawing pad out to the rear deck of the ship to sketch, so I headed aft in hopes of finding him there. I was in luck; there he sat in a folding canvas chair, his pad on his knee. He was tapping a pencil against the corner of his jaw, and he had a faraway look in his eye, as if in deep thought. My first instinct was not to disturb him, but then I remembered that a man's life might well depend on what I could learn from him. ''Good afternoon, Signor Rubbia,'' I said.

He started, looking up at me with his mouth open, then quickly recovered. ''Good afternoon, young man,'' he said, with a slight nod of his head. His distinct Italian accent gave the words a musical inflection that I could not help but find charming and exotic, raised as I was among flat-voiced New Englanders.

I held out my hand. "Signor Rubbia, I'm Wentworth Cabot. I don't think we've actually been introduced, but I wanted to tell you how much I enjoyed your talk on modern art the other night."

Rubbia shook my hand without rising from his seat. "Ah, you are not with the tour, then? I am glad to know that my lessons have been valuable to you, in any case."

"Oh, they certainly have," I assured him. "In fact, I'm sorry that I'm not traveling with your group—after hearing your comments on the French artists, I'm looking forward to seeing their work. I'm sure I'd enjoy it even more if you were along with me to tell me about what I was seeing."

At this, Signor Rubbia rose to his feet, positively beaming. "What a grand pleasure to meet such a sympathetic young man," he said, taking my hand in both his and shaking it again. "It is a pity the sea voyage will so soon be finished. Perhaps I could have found time to give you some private drawing lessons. More than anything else, learning to draw would teach you to see what another artist has seen."

"A pity indeed," I agreed, quite sincerely. I had shown some interest—and, I believe, some ability—in drawing during my school days, before my father had discouraged it as a frivolous pursuit. I was not bad at getting a general impression of a scene into a sketch, but beyond that I knew my shortcomings all too well. I pointed to the pad he had left leaning against his chair leg. "What were you drawing, if you don't mind my asking?"

"Bah, this is nothing, really," said the artist. He held up the top page of the drawing pad, a view of the stern of our vessel with the wake streaming out behind it. "I was merely keeping my hands busy. To really capture the sunlight and the sea, one wants the full palette of colors."

"Yes, I can imagine," I said, peering closely at the

sketch. "Still, this must be tricky, to get all this into proper proportion and perspective." It really was quite good, I thought, though it was evident even to my eye that it was a quick, unpolished piece of work—the artist's equivalent of a writer's first draft.

"All that can be taught," said Signor Rubbia. "Why, I could teach you more than you might think in only two or three lessons. The part nobody can teach is the little spark of genius. But if it is there, a good teacher will see it, even in an untrained artist. Here!"—he thrust the pad and pencil at me—"Do me the kindness to draw something. Anything you wish. I will know right away whether you have the capability."

"Well . . ."

"Draw!" he insisted, fixing me with a stern look that admitted no protest. He stood there with his arms folded across his chest, and I cast my eye about for something I could delineate in a few quick strokes. In any other circumstance, the offer of lessons from a real artist would have been a very appealing prospect. But Mr. Clemens would have me working double-time to help solve the mystery, and my entire purpose here was to get Signor Rubbia to tell me what he had supposedly seen the night of Robert Babson's death. Still, I saw no harm in picking up a few hints about drawing if at the same time I could learn something that advanced Mr. Clemens's interests.

Perhaps inevitably, I found a subject for my drawing standing directly in front of me: Signor Rubbia himself. I hesitated for a moment, thinking he might consider my drawing him an impertinence, but then I decided that he would most likely be more interested in assessing my ability. He might even find my choice of him as a subject flattering—unless my depiction was so wretched that he took it as mockery. Well, if that turned out to be the case, I would have only myself to blame.

He must have divined my intention, for a little smile came over his lips as he stood there in front of me, now clearly posing for his portrait. For myself, now that I had taken on the challenge, I felt an obligation to do the best job I could. I was immediately reminded that the human face and figure were among the most difficult subjects to capture accurately. I discovered unexpected asymmetries—his eyes were not exactly the same size, and my first attempt at rendering the angle of his broad-brimmed hat was not quite accurate. Neither was it easy to portray a man of his bulk without risking caricature, which he might take as an insult. I tried instead to emphasize the flowing lines of his cape, and his aggressive stance. While I was well aware of how long it had been since I'd done any serious drawing, I thought the likeness was not bad.

Finally, after perhaps five minutes, I decided that any further attempt would only worsen my sketch. I sighed and handed the sketchbook to him. "I fear it's not as good as it might have been," I said. "I should have tried something easier."

"Let me judge that," he said, taking the pad and holding it at arm's length, squinting. Was it the sun that made him squint, or were his eyes going bad? Surely that would be a severe blow to someone whose livelihood depended on his vision—and for a man so obviously vain, wearing spectacles would be a terrible concession to age and infirmity. That last thought made me wonder how reliable his claim of having witnessed the murder might be—could his identification of the prince as the murderer be mistaken? I tried to think of some way to test his vision. Then I realized that it would have to be at night and in bad weather to provide an accurate comparison. Those conditions might be difficult to arrange.

"This is not so bad, for someone who has had no training," he said, interrupting my train of thought. "You try to show what you really see, rather than what your mind tells you must be there." He pointed to my rendition of his eyes, then to his raised chin, which I had done my best to make look heroic. "That is really the hardest thing for a beginner to overcome. But of course you have no technique at all—you don't even know how to hold the pencil properly. That would make all the difference.

I could teach you a great deal, if you wished to study. Even two or three lessons would take you a long way."

"What a shame we didn't speak earlier," I said. "If we had met at the beginning of the voyage, I might have had time for a few drawing lessons."

"Oh, it is still not too late," he said eagerly. "We could meet tomorrow morning, and again in the afternoon, and then again before we reach England. I would not charge you very much—it is such a rare pleasure to work with someone who has so much of the natural ability. Not many of my students do."

I thought for a moment; it seemed impossible that I would really have the time. Mr. Clemens would surely have work for me, even if his hope to exonerate Prinz Karl turned out to be a failure. I wondered, as well, whether Signor Rubbia's praise of my amateurish sketch was not just a ploy, to persuade me to sign up for lessons. Perhaps he said the same thing to everyone he thought might give him a few dollars in exchange for half a dozen rudimentary hints on technique. Even so, it was tempting—I had enjoyed trying to capture his stance and expression, and I knew I could probably do better with instruction. "It is very tempting," I admitted. "But Mr. Clemens sometimes has me working all through the morning and afternoon—I never really know in advance what demands he will make on my time."

"Mr. Clemens?" The artist looked at me with narrowed eyes. "Are you connected with him?"

"I am his traveling secretary," I said. Suddenly I wondered if it had been a mistake to mention my employer's name—Mr. Clemens had not shown much deference to Signor Rubbia. Indeed, there had been some friction between the two on their first meeting.

"Your Mr. Clemens thinks he is clever, but he knows nothing of art," said Signor Rubbia, raising his voice. "He makes ignorant remarks, and the ignorant herd laughs at them. He cannot bear to think that someone may know things that he does not, and so he mocks them."

I glanced around, hoping no other passengers were within earshot. Unfortunately, there were a gentleman and a lady not far away from us—with a bit of a jolt I recognized them as Mr. Clemens's old acquaintances Michael Richards and his sister, Mrs. Martin—although they were at least pretending not to hear what Rubbia was saying. I lowered my voice and said, as calmly as possible, "Really, Signor Rubbia, I am not Mr. Clemens, and my opinions sometimes differ from his. But it is very uncomfortable for me to stand here while you criticize my employer, even if your complaints may be just. I have no reason to dislike you, and I would appreciate it if you did not give me one."

Signor Rubbia sputtered for a moment, but then he nodded. "You are right, young man. I apologize. I am afraid your Mr. Clemens has pricked me in a sore spot. I so often find myself fighting those who look down their noses at an artist. They do not like me because I am a fat little Italian, who speaks with the accent. They do not like me because I can do something they cannot do and can barely understand. I am not usually welcome in their homes, except perhaps to paint their wives' portraits, or to give their daughters drawing lessons." He sighed, and I found it hard not to feel sympathy for Signor Rubbia. He wasn't really such a bad fellow, and he certainly appeared to have genuine artistic talent.

"Well, Mr. Mercer certainly seems to appreciate your knowledge and ability," I said. "After all, he engaged you to guide his group through the museums, did he not?"

The little artist smiled broadly; there was a curious gleam in his eye, as well. "Yes, Mr. Mercer has been very good to me. I wish I could say that of all his group."

"I know what you mean," I said. "That one young fellow, Robert Babson, seemed to take every chance he could to attack you. He seemed to have it in for everybody—I got on his wrong side, and he did his best to make me sorry for it. A shame about his going overboard, of course.''

Signor Rubbia looked at me for a moment, then nodded. ''A shame, indeed. But perhaps there is no evil thing that does not bring good to someone. Young Mr. Babson was ignorant, and proud of his ignorance, and yet there were many young people who thought he was smart and elegant. I would not have pushed young Mr. Babson over the side, but I do not think that I will miss him very much.'' He puffed himself up as he said this, though his voice was still low. I was glad of this, since I feared Rubbia might become less talkative if he believed he was speaking for any ears but my own.

''I suppose I won't much miss him, either,'' I said, realizing that the moment I was waiting for had come. ''Do you really think the poor fellow was pushed over the side?''

''Not only do I think so, I saw it myself,'' he said, his voice full of confidence. ''I was no farther from it than I am from the rail, right there.'' He pointed toward the stern of the ship, perhaps twenty feet away.

''Really,'' I said. ''It must have been terrible. I assume there was no way you could prevent it.''

He looked at me for a moment, then said, ''I doubt anyone could have prevented it; it happened very quickly, you know. And I am an artist, not a fighter.'' He spread his hands and shrugged, as if to deny further responsibility.

''Still, with your help perhaps Babson could have defended himself,'' I said. ''It was that German who did it—Prinz Karl, the man they arrested—wasn't it?''

Signor Rubbia looked me directly in the eyes for a moment, then lowered his gaze. ''Why, of course,'' he said. ''Who else could it possibly have been?''

22 ⌒

After Signor Rubbia's statement that he had seen
Prinz Karl push Robert Babson overboard, I was
reluctant to face Mr. Clemens. My employer
would hardly be pleased to learn that his theories had
been punctured by Rubbia, for whom he had so little
regard. I decided to take a few moments to think how I
would break the news to him.

The deck was still crowded, though it was late in the
afternoon, and I knew that the lounge would be full of
noise and chatter, as well. So I headed for the ship's
library, which on my previous visits had been sparsely
occupied; on a fine day like today, it was unlikely that
many passengers would be staying indoors to read. Indeed, except for my encounter there with Miss Babson,
I had not laid eyes on anyone in the library whom I
recognized the entire time I had been on board the ship.

As I had hoped, the place was as quiet as a tomb when
I entered. There was nobody present except Mrs. Tremont, the librarian, who sat at her desk with a small book
open in front of her. She glanced up as I entered, and I
nodded to her without saying anything. I walked over to
one of the shelves and picked out a book almost at random, then slid into a soft leather armchair. I opened the
book, a selection of verse by the late Lord Tennyson, and
tried to appear absorbed in reading it, in case any of my
fellow passengers entered the room.

"Pardon me for interrupting, Mr. Cabot," said Mrs.

Tremont, who I suddenly realized had walked over to the chair without my having noticed.

"Yes, Mrs. Tremont?" I said, looking up at her in surprise, then hurriedly rising to my feet. She stood with her hands clasped over her bosom, and there was a faint smile on her lips.

"I really am sorry to intrude," she said. "I see you are reading Tennyson, and I do love his poetry, so I won't bother you for more than a moment. But perhaps you will be so kind as to ask Mr. Clemens a favor for me? And for the other passengers?"

"I will do what I can, Mrs. Tremont," I said. "What do you wish to ask him?"

She looked down at the floor for a moment, then directly into my eyes. "I asked Mr. Clemens some days ago if he would be so kind as to give a brief talk on a subject of his choosing. Many of the passengers have seen him on board and asked me whether he will be speaking. He said he would do his best to accommodate me, but we didn't set a date. Now, between the effects of the bad weather and the unfortunate incident the other night, the entertainment aboard the ship has not been up to our usual standards. But I think the fine weather has put people in more of a holiday mood, which is as it should be on a sea voyage."

"Yes, the weather has been quite delightful today," I said.

"It certainly has. But as I was saying, the weather has forced us to cancel several of our planned events, and we've had disappointing attendance at those we went ahead with. Dr. Jarvis has been indisposed, and so we won't hear him talk on London church architecture at all, this trip. And poor Mrs. Brooks had only three ladies for her flower-arranging class," she said, rolling her eyes. "You can imagine what a predicament we've been in. My lecture calendar has been a dreadful muddle, and I'm afraid the captain will think I've done a very poor job." A worried look came over the librarian's face, and I sensed that she felt that her job might be at risk, although

I couldn't see how the captain could blame her for bad weather.

She looked me in the eye and said, "We can recover in wonderful fashion if Mr. Clemens will be so kind as to speak tomorrow night, Saturday. We'll have the best turnout of the voyage for him, and perhaps it'll give him a chance to try out a few passages from the new book you say he's working on. Do you think he can fit it into his plans? I know he's by far the most notable speaker aboard, and I don't want to miss the opportunity for our passengers to hear him. I would want him to speak at about eight o'clock tomorrow, in the Grand Saloon."

"I'll be glad to ask him, though of course I can't make promises for Mr. Clemens," I said. "How soon would you need an answer?"

Mrs. Tremont lifted her chin, like some sort of small bird, and peered intently at me. "We need to post an announcement by tomorrow morning, at breakfast. I would appreciate it very much if he could give me an answer this evening, after dinner. If for some reason he can't accommodate us, I still might be able to find a substitute, though I'm sure I couldn't find anyone nearly as good on such short notice. Poor Dr. Jarvis is still feeling quite out of sorts."

"I'll go ask him now, and bring you his answer as soon as I can," I said. This, at least, would give my employer something to think about other than my news of Rubbia's seeing the prince murder Robert Babson. And if the news sent him into one of his black moods, it would give me an excuse to escape him.

"Oh, thank you very much," Mrs. Tremont said. Then she turned and pointed to the seat, where I had left the book when I stood to speak to her. "Don't forget your Tennyson, Mr. Cabot. I'll sign it out for you, if you'll wait a moment."

Mr. Clemens was pacing back and forth, smoking a rank-smelling cigar, when I reached the cabin. He whirled around to look at me as I came in the door.

"Aha," he said. "I'm glad you're back, Wentworth." And then, glancing at what was in my hands, he asked, "What's the book?"

"Tennyson's poems," I told him, tossing it lightly onto the sofa. "I've spoken to Rubbia."

"Good man, Wentworth," said my employer. Then he looked more closely at my face. "Looks as if the news isn't anything I want to hear. I guess you'd better tell me anyway." He flopped down on the sofa next to the book, knocking an inch-long cigar ash onto his trouser cuffs in the process.

"Rubbia claims that he saw the prince shove Babson overboard," I said. "He says he was no more than twenty feet away."

"Damnation," said Mr. Clemens, absently brushing at his ankles. Then he looked up at me, frowning. "Wait a minute, now. Why didn't Rubbia go straight to one of the officers and tell what he'd seen? Why did that lawyer Babson come in with Jennings and put the finger on the prince, and the next day at that? We didn't hear about Rubbia being a witness until just this afternoon."

"Why, I don't know—I'm sorry, I didn't think to ask him," I said, surprised to have overlooked such an obvious question.

"Something smells rotten," said Mr. Clemens. He got to his feet and went to stare out the porthole, then turned to look at me. "Tell me what Rubbia said, start to finish. Then maybe I can figure out what his game is."

I repeated the exchange with Signor Rubbia, including my drawing his picture, and his offer to give me lessons. Mr. Clemens listened in silence, interrupting only when I mentioned my suspicions as to Rubbia's eyesight. "That would be a problem for an artist, wouldn't it, now? It sounds to me as if he's far-sighted, though, if any-thing—you say he held the pad at arm's length?"

"Yes, and he squinted. At first I thought he was simply trying to judge the composition as a whole, but when I saw him squinting, it made me wonder how good his eyes were. Of course, the murder took place at night, in the middle of a storm, so even a man with perfect eyes might have trouble making out everything that went on.''

"If he saw it at all," said Mr. Clemens. "That's the part that smells wrong to me."

"But why would he lie?" I asked. "If he's caught lying about such a serious matter, he might be risking a perjury charge—I assume British law is the same as ours. Even if he weren't convicted, he'd have a great deal of trouble getting a position as a tour guide again. I'd think the class of people likely to patronize him would give him the cold shoulder."

"Damned if I can figure it out," said my employer. "I still think he could have pushed that boy over the rail himself, but then why would he start blabbing about the prince doing it? He must know people will question him about his story. More to the point, he'll be the leading suspect if they catch him lying about what he saw."

"Assuming they catch him," I said. "He sounds absolutely confident. Unless another witness can refute him, or some solid evidence turns up of the prince's innocence, I fear that Signor Rubbia's story will stand."

Mr. Clemens stared out the window again. "I guess this kills our hope of clearing the prince. There's no point going to talk to him now. I might as well write the poor rascal off. Still, I wonder what kind of game he was running with his claim to be from a place nobody's heard of. I suppose we'll never find out."

"Oh, if you really want to find out, you could still go talk to him," I said.

"It hardly seems worth the trouble—not with an eye-witness. I'll do better to sit in the lounge and swap yarns with Kipling and the boys." Mr. Clemens ground out his cigar. His expression was downcast, but I suspected he would recover his spirits once he was in company. A group of people always brought out his cheerful nature.

This reminded me of Mrs. Tremont's request for him to give a talk to the passengers. Perhaps it might serve to take his mind off the disappointment of seeing his detective work go for naught. I had just opened my mouth to mention the request, when there was a knock on the cabin door. At Mr. Clemens's signal, I opened it to admit Mr. Kipling.

"Hullo, lads," he said. "A fine day at last, eh?" Then he looked at my employer. "Why so down in the mouth, Clemens?"

"I've been made a fool of, Kipling," said Mr. Clemens. "Rubbia saw Prinz Karl push that boy overboard. That ruins any chance we might be able to clear him. We can bring up all the maybes and what-ifs we want to, but they aren't worth a rebel dollar against an eyewitness account."

"Really! How odd," said Kipling, settling himself on the couch. He picked up the book I'd tossed there, looked at the cover, and shrugged. Then he turned back to Mr. Clemens. "Do you think Rubbia's telling the truth?"

Mr. Clemens scowled. "Hell, no, but how do I prove it? It's my reasonable doubt against his solid word, and unless we can find somebody who saw something different, or who can prove Rubbia wasn't on deck that night, it's wasted breath. The only thing that made me defend the prince to begin with was the feeling that he was being accused not because there was any more likelihood he'd done it than half a dozen others, but because he'd made himself obnoxious to some people. But with a witness, that argument goes up the chimney." He pointed toward the ceiling, then dropped his hand to his side. He looked defeated.

"I don't think we're as bad off as all that," said Mr. Kipling. "In fact, I'd come to tell you something I think puts a rather different complexion on the matter, even after your news about Rubbia."

"And what would that be?" asked Mr. Clemens, raising his brows.

"Well, you remember I was talking to the officer on watch the night of the storm," said Kipling. "A bright young chap named Steven Lewis. It turns out I knew his uncle—Harry Lewis, his name was, a clerk in the government office at Bombay, when I was a newspaper reporter there. Small world, as they say." He paused to fish a cigarette case out of his pocket, then continued. "I remember one day Lewis and I were walking back to work from the Punjab Club, when a dreadful storm came up all of a sudden, the way they do in tropical countries. We took shelter under the eaves of a native temple, where curiously enough, there was a small troop of monkeys also sheltering. Now I don't know how often you've been around monkeys . . ."

"You can tell me that story another time," said Mr. Clemens, somewhat sharply. "What's your news, Kipling?"

Mr. Kipling was lighting a match. He looked up with a sly grin on his face. "Really, Clemens, it's a most amusing incident, and perhaps one with a lesson for us all. But I see you aren't in the mood for diversion." He lit a cigarette, shook the match to extinguish the flame, let out a puff of bluish smoke, then looked up and said, "Let's see, where was I?"

Mr. Clemens, who had been all but hopping from one foot to the other in his impatience, said gruffly, "Something Lewis told you about."

"Ah, yes," said Kipling. "If you'll remember, Harry Lewis and I were in the temple with the monkeys—"

"Damn the monkeys," Mr. Clemens cut in, somewhat more vehemently than I would have thought strictly necessary. "You don't need lessons on how to drive a fellow to distraction, do you, Kipling?"

"I've studied with the masters," said Kipling, grinning. "But I shan't keep you in suspense any longer. I asked Mr. Lewis here on the ship whether he'd seen Prinz Karl on deck that night. Of course I'd asked him before, and he'd said he hadn't, but it never hurts to go over the facts again, because sometimes a man will remember details the second or third time around. Lewis told me again that he hadn't seen the prince, but since our previous conversation, he'd been talking to some of the other ship's officers. Not to stretch things out, one of them *had* seen Prinz Karl that night."

"Aha!" said Mr. Clemens. "And where had the prince been?"

"Curiously enough, he'd seen him below decks—near the steerage. The fellow thought it odd to see a first-class passenger going that way, still dressed up in all his finery from the concert. Particularly in such foul conditions—rough as it gets in our part of the ship, the poor chaps in steerage have it much worse."

"Yes, of course," said Mr. Clemens. "Did this officer remember what time he saw the prince?"

"It was after the concert. He'd already heard about the fight, though he hadn't heard which passengers had been involved. Still, he recognized the prince—not a man you'd easily mistake for someone else, I think. And he didn't see the prince come back—he was on watch until midnight, I believe."

Mr. Clemens nodded. "Of course, the prince might have come back by another way. Or he might have come back just after midnight and still had plenty of time to murder Babson. That's probably why Jennings hasn't made anything of the report—nobody knows what time the murder took place, so the prince could have been down there to all hours and still had time to kill the boy. Still, this might be the start of an alibi." He turned to me. "What time did Rubbia claim he saw the murder?"

"He didn't say, and I didn't have a chance to press him," I said. "If we'd had more privacy, I might have, but we were out on deck. A couple of other passengers were practically within earshot the whole time, and then two or three more came along, and one of the ladies began asking Signor Rubbia about painting, so I couldn't bring the conversation back to the murder without letting the world know what I was getting at."

"Drat," said Mr. Clemens. "It would have been worth knowing, though I suppose we can still find it out if we need to."

"At least we have something specific to ask Prinz Karl about," said Kipling. "Surely he wasn't going down below decks to hide in a corner by himself. He must have been meeting someone down there—another passenger, most likely. There's got to be a damned queer story behind this sneaking around, and I'd like to find out what it is, even if it doesn't exonerate the prince on the murder charge.''

''My friends in steerage may be able to find out something,'' I suggested. ''I'll have to go ask them what they know.''

''Yes, make sure they know what we're looking for,'' said Mr. Clemens. He paused a moment in thought, then seemed to come to a decision. ''And do it as soon as we're finished here—I've got plans for us this evening. Rubbia may have seen what he says, or he may be peddling buncombe. But if Prinz Karl was prowling around below decks that night, I want to know why—blame it on an old newspaper man's curiosity. Anyhow, I'm going to do my damnedest to get the captain to let me question him, and I want you there with me. Both of you, unless the captain turns me down flat. It's time we found out what the main suspect has to say for himself. Then we'll see if we can substantiate his story—or shoot holes in it, as the case may be.''

''Well, unless there's something else to discuss now, I'll run right down to steerage and talk to the boys before supper,'' I said, reaching for my hat.

Mr. Clemens looked at Mr. Kipling, who shook his head, and then nodded to me. ''Go ahead. Kipling and I will head over to the smoker for a drink—if you come back with news, look for us there.''

I found Johnny DeWitt sitting on his bunk with a deck of cards, playing solitaire in the stark light of the bare electric bulb that illuminated the steerage sleeping quarters. In the upper berth his brother Tom lay snoring. As I entered, Johnny put his finger to his lips and pointed to the door. I followed him out to the corridor, where he turned and said, ''Poor Tom's still not up to snuff—didn't sleep a wink last night, so I don't want to disturb him now that he's actually asleep.''

"Yes, let him rest," I agreed. "Where's Bertie? It could save explaining things twice if he were here."

Johnny spread his arms with a sheepish grin. "Bertie's trying to sneak up to the top again—he's taken quite a fancy to Eliza, that Smith girl, you know. Quite a pretty little blonde. I think if he hadn't spotted her first, I'd have set my cap for her myself—though I'm usually more drawn to brunettes."

I grinned back at him. "He'll be lucky if First Mate Gallagher doesn't clap him in irons. But Bertie's never been able to resist a blonde, has he? Remember that girl Lucille, and how she ran him around in circles?" We both laughed; for a moment the image of old days in New Haven replaced the drab steerage quarters and the motion of the ship.

"Yes, Lucille certainly had him eating out of her hand," said Johnny, still chuckling. "Poor Bertie hasn't an ounce of self-respect when he's after a girl. But you didn't come down here to talk about that, did you? What's the word?"

"Well, I wanted to tell all of you, but you'll just have to pass the word to the others. Mr. Kipling talked to an officer who reported that the man arrested for killing Babson was down in this part of the ship late that night— Prinz Karl von Ruckgarten. Do you know who I mean?"

"Sure," said Johnny. "Old fellow with a beard, a bit stiff and stout, but has a jolly laugh. I saw him up on the first-class deck the first time I went there."

"Have you seen him down here? Especially that evening—it could be a question of life or death."

"Life or death, you say?" Johnny scratched his head. "Now I'll have to remember what *I* was doing that evening. That was at the peak of the storm, wasn't it?"

"Yes, Wednesday evening. We'd like to find out what he was doing down here—according to what I hear, he was decked out in full evening dress, so anybody who saw him would have noticed it straightaway, I'd think. Can you and the boys ask around and see if anyone remembers him that night?"

"Full evening dress, eh?" Johnny chuckled. "Yes, that would stand out down here. I doubt there's a square yard of silk in all of steerage, unless some merchant's got it in his case. If he was here, somebody would've seen him, for sure. Whether that fellow will talk to us about it is another story, though."

"Well, we'll have to deal with that problem somehow. Do you think you can find out if he really was here, and if so, when? Even better would be who he talked to, and when he went back up to the top decks. Mr. Clemens thinks he might have been down here on some secret business, so of course we'd love to know what *that* was—assuming you can find it out."

"That's a mighty tall order," said Johnny, a skeptical look on his face. "What sort of secret business does your boss think this German prince had down here, if you don't mind telling me?"

"It's a mystery to all of us," I said. "We think he's traveling under a false identity. There doesn't seem to be any such place as Ruckgarten, which is where he claims to be from."

"A mystery, you say," said Johnny, his eyes lighting up. "Say—what do you want to bet he's some sort of master spy? He could have been down here meeting with one of his agents, you know. The fellow could be traveling with a whole gang of socialists or nihilists."

"I can't see what a prince would be doing with that sort," I said, although I had to admit that the notion that Prinz Karl was spying might explain some of his actions.

Johnny caught me by the elbow. "But you already said that perhaps he's not a prince at all—that he might be traveling under a false identity. So he could be anything, couldn't he? What if some of these fellows who look like merchants are really anarchists, smuggling bombs and secret plans back to Europe? That would be an adventure, now!"

"I'm not sure I want any part of an adventure involving bombs," I said. "But I suppose it could be true.

You'd best be careful—if they *are* spies, they might go to some lengths to avoid detection.''

Johnny leaned closer to my ear, whispering now. ''Yes, but if their ringleader is being held prisoner, they'll be even more desperate. They might plant a bomb in the ship somewhere, and threaten to set if off unless he's freed. So we have to learn the truth as quickly as possible.''

''Yes, certainly speed is essential—and discretion, too,'' I said. Johnny's enthusiasm for the spy theory wasn't bad in itself, but I didn't need him inventing elaborate conspiracies, when the plain truth was all we wanted. ''I doubt they'd do anything to draw attention to themselves before they'd exhausted other plans. They'd wait until we'd docked, in any case. Even if they got him free through some threat of violence, here in mid-ocean, what would they do then? I don't think they plan to sail to Europe in a lifeboat.''

''I guess you're right,'' said Johnny. ''Well, I'll tell the boys and we'll try to find out if anyone laid eyes on the fellow. Dressed in full evening gear, he can't have been very inconspicuous. If he was here, we'll find out.''

''Good man,'' I said, clapping him on the back. ''Let me know as soon as you learn anything useful. And I'll let you know if I spot any pretty brunettes up on the top deck.''

''That I'll do,'' said Johnny breezily. ''These Europeans may think they have the spy business down to a science, but they haven't seen anything until they see a few Yale men at work.''

''Heaven help them,'' I said, but I smiled and shook his hand and then made my way up to the smoking lounge to report to Mr. Clemens.

23 🖎

As they'd promised, my employer and Mr. Kipling were waiting in the smoking lounge. I told them Johnny DeWitt's theory that Prinz Karl might be a spy who was meeting secret confederates down in steerage. Mr. Clemens laughed. "A fellow who draws as much attention to himself as the prince is the last man on earth I'd want as a spy for my country. Maybe the Germans have a different idea about things. Come to think of it, they *do* have different ideas about a lot of things. But I don't think we have to worry about a shipload of secret agents and assassins."

"Certainly nothing like that," said Mr. Kipling, in a low voice. He leaned forward with his hand to his chin. "Don't be so quick to dismiss the idea that Ruckgarten is a spy, though—I'd thought of it myself."

"Now you're pulling my leg again," said Mr. Clemens. His surprise was evident, though he kept his voice down. "I'd sooner believe he's a real prince than that he's a spy."

"He could be both, you know," said Mr. Kipling, glancing around as if to check whether anyone was listening before he continued. "We should certainly keep the idea in mind when we talk to him, though I doubt he'd give a straight answer to a direct query. It would explain some things that don't make sense otherwise— not that everything a man does will always make sense, of course. But let's not discuss the matter out here in public. I'll explain when we're by ourselves again.''

"Well, tie me down and paint me blue," said Mr. Clemens. "This whole thing may be stranger than I'd thought. I'll look forward to hearing what you've dreamed up, Kipling. But first, I may have to talk the captain into letting me see the rascal. I don't think the master-at-arms really wants us carrying on an investigation, no matter what he said.''

"I shouldn't think he'll cause any difficulty," I said. "He can't really believe we're likely to free the prisoner. Besides, it's in the captain's interest to bring out the truth, not to persecute a man who may be innocent.''

"It's the captain's business to run his ship efficiently and safely, and to bring it to port without any incidents that might embarrass the owners," said Mr. Kipling. "Babson's going overboard is the kind of incident that owners hate. It's to the captain's advantage to explain it as somebody else's fault, preferably a passenger's.''

"Sure, but if the prince comes up with an iron-clad alibi, somebody else has to take the blame," said Mr. Clemens. "And the owners won't be happy if the captain's wasted time on a lead that doesn't pan out. So we're doing him a favor by making sure he's not on the wrong trail.''

"We'll have to hope Captain Mortimer sees it that way," said Mr. Kipling, shaking his head. "It's a pity we don't have something more than a reasonable doubt to offer him.''

"I suppose I could threaten to deprive him of my brilliant wit and conversation," said Mr. Clemens. "I could demand to be seated at another table. Or just as easily, I could clam up and eat my dinner without talking. It'd throw the whole burden of entertaining the guests right back on his shoulders. Serve him right, too.''

"Serve you right if it turned out they liked his conversation better than yours," said Mr. Kipling, chuckling.

My employer's mention of entertaining the guests reminded me of my errand for Mrs. Tremont. "I'm embarrassed to admit that I forgot to mention this," I said, and relayed the librarian's request for Mr. Clemens to give a lecture the following night. "I promised her I'd come back with your answer right away, but it slipped my mind as we got caught up in the murder."

"I say, that's exactly the sort of thing you can bargain with," said Kipling brightly. "Tell the captain you'll give your lecture, but your price is an interview with the prince. It's considerably less than your usual fee, you know."

"I've got an even better idea," said Mr. Clemens. "I don't want to make poor Wentworth disappoint the librarian—she's been a help to me, after all. Run down, Wentworth, and tell her I'll do it. Then tonight, I'll tell the captain I have *two* lectures prepared. One will delight and entertain the audience, and send them back home telling what a fine time they had on the *City of Baltimore*. That's the one I'll deliver if he lets me talk to the prince. If he doesn't, I'll lampoon him and his crew until they wish they'd been horsewhipped instead—and then I'll *really* get rough: I'll publish the thing, with satiric illustrations by Dan Beard. What do you think, Kipling?"

"It's outright extortion," said Mr. Kipling, grinning broadly. "Best of all, you can put the proposition to him in front of a whole table of passengers, and they'll take it as just one of your jokes. But he'll know you're serious, and he'll have to give in, or look like a fool."

"Exactly," said Mr. Clemens. "If we don't hear from Jennings, or if he says *No*, that's what I'm going to do. Go ahead, Wentworth, tell the nice librarian I'll give my talk."

I set down my wineglass and stood. "Don't let the waiter clear that away. I'll be right back," I said, and left them smoking and laughing together as I went to find the librarian.

I was afraid the library might be closed already—it was less than half an hour to dinnertime—and that I would have to leave a note for Mrs. Tremont, or find out where her cabin was to give her the message. But the

Open sign hung on the door, and I stepped inside to find the librarian still at her desk.

"Hello again, Mrs. Tremont," I said. "Mr. Clemens asked me to inform you that he will be glad to speak to the passengers tomorrow evening."

"Oh, splendid!" she said, rising to her feet. "I shall be eager to hear him speak, myself."

"As will I," said another voice, and I turned to see Rebecca Babson standing in the corner behind me, an open book in her hands. She was wearing a dark dress with no jewelry, reminding me that she would still be in mourning for her brother.

"Miss Babson," I said, bowing slightly. "Permit me to express my condolences on the loss of your brother. It is always a sad thing for someone to be taken from the world while he is still young."

"Thank you, you are very kind," she said, with a downward glance that might have meant anything. She paused a moment, clasping the book to her bosom, then said, "I suppose I appreciate it more because you had what many would consider ample reason to dislike him. I heard about the trick he tried to play on you, and it made me sorry to be connected to him."

"I was very little inconvenienced by it, and to tell the truth I had practically forgotten it," I said—lying only a little. "I do my best not to hold grudges." That, at least, was true.

"I am glad to hear that," said Miss Babson. "Bobby had a knack for making friends, and a nearly equal knack for making enemies. I would have been saddened to learn that he had left the world having made still another enemy, in you." Her eyes met mine for a moment, then she looked downward again.

I was not close enough to tell whether she might be blushing, but I thought perhaps she was. The thought flashed through my mind that I would still have two or three days in her company aboard ship, and that she and I appeared to have a great deal in common. Perhaps, if Mr. Clemens did not have too much work for me, I would be able to seek her out—always assuming that she would be interested in my company. . . .

Mrs. Tremont cleared her throat, and I quickly turned to face her again, remembering why I had come here. "Pardon my interrupting, Mr. Cabot, but I need to make up a notice to inform passengers of the lecture. Did Mr. Clemens tell you on what subject he would be speaking, or will it be an impromptu talk?"

"I believe he was still deciding between a couple of possible subjects," I said. "Perhaps it would be best simply to announce it as an evening with Mark Twain."

She smiled and nodded. "Yes, I believe that will draw a satisfactory crowd."

"Then I will undertake to deliver him to the Grand Saloon at the appointed time tomorrow evening, and I hope you will be there to enjoy it," I said.

"I certainly will be there, and I intend to enjoy it thoroughly," said Miss Tremont. "We have had some wonderful speakers on *City of Baltimore*—Professor James, and Mr. Huxley—but this will be an occasion to top them all. Thank you again for passing on my request to him."

"It was my pleasure, Mrs. Tremont," I said. Then I turned to Miss Babson. "I hope I will see you at Mr. Clemens's talk, as well."

"I believe you will, Mr. Cabot," she said, smiling. I bowed to her again, and to Mrs. Tremont, and left the library. Halfway back to the smoking lounge, I caught myself humming a silly little tune. It took all my mental powers to suppress it before I returned to the company of those two austere gentlemen, Mr. Clemens and Mr. Kipling.

For once, I spent most of the dinner hour peering at the captain's table. We had heard nothing from Jennings. The group at our table had adopted a more or less invariant seating arrangement, one that happened to put me facing the center of the dining room, so I generally had a good view of the other tables. Mr. Kipling and his wife, Caroline, on the other hand, were seated directly across from me, and it seemed to me that Mr. Kipling had to draw on all his self-discipline to keep from craning his neck to see what Mr. Clemens was doing.

Unfortunately, it was impossible to hear the conversation from that distance, although the frequent bursts of laughter were clearly audible. Was the laughter more boisterous tonight than usual? I wondered as the waiters cleared my soup plate (I had chosen the *Potage aux choux*, which turned out to be nothing more than cabbage soup, tasty though it was). As my main course arrived—baked flounder with bread crumb stuffing—I could see Mr. Clemens leaning forward, telling one of his long stories, with all the others at the table ignoring their meals as they listened, finally bursting out in laughter and delighted applause. At our table, Mr. Kipling had begun describing his home in Vermont—"Naulakha, three miles from anywhere"—and Mrs. Kipling had taken over the story from him, adding all sorts of comic details about her neighbors and relations. In any other circumstances, I would have been fascinated.

The fish course went away, and the pastry came (apple fritters with hard sauce). Dr. Gillman speculated on medical applications of hypnotism, of which he had made an extensive study. The laughter from the captain's table was louder than ever, more uproarious than it had been at the young Philadelphians' table when Robert Babson was their guiding spirit. Mr. Clemens was clearly giving a fine performance, and his fellow-diners were delighted. All but one: Captain Mortimer sat there politely, not unsmiling but not wholeheartedly joining in the general merriment, either. Was he always this stiff? I had to wonder whether he was steeling himself to deny Mr. Clemens his request for an interview with the prince—perhaps he had already done so, and was patiently enduring my employer's gibes disguised as good-humored teasing.

Perhaps I was imagining difficulties where none existed. After all, I had not paid particular attention to the captain's bearing during previous meals, so I had no real basis for comparison. Still, as I sipped my coffee, I began to wonder whether Mr. Clemens's plan to threaten the captain with a satirical lecture had any chance of working. The captain of a ship on the high seas was supposedly a law unto himself. Would he contrive some excuse for calling off the lecture? For that matter, if he considered my employer a threat to incite the other passengers' opinion against him or the American Steamship Line, could he confine Mr. Clemens to his cabin for the duration of the voyage? It seemed a far-fetched notion. Still, there was no guarantee that the captain would let us visit a man suspected of murder, no matter how eminent and popular Mr. Clemens might be.

At last the captain stood, bowing to the ladies and gentlemen at his table, and the meal was at an end. As at the conclusion of one of his lectures, Mr. Clemens was surrounded by a crowd of his fellow diners, anxious for one last moment of intimacy with the famous man. At an actual lecture, it would have been my responsibility to come forward, after a few minutes, with some pretended backstage business to allow Mr. Clemens a chance to pry himself away from the crowd. It was tempting to do so on this occasion, especially because of my anxiety to learn whether the captain had agreed to let him interview the prince. But there was a chance one of the other passengers might drop some morsel of information that would help in our investigation. I reluctantly made my way down the corridor to our cabin, to await my employer's arrival and learn whatever news he had.

The wait turned out to be longer than I'd expected. At first I sat on the couch—the book of Tennyson's poems was still there—expecting him to come in the door shortly behind me. While it was common for him to be inundated with well-wishers after a lecture, it was not at all usual after a dinner. But the wait grew, and grew. I looked around our quarters, admiring how smoothly the ship's designers had disguised the functional metal hull behind flowered wallpaper and rich mahogany, turning the cabin into a small apartment that, upon first glance, might be located in a fine hotel in any American city.

The round porthole was the only obvious sign that we were aboard a ship. And only a light rocking gave any indication that we were moving across the ocean at more than fifteen knots.

After ten minutes, there was still no sign of my employer, though I had expected him to be right on my heels. Should I go back to the dining room and see if he really did need "rescuing" from the crowd? But Mr. and Mrs. Kipling would be joining us at any moment, and if I were gone, they would have to wait outside in the corridor. Besides, it was not certain that Mr. Clemens would be right where I had left him, and I would have no idea where to search if he were gone. Best to stick to the plan, and wait for him here. I picked up the book and opened it at random, thinking perhaps I would find something of interest.

I had not read much Tennyson. I remembered hearing the accounts of his death only a short while before, while I was still at Yale. One of the professors had proclaimed him the greatest poet of modern times. The first piece that caught my eye was *The Revenge*, a rousing sea-ballad of Elizabethan times that swept me away to the era of wooden ships until I was startled from my reading by a knock on the door. I looked at my watch and discovered that fifteen minutes had passed. I went to the door and opened it to admit Mr. Kipling.

"Carrie's gone to spy on the Philadelphia ladies some more," he said. "I think she enjoys it. Where's Clemens?"

"Come in and have a seat," I said. "I'm afraid Mr. Clemens isn't back yet—I thought he'd be here before now. Can I fix you drinks? We have whisky and soda . . ."

"That sounds good, but I think I'll wait for Clemens," said Mr. Kipling, strolling over to the couch I'd just vacated. "If he comes in with word that we can go talk to Ruckgarten right away, I'd either have to gulp it down or have it go to waste, and either would be a pity with such good whisky."

"Yes, of course," I said. "I can't imagine what's taking him so long, but I hope it isn't bad news. The captain seemed very stiff at the table tonight." I walked over and looked out the porthole; outside the sky was clear, and a bright moon was just visible towards the prow of the ship.

"Well, it needn't have had anything to do with our business," said Mr. Kipling. "Captains come in all sorts, but the majority of them fall into two classes: the ones who care most about their ships, and the ones who care most about the passengers. Mortimer's one of the first sort, or I'm no judge of character. That's probably why he wanted to get Clemens for his table every night. It saves him from trying to make clever talk with a bunch of people with whom he has nothing in common."

"Perhaps you're right," I said. "Still, Mr. Clemens should've been back by now. I can't help but think there's something the matter . . ."

The door flew open with a bang, and Mr. Clemens stomped into the room. "Damn right there's something the matter," he said. "Fix me a whisky, will you, Wentworth? You boys better have one, too. These no-account bastards are trying to bar the doors on us, and we're going to have to connive like thieves to figure out a way around them."

"Why, what happened?" said Kipling, standing up. "I take it we can't talk to Ruckgarten. What grounds did Mortimer give for refusing us?"

Mr. Clemens had walked over to look out the porthole while I poured the drinks. "No, he's smoother than that. First, he put me off until after dinner—during which I regaled our fellow diners with every ludicrous misadventure that's happened aboard a ship since Jonah's time, just as a little sample of what I could tell about the *City of Baltimore*, if I put my mind to it. I figured a little advertising couldn't hurt when I gave him his choice of Mark Twain lectures. He didn't like it one bit, though the others at the table were begging for more. It took me a quarter of an hour to get away to Mortimer's office to talk to him.

"That's when he pulled the dirtiest trick I've ever been bit by. He allows as how he don't object to our talking to the prince, but he wants to wait until Jennings has finished his investigation. That way, we don't inadvertently tell Prinz Karl something that would help him wriggle off the hook—assuming he's guilty. So we've got to wait until Jennings hands in his report. Which will probably be ten minutes after we land in England, damn the rotten luck."

"At which point the captain can simply hand Ruckgarten over to the British authorities, and we've no standing at all to question him," said Mr. Kipling. "Not that we really do here, to tell the truth. Sailors are always jealous of their domain. In their eyes, we landlubbers have no right at all to participate in the ship's business. It would be a courtesy to let us talk to Ruckgarten, but the captain has no obligation to grant it."

I brought over their drinks, then went back to retrieve my own. "It's too bad the prince's cabin is guarded," I said, thinking of a couple of college pranks that required breaking into the room of a classmate who had gone on vacation early. "If he was just locked up with nobody to watch the door, we might contrive some way to pick the lock."

Mr. Kipling had been about to take a sip of his drink, but at my comment he put down his glass and said, "By Jove! You know, Clemens, if you really want to talk to the fellow before the captain gives his permission, there *is* a way."

Mr. Clemens turned around, a weary look on his face. "Don't tell me you're going to lower Cabot on a rope and let him in through the porthole. That's fine for him, but you're not going to dangle *me* over that cold water. For starters, there's nobody aboard I'd trust to hold the rope."

"No, no," said Kipling. "The weak link is the guard. I'd wager anything it's a common seaman, especially on the night watches. Those fellows are the worst-paid and the least principled men aboard—I know the breed of old. For a ten-dollar gold piece and a bottle of your whisky, they'd throw their own mothers to the sharks. For no more than the price of a good dinner in New York, we could be inside that room in five minutes, and nobody the wiser.''

Mr. Clemens beamed like a man who has just opened the mail to find a bank check made out in his favor. ''Kipling, I knew you were a genius! Now, which of us is going to go down and offer the bribe?''

≈ 24

Predictably, Mr. Kipling and Mr. Clemens chose me to bribe the guard outside Prinz Karl's cabin. Back when Mr. Clemens had interviewed me as a candidate for the position of traveling secretary, he had intimated that a familiarity with bribery was one of the job qualifications. At the time I had to confess a total lack of experience in that esoteric art; but I soon learned to consider slipping a carefully folded banknote to a hotel desk clerk, theater manager, or other such functionary as natural as tipping a porter or carriage driver. On this occasion, my employer simply said, "Nobody will even notice Cabot, let alone suspect him of anything. He's the perfect man for the job."

And so I found myself strolling down one of the ship's walnut-paneled corridors, hoping that none of the passengers who passed, nodding pleasantly to me, would think it strange that I was in this section of the ship. I knew Prinz Karl's stateroom was somewhere nearby—he had told Mr. Clemens the number when we first met on shipboard—but I had not been in this section of the ship before and had no idea of how the cabin numbers ran.

Before long, I realized that Prinz Karl was in one of the larger suites at the very front of the deck I was on. I came round a corner and the sight of one of the ship's crew seated on a stool in the hallway outside the door told me that I had found the cabin I was looking for.

Coming closer, I recognized the seaman as one of the crew who had been with First Mate Gallagher when he mistook me for a steerage passenger trespassing on the first-class deck. What had their names been? Jones and Watts, if I remembered correctly. But which one was this? Well, no matter, I would find out soon enough.

"Hello," I said cheerfully. The fellow looked up from his reading—I saw it was Mr. Smythe's book, *A Christian's Duty*—and gave a wary nod in response to my greeting. A shadow of a doubt suddenly came upon me. Was this fellow going to be the inevitable exception to Mr. Kipling's confident prediction that the crew members would be easily corrupted? Or had the seaman merely picked up whatever reading matter fell into his hands, out of boredom?

"I remember you," he said, in a thick Cockney accent. "You're the gentleman Gallagher was about to 'aul off to the brig, afore you showed us you 'ad a key to that cabin. You're Mr. Mark Twain's man, aren't you?"

"That's right," I said. "I'm glad to meet you under less anxious circumstances, this time."

"Aye, I suppose they are, for you," he said solemnly, still not rising from the stool he sat on. "Any way you look at it, it's all in a day's work for me. First mate or an officer gives me my orders, and I follows 'em, and that's an end to it."

"Yes, you were just doing your job the other day. I knew better than to take it personally."

"Good, then," he said, relaxing a bit. "I 'oped there wasn't any misunderstandin', but a man can't always tell."

I moved closer to him and lowered my voice; there was nobody in sight in either direction, but nonetheless I thought it prudent not to take a chance on anyone's overhearing me when I offered a bribe. "Well, I'd have been in worse trouble if it hadn't been for that German gentleman who came along in the nick of time. He certainly saved my bacon by reminding me that I could prove I wasn't trespassing by showing my key."

"Aye, that he did," said the sailor. He glanced quickly over his shoulder at the door of the cabin behind him—if I hadn't already been certain that Prinz Karl was confined within, that would have been all the clue I needed.

"He did me a good turn then, and I feel I ought to thank him for it in some way," I continued. "This is his cabin, isn't it?"

Abruptly, the sailor rose to his feet. Looking at him face to face, I remembered how tall and broad-shouldered he was. "You can't go in there, now. Nothin' personal, but I 'as my orders. No visitors."

"Yes, I see you're here to guard the door," I said. "Do you know what he's supposed to have done?"

"Aye, they say he pushed somebody overboard," the seaman said. "Say—weren't it that same gentleman as came along and told us you were botherin' the first class? I mean, the gentleman who's gone missin'. That was an awful cheeky thing to do. Or was that some kind of joke?"

"Perhaps *he* thought it was a joke," I said, shaking my head. "At the time, I saw very little humor in it."

"Neither did I, if you don't mind me sayin' so. Live and let live, that's always my motto, but I don't 'old with goin' about and spreadin' slander or false rumors, just for amusement. The Lord commanded against it, and that's an end to it."

"I'm glad to hear you say that," I said, shaking his hand. "The truth is—I'm sorry, I realize I don't know your name. I'm Wentworth Cabot."

"Watts, sir. 'Erbert Watts." His grip was firm as he shook my hand.

"I'm glad to know you, Herbert," I said. "Now, the fact is, Mr. Twain and I believe that the fellow inside that cabin is a victim of a false accusation, just as I was the other day. Except it's much more serious, because he's been accused of murder . . ."

Just then, I heard approaching footsteps, and I stepped away from Watts a moment. To my surprise, it was Mrs. Susan Martin, the lady whose parents had befriended Mr.

Clemens in California, who came around the nearby corner. Seeing us, she said, "Excuse me, I do believe I've gotten onto the wrong deck. Oh, hello, Mr. Cabot, how fortunate to find you here. Could you tell me the shortest way to the Grand Saloon?"

"Hello, Mrs. Martin," I said. "I'm afraid I'm a bit out of my usual territory, myself, but perhaps this crewman knows the best way."

"Yes ma'am," said Watts, doffing his cap and pointing. "You're one deck down from it, and a bit aft. You go straight along this passageway, to the second crossing, and you'll see a ladder to the port side. Go up that, go forward two doors on the starboard side, and you're there."

"Why, thank you so much," said Mrs. Martin. "I should be able to find it now, I think." She smiled brightly and turned back the way she'd come.

I waited until she had turned the corner before resuming my attempt to persuade Watts to relax his vigilance. "As I said, the gentleman inside here has been accused of murder, and Mr. Twain and I aren't sure he really did it. We'd like to find out the truth. But to do that, he and I—and another gentleman, Mr. Kipling—need to talk to him. Do you think we could have half an hour with him, undisturbed? You have my word of honor we wouldn't do anything to help him escape. You wouldn't have to leave your post or let him out of the room. The door would stay closed, and we'd make certain nobody ever learns you had any part in letting us in to see him."

Watts rubbed his chin, a doubtful look on his face. "I don't know, sir," he said slowly. "I'd find myself in 'ot water if the first mate came to 'ave a look inside, unexpected like. Gallagher's got a nasty temper, 'e as—and a right long memory. It could cost me my berth, you know."

"I doubt there's much chance of that, this late at night," I said. "You probably won't see Gallagher or anyone else until it's time for your relief—when's that, midnight?"

"Eight bells, aye. Still, it's a dreadful risk for a fellow to run."

"Maybe this will make it a little easier to run the risk," I said, reaching into my pocket and extracting a ten-dollar gold piece. I held it out for him to see.

A smile came over his face, and he reached down and took my hand, covering the eagle. "Now that could make a fellow sleep more soundly," he said. "If you've got the twin to that, I think we can strike a bargain."

"I've got the twin," I said, "and it's yours when I come back with the other two gentlemen and you let us all in the door. Do we understand each other?"

"I believe we do, Mr. Cabot," he said, with a grin. "'Erbert Watts at your service, sir!"

When I returned with news of my success at bribing the guard, there was a brief discussion as to whether we ought to go separately or in a group. Mr. Clemens argued that we ought to leave his cabin separately and take separate routes to the prince's stateroom, so as to attract the least attention.

"That won't do," said Mr. Kipling. "Unless we coordinate our movements precisely—and I doubt we three can manage that—we'll arrive at separate times. Then we either have to wait outside, or our man has to open the door three times. Either way, if anyone comes by, we're likely to arouse curiosity."

"Won't the three of us in a group arouse curiosity?" said Mr. Clemens.

Mr. Kipling laughed. "You're the one who'll arouse curiosity, if that's what you're worried about. Alone or in a group, people will remember that they saw Mark Twain—unless the others with you were Lillie Langtry and Buffalo Bill, and I fear we haven't either of them aboard. If you don't want anyone to notice what you're doing, stay here in your cabin and smoke a cigar while Cabot and I go talk to Ruckgarten."

"To hell with that," Mr. Clemens said, snorting, though I could tell that he was flattered by Mr. Kipling's allusion to his celebrity. "You're right, we might as well go in a group and let the chips fall as they may. Are we all ready?"

We were, and so we trooped down the corridor toward Prinz Karl's cabin. We did pass several passengers on the way, most of whom smiled and nodded at Mr. Clemens, who returned their greetings as if he were up to nothing out of the ordinary. Fortunately, there was no one else in sight when we turned into the last section of corridor, where Watts sat on his stool, again reading his religious book. "'Ere we are," he said, standing.

"Yes, is everything in order?" I asked, reaching in my pocket for the second gold piece.

"Aye, best we get right to it, afore somebody comes along," he said. He pocketed the coin, then knocked quickly on the door. I was at first surprised that he did not have a key, but then I remembered that the prince would have been able to unlock the door from inside, in any case. Besides, with a ship in mid-ocean, there was no reason to lock the door on a prisoner not believed to be dangerous to the rest of the passengers. Even if Prinz Karl somehow eluded or overpowered the guard, there was no place for him to escape to.

"What is it now?" came a voice from inside. "Can you not let me rest?"

"Visitors," said Mr. Clemens in a low voice. "Hurry up and let us in." There was a brief pause; then the door swung open to reveal an astonished-looking Prinz Karl wearing a dressing gown.

"Only 'alf an hour, now," whispered Watts, and we nodded our acquiescence, then quickly filed inside.

"How've they been treating you?" said Mr. Clemens, dropping into a chair without an invitation.

"I suppose it could be far worse," said the prince, with a rueful smile. "At least I have a comfortable bed, and a view of the ocean, and they have let me choose my meals from the regular bill of fare. It is not quite the same as strolling the deck or sitting in the smoking lounge with a snifter of good brandy, though."

"I don't know about brandy, but I brought along a taste of good old whisky for all of us," said Mr. Clemens, pulling a bottle out of his coat pocket. "I reckon we're both going to be talking a fair bit, and my throat will need some oiling if yours doesn't."

"We do indeed have to talk a fair bit, but we'd best not dawdle about it," said Mr. Kipling. "If Jennings or Gallagher comes to look in on our friend and finds us here, we'll all be in trouble—especially the sailor outside. The sooner we're back outside, the better for all of us."

"I agree," said Prinz Karl, who had found some glasses and passed them around. "I am sorry I have no ice, but perhaps the whisky is good enough by itself. Now, Mr. Clemens, what brings you here tonight?"

Mr. Clemens poured two fingers of whisky in his glass and passed the bottle to Prinz Karl. "Curiosity, as much as anything else. We'll want to hear your story about the night Robert Babson disappeared. But first, I reckon there's a pretty good yarn attached to your claiming to come from a place that doesn't exist. I think you were about to tell it to me before they locked you up in here, and now I'd like to hear it. I'm always interested in hearing a new story."

Prinz Karl nodded. "Yes, I suppose it is time to tell that story. But it will take a little time to tell, so first let us all fill our glasses." He sloshed a little whisky in his glass, then passed the bottle on to Mr. Kipling, who took some and passed it on to me. When all of us were served, the prince nodded, then took a position in front of the large couch, where Mr. Clemens and Mr. Kipling sat. I was in a smaller leather-covered chair to the side.

"To begin with," said the prince, "I *am* a prince. Have no doubt on that score. And, as I told you, I am a second son—my older brother is capable and well-loved by our people, and blessed with a large family. So the succession is secure, and I have no ambitions on it— which is just as well for both me and my people. I have seen enough of conspiracies and revolutions in other countries to know that no good comes of them."

"What's the name of your country?" asked Mr. Clemens. "Just for our information, of course."

"It is a small principality called Mittel Reuss," said the prince, spreading his arms as if in apology. "Look on a map near Thuringia—just south of Weimar—and just there you will find it."

"I think I went through there once," said Mr. Clemens, nodding. "Go on, then—sorry for the interruption."

"Since I have no great prospects in governing our country—there is room for only one ruler, and the Prussians dictate our policies in any case—I have sought other ways that I can provide for the welfare of my nation. You could not believe it to look at me, Herr Clemens, but I have a great interest in agriculture."

"Well, I'll grant you I never saw a farmer in a silk dressing gown before," said my employer, his eyes twinkling.

"You will not see many," said Prinz Karl. "It is rarely an easy life for those who earn their living from the land. There are many such in my country, and I have made it my mission to find ways to improve their lot. I have searched for new crops and new markets for them, and over a number of years the farmers of Mittel Reuss have begun to find their lot made easier."

"Is that what you were doing in America?" asked Mr. Kipling. "Finding new crops and markets?"

"Exactly so," said the prince. "I have been especially trying to market a new strain of hops developed in my own fields, which I have been encouraging my people to plant. There are many Germans who now live in America, as you must know, and they are as fond of their beer as their brothers at home. Well, beer is nothing more than malt and water and yeast—and hops. I found the first plants of my new breed growing in a back part of my experimental garden—thus the name Ruckgarten, for that variety. Under that name they are sold, and under that name I have traveled across America."

"So the name is advertising, not some sort of disguise," said Mr. Clemens. "I guess that makes sense, but why did you give it when you came on the boat?''

Prinz Karl hesitated the slightest moment, then said, ''You do not know what name and reputation mean when you are of royal blood. My brother the prince gives his blessing to my agricultural work—he loves to see his people rich and prosperous. But to put our family name, Holdenberg von Reuss, on a basket of hops—ah, to that he cannot lower himself. He gives his blessing, but asks that the family name be kept out of it. I may style myself a prince, I may partake of all the perquisites of my rank, when I am at home. But when I travel to sell my hops, he asks that I go under a different name. And to me that is a very small price to pay. The hops are very good— the best in the world, I think—and I am not ashamed to introduce myself under their name, if I cannot use my own.''

At several points during the prince's story, I saw Mr. Clemens and Mr. Kipling exchange significant glances— though neither of them mentioned our suspicion that Prinz Karl's claim to royalty was a ploy designed to gain him entry into the first-class society. I still was not entirely convinced of his *bona-fides*, although now that we had some details, they would be easier to check. Surely one of the library's reference books would have up-to-date information on Mittel Reuss and its ruling family. If not, a few telegrams would suffice to satisfy our curiosity, once we landed in England.

If Mr. Clemens shared my doubts, he betrayed none of them to the prince. ''I'll have to taste some of your country's beer,'' he said. ''I suppose it would be bad manners to say I'm disappointed in your story, but I will say it's a lot less exciting than I had expected. Still, that explains the name. Now, I'm afraid we have to ask some tougher questions.''

''I cannot imagine your asking me anything I have not already been asked three or four times by Lieutenant Jennings,'' said Prinz Karl, confidently. ''Ask, and I will answer you.''

Mr. Clemens swirled his whisky, staring into the glass,

before looking up and asking, "Can you account for your whereabouts after the fight you had with Babson at the concert? It would help if you could name anybody who was with you."

"Alas, much of the time I was alone—brooding over my injuries and my foolishness," said the prince. "My temper has always been my downfall, ever since I was a boy. It is one reason why I am just as glad that my brother became ruler, not I—he has far more patience than I."

"Where were you—in your cabin the whole time?"

"Part of the time in the cabin, part of the time walking the decks. I find that walking helps to calm me—especially in the bad weather. It is as if my evil mood is washed away with the rain, blown off by the wind. My thoughts were turned inward, and so I did not see whether there was anyone else with me on deck. There may have been; I simply do not know."

Mr. Clemens's brow was furrowed now. "Did you by any chance go down to the lower decks, into the steerage quarters?"

The prince seemed surprised by the question, but quickly blurted out, "No, of course not, why would I?"

"That's what I wondered," said Mr. Clemens. "Would it change your answer if I told you you had been seen down there?"

"Seen!" said the prince, backing up a step. "By whom? What did this person say?"

Mr. Kipling answered him. "One of the ship's officers saw you—it was quite probably between ten and midnight, since the fellow had heard about the fight between you and Babson, and he went off watch at twelve. You were still in your formal clothes, and he saw you enter the steerage compartments. I have no reason to doubt him. But I think you ought to know that a great deal depends on what you tell us now. If we believe in you, we'll do what we can to help you clear yourself. If we do not—well, there are plenty of other things to occupy our time."

The prince looked from one to the other of the two men facing him. Mr. Clemens lounged back casually on the couch, swirling his whisky again and looking almost uninterested in the answer. This, I knew, was deceptive—he was probably thinking at full steam, trying to come up with the next question to ask. Mr. Kipling I knew less well; but there was something of the bulldog in his posture and attitude, and I for one would have been very cautious about trying to slip an evasion or prevarication past him.

After a long moment, evidently recognizing the truth of Mr. Kipling's last statement, Prinz Karl hung his head and said, "My apologies, gentlemen. I am used to being free to do as I wish without being questioned. And as it happens, my errand down in steerage was perfectly innocent—a business matter that ought normally to be kept private, if only to protect the interests of the other party. Of course, I will ask your word to keep it thus, unless revealing it is the only way to clear my name. Then, of course, I would have no compunction against revealing it on my own."

"I think we can promise that," said Mr. Clemens, and Mr. Kipling and I indicated our assent, as well, before he continued. "What, is the price of hops a state secret these days?"

The prince favored my employer with a wry smile. "I tell you, the fate of nations has sometimes depended on matters no greater than the price of hops. As it happens, there are three men traveling on this ship, on the same errand for different breweries—two from Milwaukee, and the other from St. Louis. Their business is to bring back to America what they can of the methods and ingredients of the best German beers, so as to attract the business of the German emigrants. All three had made overtures to me concerning the Ruckgarten hops. I will gladly sell to any of them, or all of them, for it is in my people's interest to have the widest possible market for the produce of their fields."

"And one of them wants to corner the market," suggested my employer. He was still slouched comfortably on one side of the sofa, but he had put aside his drink—although there was still a full two fingers of whisky in the glass.

"I believe that is the expression, yes," said Prinz Karl. "This man—he is one of the two from Milwaukee—desires his brewery to have every advantage over his competitors. He asked me to meet him late at night, hoping to avoid the notice of his rivals. And in spite of the weather, he further insisted that we meet on the open deck, so he could be certain we were not spied on by the others."

"And was his offer satisfactory?" asked Mr. Kipling. "Did you strike a bargain?"

"No, we did not," said the prince. "Perhaps that will surprise you, but you must be aware that I have not been home to speak to the hop-growers in a year. As best I can, I keep abreast of prices and conditions, but until I have set foot in my country and spoken to the growers, I cannot set prices for them. I told the man I would let him bid on the same terms as anyone else. If he offers the best price, nobody will stop him from buying as much of the crop as he can pay for. He did not like that, but it was all I could promise without betraying my people."

"Well, good for you," said Mr. Clemens. "How long would you say you were talking with him?"

"It was perhaps half an hour," said Prinz Karl. "From the time I left the main deck until I returned, it would have been longer than that."

"And then you came and looked in the lounge," I said, remembering that I had seen him stick his head in the door, then withdraw, as if he had been looking for someone he had not found. "Why was that?"

"Yes, I did look in the door," he said. "When I came up from the lower decks I thought, for a moment, that it would be good to come in and sit by the fireplace and talk with someone friendly. And then I remembered that I was unkempt and disheveled, and wet as a drowned rat, and no fit company for the first-class passengers. I came to my room thinking to change into dry clothes and return, but when I got here, it seemed too much trouble—so I did not. There, that is the whole mystery."

"Thank you," said Mr. Clemens. He reached over and picked up his glass, began to raise it to his lips, then paused. "Now, I have one last question, and then we'll leave you alone, unless Wentworth or Kipling thinks of something to ask. Are you aware that one of the passengers claims to have seen you push Babson into the water?"

"What?" Prinz Karl's eyes were wide. "Nobody has told me this. Who is telling this lie about me?"

"It doesn't matter, at the moment," said Mr. Clemens. "Did you see anyone on the steerage deck, or did anyone see you, when you were discussing the price of hops with the man from Milwaukee?"

"I do not think so," said Prinz Karl, a troubled look around his eyes. "We made a special point of trying to find a private spot—the man was very concerned that his rivals not know we were talking."

"Could you tell us this man's name?" suggested Mr. Kipling. "Then, at least, we could verify your whereabouts for part of the evening, and possibly that would clear you."

Prinz Karl paced a few steps, his hands clasped behind his back. "I suppose it is necessary," he said. "The poor man will not be happy when he learns that I have told his name—if his rivals learn what he has done, they will try to shut him out of the market, and all his secrecy will have been for nothing. But I suppose he will understand if he knows it is to save me from a criminal charge. He is Dietrich Lehrmann, of Milwaukee—you will find him traveling in steerage."

"I am surprised you haven't been confronted with the supposed eyewitness's testimony," said Mr. Kipling. "Have they interrogated you so little?"

The prince ventured a weak smile. "Not a great deal—I have resolutely asserted my innocence, and pointed out that I am an important person in my own country. I have also shown them a passport and letters of introduction bearing names and titles that have made them cautious of questioning me with too much vigor. Of course, if they think they have a trustworthy eyewitness, that may change. But I tell you that anyone who claims to have seen me kill that odious boy is lying. I had planned much subtler ways of taking my revenge—think of what the baggage handlers at Southhampton might be able to accomplish, given a small inducement. Or a properly motivated passport inspector . . .''

"I can imagine," said Mr. Clemens. "Well, boys, do you think we've heard enough? Shall we . . .''

Whatever he was going to say, he was cut off by a loud knock on the stateroom door.

"**Y**ou'd better answer the door," Mr. Clemens said quietly, nodding to the prince. "Is there someplace we can hide?"

"Over there," said Prinz Karl in a hoarse whisper, indicating a doorway covered by a curtain. Carrying our whisky glasses, and the prince's, Mr. Clemens, Mr. Kipling, and I scurried over to the doorway as noiselessly as possible. Meanwhile, the prince walked toward the cabin door, from which a repeated knocking came. "Yes, who is there?" he said, without opening it.

"Mr. Jennings," came the muffled answer. "Please open the door. I need to speak to you."

"Hellfire and damnation," muttered Mr. Clemens, as we went through the curtain into an adjoining room. We found ourselves in the sleeping portion of the prince's suite, with a brass bed, a wooden wardrobe with a mirror on the front, and a dressing table upon which there were a comb, a brush, and other toilet articles. Mr. Kipling and Mr. Clemens quickly sat on the bed, and I took the small chair in front of the dressing table, trying my best not to stumble in the dark over the prince's shoes.

Outside, I heard the prince say, "Can you come back in the morning?"

"Captain's orders," I heard faintly from outside. "He wants to get this investigation finished with."

"Aha, so maybe the old scoundrel wasn't stalling me after all," said Mr. Clemens, but Mr. Kipling shushed him as we heard the opening of the corridor door, and the sound of several pairs of feet entering. I wondered who Jennings had brought with him, but didn't dare look. Perhaps I could identify them from the voices.

Prinz Karl saved me the trouble. "Mr. Jennings, I hope you will not take long. I was just preparing for sleep. Good evening, Mr. Babson. Signor Rubbia, what is your part in this sorry business?"

"We'll ask the questions," said Mr. Babson, with a nasty edge to his voice.

"Ask, then," said the prince. "Please feel free to take a seat; but I hope you will pardon me if I do not offer you a drink."

"It would take more than a drink to buy a pardon for the likes of you," said Babson.

"Then I am glad I did not waste my time offering it to you," said the prince icily.

"Please, gentlemen," said Jennings. "Let's stick to our business. This investigation is unpleasant for all of us; we don't have to make it any worse than it is. Signor Rubbia, will you be so kind as to repeat the story you told me earlier today?"

"It is no story," said the painter, whose distinctive accent would have identified him to us even if no one had mentioned his name. "It is what I saw. It is the truth."

"Please tell us, if you don't mind," said Jennings again, patience wearing thin in his voice. I did not envy him as he tried to mediate among these prickly personalities.

"Yes, of course. Wednesday evening, you remember that was a very bad stormy night, I was restless, not able to sleep. I thought the fresh air would do me some good, just to walk outside a little bit. The stormy weather, it inspires me—it is the raging passions of nature that echo the power of the human soul. I knew it would raise up my spirits."

"What time was this?" asked Jennings.

"I don't know—after the music."

"Didn't you look at a watch?" asked Mr. Babson.

I could almost hear Rubbia stiffen with scorn. "A watch—I do not need such a thing. I am an artist, I do not work by the clock but by my own genius!"

"On this man's testimony you mean to condemn me?" said Prinz Karl sarcastically. "Take me to the gallows now—I have no hope to clear myself!"

Jennings interrupted, again in a consoling tone. "Now, now, let the gentleman tell his story—you should hear it all before you rebut him. Would you go on, please, Singor Rubbia?"

"I go out on the deck, on the left side of the boat, near the middle. The rain is heavy, but with my cloak and my hat it does not bother me. Still, I think the wind will not be so bad if I go more to the back of the boat."

"So you walked along the portside to the stern," said Jennings.

"Yes, is that not what I said? I come close to another door, and I am thinking perhaps I will go back inside after all, when I realize there is someone else outside. It is the Babson boy—your son, Mr. Babson. He acts as if he is sick, maybe from the rough waves, maybe from the drink."

"It must have been the sea," said Mr. Babson, though not with a great deal of conviction.

"Whatever the case, he is by the rail, leaning over the side. I say nothing, for fear of disturbing him, and besides, there was a little shelter here, so I thought I would wait until he left to go past him to the doorway. So I stood there a short while and waited."

"How far were you from him?" asked Jennings.

"Twenty feet, perhaps," said Rubbia, after a brief pause. "Not very far. While I stood there, I realized there was another person on deck—hiding in the shadow of the doorway behind the boy. I do not think he saw me."

"Did you see who the person was?" asked Mr. Babson.

"Not at first, but then my eyes became accustomed to

the dark, and I could see that it was this man here—this Ruckgarten, who calls himself a prince.''

"I *am* a prince, you ignorant man. And you cannot have seen me on that deck, because I was not there that night.''

"Please, gentlemen, let us not interrupt each other. We need to hear Signor Rubbia, and then you can respond to what he says.'' Jennings sounded exasperated, perhaps understandably. I wished I could see the faces of the arguing parties.

"All of the sudden, before I understood what was happening, this man rushes forward and strikes young Mr. Robert on the back of the head. The boy, he tries to defend himself, but he is sick, and Ruckgarten gives him no chance. He pushes him back like a sack of grain, with one hand on the boy's throat. I am ready to cry out, but then I realize that nobody would hear me in the storm. I know I am not strong enough to help, but I step forward in hope that I could give the boy a chance to escape. But I was too late already. Ruckgarten pushed him over the rail, and he fell into the water with a terrible cry.''

"What happened then?'' said Jennings. "Where did Ruckgarten go?''

"I went nowhere, because I was not there to begin with,'' said the prince angrily. "This is nothing but lies—can you not see that?''

"Of course he's going to say that,'' said Mr. Babson. "The man has no conscience, no shame.''

"I have more shame than you, sir,'' said the prince haughtily. "I at least do not go around the world blaming others for the things that go against my wishes. Your son was probably too drunk to keep his balance on the slippery deck. For all I know, he was so drunk that he leapt overboard on his own accord.''

"Aha!'' cried Babson. "And if you were not there, how do you know the deck was slippery?''

The prince snorted. "I did not go in the water either, but I know it was wet and cold. Do you take me for a child?''

"Did you or did you not push Robert Babson into the water?" said Mr. Jennings.

"I did not, and I never would have. He provoked me, but I know better than to return violence for violence. That is a peasant's kind of revenge. I have better ways to let a man know he has made a mistake. This time, I am almost sorry I will not have the chance to put them into practice."

Mr. Babson pounced on this statement like a hawk. "So you admit that you had a grudge against my son."

"Yes, so did many on this ship. This lying artist, for one. How do I know he did not push the boy overboard himself, then try to blame it on me?"

"It is you who are the liar, and a murderer besides," shouted Rubbia.

Suddenly I heard the scuffling of feet, and Jennings shouted, "Grab him, Gallagher!"

There was a noise of someone bumping into some large piece of furniture, and then Rubbia said, "Let me go—I will teach him not to speak so rudely."

"Gentlemen, that's quite enough," said Jennings. Then, after a pause which I was forced to fill with my imagination he went on. "I'm afraid we've gotten as far as we're likely to tonight. Let's go quietly, now. Mr. Ruckgarten, I am afraid we will have to bring these matters up again; I'll be talking to you and to Signor Rubbia again. I am not sure whether we have learned anything useful here tonight or not."

"Perhaps you have not, but I have, much to my sorrow," said the prince.

"Oh?" said Jennings. "And what is that, sir?"

"I have learned not to turn my back to this little coward. I would advise you to watch him carefully, Mr. Babson, Mr. Jennings. If he has betrayed one person, he will not hesitate to do it to another—perhaps one of you will be next. I hope that you two gentlemen will put him to the question as carefully as you have me. Then you will begin to hear a different story, and I will be a free man again. Now, perhaps it is best that you all go."

Rubbia said something vicious-sounding in Italian, and Gallagher cursed, evidently doing his best to restrain the artist; then Jennings said, "Get him out of here, men," and after a brief interval we heard the door close, followed by a burst of light as Prinz Karl threw back the curtain that had concealed us from his visitors, and turned on the electric light.

"I do not think I would have chosen this sort of entertainment for you gentlemen," said the prince, in an unsteady voice. "Still, perhaps you found it more diverting than I did." He was putting up a brave front, trying to cover up his anxiety with witty words, but it was clear to me that he was shaken by Rubbia's accusation—which, despite the prince's denials, seemed damning.

"It can't have been very diverting to a man who still claims to be innocent," said Mr. Clemens, rising to his feet. He handed the prince's whisky glass back to him. "Drink up—I'd say you need it, just now. I don't know about England, but American juries are likely to put a lot of faith in eyewitnesses."

The prince sat heavily on the bed, in the place just vacated by Mr. Clemens, and drained his glass in two large gulps before answering. "I cannot understand it. My dear God, I do not understand it. I swear to you gentlemen, on my honor as a prince, that I did not kill that boy. I thought I could end this charade very easily by sending a few telegrams, once we landed in England. I have very powerful friends and relatives. But with an eyewitness—even a lying one—you are right, this will not be easy anymore." He covered his face with his hands.

"Why do you think Rubbia is lying about you?" asked Mr. Clemens, squinting a little in the light. His voice was gentle, but even I could detect an edge of doubt in it.

"I cannot guess," said the prince, looking up with a worried expression. "I admit I made a few rough jokes against him, but I did nothing to deserve these lies. They must be paying him to say these terrible things."

"Who are *they*?" asked Mr. Kipling. "If you had enemies on board, surely you know who they are."

The prince shook his head. "I do not know of any—that does not mean there are none. I do not think that any of the commercial travelers would do such a thing. But a man in my station of life has many who hate him just because of his family. These are not good times to be of royal blood."

"Don't give up hope yet," said Mr. Clemens. "The cards may be stacked against you, but if we can find some way to put the game back on the level, we'll do it. It seems to me our two best chances for undercutting Rubbia are either to prove he was somewhere else all night, or to prove somebody besides you murdered Babson. We've still got some poking around to do in a few dark corners, but maybe we can find enough to prove you're innocent, Prinz Karl. And on that note, I think we'll take our leave. We have some plans to make and some work to do, and time's the thing we have the least of. Would you like me to fill up that glass again before we leave?"

"No, but I thank you," said the prince. "I need my own wits about me, I think." He stood and led the three of us out to the door.

I opened the cabin door a crack, and Herbert Watts turned to look at me, his face white as a sheet. "Lord!" he said, as we stepped out into the corridor. "I was sure Gallagher 'ad caught the three of you dead to rights, and me along with you. I've been shiverin' in my boots the 'ole time you were in there—'ow'd you give 'im the slip?"

"We ducked into the bedroom and closed the curtain. They didn't expect us, so they didn't search for us," said Mr. Kipling, reaching in his pocket. "It must have been quite a scare for you, though. Here's a little something extra to ease your nerves."

"Bless you, guv'nor," said Watts, touching his hand to his cap. "I've been sittin' and worryin' what I'd say

when they found you, and never findin' a good answer,
but this makes up for it all.''

Back in Mr. Clemens's cabin, my employer filled his
pipe and poured himself another glass of whisky, then
stretched out on the sofa. ''Well, I don't know about you
boys, but I had a couple of mighty uncomfortable moments back there in the prince's bedroom. At least, in
the theater, you can smoke a cigar while you're sitting
in the dark waiting for something to happen.''

''Yes, and they give you a bit of music besides,'' said
Mr. Kipling dryly. ''Who do you think's the bigger liar,
the prince or Rubbia?''

''Oh, the prince—he must outweigh him thirty
pounds,'' said Mr. Clemens. ''Still, that story about
meeting the fellow on the open deck in a howling storm
to talk about the price of hops is just dull and unbeliev-
able enough to be true—though I wouldn't be surprised
if the prince is holding part of the story back on us. I
suppose we'll have to go find the brewery man and ask
him, just to confirm the alibi, but I doubt we'll get any
closer to the truth than we already are.''

Mr. Kipling peered at my employer over his glasses.
''I think we can get pretty close without bothering to
cross-examine the brewery agent too carefully—what
was his name? Lehrmann? Remember what I told you
when Cabot here told us about his friend's wild notion
of spies aboard the ship?''

''Oh, bosh,'' said Mr. Clemens, in an annoyed tone.
''You don't take that seriously, do you?''

Mr. Kipling spread his hands. ''Why not? As Ruckgarten himself pointed out, there are lots of Germans in
America—and I'll wager most of them have family back
home. Some of them must be unhappy with the way the
Prussians have intervened in the affairs of formerly sov-
ereign states. I'd be very surprised if Ruckgarten couldn't
find sympathetic supporters among the Germans in
America.''

''Supporters for *what*?'' Mr. Clemens frowned.

"That's the part it would be interesting to know, though I doubt we ever will," said Mr. Kipling. He took a sip of his drink, then continued. "If we had the time and resources to follow it up, perhaps we'd learn something of interest—for example, whether Rubbia is an agent for any foreign government. I doubt he's everything he claims to be."

"You can go to the bank on that," said Mr. Clemens dryly. "He's barely an artist, and I doubt he's spoken three true sentences since he's come aboard the ship. That story of his stinks like a week-old mud cat."

I could not let this gibe pass. "Really, Mr. Clemens, I don't see how you can summarily dismiss everything Signor Rubbia says. As you yourself said, his eyewitness testimony is likely to carry heavy weight in court. I would be disappointed if you rejected it simply because of a personal dislike of the man, or a fondness for the man you think he's slandering. Even before I heard Signor Rubbia's account, I found Prinz Karl's alibi quite unconvincing. Besides, I must say that whatever you may think of Signor Rubbia's theories, he *is* a very talented artist. I have seen his drawings, and they are quite good."

Mr. Clemens was about to answer when Mr. Kipling cut him off. "Cabot has a point, you know," he said. "Ruckgarten's admitted telling us at least one lie, about his country of origin, and he may have told more. And Rubbia's story is not, on the face of it, as preposterous as Ruckgarten's tale of a midnight meeting in a howling gale to talk about the price of hops. The question is really whose story we're going to trust. What in Rubbia's story is so obviously false?"

Mr. Clemens stood for a moment, saying nothing, then nodded. "All right, you both have a point, men. I reckon I'm willing to accept the prince's alibi because it's so damn weak that it only makes sense if we assume it's true. If he was really trying to cover up a murder, he wouldn't offer such a preposterous fabrication. So it must be mainly true—and maybe it's even verifiable."

"Well, in that case, I suppose we should make an effort to find this Mr. Lehrmann,'' I said. "I'll get word to the Yale boys to search him out and see what he says. Maybe they can find somebody else who saw the prince down there, too. That'll at least give us a check on his story.''

"That would help," said Mr. Clemens. "But even if the prince is telling the truth, it only gives him an alibi for part of the evening. Babson's bound to point out that he could have been exactly where he said, when he said, and still have had ample time to walk up to the top deck and shove the boy overboard. We have to refute Rubbia's entire story, if we're going to get to the bottom of things. The only question is how we start.''

"The easiest way would be to prove he couldn't have seen what he said he did, because it didn't happen when he said it did," I suggested. "I wish we had a better idea of when the murder supposedly happened."

"Without a body or another witness, that's unlikely," said Mr. Clemens. "But that gives me another idea. Why don't we take a look at the supposed scene of the crime? I'm in the mood for a bit of a walk, anyway, and unless we get another storm, this is as close as we'll ever get to the right conditions.''

Mr. Kipling gave a groan. "I suppose it makes sense, though I've spent quite enough time in the dark this evening. At least we can walk around out there without worrying whether anyone will arrest us if we sneeze, or care what business we have there.''

"Oh, they may very well care," said Mr. Clemens. "If somebody else *did* kill Robert Babson, they'd be very unhappy that we haven't swallowed the idea that the prince did it after the fight. But of course, they have no way of knowing what we think—or why we're out on deck, taking a late-night stroll.''

"Late-night is right," said Mr. Kipling, taking his watch out of his pocket and looking at it. I checked my own and saw that it was nearly eleven o'clock. "We'd best get to it before it becomes early morning.''

* * *

We stepped out onto the port deck just aft of the first-class dining room. The gibbous moon I'd noticed earlier was now high above the southern horizon, and the night was clear but cool. Earlier, I had seen little reflections off the distant waves; but the port side of the eastbound ship faced north, and so was shadowed from the direct light of the moon. On an overcast night, the deck where we now were would have been only faintly illuminated by the onboard electric lights.

"Do you think this is where Rubbia came on deck?" said Mr. Kipling in a quiet voice.

"I reckon it's close enough," said Mr. Clemens. "If the story's true to begin with, this is about the right place; then he'd have gone aft." He stepped over to the rail and looked down at the waves. There was a chill in the air, and I wondered for a moment whether I should have brought my topcoat with me. But I doubted we would be outside for long; as much as my employer might be curious to see the scene of the crime, he was also fond of his comfort.

After a long pause, Mr. Clemens blew a puff of pipe smoke, then turned to us and said, "Well, let's go see if we can find the place he says it happened. Maybe the criminal has returned to the scene of the crime, and we can arrest him right there."

"That assumes a number of things, all highly improbable," said Mr. Kipling. He tucked his hands under his armpits, shivering. "By Allah, it's cold out here. Do you really need me for this, Clemens?"

Mr. Clemens clapped him on the shoulder. "Hell, if you get right down to it, I probably don't need to be out here, either. I just want a quick look at the place, to see if I spot anything that don't jibe with Rubbia's story. Go on back inside, Kipling. Tell you what—Wentworth and I will take a look, then we'll meet you down in the smoking lounge. I doubt we'll find enough to keep us more than fifteen minutes."

"Very well," said Mr. Kipling, returning the clap on the shoulder. "I'll save a couple of chairs by the fire for you lads.'' He turned and went back inside, and Mr. Clemens pointed toward the stern of the ship. I nodded and followed him.

After a few steps, Mr. Clemens stopped and said, "Here, Cabot, why don't you hang back a moment while I walk on ahead. I want to get an idea how far away you can really recognize somebody in this light. Let me get a twenty or thirty yards' lead, then follow me—I'll wait for you when I think I'm at the right spot."

"Certainly," I said, and waited while he stepped out ahead of me, walking more briskly than was his wont, doubtless on account of the cold. As he walked, I tried to match Signor Rubbia's description of the place where the murder took place with the scene in front of me. This section of the deck, at least, did not seem quite right. Several of the tall ventilating funnels were situated here, which I was sure the artist would have mentioned had they been part of the scene. They would have provided ideal concealment for an observer—or the murderer, if in fact there was any such person aboard.

When I judged that Mr. Clemens had gotten far enough ahead, I began to follow him. He was still clearly visible because of his white suit, a detail that to some extent invalidated his idea of testing the light. I would have recognized from him half the length of the ship, let alone a couple of dozen yards. Perhaps we would get a better test of the visibility when he stopped and looked back to see me.

We were at a point where the deck ran nearly straight for a good distance, with the rail to our right and the superstructure of the ship to our left. Doorways led into the ship at intervals, and the ventilating funnels stuck up from the deck, looking much like abandoned tubas. I was still trying to identify the place where Signor Rubbia claimed to have witnessed the murder, when I realized that Mr. Clemens had stopped. He was bending over a large dark object on the deck, and I barely had time to wonder what it was when I saw a sudden movement in the shadows.

Mr. Clemens was aware of it too, for he straightened and began to turn, just as a dark-clad human form emerged and launched itself in his direction without a word. My employer took a step backward and threw up an arm to ward off the charge, but he was too late to avoid the impact. He fell back against the rail, shouting "Wentworth! Help!" The attacker raised an arm and struck at Mr. Clemens's head, but he warded it off with his forearm. I was already running, but my feet seemed to be glued to the deck as I saw the mysterious attacker again raise his arm to strike my employer, who was pinned against the rail, trying to fend off the blow.

As I ran, I realized that the dark object Mr. Clemens had stopped to look at was a human body, lying inert upon the deck.

The attacker must have heard my footsteps, for he turned and glanced at me. With a muffled oath, he broke away from my employer and began to flee toward the stern of the ship. I picked up my speed, hoping to catch him before he escaped. For a brief moment the thought flashed through my head: *What if he has a weapon?* But it was already too late to worry about that.

The body—was it dead or alive?—lay directly in my path, and my instinct told me to hurdle it, exactly as I had jumped over fallen opponents on the football field. I cleared it with plenty to spare, but I hadn't reckoned with the effect of the ocean spray on the deck; when I landed, my foot slid out from under me, and I came down heavily on my back. I struggled to my feet, but by then the fleeing assailant had disappeared and Mr. Clemens was at my side.

"Jesus, that was close. Are you all right, Wentworth?" he said, taking my arm.

"I'm not hurt, just winded," I said, turning to look at him. "What about you?"

"A bit shook up, but better than that poor fellow there," he said, pointing to the still figure on the deck. "It's Rubbia; I think he's dead."

26 ⌐

"You say you didn't recognize the man who attacked you?" said Captain Mortimer. He sat behind a fine hardwood desk that would have been the envy of many an office on dry land, but his manner suggested that he would have been just as comfortable with an upended barrelhead to write on. Behind him, Mr. Jennings stood at attention. Mr. Clemens and I were in comfortable chairs in front of the desk, although neither of us was exactly comfortable. My ankle felt as if I'd twisted it, and Mr. Clemens was holding his left arm in a gingerly position. We'd both have a few bruises to show for our excursion on deck tonight. Mr. Kipling, whom we'd asked the captain to include in our conference, stood behind us.

"I wouldn't recognize the no-good son of a yeller dog if he was sitting right next to me," said Mr. Clemens, gesturing in my general direction. "It was too damn dark and it all happened too damn fast. The best I can say was that he was dressed in rough clothing—more what I'd expect a crewman or a steerage passenger to wear than somebody from this deck. Did you get a good look at him, Cabot?"

"Not really," I said, trying to remember the few details I had managed to make out in the dim light. "By the time I got close enough to see anything, he had already turned and started to run, so I never really saw his face. All I can say for sure is that he was a little above average height.''

Mr. Clemens nodded. ''Yes, about my height, I'd say, and built like a man used to hard labor.'' He rubbed his forearm where he'd intercepted a blow. ''At least, this shoots Rubbia's story all to hell. He claimed to recognize Prinz Karl from twenty feet away, in worse conditions than we had tonight.''

''Not necessarily,'' said the captain. ''You were caught by surprise, more concerned with defending yourself than with seeing who was attacking you. And Rubbia is an artist—seeing things accurately is as natural to him as running a ship is to me. But I take your point. Frankly, I'd just as soon Signor Rubbia were here to argue it with you.'' Rubbia had been stuck a powerful blow to the temple, according to the ship's doctor. He was alive, but in very serious condition; the doctor could not swear that he would last the night. We must have come upon him within moments of the attack—before the assailant could throw his victim over the side, as we assumed he had meant to do before Mr. Clemens and I interrupted him. Now he was lying in the ship's infirmary, with a man stationed at his side in case he said anything to help us learn who had attacked him—and to protect him, in case his attacker returned to finish what he'd begun.

''Amen to that,'' said Mr. Clemens. ''He could have been ten times the charlatan he is, and he still wouldn't deserve to be knocked on the head and dumped overboard—which I suspect the son of a bitch who attacked him would have done if he'd been able to lift him a bit easier. But we can do what we can to see that the killer comes to justice.''

''You call him a killer—do you really think it's the same person who murdered Robert Babson?'' I asked.

''That's the way to bet,'' said Mr. Clemens, grimacing. He turned to the captain and leaned forward. ''By the way, Captain, I'd think this attack tonight puts an end to any need to keep Prinz Karl locked up like a felon.''

''I suppose you're right, Mr. Clemens,'' said the captain. He closed his eyes and massaged the bridge of his nose with his right thumb and forefinger for a moment, then looked at my employer again. "As a practical matter, I would be unhappy if he were to insert himself too much into the public view. Mr. Babson is still very bitter toward him, and the others of the Philadelphia party appear to share the father's animosity. Prinz Karl's confrontations with young Babson still rankle, I fear. He and Signor Rubbia were not on the best of terms, either—if the prince had not been confined to his cabin, I would consider him a prime suspect in tonight's business."

"There's no way he could have gotten out, I assume," said Mr. Clemens.

"Not likely," said Jennings. "I was in that cabin questioning him not twenty minutes before the attack, confronting him with Signor Rubbia's testimony as per the captain's orders. The first mate and Mr. Babson were right there with me. And there was a good stout lad guarding the door the whole time before and after."

No sooner had these words left Jennings's mouth than I was aware that the prince could very easily have gotten out—exactly the way Mr. Clemens and I had gotten in, by bribing the seaman placed to guard his door. It seemed impolitic to mention this, unless Mr. Clemens saw fit to volunteer the information, which he showed no sign of doing. In any case, the man we'd seen on deck bore no resemblance to the prince, so that line of inquiry was not likely to bear fruit.

"Let's try another angle," said Mr. Clemens, before I could pursue the thought further. "Assume that Rubbia really did know something about what happened to Robert Babson. Maybe he was trying to blackmail the real killer, and got himself in more trouble than he could handle. Who had enough of a grudge against Robert Babson to push him overboard, and enough money to make it worth Rubbia's while to blackmail him?"

"Half the ship, on the first count," said Mr. Kipling, speaking for the first time since he'd come to the captain's office. "It's the second half of the proposition I can't make any sense of. If the blackguard who attacked you tonight was the one who killed Babson, he doesn't sound a very promising target for extortion.''

"Unless he was in disguise,'' I suggested. "If he went there intending to kill Rubbia, he might have taken pains not to be recognized in case anyone saw him.''

"I'd think a fellow dressed in rough clothes on the first-class deck would draw attention, disguise or no disguise,'' said the captain. "One of the stewards or officers would have stopped him for questioning, and I think I'd have heard about it.'' He furrowed his brow and looked at Mr. Jennings.

"I'll ask my men if anyone remembers such a fellow,'' said Jennings. "I've got them searching the ship right now, though I fear there's not much for them to find.''

"I fear you're right,'' said Mr. Clemens, rising to his feet. "Captain, I appreciate your efforts, and I'll be glad to make myself available to answer any questions you or your officers may have. But unless you need something more from me right now, I fear these old bones have taken more of a licking than they're used to. I'm going to go crawl into my bunk and give 'em a chance to recover.''

"I think we can let you and your secretary go for now,'' said the captain, standing in his own turn. "Again, I apologize that something like this could happen aboard my ship. I'd be glad to send the doctor to your cabin, if you need your injuries looked at more closely.''

"The offer's much appreciated,'' said my employer. "If a stiff drink of whisky and a good night's sleep don't fix me up, I'll go see him in the morning. Until then, good luck with your search for the killer. I'll rest easier once I know the fellow's properly locked away.''

"I'll rest even easier once he's hanged,'' said Mr. Kipling, and on that cheerful note we filed out of the captain's office and headed back to my employer's cabin.

As I had expected, Mr. Clemens had no intention of going directly to bed. Instead, he sent out for some ice, wrapped it in a towel (after reserving a fair share for drinks), and applied it to his bruises. I did the same to my sore ankle, as I'd done more than once after a football game. Then he, Mr. Kipling, and I buckled down to analyzing what we had learned in Prinz Karl's cabin—and the surprising turn of events after we had left.

"We need to look at the timing of events," said Mr. Kipling. "Rubbia couldn't have known how long he was going to be in Ruckgarten's cabin. And I can't imagine he'd have gone out on deck on a night like tonight unless he was meeting someone by appointment. Surely the fellow didn't skulk about in dark clothes all evening, waiting for Rubbia—at least not without the deck watch noticing him."

"Yes, the captain implied as much," said Mr. Clemens. "But I can think of an explanation for it. Suppose he was someone who wouldn't attract any particular notice, because he belonged there?"

"Do you mean a crew member?" I asked.

"Bull's-eye," said Mr. Clemens, pointing at me. "Possibly even the deck watch himself—after all, that's the only person we can prove was on deck the night Babson died."

"I disagree," said Mr. Kipling. He was leaning against the bulkhead, next to the porthole. Now the moon was high in the sky, and it cast a lovely light through the glass. "It's an attractive theory, on the face of it, but the last thing the steamship company wants the first-class passengers to see is a bunch of rough-looking stokers and swabbers loitering about the decks at night. The deck watch on the first-class decks would most likely be an officer, wearing a proper uniform. And if the watch saw one of the black gang up on the top decks, it *would* attract his attention—and it would be the first thing he'd remember, if there'd been an incident of any sort on deck."

"I reckon that makes sense," said Mr. Clemens, swirling the whisky and soda I'd poured him when we arrived in the cabin. "So that takes us back to the idea that Rubbia somehow made arrangements to meet the fellow after he'd gone to accuse Prinz Karl. You fellows were there listening the whole time. You heard the same things I did, unless my ears are going bad on me. What did he say—for that matter, what did *anybody* say—that would be cause for somebody to invite him out on deck and try to murder him afterwards?''

I thought for a moment, trying to recall the details of the conversation, but it was Mr. Kipling who answered. "Nothing I can think of. But I say we should press forward, nonetheless. Unless we learn that the prince is guilty, it can't hurt anyone if we do what we can to clear him—and I'm convinced that's what we ought to be doing now.''

Mr. Clemens nodded. "Right. So we're back where we started. I think the murder and tonight's attempt on Rubbia are related. And if I'm right on that, it means the killer is one of the Philadelphia crowd—I can't see how Rubbia would have been of much interest to anybody else.''

"Don't be so certain," said Mr. Kipling. "If he did see the murder, he'd be of great interest to the murderer—especially if Rubbia threatened to expose the fellow unless he was paid off. Blackmail is a very dangerous occupation.''

"Can't be as precarious as journalism," said Mr. Clemens. "I remember when I edited a Tennessee newspaper—but that's a story for another time. Let's talk about the Philadelphians for now. All my instincts say he was killed by somebody who knew him before they came aboard the ship. Granted, I could be wrong—but let's identify the most likely suspects before we go further afield.''

"Very well," I said, cupping my chin in my hand. "The jilted suitor, Wilfred Smythe, would have to be on the list. I can't see him as very likely—he was quite candid about how Bobby abused him, and I don't think a murderer would have been so willing to draw suspicion to himself. But he certainly had all the reason anyone could ask to murder Babson.''

"Yes, he's got to be a suspect," said Mr. Clemens. "What about the fellows Babson gambled with? Do you think any of them were anxious to get their money?"

"Perhaps, but they must have known they weren't going to get it if he was dead."

Mr. Clemens waved his hand impatiently. "That goes without saying—playing whist for high stakes is evidence for a dearth of common sense, but I reckon even a damn fool can figure out that a dead man ain't going to cough up his gambling losses. Now, if they were professional gamblers who wanted to scare the other deadbeats into paying up . . . but no, I don't make out any of those boys he was playing with to be card sharps. What I'm fishing for, I guess, is whether any of them were so anxious to collect that they might have confronted him about it, and maybe given him a shove that caused him to lose his balance."

"I didn't get that impression when I talked to them," I said. "Most of them spoke of him as a capital fellow— a real friend. They seemed to believe that when he married Tess Mercer he'd come into enough money to cover all his debts."

"They're worse fools than I'd thought, then," said Mr. Clemens. "Old man Mercer didn't get as rich as he is by throwing his money away—I'll lay you ten to one he'd knock down his grandmother if she was standing in between him and a loose nickel."

Mr. Kipling guffawed. "Your respect for the rich and powerful has no parallel, Clemens. You'd never be happy as an Englishman, I fear."

"I note that you make your home in Vermont, Kipling," said Mr. Clemens. "But we could jaw about that all day long—let's get back to the murder. Who else could have shoved Babson over the rail? Who had the motive?"

"Easier to list the ones who didn't," said Kipling. He gave a derisive snort. "He bullied the waiters and bartenders, cursed the crew, and insulted most of his fellow passengers. If Rubbia hadn't been attacked tonight, I'd have him as a prime suspect—especially since he tried to blame someone else for it. Even Cabot had a run-in with young Babson.''

''Yes, of course,'' I said. ''Our problem is really that we have too many suspects. And from what we conjecture of the way Babson must have died, several of them would have had the opportunity to kill him—and the means. If he was drunk enough, it wouldn't have taken much strength to push him over the rail. It could have been half an accident—an argument that came to a hard shove, with Babson losing his balance and going over. It doesn't need to be a hardened criminal we're looking for. Anyone who got angry enough or drunk enough could have taken a punch at Babson. Unfortunately, that's most of the men aboard.''

Mr. Kipling disagreed. ''The attempt to kill Rubbia would seem to rule that out, don't you think?''

''Yes, that's the one detail that alters the whole case,'' said Mr. Clemens. He carried the ice-filled towel over to the washstand and wrung out the water that had begun to collect. ''I think Rubbia had something on somebody— or at least, somebody thought he did. So Babson's killing had to be more than an accident. Rubbia's story may have been half true—but with the prince substituted for the real killer. I think he was protecting somebody from murder charges by accusing the prince. So the question is, Who stood to gain the most from Babson's death—and whom could Rubbia most effectively blackmail?''

''Those are good questions,'' said Mr. Kipling. ''But set them aside one moment—let's think a little more about the timing of things tonight. Rubbia came to Ruckgarten's stateroom and accused him of murder—not entirely convincingly, I think. But Ruckgarten didn't really refute him, either. Then, shortly after, Rubbia goes out on deck where someone meets him and tries to beat the life out of him. When did he make the appointment, and with whom? Or was it a chance meeting?''

''Or perhaps the killer followed him,'' I suggested. ''Suppose Rubbia made a habit of walking on deck every

night. Then all we need to postulate is someone familiar
with his habits who lay in wait for him.''

''No,'' said Mr. Clemens. ''Rubbia said that he walked
on the deck the night he saw Babson killed because he
had insomnia. Remember his drivel about the stormy passions of the soul? He was lucky I didn't come out of the
bedroom and whack him on the head myself. So I think
Kipling's right—it wasn't just something Rubbia did regularly. He was out there tonight to meet somebody. The
same man who attacked me, unless I miss my guess.''

''Whom neither of you saw close enough to identify,''
said Mr. Kipling. He leaned back against the bulkhead,
just to the right of the porthole, his hands gripping the
lapels of his jacket. ''A pity, really. If you had caught
him—or even just recognized him, it would solve the
whole affair without any further trouble.''

''Yes, what a shame it isn't that easy,'' said Mr. Clemens. ''I think the person he met must have been somebody who was in that room.'' He slapped his hand on
the arm of his chair. ''Who else could have known what
he'd been saying, and been in a position to arrange a
meeting on such short notice?''

''By Allah, you may be right,'' said Mr. Kipling, his
eyes lighting up.

''But that doesn't solve the whole puzzle,'' said my
employer. ''I'll swear on a stack of Bibles the fellow who
jumped me wasn't old man Babson, or Jennings, or even
the first mate. Who the hell else was there?''

''There had to be at least one more person,'' I said.
''Probably a crewman. Remember when Rubbia lost his
temper at the end, Mr. Jennings said something like *Get
him out of here, men*? He wouldn't have been giving Mr.
Babson orders. So there was somebody else we didn't
hear. I'm almost certain of it.''

''Could it have been the fellow guarding the door?''
suggested Mr. Kipling. ''They might have brought him
in with them, since there was no real need to keep an
eye on the door with Jennings and Gallagher inside.''

''I suppose so,'' I said. ''But that wasn't the man who

attacked us on deck. Watts is close to my height, and the fellow we saw was much shorter.''

"Wentworth is right," said Mr. Clemens, rubbing his bruised arm. "The bastard who came after me was strong as a bull, but he was no taller than five eight or nine. So who does that leave?"

"Suppose somebody in the room was in league with the killer?" I suggested. "He might have gone straight to him with word of what went on, and then the killer might have gone to find Rubbia."

"That's too tricky," said Mr. Kipling, shaking his head. "It assumes the fellow could find the killer right away, and then that the killer knew where to find Rubbia—and just who is this mysterious fellow who pops up out of nowhere to kill Babson and attack Rubbia?"

"There's our question, isn't it?" said Mr. Clemens. "I have an idea. Wentworth, if you aren't too worn out yet, I'd like you to go back down to the corridor outside the prince's room and see if Herbert Watts is still on duty. I'd guess he gets off sometime around midnight. If so, I want you to ask him to come visit us here. If there's anybody who can tell us who all was in that room, I guess it's him.''

I rose to my feet, somewhat more slowly than usual. Perhaps my ankle wasn't sprained, after all, but it still hurt like the devil. "Very well, I'm on my way," I said. "And while I'm gone, I suggest you send out for more ice. I think I'm going to need it." I went out the door and limped down the passageway, on one more errand for Mr. Clemens. I hoped he wasn't just fishing in an empty pond this time.

27 ⌒

Herbert Watts looked uncomfortable standing in Mr. Clemens's cabin, but he had declined my employer's offer of a seat and a drink. "I best not stay up in the first class too long, sir," he said. "We're not supposed to be up 'ere except we're on duty 'ere, so I 'ave to be back in the forecastle 'fore Gallagher misses me. And I don't use strong drink no more. *Strong drink is ragin'*, the Bible says, and I believe it's true. I saw what it done to that poor boy who went missin'."

"Well, I could still give you a glass of soda water. But I won't need to keep you long," said Mr. Clemens, looking up at the tall seaman from his reclining position on the couch. "I just have a couple of quick questions for you. No reason you can't be back in your bunk in ten minutes."

"I'll answer you best I can, sir," said Watts. He still clutched his copy of *A Christian's Duty*, Dr. Smythe's book. I was mildly puzzled that a man who seemed pious and upright in so many ways had been so quick to accept a bribe to let us interview the prince—but men had made stranger moral compromises. And I realized that piety and honesty were not necessarily the same.

"When Mr. Jennings came to the prince's cabin, we ducked into the bedroom and hid," said my employer. "So we didn't see everybody who was there, and we didn't realize until later that we might need to know. We heard Mr. Babson, and Rubbia, the Italian fellow. But who else was there?''

"Them's the only passengers, sir," said Watts. "There was two crew there besides Mr. Jennings: First Mate Gallagher, and Andy Jones, who bunks next to me. That's all—I was outside the whole time, and nobody else came in or out. I would've seen 'em if they did, sir.''

"Did anybody else enter or leave the room besides my group and Mr. Jennings's group—either before we got there or after we left?''

"No, sir," said Watts, "not durin' my watch, they didn't. Hit was dead quiet, except for you gentlemen and the party Mr. Jennings brought.''

"What about the fellow who brings Ruckgarten's dinner?'' asked Mr. Kipling. He leaned forward eagerly. "Surely he ate a meal this evening. But the plates had been cleared before we came.''

"Aye, and before I came on duty, too," said Watts, spreading his hands and shrugging. "Hit would be one of the stewards, but I don't rightly know which one 'as charge of that section of the cabins. Mr. 'Arwell, maybe, or Mr. Garner—but that's just guessin', 'cos I never laid eyes on 'im.''

"That shouldn't be hard to find out, if we need to know it," said Mr. Clemens. "One last question—think carefully about this, it might be important. When Jennings and his party came out, did they all leave together, or did they split up?''

Watts rubbed his chin, thinking, then said, "Gallagher stayed a few minutes to talk with me—tellin' me what 'ad 'appened while 'e was inside—and the others all went off.''

"Well, we're lucky he didn't stay too long," said Mr. Clemens. "We might have walked out right into his arms, and then there'd have been hell to pay.''

"Aye, I reckon so," said Watts, with a bit of a wry smile. "I was worryin' when you'd come out the 'ole time 'e was talkin'—I couldn't 'ardly pay attention to 'im for fear you gentlemen 'ud pop out the door, but I didn't want to ask 'im to repeat it all, either. It 'ad me sweatin', it did.'' The sailor shook his head as he remembered the close call, though I got the impression that he had actually enjoyed the sense of excitement.

"I can believe it,'' said Mr. Clemens. "Well, I guess that's all I need to know, Herbert, unless either of my friends here have questions for you.''

Mr. Kipling shook his head, but I raised my hand. "I have a question,'' I said. Mr. Clemens nodded, and I thought for a second how to phrase what I wanted to ask. "You seem to me to be an honest man, Herbert. I see you've been reading Dr. Smythe's book, and I get the feeling you're sincerely religious.''

Watts glanced at the tract in his hand, as if he'd almost forgotten it was there, then nodded his head in agreement. "Thank you, Mr. Wentworth. I 'aven't always been the best of Christians, but I try to lead a good life, these days. My mama was a churchgoin' woman, and she tried to bring up me and my little sisters the right way. I slid back some when I went to sea, but I 'opes to do better, God willin'.'' I could see that the sailor was pleased by my compliment.

"Now, I don't want you to take my question the wrong way,'' I said. "But I can't help wondering why a man with your beliefs was willing to let us talk to Prinz Karl? Didn't that conflict with your orders?''

Watts's mouth fell open, and for a moment he said nothing. Then he looked at the floor and said, "Well, sir, I guess I thought the poor bloke 'adn't got a fair show. My mate Andy told me 'ow Mr. Jennings and the lawyer, Mr. Babson, and that Italian gentleman all was sayin' 'e killed that poor boy, and there wasn't nobody tryin' to 'elp 'im prove 'e didn't. I thought maybe you gentlemen would give 'im a chance to get 'is neck out of the noose. That's all—I just wanted 'im to 'ave the chance to tell 'is side of the story to somebody what'll listen to it.''

His gaze remained fixed on the floor during this entire speech, but when he concluded, he looked around the cabin, as if seeking understanding. It was an awkward moment, and I found myself at a loss for anything further to ask. Then Mr. Clemens clapped his hand on the sailor's shoulder and said, "Very good of you, Herbert. We mean to help the prince, if we can. I don't know if we'll need your help again, but I'm glad to know you have the same interest we do in helping him prove his innocence. Now, I know it's late, and tomorrow's a working day for all of us, so go grab some sleep. Thanks again for all your help."

"It's my pleasure, sir," said Watts, smiling. He gave a little salute and took his leave of us.

When the door had closed behind him, Mr. Clemens looked at me and said, "That was a very interesting question you asked, Wentworth. What did you think of the answer?"

"I don't know what to make of it," I said. "I don't know what he knows about Prinz Karl, or what his notions of justice are, but I'd be curious to know exactly why he thinks the prince needs help to get his neck out of the noose. You'd think he'd be the last to question what seems an open-and-shut case—that is, Signor Rubbia's eyewitness testimony."

"Yes, you'd almost think he knew something to the contrary of what Babson and Rubbia are promoting," said Mr. Clemens. "He's not a complete innocent like some I've known, but I guess he believes wholeheartedly in what he believes. Well, unless either of you has a notion how to proceed from here, I say we get a good night's sleep and find out what we think in the morning. Anyone opposed?"

There were no dissenting voices heard, and so we all went to our beds, and to a well-earned repose. I had no doubt that I would sleep well, and my judgment was vindicated almost as soon as my head touched the pillow.

The next morning was calm and sunny, and there was a feeling of excitement in the air. Even before breakfast, there were passengers on deck, laughing and greeting one another while the crew busied themselves about their morning chores. There was a betting pool being organized on when we would first sight land, although short of the ship's sprouting wings and flying, that event would not come until the day after tomorrow. The storm in which Robert Babson had disappeared was almost forgotten—though the disappearance and alleged murder were not.

I had just stood up from the breakfast table and was making my way down the corridor to our cabin when a whispered "Cabot!" caught my ear. I turned to look who had called me, and saw the DeWitt brothers, Tom and Johnny, lurking in a doorway.

"Hello, boys," I said. "What's the matter?"

Johnny stuck his neck out a bit, looking carefully in both directions. "I think that first mate is after us again—I spotted him just as we came up on this deck, but I think we've lost him for now. We have news for you and your boss, though—Is there someplace we can talk without being rousted out?" He snatched his head back into the doorway as someone rounded the corner, but it was only one of the maids with a fresh load of towels. He gave a little nervous laugh.

I put my hand on his elbow and said, "I think we can get to my stateroom without being spotted—breakfast's just over, so everybody's moving up and down the corridors. Follow me," I said, and led them to the cabin.

I had just gotten them seated on the couch when Mr. Clemens came in. "Aha," he said. "I hope these fellows aren't just here for conversation. Not that I mind your conversation, boys. But there's a killer aboard the ship, and we haven't the foggiest notion how to find him. I hope you've learned something that can help us."

Johnny said, "Well, I don't know how much help it'll be, but we have learned something. In fact, Tom knew it all along. Tell 'em what you saw the other night."

"Well, it was the night of the big storm," said Tom, sitting up straight on the couch. "I had been seasick for two days, and I was pretty miserable. I could barely stay in my bunk with all the heaving and rolling of the ship—

it felt as if every wave was picking me up ten feet and dropping me back down with a crash.''

"I can imagine," said Mr. Clemens, seating himself in the chair opposite Tom. "In the old days, when the ships were smaller, every voyage was like that."

"Yes, well, right after six bells—I guess that's eleven o'clock, shore time—I decided to see if fresh air would help me any, so I put on my hat and coat and went out on deck. The other fellows in our dorm were sleeping like logs, and I was almost the only one stirring. It was miserable out, so I wasn't surprised, but the air seemed to do me some good, and so I walked under a stairway, where there was a little shelter from the rain. I stood there for a few minutes, just looking at the storm. It was sort of relaxing to watch, though I knew I would probably feel better once it had stopped.

"I had been there a short while, when I heard the door open and two men came out on deck. One was that German fellow, the prince, dressed up as if he was going to a ball, with a cape and everything. They looked around as if to make sure they were alone, so I didn't move—I was sort of hidden from them. They moved over near me—trying to get out of the rain, the same as I was. I thought for a moment they'd spotted me, but then they stopped and began talking."

"I'll be damned!" said Mr. Clemens, leaning forward and rubbing his hands together. "This may be a real stroke of luck! Could you hear them? Do you remember what they talked about?"

"I didn't understand a single word they said," said Tom, shrugging. "It was all in some foreign language— German, from the sound of it."

Mr. Clemens slumped back in his seat. "Well, it figures. Did you at least see who the prince was with?"

"Yes, that much I can tell you," said Tom. "He was one of the passengers who'd been traveling down below with us—some sort of commercial traveler from out West. I remember him talking about beer and grain with two of the other men."

"And are you sure the fellow in the cape was the prince?" said Mr. Clemens.

Tom nodded vigorously. "Yes, I'd recognize him anywhere—a stout fellow with a little beard. I'd seen him when I was sneaking around up on the top decks. I wondered what he was doing down in steerage, but then I realized he'd probably gone there to talk to the other man. It was obviously some sort of important business, because the fellow from steerage kept jabbering at him as if he was trying to sell him something, and the prince kept shaking his head and saying *Nine, nine*, as if that were the price or something."

"Aha, they were speaking German, then," said Mr. Clemens. "That's the German for *No*. This may clinch the prince's alibi—at least for that particular time. Would you recognize the other man if you saw him again?"

"I guess *so*," said Tom confidently. "It was pretty dark, and I wasn't making any real effort to see them—I felt sort of foolish, hiding like that, and I thought I'd wait until they left to come back out. I didn't think they'd stay out in the rain very long, and I was right. They went inside after ten or fifteen minutes—I didn't have a watch, so I can't swear how long it was."

"It's a shame you don't understand German," I said. "It would be useful to know what they were talking about. It might have been anything—for all we know, the prince was trying to hire the fellow to kill somebody for him."

Tom seemed dubious. "Well, if anybody was trying to hire someone, it was the fellow from steerage. He did most of the talking—all the prince did was shake his head and keep saying *Nein*. And I don't think they struck any kind of bargain—they didn't shake hands or anything."

Mr. Clemens slapped his hand on the arm of his chair. "Well, that's enough for me. As much as I'd like to know what they were talking about, I've got the feeling that the prince was telling the truth about that supposed meeting on deck. I still had a shadow of a doubt about it, but if you saw it, I'm satisfied. I owe you boys a drink—no, make that a dinner. When are you going to be in London?''

"Ah, but that's not the whole story," said Tom.

"Play it close to the vest, Tom," said Johnny, nudging him with his elbow. "Maybe we can parlay this into *two* dinners!"

"Hell, if it gets us to the bottom of this case, I'll buy you a week of dinners," said Mr. Clemens, winking. "What else happened?"

"Well, the two men finished talking—as I said, from the way they acted I got the idea the salesman hadn't managed to close the deal, and I guess that's right, if the other fellow was saying No all that time. They went back inside, and after a minute or two to let them get out of the way, I went in myself. I decided to walk down to the bath and get a towel to dry myself off a bit before I crawled back in bed—I figured I was going to be miserable enough with the weather and the ship rolling so much, but I might as well be dry.

"Along the way, there's a door that leads to a stairway down to the crew's quarters, and that night, there was a fellow waiting there. I didn't recognize him, or really pay him much attention at first, but I did notice him, because there he was in a big overcoat just like the one Pop got last Christmas. I thought it was odd that there was another first-class passenger down there, in addition to the prince out on deck. But pretty clearly he was a first-class passenger. I didn't have anything to say to him, so I just went on by.''

"Interesting," said Mr. Clemens. "You say you didn't recognize the man."

"No, I'm afraid not," said Tom, shrugging again. "I might know him if I saw him again, especially if he had on that coat."

"A lot of help you are," said Johnny DeWitt, in the habitual scornful tone of an older brother to a younger. "There are probably a dozen coats like that on board."

"No—that was a two-hundred-dollar coat he was

wearing," said Tom indignantly. "How else do you think I knew he was a first-class passenger? It was double-breasted, with a white fur collar, and those German silver buttons with eagles on them, that Pop makes such a fuss over—you know the coat I mean."

"Now that *is* interesting," said Mr. Clemens, putting his finger to his chin.

"Yes, and that's not even the whole story," said Tom. "I was in the bath for perhaps three minutes, drying off, and when I came back, three other men—in crew uniforms—had joined the fellow. I recognized one of them—he was that first mate, Gallagher. I didn't feel like drawing any more of that bully's attention, even though I had every right to be where I was, so I stepped back inside the bathroom door to wait for them to leave."

"And did you hear anything this time?" said Mr. Clemens.

"A little bit," said Tom. "The mate said, 'Here's your boys, mister. Where's the fellow you want us to explain matters to?' and the passenger said, 'I'll take you to him. First here's a little something to show I mean business. There'll be more after we're done,' and I heard the two other crewmen mumble thanks. Then the passenger said to follow him, and Gallagher says, 'Come along, Andy, Herb,' and they went off."

"Andy and Herb, you say!" exclaimed Mr. Clemens. "Now, I wonder how many crewmen there are with those names?"

"Not to mention that they travel in a pack with Gallagher," I added. "Was one of them a big fellow, about my height?"

"Yes, I'd hate to tangle with him."

"Oh, I reckon that fellow's bark is worse than his bite," said Mr. Clemens. "What about the other fellow?"

"Average-looking, I'd say," replied Tom, shrugging. "Looked like a working man. I only really saw him from the back. Same thing with the big man."

Mr. Clemens shot a questioning glance at me. "That

could be Andy Jones, if he was the other fellow who was with Gallagher when he was about to arrest me," I said, nodding. "But it's a fine description of three-quarters of the crew."

"Yes, but how many of them are named Andy?" said Mr. Clemens. "Tom, you may have given me the key to the whole mystery. You boys have earned yourselves the best dinner money can buy in London—or New York, or Paris—whatever town you choose to cash in the promise."

"Hold out for New Orleans," I said in a conspiratorial whisper.

"It'd be my delight," said Mr. Clemens. "You boys might have to wait a few years to collect, though."

"I think we'll settle for London," said Johnny, laughing. "Thank you very much, sir. I'm glad Tom and I could help you out."

The brothers took their leave, and Mr. Clemens returned to the porthole, looking out at the ocean. I realized that he was thinking, and did not interrupt with all the questions that had bubbled up in the back of my mind.

What was the significance of the meeting Tom DeWitt had seen? My mind kept searching for innocent interpretations of it, but there were none that convinced me. Perhaps the meeting took on a sinister aspect solely from our preoccupation with a murder. Then again, since the attempt on Signor Rubbia's life, we had excellent evidence that there *was* a killer in our midst, so our suspicion might be justified. With Prinz Karl under guard in his cabin during the attack on Rubbia, it seemed he was in the clear—although I thought Mr. Clemens was too quick to place a favorable interpretation on Tom's evidence. There would have been ample time for the prince to go back to the first-class deck and kill Robert Babson. We still had only a vague notion of when the murder had taken place.

But now we had another enigma to ponder: Who was the mysterious passenger Tom had seen? How would we learn his identity? I tried for a moment to imagine lining up all the first-class passengers to show their overcoats and letting Tom pick out the one he'd seen, but I doubted the captain would authorize such an inspection without far more proof than we had yet presented. Even if the overcoat was unique and the identification positive, we had no evidence that its wearer had done anything more sinister than pay a visit to the steerage deck and talk to some crewmen. Perhaps he was only looking for a card game—from what I'd heard, he wouldn't have been the only gentleman who enjoyed gaming with the crew.

My mind was still running along these tracks when there was a knock at the door. At my employer's nod, I went and opened it to admit Mr. Kipling and his wife. "Just the two people I wanted to see," said Mr. Clemens. "We've got a witness to back up Prinz Karl's alibi. What's more, we've got a new puzzle I need you to help me solve."

"Then perhaps our news will be of use," said Mr. Kipling, ushering his wife in the door and showing her to a seat on the sofa, where she sat with a knowing smile. "Carrie's been listening to the ladies' gossip in the Grand Saloon, and she's found an absolute pearl."

"And what would that be?" said Mr. Clemens, raising his eyebrows.

Mr. Kipling put his thumbs in his suspenders and smiled, with the air of a waiter about to bring in a special delicacy. "This morning, Carrie went to read—and, by the bye, to listen—in the Grand Saloon before breakfast, and she overheard two Philadelphia ladies speaking of a certain young woman of their party," he said. "Since the place was nearly empty, she couldn't sit right next to them, so she didn't hear everything they said, but she knew right away to whom they were referring. Unfortunately, she didn't have the chance to tell me the news at breakfast, because we naturally didn't want the rest of the table to know what we were about. But she told me after, and I thought we should come directly here and let you know . . ."

Mrs. Kipling held up her hand. "Let me finish the

story, Ruddy, or poor Mr. Clemens will die of suspense. To go straight to the point, the girl had evidently been such a fool as to let her fiancé take possession of more than just her heart.''

''Yes, that's exactly it, Carrie,'' said Mr. Kipling. He turned to face my employer, who was leaning against the bulkhead near the porthole. ''I think this opens an entire new area of inquiry, Clemens.''

Mr. Clemens turned away from the porthole and said, ''Thank you, Mrs. Kipling—that puts the icing right on the cake. Now I have a pretty good idea who killed Bobby Babson.''

''Good, I hope you'll let us in on the secret,'' said Mr. Kipling. ''I've been mulling over the evidence, and I hit the same sticking point every time—we still don't have any actual witness to the crime, unless we credit Rubbia's story.''

''Yes, and last I heard, Rubbia might not live to testify—although if he does live, he's going to have to recant, instead. Between your wife's news, and what I learned earlier today, his story ain't worth a Confederate nickel. I reckon it's time to go tell the captain I can put the finger on the man we're after. Meanwhile, Wentworth, I want you to go find somebody, and ask him to meet me here in half an hour—I should be done talking to the captain by then.''

''Certainly,'' I said. From the expressions on the Kiplings' faces, they were as puzzled as I at Mr. Clemens's claim to know the murderer. ''Whom am I inviting to meet you?''

''The minister that wrote that book,'' said Mr. Clemens. ''Dr. Charles Smythe. Be quick about it—we don't have much time.''

28 ⌒

aptain Mortimer's office, while far from small, seemed to be crowded every time I was in it. This time, six of us were there. In addition to the captain and Mr. Jennings, who as master-at-arms was the shipboard officer responsible for the investigation of Robert Babson's disappearance and presumed murder, my employer had requested the presence of Julius Babson, Robert's father and an experienced prosecutor in Philadelphia; and of Vincent Mercer, the missing man's prospective father-in-law and the *de facto* leader of the tour group of which the Babsons were part. After a brief consultation, Mr. Kipling had decided to skip the meeting in favor of me—"in case Clemens needs a big fellow's help," he said. As I already knew, Mr. Clemens had at least one surprise guest to introduce at the appropriate time.

It had been only a few short hours since Mr. Clemens had spoken to first the DeWitt brothers, then Mrs. Kipling and finally Mr. Smythe. After learning what they had to tell him, he had gone to ask the captain to convene a brief meeting, in which he promised to reveal important information concerning the case of Robert Babson. He must have been persuasive, for the captain had granted his request after only a brief interview.

The meeting had been set for right after lunch. Thus I had spent that meal picking at my food, with my mind racing ahead to various eventualities. I thought I knew whom Mr. Clemens would identify as the killer. But how he meant to prove his case was still an enigma to me. At least, it seemed to me that our original goal, of vindicating Prinz Karl, was now all but accomplished—though I supposed Mr. Babson would not yet have abandoned his belief that the prince had killed his son.

After seeing the passengers seated—except for Mr. Clemens, who elected for the moment to remain standing—Captain Mortimer said, "Gentlemen, I appreciate your finding the time to come here. Mr. Babson, we have all been distressed by your son's disappearance, but I hope we can arrive at a resolution of that unfortunate incident today."

At this, Mr. Babson sat upright and asked eagerly, "Has the German confessed? I'm glad to hear it."

"Why, no, Mr. Babson," said the captain. "Signor Rubbia, the only witness to the alleged murder, was attacked last night, while Prinz Karl von Ruckgarten was under guard in his cabin. It seems obvious that the prince could not have been the guilty party."

"I am happy that I will be able to save you from an elementary error before it is too late," said Mr. Babson. "The German's guilt or innocence in my son's death is a separate issue. There is no reason to believe that the attack on poor Signor Rubbia is in any way related to my son's murder."

The captain shook his head gravely. "There are too many suppositions for any other theory. Who except the person who killed your son had any motive to attack Signor Rubbia?"

Babson waved a forefinger. "Yes, but Rubbia had clearly identified the German as the one he saw murder Robert. The attacker may have meant to rob Rubbia; luckily, Mr. Clemens and his secretary came along in time to prevent him from achieving that, though unfortunately too late to stop the attack. Can you tell us any news about poor Signor Rubbia, by the way? Last we heard, he was still unconscious."

"That had not changed as of the most recent report,"

said the captain, pointing to a paper on his desk. "I have asked the doctor to give me immediate news of any change in his condition, and I will certainly pass word along to both you gentlemen."

"Thank you, Captain," said Mr. Mercer, his hands clasped in front of him. "The artistic portion of our European tour would be severely crippled if Signor Rubbia is unable to participate. I pray for his recovery."

"As do we all," said the captain, nodding. "But Mr. Jennings and I have concluded that the only possible motive for the attack on Signor Rubbia was his claim to have witnessed the murder of your son, Mr. Babson. The prince was under guard and so we feel that the inquiry must shift to other suspects. Perhaps one of them feared that Rubbia would recant his story, and took steps to silence him before that could occur."

"Perhaps you are correct that Signor Rubbia's testimony was the reason for the attack," said Mr. Babson, smirking. "But you have forgotten that the German might have confederates aboard the boat. One of them might have been the attacker last night. Alternately, the German might have bribed one of his guards to silence Rubbia."

The captain stiffened. "I won't hear that sort of talk about my men," he said, anger visible on his face.

Mr. Jennings stepped slightly forward from his position just behind the captain's right shoulder. "With the captain's permission, I should point out that there is an even stronger argument against that suggestion. Herr von Ruckgarten learned of Rubbia's claim to have witnessed the murder only a very short while before Rubbia himself was attacked. He hardly had time to notify an accomplice or bribe a guard, especially since the only guard to whom he had access was the one then outside his cabin door. That man would have had to leave his post, risking detection, and go find Rubbia—with no guarantee of success—in less than half an hour."

Mr. Clemens spoke for the first time. "More to the point, the man who attacked Rubbia was no taller than I am. The guard on Prinz Karl's door last night is six foot if he's an inch.''

Mr. Babson turned and looked at my employer, curiosity suddenly spread across his face. ''And just how do you happen to know that, Mr. Clemens? What is your role in this whole affair, to begin with?'' He crossed his arms over his chest, glaring at Mr. Clemens with the air of a debater who has caught his opponent in a blatant contradiction. Beside him, Mr. Mercer leaned forward a little, whispering something to Babson, who nodded.

''I'm here on the side of justice,'' said Mr. Clemens. ''You and Mercer seem to have been working overtime to make Prinz Karl shoulder the blame for your son's death. I've found out the truth, and I'm here to see that the real killer gets what's coming to him.''

''What are you implying, sir?'' said Mr. Babson. ''I don't know what sort of allegation you intend to make, but I consider your suggestion very offensive.''

''Good,'' said Mr. Clemens, nodding vigorously. ''You ought to be offended at the way your boy was killed. I reckon he wasn't a bad fellow—a bit too free with your money, perhaps, and way too hot-tempered when somebody crossed him. But he'd probably have grown out of the worst of it, especially if he'd learned to hold his liquor and his temper.''

''I'll thank you to speak more charitably of the dead,'' growled Mr. Babson, rising to his feet, but Mr. Jennings, standing behind the captain, cleared his throat loudly. Still looking angry, Babson returned to his seat.

''I should have known a lawyer wouldn't take a sensible attitude,'' said Mr. Clemens gruffly. ''Here you are, your son a murder victim, and you get all huffed up at a fellow who tries to tell you the truth about what really happened to him. Do you want to hear it, or not?''

''Let the fellow say his worst,'' said Mr. Mercer, putting a hand on Mr. Babson's arm. ''Perhaps he will grow tired of hearing his own voice—if the captain doesn't tire of it first.''

Mr. Clemens shrugged and began talking in a level

voice. "The match between your boy and Mercer's daughter must have looked pretty good, at first—though I reckon she'd have been better off with that preacher's son, Wilfred Smythe. Poor but honest—and likely to come up in the world. But she liked your boy better, for all the usual silly reasons. He was smart, he had money, he had friends, he liked to laugh and have a good time. So when she threw poor Smythe over for him, that was fine—as long as the money lasted."

"You haven't the faintest notion of my financial condition," said Mr. Babson, straightening himself to his full height.

"No, but some of the other folks aboard do. You're facing re-election in the spring, and you're up against an honest opponent who knows too much about you. And that's not all—I've heard tell you might be facing a grand jury, if he wins—this time as the object of the investigation."

Babson turned white. "That is a lie!" he said, his voice a rasp.

"Maybe it is, and maybe it ain't," said Mr. Clemens, "but from what I hear, you've thought pretty seriously about not going back to Philadelphia at all. Which is why you tried to clamp down on your son's gambling—you couldn't afford to support him anymore."

"You haven't the faintest idea what you're talking about," said Babson. He pulled a wallet from his pocket and waved it in my employer's face. "I have plenty of money!"

"Pocket money is one thing, but the kind of money it takes to buy an election is a whole 'nother animal. Bobby was eating up your money faster than it came in. He'd been giving out IOUs the whole voyage, banking on his dowry from Theresa Mercer to bring him flush again. The boys he played with didn't have any problem with that. But the girl's father did."

"Robert Babson was a fine young man," said Mercer, with a thin smile. His forefinger tapped on the arm of his chair. "I was proud that my daughter was going to marry him. I would have had no qualms about supporting them until he could get on his feet in a respectable business or profession. What else have I worked and saved for all these years, if not to see my children happy?''

''That's a fine sentiment,'' said Mr. Clemens. ''Mighty fine, indeed. I have three daughters, myself, and any fellow who comes looking to marry one of 'em is going to have a hard job convincing the old man he's worthy of the honor. So I can understand your point. In fact, if the likes of Bobby Babson had come knocking on my door, I might have slammed it in his face, no matter who his father was. Unless, of course, the father had some sort of hold over me, such as being a prosecuting attorney who knew something to my disadvantage.''

Vincent Mercer stared at my employer a long moment before saying, ''Mr. Clemens, I realize you have a reputation as a humorist to uphold. However, I must tell you that I find your remarks to be in extremely bad taste.''

Mr. Clemens returned his stare without flinching. ''Well, we're even, then. I get a bad taste in my mouth every time I think about that murdered boy—especially since I learned that the man who was responsible for his death stood aside and let somebody else take the blame.''

''I don't know what you mean by that,'' said Mr. Mercer. ''If you've nothing more than unfounded accusations to offer, I fear I must forego the dubious pleasure of hearing any more of them.''

''Then I reckon it's time to bring in somebody who can put some flesh on the bones,'' said Mr. Clemens. ''I knew this was going to be a tough nut to crack, so I made sure I had all the *t*'s crossed and all the *i*'s dotted before I told the captain I could put my finger on the killer. Wentworth, go ask Herbert Watts to come in.''

Babson had a puzzled expression. ''Herbert Watts? I never heard of such a fellow.''

Mr. Clemens smiled. ''I guess not—you probably don't even believe such a man exists. He's something foreign to your world of backroom deals and brokered elections: a man with principles. Bring him in, Wentworth.''

I stepped to a door leading to a sort of anteroom adjacent to the captain's office, where Herbert Watts waited—along with Mr. Smythe, the minister. Watts looked up, as if startled, when I opened the door, but Mr. Smythe patted him on the shoulder and said, ''Go ahead, Herbert. Just tell them the simple truth, and you'll have done your duty.''

Watts shuffled into the office, his cap in his hand, and stopped in front of the captain's desk. ''I've come, sir,'' he said in a firm but quiet voice.

''Good man, Watts,'' said the captain. ''Mr. Clemens has a few questions to ask, and I hope you'll answer them truthfully. I hope you understand that this is very important.''

''I know it is, and I'll do my level best to tell 'im the truth, sir,'' said Watts, looking sideways at Mr. Clemens. I thought I detected fear in his eye, though I had no idea what my employer might have done to give him reason for such an emotion.

''Bring up a chair, Wentworth,'' said Mr. Clemens. I brought a stout wooden chair from the far corner and set it in front of the desk. Mr. Clemens gestured to the seaman. ''Have a seat, young fellow. This may take a while, and there's no reason you should be any more uncomfortable than the rest of us while you're being quizzed.''

Watts stared at the chair a moment, then at the captain and Mr. Jennings. I realized he must be unused to sitting in the company of the ship's officers. But the captain nodded gravely, and Watts settled into the chair. ''Now, Herbert,'' said Mr. Clemens, ''I'd like you to tell us about Wednesday—when the storm was at its worst. Do you remember what you did that evening?''

''Yes, sir. Me and my mates 'ad been working like Trojans all day long, makin' everything secure against the blow and seein' that the ship was safe. Most of us was off duty that evenin' and mighty worn out, but with a blow so 'eavy, we knew we might be called out any time if the ship was in trouble. So we went to our bunks, but kept ourselves on the ready. A few of the fellows dozed off early, others whittled or played cards—not many that night, it was so rough, y'know. Me, I was readin' a tract.'' The sailor looked around at the circle of eyes fixed on him, as if looking for approval of his reading habits.

Mr. Clemens nodded. ''Well, reading's a fine way to spend an evening,'' he said. ''I'd rather you were reading my books, but I guess a tract can't hurt you if it's not too heavy. Wouldn't want to try climbing the rigging with one of those things in your pocket.''

''Aye aye, sir,'' said the seaman, but from his expression he was puzzled at my employer's levity.

Evidently realizing that his attempt at humor had gone over Watts's head, Mr. Clemens put on a serious expression and returned to business. ''Now, did anything unusual happen that evening?—besides the storm, I mean.''

''Aye. About six bells, in comes First Mate Gallagher, lookin' for me and Andy Jones. I didn't know what it was about, but me and Andy fell to, and Gallagher leads us out into the passageway. I was sort of curious, not knowin' what 'e 'ad to tell us that couldn't be said in front of the other lads. ''Ere, lads,' says Gallagher, 'ow'd you like to make some good money?' Andy and me looks at each other, and Andy asks what it's about. 'I'll tell you, but you've got to keep your trap shut,' says Gallagher. 'You'll not 'ear a dickey bird from me,' says Andy, and I promise 'im the same. 'Good,' says Gallagher, 'There's a gentleman wants us to do a job for 'im. Sort 'o rough work, but 'e's payin' American gold for it.' ''

All the while he spoke, Watts kept glancing nervously from Mr. Clemens to the captain and back. The captain's face was impassive, but behind him I could see Mr. Jennings growing increasingly disturbed at what he was hearing. Watts plowed ahead doggedly, even though he must have recognized the impression he was making.

''Well, I wasn't sure I liked the sound of the work,''

said Watts, "but the sound of the gold was more to my likin', and so me and Andy followed Gallagher up the ladder to the next deck, where a gentleman was waitin', all wrapped up in a 'eavy topcoat. And 'e told us there was a fellow makin' trouble for 'im, and 'e wanted 'im taught a lesson. Gallagher says we're the lads for it, and the gentleman gives us each a gold eagle and says there's more when we're finished. We follow 'im, and I ask 'ow we're goin' to know the fellow we're after. Gallagher says not to worry, 'e knows the bloke. It's the same one as gave us the cock an' bull before, when we was about to arrest Mr. Cabot, 'ere. Me and Andy just nodded when we 'eard that. I didn't like the way the fellow smirked when 'e tried to get Mr. Cabot in trouble, and Gallagher, no way 'e likes to be made out a fool, which is what the fellow done."

"So you figured you had a chance to get your revenge on him, and get paid for it, as well," said Mr. Clemens. "Didn't you worry he might turn you in?"

"Not with Gallagher callin' the tune, we didn't 'ave to worry. We knew 'e'd swear we was on duty some-wheres else—and we was ready to do the same for 'im. A man 'as to look after 'is mates."

Captain Mortimer had looked more and more distressed as the seaman's testimony had continued. Now at last he stood up behind his desk and interrupted the interrogation. "Good Lord, man, do you mean to tell me you and Jones contracted to kill a man for twenty dollars?"

Watts was indignant. "Kill 'im? I should think not! I'd burn in 'ell for it, and no doubt of it. There's no sum of money in this world that 'ud pay for that. I'm a Christian man, I'll 'ave you know!"

"Then what was the money for?" asked Mr. Clemens, signaling the captain to hold off. "What did the gentleman expect you to do for his gold?"

"For me and Andy, just to act gruff and put the young gentleman in mind of the spot 'e was in. 'E was a rich boy, and a soft one, even if 'e thought 'e was a tiger. Gallagher would 'andle the rough stuff, and we was there to back 'im up if the boy didn't take 'is medicine nice and quiet-like.''

"I see," said Mr. Clemens. "And then something went wrong, didn't it?"

"You might say as 'ow it did . . ." the seaman began, but he was interrupted.

"This is a complete outrage, and a bald-faced lie," said Mr. Mercer, all but spitting in his indignation. "This ruffian has evidently murdered my future son-in-law, and possibly poor Signor Rubbia as well, but he has the temerity to come before the captain of his ship and attempt to pass the blame onto me. You should be ashamed of yourself for being taken in by him, Clemens. I'll have none of it, do you understand? This man and his cronies should be clapped in irons, where they belong."

"Seems to me you're getting ahead of the story," said Mr. Clemens, mildly. "Watts didn't say he saw the boy killed, and he never said who paid him. What makes you think he was going to accuse *you* of murder?"

"Yes, Mr. Mercer, please explain yourself," said the captain, leaning forward with evident interest. "Watts has only referred to a gentleman who gave him money, but he's said no name, nor even suggested that the man was anyone present here and now. Why do you take the accusation to refer to yourself?"

Vincent Mercer sputtered for a moment, but he quickly recovered his composure and said, "It's clear enough what the filthy knave is leading up to, and I emphatically deny it. Clemens must have been coaching him—possibly to shift the blame away from that obnoxious foreigner who represents himself as a prince. I don't know why anyone would believe this man's lies, in any case. Anyone can see he's nothing more than scum from the gutters."

"Scum usually rises to the top," said Mr. Clemens, in a matter-of-fact voice. Mercer gave him a puzzled look, but the captain nodded, with a tight-lipped smile. "But I think we should hear the rest of Herbert's story, to find out what really went on that night."

"I doubt you'll learn anything of the sort from him," said Mercer, but Mr. Babson held up his hand.

"Be still, Vincent," said Babson, in a sad voice. "I want to find out what this fellow knows about what happened to my son." Mercer turned white, but said nothing more, and the captain nodded to Herbert Watts, who continued his story.

"We followed the gentleman up to the first-class deck," said Watts. "Hit was rainin' and blowin' mighty fierce, but 'e led us out on the promenade deck. Hit was dark as the bottom of a coal scuttle, an' no fit place to be, but a man don't lay eyes on gold money every day, so I was game, all right. We came on deck just abaft the stacks, on the port side, and went on aft, all in a line behind the gentleman. Presently 'e stops and says, quiet-like, 'There 'e is—you boys know your business.''

"The fellow we'd come for was leaning over the rail, pale as a fish-belly—I took one look at 'im and knew 'e was drunk as a lord—if we'd been indoors, we'd 'ave *smelt* 'im. And then 'e puked over the side. Right then, I didn't much fancy the idea of gettin' rough with 'im, 'e looked so pitiful, but I knew Gallagher would do most of the work, and me and Andy could just stand by and look mean. Anyways, Gallagher was about to step in and do what we was there for when this gentleman says to wait a minute, and 'e steps forward. 'Robert,' 'e says, 'you should be ashamed of yourself. You are a disgrace to your family.' And the boy looks up at 'im, and he tells 'im to leave 'em alone. I tell you, hit was 'ard not to feel sorry for the poor blighter.''

"Disgusting," said Mr. Mercer. It wasn't clear whether he was referring to Watts's story or young Babson's conduct.

"Gallagher looked at this 'ere gentleman, as if 'e wasn't sure what 'e was to do," said Watts, shaking his head. "I don't think 'e'd figured on the boy bein' so drunk 'e couldn't take proper care of 'imself. Wasn't 'ardly sportin' to give 'im a drubbin', I thought then. And then the gentleman says, 'You'll not spend any more time

with my daughter. I'll tell her to end the engagement.'
And the boy looks at 'im and, sick as 'e was, 'e laughs
right in 'is face. 'It's a bit late for that, Mr. Mercer,' says
the boy, smirkin'. And that's when the gentleman lost 'is
temper.''

"That is a damnable lie," shouted Mr. Mercer, jumping to his feet so rapidly that his chair nearly fell back-
wards. "I never saw this man before today!"

There was a shocked silence in the room. Now that
Watts had unequivocally placed Mr. Mercer at the scene
of the murder, there was no escaping the significance of
his testimony. "Good Lord," said Mr. Jennings. "I can't
believe it."

"Well, don't strain yourself trying," said Mr. Mercer.
"It's all lies, every word of it." He turned and started
for the door, but Mr. Jennings interposed himself between him and the exit. Mercer looked at him with un-
disguised fury. "Don't you dare try to stop me. You'll
hear from my lawyer if you lay a finger on me!"

"Vincent, I *am* your lawyer," said Mr. Babson, rising
from his seat. All his bluster was gone, and there was a
terribly sad expression on his face. I thought for a moment I saw a tear glisten at the corner of his eye. "Tell
me it isn't so, Vincent. Look me in the eye and say it
isn't!"

The captain stood behind his desk, leaning forward
with his hands on the desktop, a shocked expression on
his face. Watts stared fixedly at the floor, clearly embarrassed by the scene. Meanwhile, Mr. Clemens stood
calmly by Watts's chair, his hand resting lightly on the
sailor's shoulder, but there was a grim expression on his
face.

"I don't have to tell you anything," shouted Mr. Mercer, after an awkward pause. But his face changed as
Babson took a threatening step forward. Now Mercer
lowered his voice and pleaded, "Julius, you don't have
to believe these lies. Come with me and let them stew in
their own juices. They have no proof of anything."

"I think we'd better both sit down and hear the rest

of this man's story," said Babson firmly. "I tell you, Vincent, if you leave this room now, you will have forfeited any claim to my friendship."

The banker stared around the room, as if searching for an ally. Then he looked at Jennings, standing firmly in front of the door. I had risen to my feet as well, ready to assist the officer if the need arose. Finally, Mr. Mercer hung his head and returned to his chair.

Mr. Clemens nodded. "Now, Herbert, why don't you tell us what happened when the gentleman lost his temper. What did he do?"

Watts began speaking again, almost as if the interruption had never occurred. "The gentleman lost 'is temper bad, when the boy said that about 'is daughter. 'E stepped up to 'im and said, 'You better not 'ave touched 'er, you 'ear me?' The boy, 'e just snickered and said, 'What'll you do about it if I 'ave?' That's when the gentlemen 'auled off and took a poke at the boy. The boy blocked it with 'is arm, not fightin' back but just blockin' the punch, y'know? And that's when Andy decided 'e'd better start earnin' 'is money and stepped in. 'E put a 'ammerlock on the boy and said, 'Easy now, and you'll not get 'urt,' and I think he meant it. I tell you gentlemen right now, I was ready to throw down my gold eagle on the deck and walk right away. But the boy started to squirm, and 'e cursed—I don't know if it was Andy or the gentleman 'e meant it for, but the gentleman must 'ave took it personal, cause 'e waded in and gave the boy a good whack right on the Adam's apple. Andy let go, and the boy went down and started to gag, and the gentleman gave 'im a kick square in the belly, and then another in the 'ead. That last one knocked the boy's 'ead into the rail, and 'e just stopped movin'. Me and Andy just stood there, not knowin' what to do. But Gallagher knelt down and listened for the boy's 'eart, and then looked up at us and said, "E's gone.' And so 'e was."

"Merciful Lord," said Captain Mortimer. "Is this true, Mr. Mercer?"

"I deny every word of it," said the banker loudly. I

could see beads of sweat on his brow. "This villain has murdered my daughter's fiancé, and now he tries to throw the blame on me. I demand that you put him in irons, and deliver him to the authorities for trial as soon as we land in England." Mr. Mercer looked around belligerently, his muscles tensed. For a moment I thought he was ready to flee, but somehow he kept his seat.

"Thou shalt not bear false witness against thy neighbor," said Herbert Watts, in an utterly calm voice, and if I had had any doubt about his testimony before, I had none now.

For his part, Captain Mortimer sat at his desk, his arms folded, looking from his crewman to the passenger, and at last he said coldly, "Mr. Mercer, I suggest that you refrain from trying to teach me how to run my ship. For now, I am going to listen to this man's story, and I can assure you that when I am satisfied of the truth of the matter, I will take appropriate action to secure the persons of the most likely suspects."

Mercer sat bolt-upright, stiff as a board, saying nothing. Next to him, Mr. Babson's hands were over his face. "No," he said in a barely audible voice, and again, "No."

"Speaking of false witness," said Mr. Clemens, taking charge of the proceedings once again, "where does Giorgio Rubbia come into this? Why did he suddenly crawl out of the woodwork and claim to have seen Prinz Karl shove the boy overboard?"

"Well," said Herbert Watts, "when we realized the boy was gone, the gentleman"—here he pointed directly at Mr. Mercer—"went all frantic, 'e did. 'We must keep this quiet,' 'e says. 'You're all accomplices, and we'll all 'ang together if we don't.' Well, the rest of us didn't know what to do, 'avin' taken 'is money, but when 'e asked us to all 'elp 'im throw the boy in the water and let people think it was a haccident, it seemed to make sense. So we all four turned to and 'eaved the body up over the rail—over it goes, splash. Mr. Mercer sees 'e's got some blood on 'is 'and, and 'e takes out 'is pocket 'andkerchief and wipes it off and throws it away, and just as 'e turns around, there's that Italian fellow, the painter, lookin' at us, and my 'eart like to stopped. *Now we're in for it,* says I to myself, and Mr. Mercer says, 'What did you see, Rubbia?' And Rubbia says, 'A man might see almost anything out 'ere; let's go talk about it.' Then the gentleman, Mr. Mercer, gives us each another twenty dollars, and tells us again not to say anything about what 'appened or we'll all 'ang, for sure. And then 'e went away with the painter, and that's the story.''

Captain Mortimer looked at Mercer again. After an uncomfortable moment of silence, in which I realized for the first time that Mr. Babson was in tears, the captain said, ''Mr. Mercer, how do you respond to Herbert Watts's account?''

''It is an outright fabrication,'' said the banker, who seemed unaware of Mr. Babson's distress. ''Rubbia has plainly testified that he saw the so-called German prince push poor Robert overboard. Unfortunately, he is presently in no condition to refute this sorry fellow's story. I suggest that this man knows more than he's said about the attack on Signor Rubbia, as well. I find it hard to credit that you would accept his testimony at face value. He is evidently deluded by some sort of religious mania. There is not a shred of evidence to connect me with this alleged incident.''

''Oh, I almost forgot about that,'' said Herbert Watts. ''Remember 'ow I said the gentleman wiped the blood off 'is 'ands with 'is pocket 'andkerchief? 'E threw it away, but the wind blew it back on deck. I thought it better not lie there, and picked it up—and then, later, I thought I'd better keep it, just in case I needed a trump card. 'Ere it is.'' He reached into his pocket and pulled out a crumpled, blood-stained square of white linen, placing it on the captain's desk. Even from where I sat, I could see the embroidered monogram *VM* in one corner.

29

"Poor Watts will have to stand trial, but I don't think he's in danger of the gallows," said Captain Mortimer. After the meeting in which Mr. Mercer had been exposed as the murderer of Robert Babson, the captain had sent out for whisky and a siphon and sat us down to hash over the day's events. "Watts went along not intending to harm anyone, and he and Gallagher took no part in the actual killing—though I fear they'll face charges as accessories before and after the fact. But perhaps Watts's having testified against Mercer will convince a judge to be lenient with him." He shook his head sadly. "What a terrible scene that must have been."

"It was fearful enough in Watts's description from what you say," said Mr. Kipling, swirling the whisky in his glass. "Curious, isn't it? A poor half-educated fellow who can barely speak a proper sentence can bring more of a chill to your blood in five minutes than Lord Lytton can in three volumes."

"The plain truth is always more frightening than made-up bogeymen and monsters. I reckon Andy Jones is thinking about that right now; odds are, he'll be climbing that ladder to the gallows along with Mercer," said Mr. Clemens. He took a cigar out of his pocket and began searching for a match. We were all silent for a moment, thinking of what awaited Mr. Mercer and his hired toughs when the *City of Baltimore* docked in Southampton on Monday.

"Yes, I'd think Mercer and Jones will hang," said the captain, a stern expression on his face. "Even if poor Signor Rubbia recovers, Jones's laying hands on Robert Babson makes him a direct accomplice to the murder, even if he didn't strike the fatal blow. Some judges might find extenuating circumstances, but you won't see me arguing for leniency. There's no excuse for crew to attack one of my passengers, no excuse at all."

"Can it be proven that Jones attacked Rubbia?" asked Mr. Kipling. "Has he confessed?"

"Not yet," said the captain. "Mr. Jennings is quizzing him right now, and perhaps he'll make a clean breast of it. Jones was in Ruckgarten's cabin when Rubbia confronted the prince, and he heard the prince suggest that Rubbia would tell a different story under hard questioning. He must have decided that the threat had to be taken seriously. Watts says that Jones followed Rubbia and Mr. Babson toward the upper deck when he left the cabin, instead of going back to his own quarters. He didn't think anything of it at the time, but in retrospect it's a telling circumstance. Jones had no business in that part of the ship."

"What will happen to Gallagher?" I asked. The first mate had been put under arrest along with Mercer, Watts and Jones; all four sat in the ship's brig. No comfortable cabin arrest for them.

"If I were the judge, he'd never again see the light of day outside a prison," said Captain Mortimer, in a voice that brooked no denial. "That's assuming there's not enough evidence to hang him. He was dead wrong to take one passenger's money to play roughhouse with another, no matter how the boy had offended him. But if the judge is lenient, he may escape the worst—Watts said that Gallagher never laid hands on Babson, and that may save him from the gallows, in the end."

"And Mercer's money may save him," said Mr. Kipling. "A rich man can often buy his way out of trouble—

even this kind of trouble. He'll certainly have the best barrister he can hire.''

"It won't be Babson, that's for sure," said Mr. Clemens.

"No, certainly not," said the captain. "But Mercer is trying every excuse in the book. His latest story is that Jones killed the boy, that he was dead even before he kicked him, and that it was Gallagher's idea to throw the body overboard. By the time he's done, he'll be claiming that he was trying to save the boy from the murderous crewmen." He snorted in disgust.

"The whole thing is a tragedy," said Mr. Clemens. "Here we have half a dozen lives ruined—not even counting Rubbia, supposing he survives. And how many more permanently shadowed by the tragedy? Mercer's poor wife and children, and the Babson boy's family, too—though I think Babson senior brought much of his misery on himself.''

"I'm afraid you're right," I said. "I wondered from the beginning why he was so intent on proving that Robert was murdered. Wouldn't it have comforted him more to believe that his son was the victim of an accident?"

"Not necessarily," said Mr. Clemens. "I know how it feels to lose a child—my little boy Langdon died when he was barely two years old. I wanted to blame everybody and everything except myself, even though I knew I was the one most to blame. The same may be true of Babson—I don't know for sure. All I can say is that a young man doesn't get that wild all by himself, and the father must know he carries some of the responsibility for it. But Babson did accomplish one thing. If he hadn't insisted that his son had been murdered, and pressed the investigation, we'd never have learned the truth—terrible as it is.''

"It is a terrible thing, yes," said the captain. He stood up and walked out to the front of his desk, then leaned against it, his hands on the desktop. "The one thing I cannot for the life of me understand is why Signor Rubbia would come forward to accuse an innocent man of murder. What could he possibly have hoped to gain by it—other than an enemy for life, if the prince managed to clear himself?''

"It may not have been his idea to begin with," said Mr. Clemens. "It was Robert Babson's father who picked Prinz Karl as the likely suspect, if you'll remember. That fight after the concert gave him a believable motive, and at the time we weren't entirely certain of the prince's *bona fides*. In fact, we may not be really sure of them until we're in port.''

"We'll find out shortly thereafter," promised the captain. "It won't be a mystery once my directors learn what's happened. A few telegrams, and they'll have him sorted out.''

"I'll be curious to know the answer myself," said Mr. Clemens. "Not that I put any stock in titles and the like, but it's taken on an interest independent of the murder. Anyhow, I suspect that when Babson started making a stink about his son being murdered, Mercer must have panicked. He wasn't sure whether an investigation would point to him or not. He had four witnesses to worry about, and he couldn't be sure the bribes he'd given them would keep them quiet if the pressure got too high.''

"You think he bribed Rubbia?" said the captain.

Mr. Clemens blew a puff of cigar smoke and nodded. "It makes sense that he did. Rubbia was the only one who didn't have to worry about being put in the dock if the case ever came to trial. And Rubbia had Mercer over a barrel. So when Babson started talking murder, Mercer must have been willing to do anything to dodge suspicion—at least long enough to get to shore, where he'd have a chance to disappear before the investigation got back to him. So he must have bribed Rubbia to claim he'd seen the prince do it. Rubbia didn't like the prince, to begin with—they were like fire and powder from the first time they met.''

"Didn't Rubbia know he was risking a perjury charge?" I asked. "He must have known he would be exposed if the prince could establish his alibi, or if any of the other participants confessed."

"Rubbia likely doesn't know English law," said Mr. Kipling. "Perhaps the prospect of money blinded him. Or perhaps, like Mercer, he assumed he could fade away, and never face the consequences."

"Not as a material witness to a capital crime he wouldn't," said Captain Mortimer, with a grim smile. "He'd never have been allowed out of the jurisdiction until he'd testified in court. If he showed any sign of bolting, he'd have been in a cell, just as tightly guarded as the accused."

"More tightly, if the prince really is who he claims to be," said Mr. Kipling. "Poor Rubbia. He almost talked his way into being the next murder victim. I hope he lives to tell the true story in court, and then to set his life back on the proper road."

I thought of Signor Rubbia's offer to give me drawing lessons, and his encouraging my interest in art, and I hoped that he would recover to pass on his knowledge and skills to other students and art lovers. Perjurer or not, I couldn't find it in my heart to hate him.

"I'll drink to that," said Mr. Clemens, raising his glass. We all solemnly echoed his gesture and drank. Then he grinned and said, "With any luck, maybe he'll even give up the art tour business and become an honest horse trader, or a sincere spiritualist."

Mr. Clemens's lecture was scheduled for that evening, and after a brief consultation with the captain and the librarian, Mrs. Tremont, it was decided that (in spite of the events of the last day) it would be best to go ahead as planned. Mrs. Tremont had reported greater interest in this event than anything she had scheduled for the entire season, so it would have been too great a disappointment to postpone it. With the ship due to arrive in England midday on Monday, the only other possibility would be Sunday evening. That would force many passengers who wished to attend the lecture to stay up late to complete their last-minute packing for debarkation—not to mention depriving those passengers who were strict in observing the Sabbath—of their only opportunity to see my employer speak. Besides which, the lecture might give the passengers some subject of conversation other than the murder, for by now the entire ship knew that Robert Babson had been killed and that Mr. Mercer had been arrested for it.

Since Mr. Clemens's half-serious plan to turn the lecture into a satire on the *City of Baltimore* and its crew was no longer relevant, he sat down after our meeting with the captain to decide on a subject. He used to say it took him three days to work up an impromptu speech, and here he was with only a few hours for the same preparation. (Of course, most of the last three days, his mind had been occupied with solving the murder.) He was shuffling through his notes for various set pieces he could deliver with no rehearsal, when there was a knock at the door. "See who that is, Wentworth," he said, and I went to open it.

To my surprise, there stood my Yale friend Bertie Parsons, with Mr. Jennings close behind him. "Hullo, Cabot," he said. "This fine gentleman was about to eject me from the upper deck, but I managed to persuade him that Mr. Clemens would want to hear what a fellow Yale man had to say. Does your boss have a minute free?"

"I guess I do," said Mr. Clemens, getting to his feet. "Come on it and sit down. You too, Jennings. Would you fellows like a drink?"

"Thank you, but I'm on duty," said Mr. Jennings, who remained standing.

"It would be against my principles to refuse such a generous offer," said Bertie, plopping himself on the sofa, across from Mr. Clemens. "Whatever you've got is fine."

"Give him whisky, then, Wentworth," said my employer, returning to his chair. The light from the porthole fell directly over him, and his white suit was dazzling. "What can I do for you, Bertie?"

Bertie looked at Mr. Jennings, then back at Mr. Clemens. "Well, the DeWitt boys and I heard that you were going to give a talk tonight, and we thought it would be bully to come hear it. But when a fellow from steerage tries to come up to the Grand Saloon, half the crew seems to be looking to send him back down. So I wondered if you could put a word in the captain's ear to let us come hear you talk?"

"Damn right you can come hear me!" exclaimed Mr. Clemens, jumping to his feet again. "In fact, I won't give the talk unless you—and anybody else aboard who cares to hear me—can come to the lecture. That includes steerage, and the stokers, too. Do you hear that, Jennings? Go tell the captain!"

"I don't think he's going to like that, Mr. Clemens," said the officer, who looked uncomfortable. "Besides, I can't leave this young man unattended."

"I'll keep an eye on him. He's not going anywhere else—not while the whisky's free here, anyhow," said Mr. Clemens, glowering. "And unless you're slower than molasses, not even a Yale man is going to drink up my whole supply in the time it takes you to get to the bridge and back. Hurry, now!"

Somewhat flustered, Jennings turned and walked briskly out the door. Just before it closed, Bertie said nonchalantly, "You haven't seen me drink before, have you, sir?"

There was a perceptible pause in the closing of the door. Then Mr. Clemens said, "You don't know how much whisky I keep on hand, do you, son?"

The door closed, and we heard Jennings's footsteps receding rapidly down the corridor. Evidently he had decided that it was a good idea to get his answer and return as quickly as possible—just in case Bertie's capacity was larger than he anticipated.

After a period of amiable chatter—Mr. Clemens seemed far better informed of current events at Yale than either Bertie or I, who were both alumni—we heard a gentle knock on the door. "That'll be Jennings again," said Mr. Clemens. "Let him in, Wentworth."

But to my surprise, when I opened the door, there stood Mrs. Tremont, the librarian. She smiled shyly and said, "May I come in?"

"Certainly, ma'am," said Mr. Clemens, jumping to his feet. "What brings you to an old man's humble cabin on a Saturday afternoon?" He bowed low, taking her hand and kissing it in the European style. The librarian blushed, but was clearly pleased at his flattery.

Mrs. Tremont recovered her composure and said, "Captain Mortimer has sent me to speak to you, after Mr. Jennings informed him of your request to admit the steerage passengers and crew to your lecture tonight."

"I see," said Mr. Clemens. "I reckon he means to refuse me, and thinks I'll take rejection easier from a sweet little lady than from a bluff old sailor. Well, that just goes to prove he don't know Sam Clemens. You can go back to your books, and I'll go straight to the bridge and show him just how stubborn a Missouri mule can be." He crossed his arms over his chest, all gallantry forgotten.

Mrs. Tremont shook her finger, like a kindly teacher reprimanding a naughty schoolboy. "Really, Mr. Clemens, you should learn what my news is before you compose your answer to it. I have not come to refuse your request—quite the opposite, in fact." She smiled and cocked her head to one side.

"I'll teach him not to . . . What did you say?" Mr. Clemens stopped in mid-rant as the import of Mrs. Tremont's message penetrated his consciousness. "Then why did he need to send you here?"

"For two things," said Mrs. Tremont, moving into the room. "May I have a seat?"

"Of course, of course," said Mr. Clemens, now obviously flustered. He showed the librarian to a comfortable chair, while Bertie and I stood looking on, amused at the turn of events.

"To begin with," said Mrs. Tremont, "Captain Mortimer is delighted at the notion of letting the steerage passengers and those of the crew who can be spared from work hear your lecture. They so rarely get to hear any of our speakers, let alone such a famous one as Mark Twain.''

"I'm flattered, Mrs. Tremont," said my employer, with a little bow. "Then I'll double my efforts and try to be especially diverting tonight."

"I am pleased to hear you say that, Mr. Clemens," said Mrs. Tremont. "That raises the second reason for my visit. Since the Grand Saloon cannot hold all those who might wish to hear you speak, the captain wonders if you might be willing to give *two* lectures tonight—let us say at eight and ten o'clock? That way, none of the crew will have to miss you on account of work, and we can accommodate everyone."

Mr. Clemens slapped his knee and laughed. "I should have known there'd be a kicker to the story, but I guess I brought it on myself. Sure, two lectures aren't much more work than one. Tell the captain I'll do it, and I leave it up to you to get me a full house both times."

"I can promise you my best efforts, Mr. Clemens," said the librarian, getting to her feet. "And I shall be on hand to hear you—both times, in fact."

"Mrs. Tremont, it will be my pleasure," said Mr. Clemens, bowing and showing her out of the stateroom.

30 ⌒

Mrs. Tremont was as good as her word. The Grand Saloon was full for the first lecture. Many of the first-class passengers looked askance at the humbly dressed steerage passengers and the rough-looking crewmen, but once Mr. Clemens ambled out to the podium and began to speak in that slow, drawling voice, they followed his every word. Bejeweled ladies in satin, and burly stokers, whose faces bore traces of coal dust despite their best efforts at cleaning up, laughed together at his stories, and at the end they stood and applauded as one.

Having accompanied Mr. Clemens on an extensive lecture tour, I knew many of his routines of old. But here, as on his riverboat lectures, he made an effort to introduce new material appropriate to the audience and the occasion. So he gave us a sketch in which he imagined Noah trying to persuade a strict German inspector to certify the Ark as seaworthy. His imitation of a German accent had Prinz Karl (in a choice front-row seat) nearly falling from his chair with laughter. He repeated, with ludicrous embellishments, his tall tale of the ship cemented to the sea bottom by barnacles. And he told of his first Atlantic voyage, on the tour ship *Quaker City*, comparing its primitive conditions to the luxury of a modern liner like *City of Baltimore*—taking the occasion to compliment both our captain and the ship itself, to much applause from both passengers and crew.

I had wondered whether the recent scandals would hurt the attendance at the lectures, but that did not seem to be the case. Mr. Mercer was of course absent, presumably under guard; so were the three crewmen he had bribed to intimidate Robert Babson before he lost control of his temper. Neither was I surprised that Julius Babson, the victim's father, was absent, along with the rest of his family. Learning that his old friend had so thoroughly betrayed and misled him must have been a terrible shock. I wondered whether the rumor that Babson might decide to remain in Europe to avoid prosecution for his supposed offenses might not turn out to be well-founded.

If so, what would his daughter Rebecca do? Would she remain in Europe, or return home to take her fate in her own hands? I hoped at least to speak to her again before we landed in England and went our separate ways. It seemed my fate to meet attractive young women on my journeys with Mr. Clemens—many of whom I would have welcomed the opportunity to know better. But between the constant travel and the strange circumstances that had involved my employer (and, perforce, myself) in a series of murder investigations, none of the relationships had progressed beyond the stage of casual acquaintance. Perhaps this was only the natural consequence of my decision to pursue a traveling life rather than the sort of steady profession my parents urged upon me. If so, I was willing to accept my side of the bargain.

In the intermission between the two lectures—perhaps twenty minutes, just enough time for Mr. Clemens to rest his voice—I went to join him "backstage." This was actually a nearby room normally used for small meetings, where he could sit down and drink a glass of water between the two lectures. "How'd it look out front?" he asked me.

I assured him that it was going very well—which was the truth. I had never seen him have the slightest difficulty winning over a crowd, though he had as many trepidations before a performance as any rank amateur going on the stage.

''Well, I did the best I could on short notice,'' he said, visibly relaxing. ''Do you think very many people will stay to see the second lecture? Should I try to change it?''

''The room almost completely emptied out when you were done,'' I said. He looked startled by this, so I hastily added, ''It was the captain's doing. He jumped up on stage and ordered everyone out so there would be room for those who wanted to see the second show. So don't worry about any repeaters except Mrs. Tremont—and me. We won't be at all disappointed if you repeat yourself verbatim, I'm sure.''

''All right—I want it to be a good show,'' Mr. Clemens said. He was about to say something else, but was interrupted by a knock at the door. ''Who's that?'' he wondered. ''Go answer it, will you?''

I opened the door to discover Michael Richards and his sister, Susan Martin. ''Hello,'' said Mr. Richards. ''Does Mr. Clemens have a few minutes before he has to give his lecture?''

''For two old friends, sure I do,'' said Mr. Clemens, rising to his feet. ''Come on in and chat a bit—it seems as if I've seen you every time I turn around, but I've been so busy I've hardly had time to talk to anybody.''

''Yes, you certainly have been busy,'' agreed Mrs. Martin brightly. Mr. Clemens showed her to a seat, and she looked up at him and said, ''We've had an awfully hard time trying to keep up with you.''

Mr. Clemens's eyes narrowed. ''Wait a minute—you two *have* been just about everywhere I've been, lately. Don't tell me it hasn't been a coincidence—that you've been following me!''

Mr. Richards laughed. ''Yes, I'm afraid we have been. That's why we wanted to come see you—partly to explain, and partly to apologize.''

Mr. Clemens looked puzzled. ''Explain? Apologize? I could certainly use some explanations. But I don't know what you've done that needs an apology—not yet, at least.''

Mrs. Martin smiled. "When Michael and I learned that you were on board, we ended up chatting about the old days, and how we'd both thought we'd grow up to become writers, because of you. Of course, things didn't work out that way. I have my marriage, and Michael has his career, and time flies—as I'm sure you know."

"But meeting you made us think, *Why not now?*" said Michael Richards. "We've got a long ocean voyage, and plenty of time in Europe. Since your first book was about your adventures in Europe, perhaps we could do the same sort of thing. So we sat down and began working on it, although at first we weren't quite sure what to write about."

"Yes, that's always the hard part," said Mr. Clemens, looking from brother to sister in some perplexity.

"Well, you can't imagine how pleased we were when we learned there had possibly been a murder on board," said Mrs. Martin. She saw my shocked expression, and her hand flew to her mouth as she realized what she'd said. "Oh, dear! Of course I don't mean that we were pleased because the poor boy was dead, but because now we had something to write about. And it didn't take us long to figure out that *you* were trying to solve the mystery."

"We'd heard about the mysteries you'd solved back in America," said her brother. "So we decided to spy on you and see how you managed to solve this one. And of course, that meant following Mr. Cabot here, as well."

"You've been spying on us?" I said. Now I was as puzzled as Mr. Clemens. I had noticed the two passengers in my vicinity several times, but now, casting my mind back over the last few days, it did seem that one or the other had made an appearance far more often than chance would allow.

"Yes, and that's what we came to apologize about," said Mrs. Martin. "We couldn't let you know while we were doing it, because you might have tried to evade us. Of course, now that you've solved the mystery, we won't need to do it anymore. But now we have such a fascinating story to tell—it gives our book all the interest we could possibly have hoped for. And we hope you'll be so kind as to take the time to tell us all about your investigation before we dock in England. We want to get it right in our report.''

"Good Lord,'' said Mr. Clemens, shaking his head in disbelief. "I've been a character in a book before, but it's always been in my own books. I hope it isn't too much to ask you to send me a copy? I'll send you back a copy of my next book in exchange.''

"We'd be delighted to send you a copy,'' said Mrs. Martin. "It's the least we can do for the man who made us believe that we could be writers—and who gave us all our best material. And we certainly look forward to your new books—we try to buy them all when they come out.''

"Good, then it's a deal,'' said Mr. Clemens, shaking hands with the brother and sister. "Well, I'm glad you let me in on your little secret.'' He laughed, and then a twinkle came into his eye. "Now let me tell you *my* little secret. I noticed you two hanging around—it seemed you were right there every time Wentworth or I were about to pick up some clue or another. I thought the only reason you'd be watching me so closely was that you were up to your ears in the whole mess—so for a while you two were on my list of suspects! I never could figure out your motive, but if I had, you two would have been in the brig!''

Mrs. Martin's eyes grew big, and Mr. Richards began to sputter, protesting his innocence. Then the sister laughed, and put her arm around her brother's shoulder. "Well, Michael, I think we've just had our legs pulled. I suppose we shouldn't expect anything else from Mark Twain. But we'll get back at him—just wait till he sees what we say about him in our book!''

Mr. Clemens chuckled. "I reckon it'll be a real eye-opener to see what I look like to somebody else. I hope the resemblance is close enough to for me to recognize.

If it's close enough, maybe I'll get rid of my mirror, and use it to shave by.''

Mrs. Martin smiled broadly. "Do you see, Michael? He hasn't changed a bit.''

"I certainly hope not," said Mr. Richards. "It would be a shame to learn he'd changed all his best stories, just when we've gotten old enough to stay and listen to them!''

There was another knock on the door; I opened it to find Mr. and Mrs. Kipling. "Come on in," said Mr. Clemens. "If we get a few more, I can give my lecture right here.''

"I'd advise against," said Mr. Kipling, with a chuckle. "The Grand Saloon is close to full, and I wouldn't be surprised if you could fill it up a third time. We asked Colonel Fitzwilliam to save us seats. But I thought you'd like to hear the latest news. Mr. Jennings tells me that Signor Rubbia is conscious, and he has apparently recanted his claim that the prince was the killer. I think he's ready to tell all.''

"Good," said Mr. Clemens. "That ought to wrap up all the loose ends. And I'm just as glad the captain's only got one murder to account to his directors for. Of course, I'll put in a good word for him and for Jennings—they both did their best, and none of what's happened should be held against them.''

He reached in his pocket and pulled out his watch. "Now, I guess you'd better go grab whatever seats are left, if you want to see the show. It's almost time, anyhow.''

"Oh, we've seen quite a show already," said Mrs. Martin, with a bright smile. "We won't be a bit disappointed, even if we don't get seats tonight.''

Mr. Clemens stood and stretched. "I reckon this is the last time I'll think of an ocean voyage as a chance to relax. What with a murderer to catch, and entertaining the guests at the captain's table every night, and two shows on a Saturday, I've been working overtime, and my wallet not one cent the fatter for it. It'll be a wonder if they don't have to put me in bed for a week, once we land in England.''

I opened the door to let our guests file out, then turned to Mr. Clemens. ''Your wife and daughters would be quite disappointed if you were to collapse the minute you were reunited with them,'' I said.

''No, they know me too well to be surprised at anything I do,'' replied Mr. Clemens. ''But for Livy and the girls, I think I can manage to stay awake. Now, let's go see whether I can keep an audience awake when I'm about to fall asleep myself. It'll be a hard test.''

As I would have predicted, he passed it with flying colors.